Praise for the Novels
of Laura Fitzgerald

Dreaming in English

"If you want to stand up and cheer, read *Dreaming in English.* I loved the compelling, sweet love story. And I loved the way Laura Fitzgerald, through the eyes of an Iranian immigrant, made me fall in love with America all over again."

—Cathy Lamb, author of *Such a Pretty Face* and *Julia's Chocolates*

"A delight sweet as a sugar cube melting on your tongue as you sip hot tea, *Dreaming in English* beautifully showcases Fitzgerald's trademark charm and grace in illuminating cultural differences and human universals."

—Monica Pradhan, author of *The Hindi-Bindi Club*

"A warm, winning novel. Laura Fitzgerald elegantly crafts a story that will tug on your heartstrings while making you smile. Fans and new readers will be delighted."

—Mia King, author of *Good Things* and *Sweet Life*

"You'll cheer through every page of this enchanting book for the kind and beautiful Tamila Soroush as she fights to hold on to the man of her dreams and her newfound American freedom (not necessarily in that order). Once you know Tami's story, you'll never again take for granted the simple joys of wearing a sleeveless dress on a sunny day or of publicly kissing someone you love."

—Claire LaZebnik, author of *Knitting Under the Influence* and *If You Lived Here, You'd be Home Now*

"What a delight to dive back into the world of Tami Soroush, an artistic and charming young Persian woman intoxicated with America and the possibilities for a new life. Laura Fitzgerald has given us another beautiful, heartfelt tale about love, family, and freedom."

—Carol Snow, author of *Just Like Me, Only Better*

"A warm, gentle, yet unsparing story of one immigrant woman's quest for her inner strength and worth in America. Sprinkled with unexpected revelations and twists, Tami Soroush's funny and moving journey to find her place in a foreign land—and the formidable obstacles she must face—will keep readers turning the pages late into the night. *Dreaming in English* is an endearing tale of family and love that made me laugh, cry, and at times sent a chill across my skin. I rooted for Tami all the way through to the last tension-filled scene." —Anjali Banerjee, author of *Haunting Jasmine*

"*Dreaming in English* is exactly the kind of book I'm always hoping to find and rarely do: a generous, honorable, illuminating tale about family, love, and a woman's journey to her truest self. If there is a more winning character in recent memory than Tamila, I have not met her. If only we could be friends in real life!"
—Barbara O'Neal, author of *The Secret of Everything*

"*Dreaming in English* is the insightful story of a young Iranian immigrant navigating love, prejudice, and her own conflicting emotions as she assimilates to Western culture. With compassion and wisdom, Laura Fitzgerald imbues Tami with hope and charm in this bittersweet look at what it means to be Iranian in today's America."
—Jennie Shortridge, author of *When She Flew*

Veil of Roses

"Every mother, every daughter, and anyone who's ever been in love should read this book! Grab the tissues. It's a triumphant tearjerker!"
—Vicki Lewis Thompson, author of *A Werewolf in Manhattan*

"With simple but heartfelt prose, this book is a marvelous read for any woman who has had to choose between love and family or has watched her freedom and choices dwindle before her eyes."
—*The Tampa Tribune*

"Evocative, poignant, and truly lovely. Laura Fitzgerald gives us a glimpse of a culture that's terrifyingly different—and yet heartbreakingly the same as our own."
—Alesia Holliday, author of *Seven Ways to Lose Your Lover*

"A fun, romantic, and thought-provoking debut novel from a promising author." —*Booklist*

"A gorgeously authentic voice. Fitzgerald's narrative is infused with wit, warmth, and compassion. If you like cross-cultural books, you won't want to put this down."

—Kavita Daswani, author of *Salaam, Paris* and *For Matrimonial Purposes*

"In this winning debut, Fitzgerald has crafted the powerful story of one woman's courage to look beyond the life she has been given—*Veil of Roses* is a poignant and uplifting novel full of charm, wit, and grace."

—Beth Kendrick, author of *Fashionably Late* and *Nearlyweds*

"Watching Tami find her voice through such small comforts as being able to sit alone in a house, walk to school unescorted, or buy lingerie with her sister will leave readers rooting for her."

—*Publishers Weekly*

"After picking up *Veil of Roses*, I did everything one-handed for two days, I was so unwilling to put it down! Charming and heartbreaking and hopeful and funny, this is the rare book that completely transports the reader. Laura Fitzgerald is an amazing talent." —Lani Diane Rich, author of *The Comeback Kiss*

"Poignant and warm, *Veil of Roses* is a story about having hope, finding love, and embracing freedom. I loved it."

—Whitney Gaskell, author of *Testing Kate*

One True Theory of Love

"A gorgeous book. At times cheeky and poignant but always very real." —*Arizona Daily Star*

"An engaging read that's tough to put down . . . the book seems to pick you up and carry you right along." —*Tucson Weekly*

Other Novels by Laura Fitzgerald

Veil of Roses

One True Theory of Love

Dreaming *in* English

LAURA FITZGERALD

NEW AMERICAN LIBRARY

New American Library
Published by New American Library, a division of
Penguin Group (USA) Inc., 375 Hudson Street,
New York, New York 10014, USA
Penguin Group (Canada), 90 Eglinton Avenue East, Suite 700, Toronto,
Ontario M4P 2Y3, Canada (a division of Pearson Penguin Canada Inc.)
Penguin Books Ltd., 80 Strand, London WC2R 0RL, England
Penguin Ireland, 25 St. Stephen's Green, Dublin 2,
Ireland (a division of Penguin Books Ltd.)
Penguin Group (Australia), 250 Camberwell Road, Camberwell, Victoria 3124,
Australia (a division of Pearson Australia Group Pty. Ltd.)
Penguin Books India Pvt. Ltd., 11 Community Centre, Panchsheel Park,
New Delhi - 110 017, India
Penguin Group (NZ), 67 Apollo Drive, Rosedale, North Shore 0632,
New Zealand (a division of Pearson New Zealand Ltd.)
Penguin Books (South Africa) (Pty.) Ltd., 24 Sturdee Avenue,
Rosebank, Johannesburg 2196, South Africa

Penguin Books Ltd., Registered Offices:
80 Strand, London WC2R 0RL, England

First published by New American Library,
a division of Penguin Group (USA) Inc.

First Printing, February 2011
10 9 8 7 6 5 4 3 2 1

LIBRARY OF CONGRESS CATALOGING-IN-PUBLICATION DATA:

Fitzgerald, Laura, 1967–
Dreaming in English/Laura Fitzgerald.
p. cm.
ISBN 978-0-451-23214-4
1. Iranians—United States—Fiction. 2. Women immigrants—United States—Fiction.
3. Marriage—Fiction. 4. Families—Fiction. I. Title.
PS3606. I8836D74 2011
813'.6—dc22 2010036658

Set in Bembo
Designed by Alissa Amell

Printed in the United States of America

Dear Laura,

There MUST be a sequel to Veil of Roses. *I keep reaching for the book that isn't there and yearn for a continuation of this wonderful story. I'm 86; please hurry.*

—Margaret Tobin, Albuquerque, NM

This book is dedicated to my wonderful readers, who convinced me there was more to the story. Enjoy!

I did it, Maman.
I am here, now.
I have found a way to stay.
I have even found love.
I was married by Elvis Presley
At the Chapel of the Blue Suede Shoes
In the City of Sin.
If you'd been here, Maman,
I would have been married in my sister's home.
You would have washed my hair with your lavender soap
And laced flowers in my hair,
Making for me a veil of roses.
Go, you said. Go and wake up your luck.
But what about you?
At last, Maman—what about you?
Come, I say to you now.
Come, Maman Joon.
Come, and wake up your luck.

Part One

GO AND WAKE UP YOUR LUCK

Chapter 1

My mother wouldn't let me cling to her; she made me stand tall. My world—the only one I knew, the only one I remembered—stood still for that last moment at Mehrabad Airport while she brushed away my tears and told me, *Go, my daughter. Go and wake up your luck.*

At her urging, I did.

All by myself, I flew halfway around the world, more than twelve thousand kilometers, from Tehran, Iran, to Tucson, U.S.A., worrying the entire time. You name it, I worried about it—first, that the dangerously outdated IranAir aircraft would simply break apart midflight. That when I spoke in America, my English would not be good enough and people would laugh at me. I was scared to see Maryam again after fifteen years of only across-the-ocean phone calls, concerned that our sister relationship would be too different, or else that it would be too much the same. I was terrified by the possibility that I might never see my parents again, and equally anxious that I would fail in my quest—my mandate—to find a husband in America before my tourist visa expired, and that I'd have to go back. I was afraid I *would* find a husband, only he'd turn out to be maybe not so nice. I feared that Americans might not see me for *me*, that they wouldn't understand I was separate from my government, that even if some crazies in Iran thought America was Sheytan-e Bozorg, the Great Satan, I did not. I was afraid I would not be given a chance.

Oh, how much has changed in three short months!

This time when I fly into Tucson, I'm not alone. I'm with Ike—my beautiful Ike, with his easy smile and ocean blue eyes. He's my husband now! We got married yesterday in Las Vegas. Everything has happened so fast there has hardly been time to think. I've been too excited to eat and far too excited to sleep, and this time, when things get bumpy during the plane's descent, Ike is here to take my hand.

"Scared, Persian Girl?" He asks this with a tease in his voice. While I'm Tamila Soroush to everyone else, to Ike I am and always will be his Persian Girl. "You're not scared of a little turbulence, are you?"

I rest my hand on his warm, sure skin. He's been quiet on the flight back, studying me closely when he thinks I'm unaware, probably wondering just who this is, this woman he's married, and I'm glad now for his light tone and gentle joking. "I'm not afraid of anything anymore," I say.

But Ike knows me better. "Oh, yeah?" He grins at me,

a sweet, naughty-boy smile. "Kiss me, then," he says. "Kiss me right here, right now."

At this, I blush. All around us on the airplane are other people—people going home; people leaving home; people traveling for work, for fun, for family, for love. The airplane is a bullet shooting through the sky. Life is happening all around me. We are all moving all the time, and I realize—*finally,* I realize—that I am no longer in a holding pattern, waiting for my life to begin. Like everyone around me, like Ike beside me—I, too, am hurtling toward my future, one which, if all goes well, *inshallah,* will take place in the land of the free and the home of the brave. And yet, when it comes to kissing Ike in public, I don't feel very courageous. For in my homeland of Iran, the country that has woven itself into my psyche, for both better and worse, love happens mostly behind closed doors.

"Okay," I admit, "I maybe still have some fears."

"You know the best way to get over them, don't you?" he says. "Through repetition. You're going to have to kiss me over and over again. Public displays of affection, it's called."

I feel myself blush as I give my new husband a friendly kiss on his cheek.

"Well," he says matter-of-factly, "I suppose that's a start." When he runs his fingers up my forearm, my skin tingles with possibility. Although the air on the plane is stale, I have never felt so alive. Alive, and suddenly worried.

"What about you?" I ask. "What are your fears?"

"Me?" He scoffs. "I'm not afraid of anything. I have no fear. None. Zilch. Nada."

I give him a look that asks, *Really?*

"I swear, Persian Girl," he says. "Perfect love drives out all fear."

"Wow," I say. "That's very profound." Not to mention incredibly sweet. But I know Ike a little bit by now. "Did you come up with this yourself?"

He grins. "It's U2. Do you know who U2 is?"

"U2 is a band from Ireland, and they are very socially conscious, yes?" I ask. "They have a campaign called Red that raises money to help poor people."

"Very good!" Ike says. "Although actually they raise money to help fight AIDS—in poor countries. So you were close—very close! But I'm surprised U2 isn't banned in Iran. They're kind of revolutionary, I'd think."

"Everything's available on the black market, no problem," I say. "But I know about them from here, from my English class. Danny taught us the song 'Pride,' which is about Martin Luther King, Jr., yes?"

Danny's my English teacher. He's a hippie-style person who plays the guitar for us and teaches us American folk songs and other songs, too. The way he played the song "Pride" was using only an acoustic guitar, and he sang it with sorrow in his voice. I liked his humble version better than U2's loud one.

"Partly it is, indeed," Ike says. "It's a very cool song." He sings, "*Free at last they took your life. They could not take your pride. . . .*"

My new husband does not have a very good voice, I'm sorry to say. I try not to wince at how off-key he is.

"Ike?" Thankfully, he stops singing. "Aren't you afraid for what your parents will say about our marriage?"

As of yet, they know nothing about it. Ike left a voice mail for his parents before he boarded the airplane to Las Vegas, saying only that he was going to meet some friends. And then he married me. He's a planner by nature, and I'm very much aware that marrying me was not in his plans. Surely his parents will be aware of this, too.

If that's a flicker of doubt I see in his eyes, he quickly pushes it away. "They're going to love you, Tami."

"And if they don't?"

"They will," he insists. "How could they not?"

"Um—because I married their son in order to get my green card?"

"No, no, no." Ike corrects me. "You married their son because you love him."

"Yes," I agree, for this is true, too. "But I worry they'll overlook that point."

Ike assures me they won't. Then he looks away, out the window. He's watching our descent as if he's landing in a new city to which he's never before been—which isn't the situation. We're going back to the same Tucson we left. It's the two of us—married now—who are different.

The final buckle-up bell sounds, and Ike unconsciously tightens his seat belt.

"Are you ready?" I ask him.

He takes my hand. "Ready for what?"

I can't help but smile. "For what comes next."

"No." He grins. "But what the hell, let's do it anyway."

* * *

What comes next is telling his parents we're married, and even if Ike isn't nervous, I certainly am.

I've never met them, and from what Ike has said, he's told them very little about me. Here is what I know about these people who are now my family: His father, Alan, owns a small construction company and a number of rental properties. Ike is close to his father and often helps him on construction jobs. His mother, Elizabeth, used to be a full-time nurse but has worked just one or two shifts per week since Ike was young. Besides Ike, who's the eldest, there are four girls in the family—Izzy, who's eighteen; Kat, who's sixteen; Paige, who's fourteen; and Camille, who is six and was adopted from Guatemala when she was a baby. Ike lives in a backyard studio guesthouse that he built with his father, and the girls share bedrooms.

Ike and I hold hands as we walk through Tucson International Airport. Holding hands in public is new for me, and it feels both utterly innocent and profoundly naughty at the same time. I pause for a moment under the sign that greets arriving visitors and take in its message with new eyes: WELCOME TO TUCSON.

Welcome to Tucson.

Welcome to America.

My family lived in the United States before, back in the 1970s, when my father was a graduate student at the University of California–Berkeley. We went back to Iran soon after the Shah was deposed and the Ayatollah Khomeini returned from exile. My family's happiness ended at that point. My Western-leaning parents, who'd seen a successful democracy in action, who understood the wisdom of a separation between church and state, got caught up in the clampdown that followed. More than that—my mother was arrested and jailed for five months. Permission to leave has been denied them again and again, and so now they're destined to live out their lives in Iran's repressive religious regime. For so long, their only hope has been to see their daughters settle once more in America.

Maryam made it out first, fifteen years ago, when she married Ardishir. Now it's my turn. I'm so glad to have my chance; I almost didn't make it.

Although my family is modern, they encouraged me to agree to an arranged marriage upon arriving in America. It was the only way I would be able to stay beyond the three months my tourist visa granted. And so I agreed, but on what was to be the morning of our wedding day, my hastily-agreed-upon fiancé, Masoud, a developer from Chicago, handed me a contract which demanded that I bear his child immediately—before filing my green-card paperwork—and that I give up all rights to the child in the event of a divorce.

I couldn't do it. I'd come to America for my parents, yes, and I'd come for myself, too—but most of all I'd come for the children I hoped to have one day. That they would never know repression. That they would be raised in freedom. I couldn't let them have a father like Masoud Fakhri, who would so coldly cut their mother from their lives. If I signed his contract, my children and I would be hostage to his decisions, his whims, his vices, his control. He could divorce me at will and take from me my children.

And so for them—for the daughters and sons I hope to have one day—I said no.

When I walked away from this marriage, with my visa just days away from expiring, I resigned myself to going back to Iran, defeated, to a homeland where I never really felt at home. And then Ike, my handsome American Boy, Ike—the only one I'd wanted, the one I was sure I could not have, the one I'd secretly met for coffee day after day on my way home from English class—knocked on the door of my hotel room in Las Vegas, where my friends and I were celebrating the wedding of our classmates Agata and Josef.

This was yesterday, when Ike came for me, and I got that flutter of excitement I always get when I watch the end of romantic American movies—after it has all fallen apart and when it seems that love is not meant to be and that life has turned out to be nothing more than a cruel dictator of fate, but then . . . *but then* . . . something happens to change all that.

For me, it was a knock at the door.

Ike came for me, and the storm clouds parted. The angry gods softened toward me, and Ike declared his love. I've been pinching myself ever since, to remind myself it's not just a dream. It's true. *I'm married to the man I love.* Thanks to him, I got my freedom. The question that remains: Can I keep it?

So many things can and might go wrong, especially with our immigration interview. Will the authorities believe our love is for real? Maybe, or maybe not. But on this, my first full day as Ike's wife, standing beneath the WELCOME TO TUCSON sign, holding his hand, I allow myself to be hopeful.

"What are you thinking, Persian Girl?" he asks.

What I'm thinking is how nice it will be to put the past behind me.

What I'm thinking is how far I've come, and not just in miles.

What I'm thinking is *wow.* Just . . . *wow.* Did this really happen? Am I really here?

I look into my new husband's true-blue American eyes and squeeze his hand. But I don't answer him, for what I'm thinking is too big for words.

What I'm thinking is: I just might get my happy ending after all.

Chapter 2

There are a few reasons I didn't originally tell Ike about my visa situation. Perhaps the first reason, the simplest reason, was that I was embarrassed. Arranged marriages are not something Americans understand. They're not burdened by their culture or history in this way. For them, it's *first comes love, then comes marriage.* Or else it's love, even living together, without the marriage. But it's never marriage without the love—at least not at the beginning!

Also, as I mentioned, Ike is a man with a plan. He has his future precisely mapped out, and marriage was not in his plan. Someday, yes. Now, no, and I didn't want to put him in a difficult position. If it hadn't been for my sister, who went to see him yesterday without my knowledge, Ike still wouldn't know of my dilemma. I'm so thankful she did!

And I'm thankful Ike didn't just let me go, even though our marriage will cause a change in his plan.

When we get to his scooter, which is sandwiched between two large motorcycles, Ike climbs on first. I hand him my travel bag, which he sets on the floorboard. He has no bags of his own, because he was in such a rush yesterday to get the last flight to Las Vegas that he didn't even stop at home, instead going directly to the airport after his shift ended at Starbucks, which is where Maryam went to see him.

"Here." He hands me the one helmet he's brought. "We've got to make sure you stay alive long enough to file your immigration paperwork."

As I climb on, I nudge him. "Very funny, mister."

"Seriously," he says. "No need to tempt fate." As I'm putting on the helmet, he sings, "*I don't mean to start any blasphemous rumors, but I think that God's got a sick sense of humor. And when I die, I expect to find him laughing.*

"Depeche Mode," he informs me. "An oldie but a goodie."

As I listen to the laughing-God lyrics of this song, it occurs to me that I know very little (make that nothing!) about my husband's religious views. "Ike, do you believe in God?"

"Let's just say I try to live my life in such a way that if I learn after I die that there really is such a thing as heaven, I'll be pleasantly surprised," he says.

"If you ever go to Iran with me for a visit, this is not something you should say, okay? You could get in big trouble."

"I highly doubt I'll be going to Iran anytime soon," he says.

"You could, you know," I say. "My parents would love to meet you."

"No offense to your parents, but I'd never willingly put myself in a situation where I'd give up any of my rights," he says. "And wouldn't I have to convert to Islam or something?"

Oh, that. I'd forgotten about that. "That's mostly just a technicality."

He laughs. "That's one hell of a technicality, Tami."

He backs the scooter out of its parking spot, and for a moment I'm so happy, reminded of our previous scooter rides—my body on fire from his nearness, my arms tightened around his waist, pretending it was necessary to keep my balance. Before, I was terrified of getting caught sneaking these rides, afraid it might ruin my chances of finding a husband. But now he *is* my husband.

As he makes the twenty-five-minute drive to his house, however, my happiness is replaced by nerves. Again and again, I chant to myself, *Please let them like me. Please let them like me.* Six miles of this!

His family lives in a neighborhood called Winterhaven, where every December all the residents are required by the homeowners' association to decorate their yards with holiday lights and displays, and people come from all over the city to walk or take horse-drawn carriage rides through the streets. Ike turns off Tucson Boulevard onto a street called Kleindale and in less than a block, pulls over and parks in front of a quiet brick house that looks similar to all the other houses on the street. This neighborhood is different from Maryam's in that the front yards have grass and the houses are brick, smaller and all one-story.

"Here we go," he says, sliding off the scooter. "Home sweet home."

I'm making him leave his childhood home. Dear God, what have I done?

I remain on the scooter, unable to face his family. "I'm too nervous, Ike."

"My parents are going to love you, Tami," he says. "They're going to welcome you into the family with open arms. That's the kind of parents they are. And you're going to love my sisters, and they're going to love you, too. Trust me, there will be a . . . plethora of love."

"You're sure? They won't think I'm . . . ?"

"They won't think you're what?"

A thief . . . stealing away their most precious son?

"I don't know," I say, although this isn't true. I do know. I just don't want to say it. "Too . . . foreign?"

"Exotic, maybe." Ike smiles. "And sexy. But foreign? No. That's not how they'd ever—"

"I don't want your parents to think I'm sexy, Ike!"

He laughs. "Tell you what. Just keep that helmet on, and there's no fear of that."

Laughing, I pull it off and shake out my long brown-black hair.

He gives me an appreciative look. "Ah, well, now. No denying it—you're sexy," he says. "My sisters are going to go nuts for your hair. I should warn you, they're a touchy-feely bunch. They're probably going to want to braid it."

Touchy-feely. This is a cute word.

"The first time they meet me?"

"Another thing about my family—we're very casual."

"Your parents know we're coming, right?"

"I told my mom I'm bringing a friend to dinner." He extends a hand to me. "Come on, friend."

I slip my hand into his and climb off the scooter—and there we are, holding hands in public again. Take that, you government goons! The streets of Tehran are filled with many things, but affection is not one of them. "Do they know this friend you're bringing is female?"

"Yes, dear, they know my friend is female," he says. "They just don't know she's my wife." His plan is for us to tell them after dinner, after they've had the chance to get to know me a little bit.

"I should have brought something," I say. "Flowers, or sweets, or—"

"There's no need for that," he says.

But even if his family is casual, mine is not. We'd never go to someone's house without an offering, and yet here I am. Am I changing already, as an American wife? But I'm *not* an American wife—I'm the wife of an American, and I should have insisted that we stop and get something. Yet before I know it, we're at the front door, and we walk inside to what I can immediately tell is happy, half-organized chaos. Book bags are strewn by the front door. Shoes are everywhere. Plastic shopping bags from Target have been brought in and left lying in the middle of the living room. Spanish-sounding music plays in another room, and there's a delicious smell coming from the kitchen.

"Ah, lasagna," Ike says happily. "My favorite."

Lah-zan-ya. I practice the word in my head. I have not yet eaten this food.

Sitting together on the couch are two girls. One is dark-skinned and young enough that she must be the six-year-old adopted girl, Camille. The other I guess to be Paige, the fourteen-year-old. She's reading to Camille from a book written by a doctor named Seuss, *Oh, the Places You'll Go.* They glance at us and then continue on.

"It's Squirt and Baby Squirt!" Ike says. Camille smiles, while Paige wrinkles her nose at him. Ike introduces me, and we exchange smiles, but before anyone can say anything, there's shouting from another room.

"Who took my cell phone?"

Ike grins at me. "That would be my sister Kat. She's the drama queen of the family. Come on—I'll introduce you to my mom."

He stoops to pick up the shopping bags and carries them to the kitchen. Paige continues reading to Camille, and as Ike walks by, he recites the story from memory. *"And when things start to happen, don't worry. Don't stew. Just go right along. You'll start happening, too."*

Ike's mother, wearing denim Capri pants and a green linen blouse with a white camisole under it, is tall and a bit on the heavy side—not in a way that makes her seem weak or unhealthy, but in a way that makes her seem sturdy and competent. She has thick, shoulder-length brown hair with gray streaks in it, worn back in a barrette. She's sitting on a stool by the counter, slicing red onion for a salad.

"Mom, I'd like to introduce you to someone," Ike says from the doorway, "This is Tami. Tami, this is my mom."

As we approach from the doorway, she points her chopping knife at me. "So *you're* the one my son rushes off to Vegas to be with. The girl from Iran."

Inwardly, I cringe. "Oh, I, uh—" I glance at Ike. He's smiling. "Yes, ma'am. I am. I'm the one."

"Please don't call me ma'am. It makes me feel so old!" she says. "Call me Elizabeth, why don't you?"

"Thank you," I say, at the same time thinking, *I can't call her Elizabeth!* "Or maybe . . . Mrs. Hanson?"

"If you must." She smiles. "I've certainly been called worse, especially by my sixteen-year-old lately!"

Ike unloads the bags, setting the items on the counter. Soap, shampoo, suntan lotion, toothpaste, hair clips. I'm embarrassed when he sets down a box of tampons, but he's unfazed, and I'm suddenly glad he lives in a house with five females. It will make the womanly aspect of our relationship no big deal to him.

"Was Vegas fun?" Mrs. Hanson asks me.

I married your son!

"Yes, thank you," I say. "I had a very good time."

"I suppose gambling is illegal in Iran," she says. "Did you have a chance to do any while you were in—"

"Who took my cell phone?" A teenage girl storms into the kitchen. Her blond hair is very straight and falls all the way

down her back. "Do *you* have my cell phone, by chance?" she asks me.

It warms my heart to see Ike's teasing eyes on this younger, female version of him. I smile at her—she's my sister now, too . . . my sister-by-marriage! "Sorry, no."

"Kat, meet Tami," Ike says. "Tami, meet my sister Kat."

Kat stretches out her hand to shake mine. Her grip is that of an equal, and I marvel at how a sixteen-year-old can have the confidence and presence of someone much older. When she's not yelling about her cell phone, that is.

"Why don't you call yourself with the landline?" Mrs. Hanson suggests.

"I can't find that, either!"

Ike pulls out his phone, dials hers, and within seconds, we hear, *I know what boys like. I know what guys want. They want to touch me. I never let them.*

I laugh, as I have not heard this song before.

"The dryer!" Kat says, and heads to the laundry room to retrieve her phone.

"Girls and their cell phones." Mrs. Hanson shakes her head. "Do they have cell phones in Iran? They must, I'm sure."

"Yes, of course." Tehran is a vibrant city of eight million—of course we have cell phones. (And no, we don't ride camels!) We also have shopping malls and movie theaters and beautiful parks. Except for the many backward restrictions we're forced to endure, we're quite modern. We like to think so, anyway.

"Were you two planning to stay for dinner?" Mrs. Hanson looks at me to answer.

"Oh, I, uh . . . Didn't Ike . . . ?" I look to him.

"I told you we were," he says. "On the phone. Is Dad around?"

"Did you see his truck out front?" Mrs. Hanson says.

"No, I didn't," Ike says.

"Well, then, you know he's not home."

They grin at each other, and I envy this easy, teasing exchange. My father is funny, or likes to think he is, but my mother always seems so fragile, as if a deeply felt laugh or cry might cause her to crack open, to shatter. With her, we are smooth. Soft. Measured, in our emotions and our words. But Ike and his mother appear to be the opposite of this.

"Come on." Ike reaches for my hand. "Let me show you my bachelor pad."

"It's very nice to meet you," I say to Mrs. Hanson.

"You, too," she says. "My son was right. You *are* beautiful."

"Inside and out," Ike says—so sweet!—and on the way out the back door, I breathe a sigh of relief. His mother seems to like me just fine, and so far, I like her very, very much.

Between the main house and Ike's guesthouse is a green-grass backyard. Also in the yard is an in-ground pool with a diving board, and on the diving board is a tall, very thin teenage girl in a bikini, and also a tan, muscled, shirtless boy in swimming trunks that are called board shorts. He's behind her, with his hands around her waist, cheerfully forcing her to the edge of the diving board. The girl shrieks happily as she readies herself to be pushed from it. Several other teenagers are either in the pool or sitting at its edge, their feet dangling in the water.

"That's my sister Isabel," Ike tells me and calls to her, "Hi, Izzy!" She waves as the boy forces her closer to the edge. "Izzy, this is Tami."

Izzy starts to say hello, but before she can, the boy pushes her off the diving board amid laughter from the others. I laugh, too. How many years I have dreamed of moments such as this, with myself as the free-spirited girl, the center of attention, laughing in the sunshine and being touched by a boy as if it were no big deal. I left my backpack with my camera in Ike's living room beside the front door, and it might not be proper to take pictures of people I just met, anyway, but I take a few in my mind: Of the loosely tied strings of Izzy's bikini bottom. Of the boy's weight-lifter muscles. Of the intertwined feet of another boy and girl who lounge in the pool on matching inner tubes. Of the splash of water, frozen in midair. Of Izzy, as she pops up from underneath the water with her hair slicked back like a model's and with her smile showing her teeth so American-white.

"Sorry 'bout that!" she calls to me, glowing with happiness and good health. "Hi, and welcome!"

Welcome.

There's that word again, my favorite in all the English language. It's how I've felt, every single day since my arrival in America. Welcomed. It's how I never felt in Iran, not even for one day.

Ike does not have posters of bikini-naked women on his walls, thank goodness.

Another good thing: He is not very messy. I was curious about this. Because he'd left in a hurry to catch his flight to Las Vegas, he wouldn't have had time to straighten up, and yet, besides a towel on the floor and a few shirts hanging on the back of a kitchen chair, his apartment is very neat. It's masculine, with beige and maroon the main colors, and the furniture is modern. His stereo is a Bose, which I know is expensive because my brother-in-law, Ardishir, buys only the best of everything, and he has a Bose stereo.

Ike watches me as I look around. "So, do I pass the test?" He closes the door behind us, but the noise from the backyard still comes in. I don't mind. In fact, I like it. I always wished to grow up in a loud house.

"Of course you pass the test, Ike!" *The real question: Will I?* "You don't have a TV?"

"I watch movies with my family; that's about it," he says. "I never watch it alone."

"What *do* you do when you're alone?" As I say this, I wonder if it came out like I was flirting. I can't always tell, and I didn't mean for it to—it's just that there are so many things about him I still don't know.

"When I'm alone, I think about you," he says, tilting his head at me the cutest little bit.

I smile, and smile, and can't stop smiling. I've been this way ever since yesterday. It's because of the *fact* of his love, the affirmation, the confirmation of it. But did it come too easy? He bestowed his love on me; I didn't earn it. *But I will. I'll be the best wife ever.*

"This is so nice here, Ike," I say, looking around. The ceiling has exposed beams, while the floors are stained concrete. This is modern style, I know, but the walls are thick adobe, which is traditional here in the desert. It's a nice combination, to mix the old and the modern. "You built this all by yourself?"

"Me and my dad, yep."

My father-in-law. Mr. Hanson.

"What kind of furniture is this?" I gesture to a wood-framed, leather-seated rocking chair. It matches his bed and small dining table, and I know it's a particular style, because I've seen it several times since being in the U.S.

"It's Mission style," he says. "Made by the Quakers or the Amish or some such group. The Amish, I think. I got it as a gift from my parents, so I didn't think too much about it."

Quakers, I say in my head. *Amish. Ah. Mish. Amish.*

"You'll have to tell me about these groups sometime."

He laughs. "There's so much you don't know, isn't there? Every day must be an adventure for you. The Quakers, the Amish . . . they're both very . . . well, I'm not sure they're entirely American, but they're certainly not Middle Eastern, I'd suppose."

"I'll look them up on the Internet and let you know," I tell him.

"You do that often?" he says. "Look up American-ish stuff you don't know?"

"Of course," I say. "Did you know, for instance, that the first hot dogs in America were sold in the 1860s from street carts in New York City? And that Americans eat on average over sixty hot dogs per year? And that your president Franklin Roosevelt served hot dogs to the king of England when he visited in 1939?"

"Why, no," Ike says. "I had no idea. Did the king like the hot dogs?"

"He loved them." I laugh. "I can tell you many very interesting things about cotton candy, too. Or should I save that for another day?"

"Have you ever played Trivial Pursuit?" Ike says. "You really should."

"No, I haven't, but Ardishir tells me the same thing."

"That would be fun," he says. "Let's do it."

"Okay. Do you play chess? I like chess."

"Chess, sure. And I'll teach you to play strip poker. You'll like that, too," he says. "Or, at least, *I'll* like that."

When I agree to this, Ike laughs. "You don't know what strip poker is, do you?"

I shake my head. "I've heard of poker. It's a card game. But strip? No."

"For every round you lose, you take off an article of clothing. So if you lose too much . . ." He watches me, waiting for me to get his meaning, and as I feel my face redden, he grins. "Sound fun?"

This is not a question I could answer—ever! I'm very shy

about things like this—so instead, I move closer to a window ledge that's lined with postcards. Ike follows, wrapping his arms around me from behind, which causes my temperature to rise by what feels like several degrees. "Do you mind?" I say, meaning does he mind if I pick up the postcards.

"Of course not. Do *you* mind if I kiss your neck while you look at them?"

Blushing, I say, "No!"

I pick up the Eiffel Tower one first. Paris. *Wish you were here. J.*

It's a woman's handwriting. I wonder, who is this J. person? But it's easy enough to disregard the question when Ike's lips are so soft on my neck. However, when I pick up the Venice postcard and read, *Really wish you were here! J.*, it's not so easy to ignore anymore.

"Who's J?" I ask.

"Those are from Jenna," Ike says. "Remember? I told you about her."

"This is not a name I've ever heard before, Jenna."

"She's my old girlfriend," he says. "My old set-it-free girlfriend. You know, the one who went on that huge trip to Europe after college. I told you about her."

"Oh, right." I remember now. This girlfriend gave Ike an ultimatum: Marry me, and I'll stay. Don't marry me, and I'll go. Ike decided to let her go. "But the set-it-free part—what does it mean, please?"

"It's stupid." He grins, embarrassed. "But there's this . . . well, when it ended, as it was ending, my mom reminded me of this saying, which is totally a cliché, but also, you know, it happens to be true—I guess that's what a cliché is, right? A true but overused expression—"

"Every expression is new to me," I remind him.

"Well, then you might appreciate it," he says. *"If you love something, set it free. If it comes back to you, it's yours. If not, it was never meant to be."*

This is sweet, and sad.

"This saying reminds me of a bird," I say. "Of letting a bird out of its cage and hoping it will fly back to you, but knowing it might not."

"That might be where it comes from," Ike says. "And it definitely fits Jenna because she's flightier than hell. So anyway, I . . . set her free, and she didn't come back, so . . ." He gathers up the postcards, tears them up, and throws them over his shoulder so they fall to the ground, the poor things. "It wasn't meant to be."

I appreciate his words, but his matter-of-fact tone does not ring true. He loved her, and he hoped she'd come back. Luckily for me, she didn't.

When we hear Mr. Hanson's truck pull into the driveway, my heart begins to race. Ike suggests we go back to the main house, and on the way, we pass by his mother on the back patio. She's setting a stack of dishes on the table.

"Need help?" Ike asks.

"Nope," she says. "Fill a pitcher of water before dinner, though, if you would."

He agrees, and as we enter the house through the kitchen, I hear a child's squealing from the living room. Ike grabs a can of Budweiser beer from the refrigerator, and at the doorway to the living room, he makes a motion as if he's offering to throw it to his dad.

"Ah, just what a thirsty man needs," Mr. Hanson says. He looks like Ike, plus twenty-five years—trim, solid, with his shirt tucked into his jeans, although Ike is a little bit taller. "Toss it here!"

"No, no!" Camille screams. Mr. Hanson is holding her by the ankles, upside down. If he lets go to catch the beer, she'll fall and land on her head, but from how she's laughing, I can tell she's not worried. I don't think this is the first time they've played this game.

"Ready?" Ike says. "Get ready to catch it."

"No-o-o-o-o-o!" Camille giggles.

"Oh, all right," Ike says. He crosses the room, bends to tickle Camille's stomach, and in one swift move grabs her by the waist, takes her from his father, and tosses her over his shoulder. After this, he hands the beer to his father, who pops open the can and takes a long, satisfying swallow.

"Where's Camille?" Ike says, looking around, twisting her sideways and back again.

"I'm right here!" She kicks her feet.

"I hear her, but I don't see her," he says.

"I don't see her, either," Mr. Hanson says. "In fact, I haven't seen her since I've been home."

"Yes, you have, Daddy!" She kicks twice as hard, and Ike flips her over so she's back on her feet in front of him.

"Oh, *there* you are," he says. "Why didn't you say something?"

Was my house ever this lively? Ever, even just once?

"Do it again!" Camille says to her father.

"Do what again?" he says.

"Again! Again! Again!" Camille jumps on him, nearly knocking him off balance, nearly spilling his beer.

"No, honey, I just got home. Let me relax for a minute. Let me meet your brother's friend." He acknowledges me with a nod. "Hi, there. I'm Alan."

"Dad, this is Tami," Ike says. "Tami, this is my dad."

My heart pounds from the information he left out—*this is my wife.* For his part, Ike's father gives no indication that his son having a woman over is in any way out of the ordinary. He extends his hand with a crinkly-eyed smile. "Nice to meet you."

"Thank you," I say. "It's very nice to meet you, too."

"Will you play Uno with me, Daddy?" Camille says.

"After dinner," Mr. Hanson says. "I'm going to go say hello to my wife now, if you don't mind."

Camille tries but fails to roll her eyes as he leaves the room. "Ike, will you?" She looks at me. "She can play, too."

I smile. Does this mean she likes me?

"Another time," Ike says. "We wouldn't be able to finish before dinner, and Tami and I have something to do afterward."

She pouts. "No one will play with me."

"You poor thing," Ike says. "You have such a hard life, don't you?"

Camille smirks at him; she knows she's got a good life.

She's acting a lot like Iranian girls her age do, before they're made to understand the world does not, in fact, revolve around them.

"*Dinner!*" we hear yelled from the back porch.

"Can I sit next to you?" Camille asks Ike. "Even though she's here?"

Ike laughs. "Guess what? I have a left side and a right side, so you can sit on one side and Tami can sit on the other. How does that sound?"

"I call the right side!" she says.

"Tami, is that okay?" Ike asks. "I know you really wanted to sit on my right side."

I smile. "Camille can sit on your right side."

"Isn't she nice?" Ike says to Camille. "Isn't she the nicest person you've ever met?"

Camille nods. "Next time, I'll sit next to her."

At dinner, I'm one of many, part of a festive group. Izzy's friends stay—they've changed out of their swimsuits, but their hair is still wet and they're glowing from their healthy afternoon in the sun. A girlfriend of Kat's has also come for dinner, and I have the feeling there's always someone over, that there's always something going on. Their home is a place people want to be, and I feel such gratitude to be part of it—tonight, and hopefully forever. Looking at everyone up and down the large, long table stretched across their covered back patio—fully half the people here are guests—I think Ike might be right. His family indeed might welcome me with the open arms he said they would. That's the sort of people they seem to be.

I sit toward one end of the table with Ike and his parents (along with Camille, to Ike's right, of course), while Izzy and Kat and their friends sit toward the other end. Paige sits next to her father, across from me. For the first few minutes, we pass dishes around and fill our plates. When his father asks if I'd like a glass of wine, Ike correctly senses my uncertainty as to whether I should accept and announces that he'd like a glass, so I say I'll have one, too. I haven't had much wine in my life. In the teetotaling country of Iran, I hardly drank alcohol at all, and here, the few times I have, it's been margaritas or beer or champagne. I do like the smooth taste of the wine Ike's father serves, although I take only a few polite sips. I have what my friend Eva calls *low tolerance*, and I certainly don't want to get drunk in front of my new in-laws!

Mr. Hanson, with the watchful eyes of a poet, listens far more than he speaks. I feel that the least of my gestures has significance to him, as he takes in how I cut my lasagna and lettuce into small bites, at how I smile at what everyone says, at how I pause to form in my head the answers to Mrs. Hanson's many questions before I say them out loud. It makes me nervous to be studied so closely, and so I keep my eye contact mostly away from Mr. Hanson, but when I do meet his eyes, they reflect back a decency that's similar to his son's.

Mrs. Hanson asks mostly the same questions everyone

asks me: How am I finding America? Do I miss my parents? What's the most surprising thing about the U.S.? What's it like to live in Iran? Isn't it awful how women there have to wear headscarves? My standard answers come out easily and coherently, as I tell her that I love America; that I miss my parents tremendously; that the most surprising (and refreshing!) thing about America is how everyone mostly just leaves everyone else alone. I tell them living in Iran is in some ways wonderful, but that unemployment is very high and Tehran is crowded and polluted and yes, it's too bad women have to wear *hejab*, but we don't walk around obsessing about it as much as Americans seem to.

It's only when she asks how much longer I'll be visiting that I trip over my words.

"Oh, um . . ." I look to Ike.

He puts his hand on my thigh. "We're working on that."

I freeze. He shouldn't have said that! The plan is to tell his parents after dinner—he needs to stick to the plan! Sensing Mr. Hanson's eyes on me, I make myself unfreeze.

"This lasagna is delicious," I say to Mrs. Hanson. "Please, how is it made?"

Camille's mouth drops open. "You don't know how to make lasagna? Even *I* know how to make lasagna!"

"Camille's favorite TV show is *Top Chef*," Mrs. Hanson says, and goes on with a funny story about how Camille made breakfast in bed for the whole family recently and left the kitchen a disaster area. I almost feel safe again until from the other end of the table, Kat calls down to Ike, "Hey, did you win any money in Las Vegas?"

He shakes his head. "You know I don't gamble."

"Hello," she says. "You go to poker night every month."

Ike grins. "Besides that."

"What *did* you do?" Izzy says. "You were only there for, like, a day, and none of us knew you were going."

"It was a last-minute trip." Ike gives me a quick glance and then reaches for the bottle of wine and pours himself some more. "This is good wine, Dad. Is it the Sonoita wine you were telling me about?"

"So why'd you go?" Izzy persists. "All anyone does there is quickie weddings and gambling. You didn't get married, did you?"

She says this in a joking tone, but while the younger people laugh, I freeze again and Ike gives her a look. Half the look tells her it's a ridiculous idea and the other half tells her to be quiet.

It is the second part of his look that makes his mother suspicious. "Ike?"

"There are lots of shows there. Did you see any shows?" Paige nods at me encouragingly. Sensitive girl that she is, she must have noticed the panic I've been trying to suppress.

I smile at her gratefully. "There was a show we *almost* saw with men who paint their whole bodies blue! So very strange! I can't imagine why—"

"Ike?" his mother says again.

A long moment passes as Ike looks from one to the other of his parents. Then he takes a big breath and again takes my hand. I squeeze hard to tell him this is *not* a good time. But he smiles at me to tell me he knows what he's doing, and then he clears his throat. "Actually," he says, "I have some news that I think you'll find very exciting. Tami and I *did* get married while we were in Vegas."

Camille smiles and claps. Paige's eyes widen. She looks immediately at her mother.

Mrs. Hanson gasps.

Ike's other sisters stare at him openmouthed, trying to figure out if he's making a joke.

And his mild-mannered father swears.

"Jesus *Christ*, Ike," he says. "Just exactly how drunk were you?"

Chapter 3

They'll love you. They'll welcome you into the family with open arms.

My hopeful heart withers as Ike's earlier words come back to haunt me, or taunt me, and I feel myself literally shrink. They don't love me, not one little bit.

Jesus Christ, Ike. Just exactly how drunk were you?

Is that who I am? Someone who could only get someone to marry her if he's too drunk to know any better? *But, of course they'd think that. They don't know me enough to know his reasons.*

Tell them, Ike. Please, please tell them fast and make them understand.

"I was stone-cold sober." Ike looks at his father evenly, man to man, slipping his hand from mine as he does. "It was somewhat spur-of-the-moment, yes, but I assure you it was a clearheaded decision."

Mr. Hanson takes a moment, and then says in a tone that matches Ike's, "Deciding whether to spend the rest of your life with someone is not a spur-of-the-moment decision."

"It can be," Ike says. "When it's right, it's right."

"It's okay," Mrs. Hanson says softly, and for a second I'm hopeful. But then she continues. "People make mistakes, and what's done can be undone. You'll just get it annulled."

I don't know this word—*annulled*—but I don't think it means anything good.

"It wasn't a mistake," Ike says. "I love Tami, and I intend to spend the rest of my life with her."

Mr. Hanson sets down his fork. "Girls." He looks at each of his daughters in turn. "You're all excused." Without another word, they and their friends stand, gather their plates, and file indoors. Paige gives me a sympathetic glance as she leaves. Camille remains in her chair and looks at her father with her beautiful big brown eyes until he says, "You, too, Camille."

Grumbling, Camille follows the others inside. I look after her wistfully, wishing I could join her, wishing I could be just about anywhere but here. Then I realize that's not true—there are many worse places I could be. Like in Iran. This difficult moment is just something to be gotten through, and then Ike and I can get to the good parts. *Of course they're concerned. They have every reason to be. They don't know me. They don't know me at all.*

I sit up straighter in my chair. "I love your son. I love him very much."

"Just who exactly *are* you?" Mr. Hanson says. "I've never even heard of you before tonight."

"Yes, you have, Dad." Ike gives him a stern look and then gives me one of apology. "He has."

"Well, hardly," Mr. Hanson grumbles.

"Is she pregnant?" Mrs. Hanson says to Ike and then asks me, gently, "Are you pregnant, honey?" Her eyes flick to my glass of wine and then back to Ike. Because she seems ready to accept this possibility, part of me wishes I were, in fact, pregnant. But Ike and I only had sex for the first time last night, and he used a condom. So, no, I'm not. Which is good, because the thought seems to horrify Ike.

"She's *not* pregnant." He shudders. "Just let me explain, okay? It'll all make sense once I do." He proceeds to tell them about my immigration situation and how if I'm married to an American citizen, I can apply for permanent residency and how otherwise I'd have to go back to Iran and how neither of us wants that.

"You're right. It makes perfect sense now." Mrs. Hanson's face is pomegranate red. "You're being taken advantage of by this girl."

"I'm not being taken advantage of." Ike's face is tight. "I've known her for three months, and I've been crazy about her the whole time."

"Three months." Mrs. Hanson says it as scornfully as if Ike had said three days. "Do you even know her middle name?"

Floundering, Ike looks to me.

"I don't have a middle name," I say.

"That's not my point," Mrs. Hanson snaps. "Ike, what *do* you know about her?"

"I know that I love her." He takes my hand again. "I know that if I let her leave, I'd regret it for the rest of my life."

My heart swells.

"Oh, for God's sake," his mother says. "Get a grip, would you?"

Mr. Hanson leans toward Ike. "I'm sure she's a lovely person. But, son, how much of this is just a result of . . . well . . . of you not wanting to be left again?"

Ike startles. "What're you talking about?"

"If you remember, you said these same sorts of things after Jenna left."

My heart gasps. This *Jenna* keeps coming up—twice in the past hour! I'd had the impression the relationship ended long ago, and yet there were those postcards, and now there's this comment.

Ike's face is flushed, angry. "This is utterly, completely, a hundred percent different."

"Is it?" Mr. Hanson says. "Don't you think you maybe rushed into this with her because you took too long to make up your mind about—"

"I *let* Jenna go," Ike says. "I *want* Tami to stay. It's not the same at all." He keeps a firm grip on my hand.

"It would have made inherently more sense for you to have married Jenna," Mrs. Hanson says.

"I didn't *want* to marry Jenna."

"We're not saying you should have married her, either," Mr. Hanson says. "Only that it would have made more sense than this does. You knew her a lot longer. You—" He stops himself, but it's quite simple to fill in the blank. *You loved her a lot longer, and maybe more.* "Your words at the time, if you remember, son, were that you weren't ready to be married and you resented how she'd basically—your words—*put a gun against my head to get me to commit.* How is this not the same thing?"

"This is different." I've never heard such harshness from Ike before. I hate to hear it and hate even more that I'm the one who caused it. "Jenna's ultimatum was contrived. Tami's isn't. She didn't even *give* me an ultimatum. *I asked her.* Happily. Voluntarily. With total delight! I wish—" His strident voice softens. "Show a little faith in me, would you? I'm a relatively smart guy with a pretty decent head on my shoulders. I'm not an idiot. I realize this isn't exactly normal. But it's what the circumstances require. And within the context of things, I'll tell you the marriage itself is more of a formality, or a technicality, than anything. You're going to see us taking things slow."

"How is marriage just a technicality?" Mrs. Hanson says.

"And how is marrying a girl you hardly know taking it slow?" says Ike's father.

"Well, for one thing," Ike says, "we're not going to live together right away."

His mother gasps and covers her mouth.

Ike continues, "We're going to—"

"What kind of marriage *is* this?" She's practically wailing.

"It's the kind of marriage Tami and I want."

"It's a sham!" she says. "It's a fraud! *She's taking advantage of you*—how do you not see it? Anyone can see it! Ike, come on! *Get it annulled.*" She looks at him earnestly. "We'll help you. We'll get you a lawyer. We'll find you the best lawyer in town, but please. *Get it annulled.*"

"I'm not getting it annulled." Ike glares at his parents. "Our marriage is a contract, and I'm not about to break it."

"It happens every day in business," Mr. Hanson says.

"This isn't business," Ike says. "It's love."

"Oh, Ike." His mother looks at him with pity. "I've never seen you so pussy-whipped."

Pussy-whipped. This is not a word I know.

"MOTHER!" Ike pushes back from the table. "This is *bullshit.*"

"Calm down," his father says. "Sit back down."

"No, I won't," Ike says. "You've insulted my wife. I expect better from you."

"We expect better from you," Mrs. Hanson says. "We expect better *for* you."

Ike raises his palms like he's a traffic officer halting a quickly oncoming car. "Enough," he says. "I expect your support, no matter what. I expect that my parents, at all times, *no matter what*, will support me."

"Whoa, whoa, whoa," Mr. Hanson says. "We do support you."

"But we *don't* support this marriage," Mrs. Hanson says. "And we certainly don't support . . . *her.*"

I've been the recipient of much disgust in my life, but

I've never in all my life felt so . . . small. I feel like I might blow away, and there isn't even a breeze.

"You plan *everything*, Ike," Mr. Hanson says. "You're the opposite of impulsive, and so when you do something like this, it causes us to—"

"I want your blessing," Ike says flatly. "That's what I want from you. I know what we've done is unconventional, but I love Tami, and I want you to trust that I know what I'm doing, and I want you to accept her into this family."

Mr. Hanson stares hard at Ike and prepares to say something, but before he can, Ike's mother does. "This marriage *isn't* blessed," she says. "It's the biggest mistake you've ever made. And, no, we will not be welcoming this . . . *person* . . . into our family."

An intensely serious Mr. Hanson watches his son, waiting for his response. I see the instant in which Ike decides that by his silence his father agrees with what his mother has said—that I'm not welcome. It comes directly before he holds out his hand to me and helps, almost pulls, me up, so that I'm standing by his side.

"Her name's Tami," he says. "Remember it, because she's not going anywhere."

Chapter 4

"Well, that was fun," Ike says grimly as we leave his parents' house. We're driving in a big, beat-up white pickup truck with the letters *GMC* on the front, which is Ike's other mode of transportation besides the scooter.

"That was *awful*, Ike." He grips the steering wheel so tightly that his knuckles are white. I put my hand on his thigh. "I'm so sorry. I—"

"Don't."

I take my hand back.

"Not that." He reaches for my hand and puts it back where it was. "Don't apologize. I'm the one who should apologize to you. I guess I shouldn't have told them with you there—but really, I had no idea they'd react this way. They've honest-to-God supported every single thing I've done before, even things that later proved to be stupid beyond reason."

This doesn't make me feel any better. "What does *pussy-whipped* mean?"

A smile breaks through. "Never you mind."

"What does *annulled* mean?"

His smile fades, and he takes his right hand off the steering wheel and covers mine. "Never mind about that one, either."

"It means to cancel our marriage, doesn't it?"

"That's not going to happen. But *how did I not see this coming*?"

Even if Ike doesn't know the answer to that question, I do. We'd been in a little bubble of happiness all by ourselves for twenty-four hours—it had been all good, and when things are all good, you think they'll stay that way. But that kind of happiness never lasts—and when the bubble pops, you feel like it was all just a lovely dream. Like it was stolen time, and for stealing that time of course there's a price you must pay. If I've learned anything in this world, it's that happiness has a price. You just don't always know what it will be.

I sigh to have been reminded of this, and I wish so much it wasn't true.

But it is.

In my life, and in my family's life, it has always been true.

At the intersection of Speedway and Tucson boulevards, Ike turns left onto Speedway. When we get to Country

Club Road, where he should turn right to go to my sister's house—that had been the plan, to see first Ike's family and then mine—he keeps driving straight.

"Did you forget to turn?" I ask.

"I want to show you something." He continues to Magnolia Avenue, the next big intersection, and pulls into the shopping plaza on the right. He parks in a spot in front of a corner store with a sign in the window that says AVAILABLE. He turns off the ignition and stares through the windshield at the vacant storefront. "Here she is. My perfect anchor spot."

"Is this—? Oh, Ike! Is this it? Is this going to be your coffee shop?"

"That was the plan." But instead of sounding happy, he says this like he just lost his closest friend. He takes a huge, miserable breath. "I did *not* see this coming."

"Ike?"

He keeps looking straight ahead. From the side, I see that his swallow comes hard. Then, finally turning to me, he says, "Want to get out and see it?"

"Of course!" I climb down from the truck, approach the store, and peer in the window. It looks to have been a restaurant, as there's an ordering counter and some food display cases. "It looks nearly ready to go."

He comes up, wraps his arms around me from behind, and looks over my shoulder into the abandoned restaurant. I lean back into him, feeling like a puzzle piece that has just been connected with its rightful partner. "There's a ton of work to be done. It's kind of a dump. But the location's perfect." He tells me how when Starbucks looks for locations, it looks to open them in shopping plazas where there's already a grocery store, and he points out the Trader Joe's directly across from this space. He goes on to describe how he'd change the layout, what sort of furniture he'd buy, what sort of lighting he'd have.

"I always thought I'd go modern with the design," he says. "But then—well, remember how you said I could use your 'capturing freedom' photographs as my artwork? That made me want to go cozier. And then I thought, maybe classier, too. So I'm going metal, wood, and glass, with a big wall fountain right there." He points out the spot against the far wall.

I hardly heard anything beyond the mention of my photographs. "You really want to use my pictures?"

"Absolutely," he says. "And I want you to sign them, and I'd like to sell them, too, if you're okay with that."

"If I'm okay with that?" I repeat. "Of course I'm okay with that!"

When I first arrived in America, Ardishir gave me his camera, and I took so many pictures. I took a picture of a teenage boy with three earrings in his ear and one in his lip. I took another of a barefoot, shirtless black man with crazy braids riding a unicycle and playing a flute. One of a car with pink daisies painted on it. Still another of my friend Eva from the waist down—of her miniskirt and thigh-high boots. Girls' bare shoulders. Front doors open to the world. Public hand-holding between gay men. Line dancing at a country-western bar. Cheerleaders doing cartwheels across the campus lawn.

You're looking for freedom in all its often overlooked details, Ike had observed. *You're photographing tiny acts of everyday rebellion.*

He was right. And even after three months, I still see freedom best that way, in its small, everyday forms.

I look once more through the window of the coffee shop and visualize all that he has described for me—the high-class coziness, the wall fountain. But mostly, I imagine my photographs on the walls. I will have them enlarged and very nicely framed. I'll make them grand, very professional. *I will be an official artist.*

I turn back to Ike and throw my arms around him. "Thank you!"

He accepts my hug but not my thanks. "There's one big, deal-breaking problem. My parents were supposed to match my investment dollar for dollar, to the tune of a hundred thousand dollars. I've spent the last three years of my life remodeling and flipping houses with my dad to earn my share, and that was in a rising housing market. God knows how long it would take me to earn the rest, but after to-night . . ." His eyes contain acute pain. "There's no way they're going to give me the money now."

"Oh, Ike." I did this. I caused him this pain. "I'm so sorry."

"Don't ever say you're sorry for marrying me."

"But I am if it . . . What can we do to make things better with your parents?"

He considers that for a moment. "I don't know that we can do anything."

"But this is your dream, Ike. You can't just give up on a dream."

He gives a halfhearted shrug. "There'll be other locations. Other opportunities."

He doesn't sound like he believes this, though, or that he can stand the wait.

I step away from him and go around the corner of the store, as if I want to look inside it from a different angle. But what I really want to do is kick the plate-glass window, or knock over one of these chained-down, leftover wrought-iron tables, or . . . or *something.* Something violent and destructive on purpose, because in marrying Ike—in making *my* dream come true—I've done something unintentional and yet vicious. I've ruined his.

I steady my breath and then look across the abandoned café and study my new husband. He leans against a concrete pillar on the covered patio with his arms crossed, staring through the window that separates him from the dream he was so close to realizing. That he *would* have realized, had I not come along. He catches my gaze and gives me a smile that's so sad I simply can't bear it, and so I go to him resolutely. "Maybe your parents are right, Ike."

He looks at me as though he's not at all surprised by what I've said. As though he knew I'd say such a thing. "My parents mean well," he says. "But they're not right."

"If you want to have our marriage annulled, I'll understand." I say this firmly, but inside I'm quivering, for this is *not* what I want.

Thankfully, Ike doesn't either. "Are you crazy, Persian Girl?"

"You didn't know this was going to happen," I say. "You would've made a different decision if you had."

He shakes his head no. "I don't think so."

"This is your *dream*, Ike. You can't give up on it."

We've been holding hands as we've talked, but now he grips my forearms. "Listen carefully. I'd also like to go parasailing. And bike across the country, and hike the Appalachian Trail. I'd like to buy a Harley, and live in Spain for a year. Opening a coffee shop isn't a dream, Tami. It's just one of the many things I'd like to do at some point in my life."

"*All* those things are dreams, Ike. You're a man of many dreams."

"But they're not—" He stops, frustrated, and looks away, struggling to find the right words. When he looks back at me, his eyes are earnest. "When you said good-bye, when you told me you were going back to Iran and would probably never come back, I thought I'd lost you. I felt so . . . hollow. Nothing meant anything anymore. You call them dreams, and maybe they were at some point, but after losing you, they all just became things on a list. Even opening the coffee shop didn't mean what it used to."

He takes my breath away, Ike does.

"Once I met you, my dreams changed," he says. "Everything I want to do in my life, I want to do with you by my side. That's my new dream. *You're* my dream."

"Ike."

My eyes fill with tears, my heart with wonder. I'm twenty-seven years old, which I realize is a little late in life to have fallen in love for the first time, but that's the situation I'm in. When I've imagined going back to Iran, part of me has thought I'd feel as if Ike were still with me, like an angel on my shoulder, whispering love into my ear, and another part of me—the more realistic part—has thought that I'd mourn his absence every day for the rest of my life. This love—it's overpowering. I'm so glad to know I'm not alone in it.

But still.

"I know how much your parents mean to you," I say. "And they're right that we hardly know each other."

"We know enough." He touches his finger to my lips to silence me. "We know we belong together."

I kiss the finger he has pressed against my lips and then with my hand move it aside. "Let's at least live together to show them our marriage is for real. Let's at least do that."

"Taking things slow was the one condition you had when it came to marrying me," he says. "You can't just drop it now."

One of my dreams is to live alone. All by myself. I know this may not seem like such a big dream, and maybe it's only a silly little dream, but there it is. I want to live alone.

These words popped out of my mouth in the hotel room in Las Vegas. I had no idea how badly I wanted it, until Ike proposed and I found myself saying it to him. It seemed right at the time.

He was confused at first, thinking I meant I didn't want

to marry him, but that wasn't the situation at all. There's no one in the world I'd rather be married to than him.

I want for us to date, I'd said. *Really, truly date. Go to dinner. See a movie. Maybe even dinner* and *a movie.*

That last part was a joke from a conversation we'd once had, but otherwise I was serious—because Ike had been forbidden to me. All we'd had were stolen moments between the time my English class let out and the time my sister got home from work. Maryam was afraid Persian men would think I was immoral for spending time unsupervised with an American man, or not serious about marriage. And so seeing Ike—loving him—was my secret. And as thankful as I now am to be his wife, the fact remains that we skipped over the whole boyfriend-girlfriend part. The fact remains that we have yet to go on one official date together.

For three months, we met for coffee after my English class and day by day, we'd flirt. We'd tease. We'd look at each other with yearning in our eyes. But we never dated. Ike asked, but I couldn't say yes. I was looking for a husband, not a boyfriend, and dating—an American man, no less—was a luxury I couldn't afford. Instead, I'd leave him and go home to meet one Persian man after another, trying to find one suitable for marriage, all the while dreaming of Ike.

I want to hold your hand and walk down the street with you and not be afraid of showing the world how I feel. To treasure every moment of falling in love. To learn to kiss you without fear. . . . And I want to live with you someday, when we're ready. When I'm ready.

I'd said all this, just yesterday. And I'd meant it. It seemed like a good idea at the time. But now, with Ike's parents against our marriage, thinking I have somehow tricked him, I realize that living alone is not only wrong, but selfish, too.

"I have no idea where that all came from," I say. "The words just came out of me."

"They came from that place in the soul that knows you best," Ike says. "That place you're never supposed to ignore."

"But, Ike—your parents love you," I say. "And if there's anything we can do to help them not be so upset, we should do it."

He shakes his head. "Our marriage is between you and me. What we do and how we do it is nobody's business but ours. We create our own path. That's what this marriage is—it's our path. Others can join us, or support us—or they can get the hell out of the way. Time will prove, in the end, whether it is, in fact, the right path. *But we don't change the path*—unless and until we decide *on our own* that we want to and that it's the best thing for our marriage."

He sounds perfectly sure of himself and he looks it, too. As he's talked, he's straightened his shoulders and puffed out his chest and raised his chin. He's so strong, this new husband of mine.

"You really don't mind having your parents be so upset?"

"Of course I mind," he says. "It hurts like hell. But I have to believe they'll come around eventually." He shrugs. "Ideally, when you get married, everyone's happy. But that's not always the case, and so then you've got to make a choice about who you're going to keep happy. For me, it's a no-brainer: You choose your spouse. That's what marriage means: I choose you above all others."

I squeeze his hands, trying to press my love into him. "I choose you, too, Ike. I just . . ." I sigh and look to the available storefront. "I want you to have your coffee shop. I don't want you to have to sacrifice it for me."

"Never mind the coffee shop," he says. "This is larger than that. We can't let anyone ruin things for us," he says. "Nothing and no one." He brushes a lock of hair off my shoulder. "The world's going to try and break us, Tami. It tries to break everyone. We just can't let it. That's how we win, right? As long as we stick together, as long as we fight for each other, we win. Even if we lose, we win. Right?"

Even if we lose, we win. As long as we fight for each other, we win.

He's a philosopher, too, my husband. "Right, Ike."

"So . . ." He pulls me close. "Are we together in this?"

"Yes, Ike. We're together in this."

"Are we united?"

I've only been married to him for a day, but already I can't imagine not being with him—together, united. Being in love is new to me, but this feeling of camaraderie, of shared purpose—well, this is something even better than being "in love."

This is love itself, and to me it feels as old as time and as necessary to life as food or air or water. There are lots of things I don't know very much about, but one thing I do know: This kind of love *is* worth fighting for.

"We're united," I say. "Absolutely."

Chapter 5

With our new sense of shared purpose, we go to my sister's house. Although we hadn't set a specific time because we weren't sure how long things would take with Ike's parents, Maryam and Ardishir are expecting us, and on the drive over, I find myself relaxed for the first time since our airplane touched down in Tucson. Relaxed and almost giddy, because I *know* Maryam and Ardishir are happy for us, and I can't wait to give Maryam the biggest hug of thanks for going to Ike and telling him of my situation. She *saved* me.

But my excitement turns to worry as we pull up to their house, for Maryam is standing on the front walkway with her hands on her hips, her long black hair loose, and her eyes wild. She's wearing a skirt and high heels and is glittery in her jewelry, but her face is furious. Ardishir holds two grocery bags and is halfway to the house from the car, but he's stopped still because Maryam is blocking his path.

She yells, "The whole reason I asked you to go to the store was to get me some nacho cheese sauce! How could you have forgotten this? I even sent a text message to remind you!"

Ike turns off the ignition and we remain seated in the cab of the pickup, watching. They've seen us, but Maryam is too mad to care about the impression she's making on Ike, while Ardishir gives us a close-lipped smile of apology.

"You think this is *funny*?" Maryam yells at him. "One thing I ask you to do—ONE THING! And this is what happens? After all I do for you?"

The neighbor lady next door pretends not to listen as she waters her yard. I'm dumbstruck. This is so unlike my sister. She's usually so refined and concerned about behaving in a high-class manner.

"Do you want me to go back to the store?" Ardishir's voice is even.

"YES, I want you to go back to the store!" she screams. "How are we supposed to have tortilla chips without nacho cheese sauce?"

I'm by now so mad at Maryam that it's all I can do not to jump out of the truck and begin defending Ardishir. Having lived with them for three months, I can say without hesitation that Ardishir treats her very well. My sister is a bit of a Persian Princess—it's not true that this nacho cheese sauce is the only demand she's made of him; it's always,

Ardi, can you rub my feet? And, *Ardi, will you scratch my back?* And, *Since you're going to the kitchen anyway, would you mind getting me a glass of water?*

All the time, she makes these requests. Yet I've never known her to send him away like this, and certainly never to scream at him this way. This is not how we were raised. Voices remain lowered in our family.

"I don't know why she's acting like this," I whisper to Ike. "And what the heck is nacho cheese sauce, anyway?" In my three months of living with Maryam, I have never heard of this before.

Ike laughs. "Trust me, you don't want to know. She probably thinks she's going to make a good impression on her new American brother-in-law by serving crappy processed food." Ike's voice is amused. "Either that, or . . ."

His voice trails off as the scene on the front lawn continues. Ardishir, in a very levelheaded manner, like he is dealing with a crazy person who's brandishing a gun, asks, "Do you want me to take the bags inside, or what do you want me to do with them?"

"Give them to me," she growls. "Just . . . *give* me them. I'll take them in my*self*."

Still stunned, I watch as Ardishir hands her the grocery bags and returns to his black Lexus.

To his back, Maryam yells, "Bananas, too! Get me some bananas or don't bother coming home!"

A little smile crosses Ardishir's face as he climbs into his car—thank goodness Maryam doesn't see it! He backs out of the driveway and smoothly drives away. Ike and I watch

Maryam storm back inside; then he says, "Man, she's got some serious cravings going on."

"Cravings? What do you—?" All of a sudden it occurs to me. "You think she's pregnant?"

"My mom had raging hormones like that every time she was pregnant," he says. "Let me tell you, it was not a pretty sight."

"Oh, my God!" I clutch his arm. "Do you really think that's it?"

"Why else would Ardishir put up with that shit?"

"He's a very patient person."

"Nobody's *that* patient," Ike says, laughing. "Nobody *should* be, unless there are some seriously extenuating circumstances."

Maryam pregnant.

I look out the truck's window. It's dark, but Maryam's house is lit with spotlights, and I remember back to my first night in America, when in the airport bathroom, Maryam stuffed me into a low-cut red dress and open-toed sandals and then brought me here. Waiting for me were Persians like her, who had already established themselves in America, and that night from the street, we could hear the music and through the open-curtained windows we could see them dancing. I saw how open and free they were—no need to hide behind high walls and thick curtains—and suddenly, all my years of idle dreaming—all the *might I*'s, the *can I*'s, the *will I be able to*'s—all those half-formed questions, half-formed desires—had an answer, and the answer was *yes.* In America, everything was possible.

I married the man I love. That is a dream come true.

Maryam being pregnant would also be a dream come true.

I look out the truck's window and through the living room window's sheer curtains make out my sister's form. She sits on the couch in her living room, alone with only her raging hormones to keep her company. I'm glad she's alone, for I want her all to myself for a little while. I want to find out if it's true, if it could really be true that she's pregnant, and if it is, I want to hold her close and for us together to celebrate the happy possibility that maybe—just maybe—whatever curse has befallen my family has finally been broken.

Ike agrees it's best for me to go inside alone. He'll return to his parents' house and talk with them some more, and we'll see each other tomorrow and the day after and the day after—every single day for the rest of our lives.

When I get inside, I find Maryam still sitting on the couch. She's flanked by the grocery bags and staring at the television screen, which isn't even turned on. "Maryam?"

Dazed, she turns to me. "Did that really just happen?"

I burst out laughing. Whoever that beast was, she's gone now. Only my chastened sister remains. "That really just happened."

"I need to call Ardishir," she says. "I need to apologize. And Ike! Oh, what must he think of me?"

"Ike thinks maybe you're pregnant," I say. "He says this is how pregnant women sometimes act. From hormones."

"Really? They do?" Immediate relief floods her face.

"You *are*? You're pregnant?"

Her eyes light up as she nods. Yes, she's pregnant!

I'm instantly a crying mess. I rush to the couch and we embrace. "Maryam, this is such good news! When did you find out? How far along are you?"

"More than three months," she says. "Fifteen weeks, the doctor says."

"But you're not even showing! Let me see!" She lifts her untucked blue blouse to reveal a precious little pooch of baby. "How could you have kept it a secret from me when I was living right here? You've been pregnant the entire time I've been here!? Oh, you and Ardishir must be so happy!"

"We haven't known for sure for very long," she says in apology. "I wouldn't even take a pregnancy test for the longest time because—well, just because." She sighs. "It's hard to keep getting your hopes up for something you don't think is ever going to happen. You know?"

I know. Of course I know. "Have you told our parents?"

Maryam's no is very firm.

"Oh, but why not?" I ask. "They'll be so excited!"

"It won't change a thing," she says. "Not one stupid thing."

I pull back. "What do you mean?"

She gives me a long look.

"What, Maryam? Tell me what you meant."

"It's nothing," she says. "I'd rather talk about your marriage! Tell me, was it—"

"Why aren't you sharing such good news with our

parents?" I say. "We should do all we can to give them happiness."

"I don't want to talk about it right now." Then she adds, "Poor Tami. Nobody ever tells poor Tami the truth, do they? You're our baby. We all want to protect you."

I sit back, stinging from her comment, even though I know it's true. After all, it was only a few days ago that I learned what really happened to our mother when we returned to Iran from America in 1979. Only weeks after we moved back, she was arrested at a rally protesting the new law that mandated the veiling of women. She was on the outskirts of the crowd—not an organizer, but simply one of many, and yet she was singled out in the worst of ways. Arrested. Thrown into the horrible Evin Prison and not allowed a lawyer for many weeks. No one knows what happened to her there. She doesn't talk about it.

Throughout my childhood, this was kept from me. I'd grown up thinking the hours, days, and years my mother spent sheltered indoors or in our courtyard garden were from regret—sadness at having made a bad decision to go back to Iran and getting stuck there. I knew nothing of how she suffered. I'd had no recollection of the time she was gone, but since recently learning of it, flickers of memory have emerged about the day she came back.

It happened suddenly, in my memory. I was actually in my parents' bedroom, at my mother's dressing table, with her curlers amateurishly spindled through my hair. I was holding her blue perfume bottle with its puff nozzle that I so adored, spritzing myself. Although the perfume was gone, with each puff, the smell of my mother came out of the bottle, and I chased it with my nose.

There was sudden action from the living room—startled voices, the sounds of grown-ups. My grandmother was there—my mother's mother—and my uncle, my mother's brother who now lives in London. There were others, too, but if I knew them then I don't remember now. There were loud cries, and a blur of grown-ups moved past the half-open door of the bedroom in which I played. My mother was in the middle, I think—I'm almost sure of it. Passing by, my grandmother looked at me, put her finger to her lips. *Stay quiet, Tami Joon. Stay silent,* she whispered as she closed the bedroom door.

Much, much later, I was led to the living room, to my mother, who'd been freshly bathed. I approached tentatively, held back a bit. My mother had thinned—her wrists, her neck, her waist—while her cheekbones had grown more pronounced. Yellowed bruises were covered with makeup. I knew her, but I didn't know her. She'd been cracked and patched back together like Humpty Dumpty, one of my favorite rhymes. And I, in playing with her perfume bottle, had taken on her smell. When she clasped me to her, her breath came in sobbing heaves. They had to pull me from her, and they made me go away again so as not to cause her further upset—she, who'd already been kept from me for so long.

I understood very little that day, as a child of not even four.

The one sure thing I understood was how I'd made my

mother cry. I'd made her sad, and her sorrow never went away. I believe now that she was crying not only from how she missed me, but from how she missed herself, too. Gone was the most beautiful woman in Tehran, the one with the carefree heart and the smile given freely to all, the one who loved to dance and put on fancy party clothes and enchant my father with her magical perfume. When she wore it, he'd playfully nip at her earlobes, lift her dangly earrings, and kiss her neck—again and again, until she'd swat him away with a look that promised more playfulness later.

"So you be the one," I say to Maryam now. "You be the one who tells me the truth."

My sister's sigh is deep and her voice quiet. "You don't remember how Maman was before, but I do. At night when I was little, she used to chase away the monsters under our beds. She had a smile that brightened the whole room, and her spirit filled the house with lightness. And now . . ." Her voice fades. "Well, she hasn't chased away our monsters in a long time, has she?"

I used to spend hours upon hours watching our home videos from the time before, and besides being the one who chased away our monsters, my mother was a tickler. She was a hugger, a teaser, a twirler-arounder. But none of these is the mother I know.

My mouth has soured at my sister's words, at my realization that there are so many pieces of my mother I know nothing about. "Poor Maman," I say.

"Poor *us*." Maryam's voice is harsh. "When I first came to the U.S., I was so homesick. I cried every day for months. . . . Poor Ardishir!" Now she's half laughing and half brushing away her tears—what a roller coaster of emotions this pregnancy has brought her! "I think he would have sent me back those first months if he could have!"

"Oh, no. Not Ardishir."

"He was so nice to me," Maryam says. "But I just begged Maman over and over to please come, that there was no reason for us to be separated from each other like that."

"You know it's not her fault," I admonish. "You know it's the government that won't allow them to leave."

"The government has nothing to do with it," she snaps. "It's her. She's too . . ." She stops and shudders. "It's her fault. It's her fault for not even trying. She won't even try to come."

The blood rushes to my head and I feel like I might faint. Maryam all of a sudden looks very far away. What she said isn't right. *It isn't right.*

"They *can't* come," I correct her. "They can't get their visas. You know this, Maryam."

"You said you wanted to know," she says. "I'm just telling you. Baba's got their visa paperwork all filled out—he's had it filled out for years—but Maman won't let him submit it. *She's* the reason they're not here, not the government. She's afraid of getting arrested again, or of their application being rejected, or of something else equally stupid. Who knows? She won't talk about it."

Have I been living in an alternate universe for my entire life? How can any of this be true?

"But it's our family's dream." I'm near tears. "Right?

To all be together in America? Has that stopped being the dream and somebody forgot to tell me?"

"Of course it's still the dream." Maryam's fists are clenched. "And now I'm having a baby, and they won't be here." Tears pour from her eyes. "They should be here. I need my parents to help me. I don't know what to do with a baby! What am I supposed to do with a baby?"

I can't believe this. *I can't believe this.* How could my mother not want to hold her grandchild, this proof that there's at least some beauty in this world? Don't we all sometimes need affirmation of that?

"We have to tell them you're pregnant," I say. "That will get her to come." Maryam's no is very firm, but I persist. "She'll want to know her grandchild."

Maryam shakes her head. "I don't want her to know. Not yet. Once I tell her, I'm just going to get even more angry with her. I know I will. I already have this ball of anger inside me—it's bigger even than this baby is—and that's not good. This baby should know nothing but peace and calmness and joy. This baby should know nothing but love."

Her breath catches in her throat from emotion, and while she tries to slow her breathing, I grapple with how little I know these people I love. I had no idea of the depth of Maryam's anger, no idea of the depth of my mother's fear. And what does this say about my father?

"For years, I tried all these things to get her to change her mind." Maryam's voice is far away as she remembers. "I tried anything I could think of to convince her to come.

Nothing worked. For a while, I called every day. I begged, I pleaded. Then for a long time I didn't call at all. For years, I told her I wouldn't have a baby until she was here to help me. I thought, you know . . ." She sniffles. "It's a mother's duty, isn't it? To be there for her daughter when her daughter needs her?"

"She'd love to be here." I'm sure of this. "You have to tell her so they can arrive in time."

She shakes her head. "She's a bad omen. A curse."

"Maryam."

She looks at me very directly. "Tami, this is my third pregnancy."

I gasp, for I had no idea. *No idea.* Who are these people I call my family?

"I told Maman about my first two," she says. "I thought—of course she'll come! But she's so wrapped up in her own sadness that my babies didn't even matter to her."

"You don't know that." I feel compelled to defend my mother, even as I can't begin to understand her. "You don't know what she's been through."

"I know she's not here." Maryam gives me a firm look. "Listen, I can't have stress in my body right now. I can't have anything negative in my heart. I told Maman both times before, and I lost both babies." Her voice breaks. "I can't lose this baby."

My poor, poor sister, all alone for so long with no family. "You won't lose this baby," I assure her.

"I've already had some spotting," she says. "Remember that night when Eva was over for dinner and I ran from the table crying? Well, that's what was going on. I thought I was losing this baby, too."

But she didn't *say* anything! I'm her sister, her only sister! Why wouldn't she share this with me? "Everything's okay now?"

Maryam nods. "I had an ultrasound, and the baby was fine. She had a good strong heartbeat, and I haven't had any more spotting or other bad symptoms since then."

"She? It's a she?"

Maryam smiles. "We don't know yet, but it *feels* like a she."

"Oh, Maryam! This is so exciting!" I'll be Auntie Tamila, and Ike will be Uncle Ike. I'll help take care of the baby, and Maryam, too.

"I can't believe I almost missed this, Maryam! Thank you so much for going to Ike and working things out for me." I brush the bangs from my beautiful sister's face and forgive her months of bossiness and rules and pushing me to marry men who were so clearly unsuitable. She couldn't stand the thought of being alone without family except for Ardishir again, especially not with a baby on the way. And I couldn't have stood being back in Iran with a new niece or nephew here. *Family should be together.*

"I'm here now," I comfort her, promise her. "I'm here now for good. It doesn't matter if Maman's not. I'm here, and I'll help you. You're going to be a great mom, and she's going to be the prettiest baby ever. She's going to be perfect. And we're going to be happy. We *are* happy, right?"

At last, the gleam in my sister's eye is the look of excitement a pregnant woman should have. She throws her arms around me. Her hug tells me the answer is yes, but she warns, "Don't say it out loud. That's just asking for trouble."

"What will you name my beautiful little niece?"

She laughs and takes my hands in hers. "I don't know yet. What name would *you* choose?"

"Hope," I say instantly. "I think you should name her Hope."

"An American name," Maryam says.

"Persians need to have hope." I squeeze her hand. "Her name will remind us of this."

Until Ardishir returns with the bananas and the nacho cheese sauce, my sister and I chat about happy things—about how we will turn my bedroom into the nursery, and how we'll shop for her maternity clothes, the merits of an American name versus a Persian name, and about how I will go with her and Ardishir for their upcoming sonogram. We talk about all the good things that are to come.

As we talk, I feel a huge new appreciation for Ike. We didn't have time to buy rings before we got married, or get each other gifts, but in marrying me, he gave me so many: The gift of love. The gift of America. The gift of keeping sisters together.

It's only later, when I'm alone in my room with my candle lit and my Googoosh music seeping into my heart, that my thoughts turn again to my parents. To my mother, in particular. What I said earlier isn't true. It does matter that my parents aren't here. It matters a lot.

Our family's dream is to be together in America. Until

tonight, I thought it was a dead dream, one that could never come true. But if it can . . .

If what Maryam says is true, then they must come. If it's not the Iranian government holding them back, but only my mother's fear, then that's something she has to overcome, because our family's dream is to be together in America, and we cannot kill our own dream.

We cannot kill our own dream.

We've got to try, and try, and keep on trying. It's our duty.

It's what we owe one another.

Chapter 6

The next day, I wake at dawn. My first thought is of Ike, and my vision of him is clear. He's sleeping like a prince, shirtless, covered with only a sheet. His precious ocean blue eyes are closed, graced by delicate black lashes. On our wedding night—the one night we've spent together—I remained awake long after him, trying to memorize his face. He has a tiny scar at the corner of his eyebrow, left over from a childhood bout of chicken pox. I hadn't noticed it before, hadn't known about the chicken pox, either. *They might ask you about that.* I pushed the thought away, because my curiosity for him is pure. I want to know everything about him, even the smallest things. Paper or plastic? Whole wheat or rye toast?

But it's true—they might ask me about that scar. At our immigration interview, they'll ask us lots of questions, some easy to answer and others not so easy. *You didn't move in together right away after your marriage—why not?*

That's one we'd have trouble answering, and how stupid and selfish would it be to lose America because of some silly-brained idea that it might be fun to "date" my husband instead of to live with him right away? I imagine myself saying, *I'm sorry, Baby Hope. I'd love to be there for you, to cuddle you and play with you and help your maman, but . . . well, I wanted to do things the American way when it came to getting married. Never mind that I lost my freedom as a result.*

Maybe I did have some secret desire to live alone, but that was before I married Ike. Before we made love. Before we sat together in front of his parents and endured their anger and made our pact to walk together on our path. We're comrades now. Kindred spirits. United in a way we weren't even a few days ago. I simply can't get enough of him and his tender strength. Kissing him, giving myself over to him, is like a prayer; it affirms God.

The person I want to talk with about this is my friend Rose. She's been on my mind so often as the past week unfolded—first in all its horror and then in all its beauty. The last time I spoke to her, I was still engaged to Masoud, still intending to move to Chicago with him. Rose and I said our sad good-byes—and now, on this beautiful Tucson morning, I want to say hello again.

I dress quickly. Usually, Maryam is the first to awake in the household, but I'm glad to learn from Ardishir, when I find him in the kitchen, that she's still asleep. This saves me from having to explain why she's never heard of Rose.

Five, perhaps ten years older than my mother, Rose has never married. We became friends when she found me foolishly hiding a pair of shoes in her front-yard bushes. They were a gift from Ike, and at the time, my friendship with him was a secret from Maryam, and so I needed to hide my shoes. Rose was very kind, very accepting of me, even though it was such a silly thing, and as the weeks and months went by, I found myself confiding in her like she was my mother—not the quiet, sad mother I have, but the generous, happy mother for which I've always yearned.

I take the same route to Rose's house that I always take to English class, which winds through the large-lot homes in the historic El Encanto neighborhood. The houses, the yards, the cars in driveways—the street signs, the birds calling, the sounds of traffic from nearby boulevards—none of it is new to me, yet it all feels so different. But I think it's me who's different this morning. I'm no longer a guest in this neighborhood, in this town.

I live here now. Tucson's my home. It's where I'll raise my family.

I cross Country Club Road at Sixth Street, then continue through a church parking lot on my way to Third Street. As I walk past the lively playground of an elementary school, I overhear two girls teasing a third: *Jake and Ella sitting in a tree. K-I-S-S-I-N-G.*

Curious, I stop in midstride and turn my attention to Ella, the redheaded girl getting teased. She looks forward to falling in love; I can see it by the coyness in the smile on her freckled nine-year-old face. I shake my head in wonder, in openmouthed awe. I think, as I so often do: *This would never happen in Iran.*

Nine-year-old girls in Iran do not shout gleefully on playgrounds in public view of passersby. They do not draw attention to themselves; they do not go to school with boys. They do not swing their long red hair and expect with Ella's certainty that romantic love is in their future. And they do not sing of sitting in trees with boys, kissing and producing babies! In the Islamic Republic of Iran, there is nothing innocent about a moment such as this. I know—I was a teacher there. I gave it up, because it was just too hard, taking part in a system of forced prayer, forced *hejab*, forced adoration of those who martyred themselves for the regime. Life either is or isn't precious—you have to choose what you believe—and I believe it is, or should be. It was too hard being part of a system I didn't agree with, one in which girls receive world-class educations and then are smothered as they try to use them to better their world.

Today, I wonder what it would be like to be a teacher in America.

Here, I think I might like it.

Here, everything seems possible for these girls in front of me.

With my ever-present camera, here are the pictures I take: Ponytails. Bony knees. Short plaid skirts. That neon-pink Band-Aid on Ella's bare arm. I blur out the boys in the background and keep my focus only on these girls and the way their white socks fold down to their ankles. The easiness of their smiles. They are unburdened, these girls. So fortunate as to take their good fortune for granted.

After I finish taking my pictures, I lower my camera and catch the eye of a sad-looking boy. He clutches the fence, as if desperate to escape the playground—indeed, as if desperate to escape his life. Back in Iran, I never paid much attention to boys. The stories I imagined for them—the lives I imagined they would one day lead—never seemed as sad as the ones I imagined for girls. But this American boy seems so lost. So lonely. So in need of something no one's giving him.

I can't give him much, but I give him what I have: My best pretty-lady smile. I also wave, but he just stares at me and continues to clutch the fence, and so I go on, his eyes haunting me long after I've left him behind. I wonder how anyone can be sad in America, and then I chastise myself. Everywhere in the world, there is happiness, sorrow, fear, longing, and love—and hate, too. These emotions are universal; only the particulars are different.

Even though it's not yet eight thirty, I know Rose will have been awake for hours. However, she doesn't answer her door, so I go up her driveway, past her not-so-new Honda Civic, and peek through the painted-pink iron gate. It's there, in her backyard, that I find my Rose, on her knees before a flower bed, tending her garden.

"Excuse me, Rose?" My voice sounds loud in the still morning air, but it doesn't reach her old-lady ears. I raise my voice and call again. "Rose? Excuse me, please. Hi! Hi, Rose!"

Finally, she turns, and the pleased look on her face warms my heart. "Oh, my—Tami!" she says. "Is it really you?"

"It's really me!"

Rose works herself to her feet and comes to greet me, removing her gardening gloves as she does. "I've been watching the airplanes in the skies all week, wondering which one you were on." She stops before me, reaches through the gate, and caresses my cheek. "How are you still here?"

"Rose, you'll never believe it—I married Ike!"

"No! Tami, really?"

"Yes, and I get to stay right here in Tucson!"

"This is wonderful! The best possible news!" She covers her heart with her hands, overjoyed; then she quickly reaches to unlatch the gate. "Come in! I'll put some water on. Let's have tea, and you can tell me all about it."

Rose is so thoughtful—she bought a box of sugar cubes just for me so I can have my tea the Persian way when I visit her, where you place the cube in your mouth and let the hot tea melt it into pure sweetness. As I step through the gate, I clasp her cool, fragile hand, careful not to crush it in my excitement. "We can have tea together all the time now, Rose!"

She gives me a confiding look. "I'll confess, I was terribly sad at the prospect of not seeing you any longer. Your parents must be so pleased."

Ah, my parents. "I don't know *what* my parents are thinking, Rose. I really just don't know."

She tilts her head, curious, but when I don't continue she encourages me to have a seat at the wrought-iron table while she goes inside to get our tea. I like it that Rose pushes me just as far as I want to be pushed, but never further.

My heart has grown heavy, as it always does when I think of my parents half the world away, and it's heavier than usual because of what Maryam told me last night. I dread the phone call to them that I'll soon have to make. Our relationship feels newly false—although I suppose it's been false all along and I just never knew it. A part of me wishes I still didn't.

But I don't want to be sad. Not today. I'm a new bride, my sister's pregnant, and I'm having tea with one of my favorite people in the world. I should be happy, and I almost succeed, except as I look around Rose's backyard, the fresh-dirt smell of her garden reminds me of our courtyard at home, where my mother grows her rosebushes and takes her tea in the afternoons if the weather permits. She so seldom ventures beyond it that I've come to think of it as her pretty little prison cell. Genteel, a decaying glory, it reflects her, too, with its chipped concrete birdbath and mossy walls. Leaves fallen from the tree breezes are trapped there, gentle dervishes, spinning idly around the courtyard, going nowhere in the end, unable to escape their fate.

But Rose's garden is delightful. The word for it, I think, is *whimsical.* First, it's so colorful with spring flowers unfolding into their full beauty. Then, it's colorful with personality. This garden could belong to no one other than Rose. There's an old ladder painted deep pink with a potted plant on each step. She uses old tires for planting beds and has Mexican tin-can lanterns strung throughout. Her three cats roam freely. There are two altars in her yard—one created in honor of her parents, who have died, and the other a Christian one which depicts Mary, the mother of Jesus, whose lifeless body is draped over her lap. Rose is Catholic, like Ike's family. She has a little pond with very large goldfish. My favorite part of her yard is a saying she has painted on the archway to it: ONLY MY GARDEN KNOWS THE SECRETS OF MY SOUL. While I wait for her, I wonder what Rose's soul secrets might be.

She soon returns with our tea, and as it cools, she asks me to fill her in on what's new. Laughing, I tell her I don't even know where to begin.

"How about pick up your story from the last time you visited me," she says. "That was the day before you were to be married to that gay man from Chicago you were afraid wasn't very nice."

"It turns out I was right about that."

"And you also said Ike wasn't ready to be married." Her eyes twinkle. "It looks like you weren't so right about that!"

I update her on everything—Masoud's day-of-wedding demand that I forfeit my rights to my children in the event of a divorce, about Maryam telling Ike of my visa predicament, about Ike's showing up in Las Vegas and his sweet proposal, of his parents' reaction to our marriage, to Maryam's pregnancy, to my most immediate dilemma of convincing Ike we should, in fact, move in together right away even though that's the exact opposite of what I said just a few short days ago—and when I'm done, I sit back, exhausted.

"Whew!" she says. "You've had quite a busy week!"

"And an emotional one," I say. "So many highs, so many lows. I'm really very exhausted."

I look around her yard again, resting my eyes on the striped-fabric hammock under a tree near the little waterfall and goldfish pond. The very sight of it makes me yearn for the chaos in my life to take a break. I wonder if there might be a way for time to stand still, just for a little while. Just so I could catch my breath.

I'm still looking wistfully at the hammock spot when Rose pats my hand. "Have you seen my guesthouse, Tami?"

"Only the outside." I look to her tiny pink adobe guesthouse and its sweet windows, with green-painted trim and blue-painted flower boxes that contain red geraniums. A French door opens to the backyard, and there's also a second door that can have the bottom half closed and the top half open. You can lean against it from inside and have a pleasant conversation with a neighbor—it reminds me of Dorothy's farmhouse in *The Wizard of Oz*, a movie we took back with us to Iran that I've seen perhaps one hundred times. The second door opens to a small patio at the rear of the guesthouse.

"Let me show you the inside." Rose leads me to it, and right from the doorway, I fall in love with its brick floors, multicolored walls, and the hand-stenciled tile sign that reads, LET US LINGER HERE A WHILE IN THE FOOLISHNESS OF THINGS. I read that over again and think *yes*, that is exactly what I want to do—to linger in this delicious moment of my life. I love the little messages Rose paints on her walls and in her garden. To me, they're like invitations to a magical world.

"What do you think of it?" she asks. "Other than the fact that it's so small?"

"Oh, it's beautiful!" I scan the one-bedroom house again. The kitchen area has open shelves with bright dishes and there are tissue-paper flowers in a vase on the kitchen table for two. "There couldn't be a sweeter place."

"Why don't you stay here for a few days?" she says.

My heart skips a few beats. "What do you mean?"

"It's going to take at least a few days if not a week or more for you and Ike to find a place, get his credit checked, and get your utilities hooked up, right?" Rose says. "All those things take time. And meanwhile . . ." She raises her eyebrows mischievously. "Meanwhile, you could have a mini vacation here and maybe get this living-alone business out of your system."

"I don't think I *do* want to live alone anymore," I say. "I think I'm over that idea."

She shrugs. "Then Ike can stay here, too."

I break into a broad smile and walk onto the private patio, with Rose following. Glass-shard wind chimes sprinkle the air with their light sound, and two hummingbirds busily gather their nectar from the potted honeysuckle plant. A red robin perches on the frame of one of the patio's two chaise lounges, and I imagine myself with a pretty pot of tea, sitting there—successfully reading an American novel, with the robin reading over my shoulder. I can picture it perfectly. And to have Rose so near! Rose, who always makes my heart feel at peace.

I turn to her, having realized that what I most wanted when I made my big declaration to Ike wasn't, in fact, to live alone at all. It was to have a choice.

"If it's okay with Ike, could we pay you rent and stay longer than just a few days?"

"You'd like to live here?"

"To live here, yes. To linger here," I say. "If that's all right with you."

"I'd love that." She's teary-eyed.

All of a sudden, I'm crying, too. She puts her arms around me, and I cry and cry and can't stop crying. At first my tears are happy ones, but too soon I'm heaving with sorrowful ones, and angry ones, and relieved ones, and, finally, tired ones. Rose pats my back and shushes me in a way that tells me I can keep on going as long as I need to. At long last, I get control of myself and step back.

"I'm sorry! My gosh!" Embarrassed, I sniffle and wipe away my tears. "I think I really do just need to catch my breath."

"You're closing one very big chapter in your life," she says. "It's natural to have such strong emotions."

I take her hand, appreciative of her perspective. She's right—I *am* ending a big chapter. I'm beginning another one, too, and I can't think of a place I'd rather start it than right here, in this magical place, near my good-hearted Rose.

Chapter 7

I'm back at Maryam's house, and when Ike calls me on his break at work, I tell him about Rose's offer to let us live in her guesthouse, and after I convince him that this is what I really want to do, he agrees to pick me up after work so I can show it to him. I spend the afternoon alone, as Maryam and Ardishir are both at work. Besides preparing a dinner of chicken shish kebab for them, I don't have much to do. I could call my parents. . . . I *should* call my parents, but I'm not ready to talk with them yet. I don't know what to say to Maman. All I want to do is ask a question that seems both childish and pathetic: *Don't you want to be with me?*

Rather than face that uncomfortable conversation, I call my Russian friend, Nadia.

"Nadia Joon!" I say when she answers. "How are you? How is your baby?"

"Tami! Everything is good! No baby yet—but the doctor, he says any day!" Before, when Nadia lived in Tucson, being abused by her horrible husband, her voice was tinged with shame and regret and sadness, and she spoke softly, as if what she had to say was not important. Not anymore. Today, her voice holds happiness. "You are in Chicago?" she says in her thick accent. "And your vedding—how vas it?"

"My wedding was wonderful, Nadia, but you'll never believe what happened. You'll never guess who I married!"

"Your husband, he is Masoud, *da*?"

"No, Nadia! I didn't marry Masoud. I married Ike!"

"Vat?" she says. "How is this possible? How is this good news possible?"

As I share the details of what happened, she cries with joy for me, and my heart bursts anew with love for Ike, love for Nadia, love for my life here in America. This is a story I'll never get tired of sharing. Already I'm imagining how much fun it will be to tell our children one day. *Your father was like a knight in a fairy tale*, I'll say. *He rode in on his white horse and saved the damsel in distress.*

Things for Nadia are going well, too. Since arriving in San Francisco a few weeks ago, she's been staying with Maryam's very kind friend, who took her to an organization for Russian immigrants. A lawyer there helped her file for divorce from her husband, and also, she met some women she plans to live with after her baby is born, a group of single mothers who help each other out. She met an older Russian man who owns a health club and will give her a job. It would only be cleaning the locker rooms and sports equipment, but she'd be able to leave her baby in the on-site nursery and get her meals at a fifty percent reduction. So this is what she plans to do, and I'm so happy for her.

Nadia squeals with joy when I tell her about Maryam's pregnancy. "This is such good news! If I have girl, for honor I vill give her your sister's name. Please tell her *spaseeba* from me. Tell her very much thank you. I owe her *everything.*"

She says this because Maryam—who had never met Nadia but who'd heard from me stories such as how her husband broke her arm by pushing her down the steps of their trailer home—helped her get away by giving her some money and also asking a friend if Nadia could live with her in San Francisco until she can live independently.

"Maryam will be so honored if you name the baby for her," I say. "But really, you saved yourself, Nadia Joon. You made a good decision when you were offered the chance to leave. You were very brave."

We talk for a bit longer, and then she has to hang up because a friend is picking her up to help with some errands.

The last hour before Ike gets off work feels like forever, but at long last, I hear the sound of a vehicle pulling into the driveway. I switch off the television and jump up from the couch. I fluff my hair and smooth my skirt before rushing to open the door. I throw it open, a huge smile on my face.

"Hello!" I say. "I've missed you so much!"

Only then do I realize it's not Ike standing behind the big bouquet of flowers. It's—oh, my God—it's *Haroun*, my obsessive-compulsive almost-fiancé. Someone I was days away from being engaged to. Someone I hoped never to have to see again.

What on earth is he—*oh, my God*—doing here?

"Haroun! What are you . . . Oh, my, hi! I can't believe it's you! I can't believe you're here!" I keep my smile pasted on my face, but inside, I'm panicking. He's a part of my past I'm longing to leave behind.

"Hello, Tami." He beams at me. "You're looking especially lovely today."

"Thank you." My heart pounds. *Shut the door, shut the door,* but of course I can't do that.

"May I come in?"

"Of course. Please!" I unlock the security door and push it open for him.

"These are for you." He steps inside, into the foyer, and hands me the beautiful bouquet. I can't help but admire how smartly he's dressed, in a dark gray suit, white dress shirt, and a deep purple tie. "Your sister and brother-in-law aren't home?"

"No," I say. "They're at work."

This is when I should invite him to sit down and offer him tea, but I can't bring myself to do it. In fact, I leave the front door open in hopes that he'll be heading back out very, very soon.

"Today, of all days?" He gives me an odd look. "I would think they'd want to spend this last day with you."

Oh, right. He thinks I'm flying back to Iran tomorrow. After my brother-in-law broke the news that I'd chosen Masoud over him, he later called him—this was just days ago, although it feels like forever!—and asked if Haroun would still marry me. Unsurprisingly, his answer was no—which meant, to all of us at the time, that I'd be leaving for Iran when my tourist visa expired. I don't know how to tell him all that's happened. It won't be as enjoyable as it was telling Rose or Nadia; that much is certain. In fact, I'd prefer not to tell him at all, and I really don't think I should have to—I didn't summon him, after all, but rather he came uninvited, which is very odd for him and which he really shouldn't have done. But from his kindness so far, I suspect he wants me to know there are no hard feelings in spite of how things ended for us, and for this I'll be very glad.

"These flowers are *lovely*, Haroun." To be polite, I sniff them. "It's very kind of you to bring them."

His Persian brown eyes shine brightly. "Are you all packed?"

"I am." I neglect to add that I'm packed to move to Rose's guesthouse, not back to Iran.

"Tami . . . ?" He peers at me, trying, I think, to be serious, but a smile slips through. "I've been thinking."

Haroun thinking. This can't be good. "About?"

Suddenly, there's a charge to the air, like something important is about to happen. I've felt this several times recently—when Masoud showed up on the morning of our wedding day and insisted we talk about the terms of our marriage. When Ike appeared at my hotel room in Las Vegas. When he dropped to one knee and . . . oh, God.

In front of me, Haroun drops to one knee.

"Haroun," I say urgently, panicked. I look around the room, hoping beyond hope that Ardishir or Maryam or someone—*anyone*—will save me from this moment. Eva would tell him to get the hell up and get the hell out. Where is she when I need her? "What are you *doing*?"

"I told you," he says. "I've been thinking."

Get up, get up.

"The floor's dirty, Haroun. It hasn't been vacuumed in several days."

If anything will get him off his knees, this will, as he's obsessed with germs.

"I don't care," he says, although his neck veins tighten. I notice, too, that he didn't try to take my hand, although maybe it's because I'm holding the flowers. The flowers!

"Let me get a vase." I start to step away. "Why don't you have a seat on the couch while I do?"

"No, please!" He grabs my hand.

"Haroun! What are you doing?"

"Forgive my forwardness," he says. "Do you mind?"

"No, but the germs!"

"I'm going to change, Tami," he says. "I want to change my life. Embrace it fully. I can't let—" He grips my hand harder. "I have to get better. I have to *be* better. Life is so fragile. It can be lost in an instant, and because it's so fragile we must . . . kiss every moment with laughter and joy."

Kiss every moment with laughter and joy? Is this the same man who just weeks ago told me I might get mad cow disease from eating a rare steak?

"Are you all right, Haroun?"

"I'm wonderful, Tami." He adds meaningfully, "And so are you."

Please stop, please stop, please please stop.

"Haroun, have you, um, talked to Dr. Haji about these changes you're experiencing?"

"I have," he says. "We adjusted my medication, and I feel better every day. The world is so beautiful, isn't it?"

"Yes, Haroun. It is."

"The greens are so green and the blues are so blue and the reds are so red and the yellows—"

"Are so yellow. I get it, Haroun." I wonder if perhaps Dr. Haji didn't *over*medicate him.

"But why are we talking about doctors and medicine at a time like this?" he says. "I'm *here*, Tami. And I *will* marry you. I'll save you from a lifetime of repression in Iran and I'll treasure you every day for the rest of my life. I'll—"

"Get the hell away from her!"

Ike's voice bursts from the doorway as he bolts toward Haroun. *"Or I'll kick your ass so bad you won't—"*

"Ike!" I get between them and press my hand against Ike's chest as Haroun scrambles to his feet and backs hurriedly away. "Don't! What are you doing?"

"This is the guy, isn't it?" Ike glowers at me. "The guy you were supposed to marry? The asshole who tried to force you to sign that contract?"

He means Masoud. I haven't exactly told Ike about Haroun yet.

"No-o-o-o-o-o-o." I draw out my breath as I say it. "This is Haroun. He's . . . actually . . . very nice."

"Who are *you*?" Haroun demands, a little braver now that he has me as a buffer.

"I'm her *husband*."

Shocked, Haroun stares first at Ike and then at me. I stare back with my mouth dropped open, as if it's news to me, too.

"Her *what*?"

"Her *husband*." Ike brushes my hand off his chest and starts to go around me. "You got a problem with that?"

"Ike, please."

"Ike please *what*?" he says to me.

"Don't talk to her that way," Haroun says.

Ike pokes Haroun in the chest. "You *don't* tell me what to do."

"Ike, no. Please, listen," I say. "Haroun is—" Oh, God. What is Haroun?

The desperation on Ike's face borders on betrayal and simply breaks my heart. "Is he . . ." He stops to swallow hard. "Is he your *boyfriend* or something?"

"No!" I say. "God, no!"

"But I am," Haroun says.

"No, you're not!" I say, and then, to Ike, "He's not!"

Haroun asks Ike, "What do you mean you're her husband?"

Ike snarls, "What do you think I mean, dumb-ass?"

Fruitcake, I think. *He's a fruitcake, not a dumb-ass.*

"You were supposed to marry a Persian," Haroun says, confused. "Ardishir told me. I distinctly remember."

"This is someone different," I say.

Now it's Haroun who looks betrayed as he fumbles about, wiping his hands on his pants and brushing off the knees of his trousers. He's reverting, the poor man. "But . . . how? Where'd you find him?"

Where did I find him?

"At Starbucks."

This is a truly stupid thing to say. I realize it as soon as the words are out of my mouth.

"What, you just . . . picked him out of a crowd and somehow convinced him to marry you?"

"Haroun, please, it's not like that."

"What am I supposed to think, Tami?" His voice catches on my name. "That *anyone*, just some random stranger off the street, is better than me?"

"Of course not, Haroun," I say. "Ike is—"

"*Not* a random stranger," Ike says, seething.

"I thought we had something special," Haroun says, giving me a look that asks, *Didn't we?*

Ike raises an eyebrow and waits for my response.

"You were . . . a good friend to me," I say.

"We were more than that," Haroun says.

I shake my head. "No, Haroun."

His look darkens. "Then you used me."

"Used you? What are you *talking* about?"

"To get your citizenship," he says. "You used me."

"You knew about my situation," I say. "You knew the whole time. Of course that was part of the deal. I wouldn't have agreed to an arranged marriage otherwise. I mean, I hoped we'd grow to love each other over time, but—" *But you see imaginary bugs and suffer imaginary bites and refuse to fly in airplanes because of all the germs in the recycled air.* "But neither of us was in love."

The hurt look he gives me tells me I'm wrong about that.

"Haroun?"

It's the strangest thing. He doesn't physically move, but his eyes develop black circles underneath them and his face turns gaunt. It's as if a sickness on the inside is manifesting itself on the outside. He doesn't even look like himself anymore. He looks mean. Like a stranger. Like a very mean stranger.

"You used me." His voice is perfectly flat.

"I didn't." I shake my head, at him and then at Ike. "That's not how it was."

"You led me on and then you dumped me when someone better came along. Then you dumped him when *this* guy came along."

"That's not true! That's not what happened. I've, I—" *I loved Ike from the moment I met him. Even before that. He was already in my heart the first time we met.* "I knew Ike all along."

There is an abyss of blackness in Haroun's eyes. "What did you say?" When I freeze up, he asks Ike, "How long have you known her?"

"The whole time she's been here." Ike seems to say this more in defiance of Haroun than in support of me. I don't like this—how either one is acting. It feels off. Wrong. Bad.

"You knew him while you were dating me?" Haroun says.

"You and I were not exactly dating," I say.

"We were deciding to get married," Haroun says. "I'd call that dating."

"And Ike and I were definitely not dating," I say, looking to Ike both in apology and for confirmation.

"No," he says grimly. "We were falling in love."

Our eyes lock on this undeniable truth and for a moment, we're alone in the room, alone in the world, alone, together, in our love. Our love is the easy, indisputable part. It's everything else that's complicated.

"Don't let her fool you," Haroun warns Ike. "She used to look at me that same way, too."

I laugh. This is almost funny.

"I never did," I assure Ike.

"She's going to do the same thing to you that she did to me," Haroun says.

"What same thing?" Ike asks.

"Please don't ask him anything," I say. "Don't talk to him. His view of things is . . . not quite normal."

"She'll dump you," Haroun says. "As soon as you're not useful to her anymore. As soon as you've served your purpose."

Ike, already pale, loses his coloring completely. I'm sure he's hearing echoes of his mother: *This marriage is the biggest mistake you've ever made.*

"It's not like that," I say desperately. "Ike, you know this isn't true."

He says nothing.

"Ike." I put my hand on his arm. "I love you! You know this!"

"Another lie from the mouth of the beautiful Tamila Soroush," Haroun says. "Don't believe it. She doesn't love anyone but herself."

"Please be quiet," I snap. "I've had enough of you."

"*You* can give me back my flowers."

"Oh, my God. Take them." I practically throw them at him. "Now go. Please! Would you just go?"

"Gladly." Haroun bumps shoulders with Ike as he passes and then brushes away Ike's invisible germs. At the doorway, he turns to me with bitter eyes. "You can't do this," he says. "You can't treat people this way and expect to get away with it."

"I'm only trying to live my life, Haroun."

He glares at me. "So am I, Tami. SO AM I!"

I close the security door behind him and watch as he takes a handkerchief from the pocket of his suit, lifts the lid of the green garbage Dumpster at the end of the driveway, and tosses the bouquet of flowers into it. He gets into his black late-model Mercedes, and as he drives away in his squeaky-clean car, I wonder, *Did this really just happen?*

From the look on Ike's face when I turn back to him, I have my answer: Yes, it did, and he's none too pleased about it.

Chapter 8

"Shit, Tami," Ike says. "What was *that* all about?"

I laugh. I can't help it. Nerves, probably.

"It's not funny," he says. "Who the hell *was* that guy?"

"He's just . . . well . . ." I twist my hands nervously and try to find the right words. How do I explain Haroun, a nice man, a willing man . . . and yet, not one I loved. "It was supposed to be an . . . arranged marriage kind of thing."

Ike nods slowly a few times, digesting this, and doesn't say anything for a long, long, too long moment.

"I would have told you about him," I say. "I meant to. It's just . . . Haroun was never my official fiancé like Masoud was. He was more of a . . . maybe-fiancé."

Ike presses his palms against his eyes, grimacing like he has the world's worst headache. "*Gah!* You talk about these guys like they're items you're ordering from a menu. *I think*

I'll have the halibut today, not the ravioli. This is too much. *Too much.*"

I'd move to him, put my hands on his wrists, pull his hands away from his eyes so he can look into mine and see *me* again instead of the horrible person Haroun has made me out to be. Only I can't, because what does he mean by *this is too much?* Does he mean our two-day-old marriage is too much?

"Ike?"

He gets his composure soon enough and drops his hands from his face. "It's just—God. I spent the whole friggin' night last night trying to convince my parents that I know what I'm doing with you, and then—" He pauses to laugh at himself like what an idiot he's been. "And then there's this guy, who I know nothing about, on his knees proposing to you, and he knows nothing about anything, either. And he gives me basically the exact same warning as my parents. It's just a little hard to process. You know? It's too much, too fast, too soon. All of it. Too much. This isn't how my life is supposed to be. I like simple. Uncomplicated. I can't even think straight at the moment."

I take his hand. "Can we sit down?"

He nods, and when we get to the couch, we sit close and hold each other—tightly, preciously, with abandon. When we separate, he says, "This is how I know it's right. This feeling can't be faked."

"I'd rather leave the U.S. forever than have you doubt my love," I tell him. "And *that's* why I didn't tell you about my situation, because I didn't want you to think exactly what you're thinking."

"I don't doubt your feelings. I just . . ." He sighs. "I don't like surprises, I guess. That guy was quite the surprise." He peers at me. "When did all this happen? When did things with him fall apart? How recently were you supposed to marry him?"

Bad questions. Bad, bad questions.

"Recently," I say.

"How recently?"

"Very," I say.

"Like . . . last week?"

"Well . . ." I calculate back. It was, in fact, about ten days ago, even though it already feels like another lifetime. "That's about right."

"So in the span of, let's see, about a week, you were engaged to three different men?"

My eyes tear up. I wasn't trying to hurt anyone. I really wasn't. I was just trying to help myself. But in doing so, I've been horrible to others. I've been so, so, horrible.

"I try to be a good person." This comes out in a near-whisper.

"Oh, you are. You are!" Ike's irreplaceable blue eyes sparkle. "You're my favorite person in the world."

My heart, which had been shrinking, expands again to make room for his love. "You're my favorite person in the world, too."

"You just happen to have very short engagements."

I give him a look that says, *Very funny, buster.*

"But seriously," he says. "What sort of trouble can this guy cause?"

"Haroun? None." Of this, I'm fairly certain. "Even today, he was being honorable. He was offering to save me from having to go back. I think he's one of the good guys. One of the crazy-but-good guys."

"*Would* you have married him?" Ike asks. "If we weren't already married, I mean. If you were faced with going back to Iran tomorrow or marrying him today, would you?"

Don't ask me that.

He raises an eyebrow. "Well?"

"Ike . . ." He's not going to like my answer, for I would have married Haroun. Absolutely, I think. And I would have done my best to make it work. "Until you've lived under a repressive government, Ike, please don't judge me. You can't fully understand what living in a place like Iran does to you—you can't really even understand until you leave it, and not even then, sometimes. It . . . keeps you small. All your thoughts, your hopes. Your mind. Your heart. Your dreams. They shrink to fit what's allowed. At least mine did. My worst day in America was better than my best day in Iran, because at least here, no matter what, I'm free."

Free to succeed or fail, to choose or not choose.

Free to just . . . be.

"I regret saying anything harsh about him, then." Ike gently brushes a strand of hair off my shoulder. "Coming here was a decent thing for him to do."

"It was," I agree. "And I should apologize to him. It can't have been pleasant, what happened just now. He was only trying to be nice."

Ike smiles. "Maybe you should send him flowers."

Funny husband. "He'd probably just throw them in the Dumpster."

He pulls me to him for a hug, and just like that, it's okay between us again. It's his heart beating against mine. It's me tucked into him. It's him not letting me go. We stay like that until another black car pulls into the driveway. This time, it's Ardishir, home early from work.

"Another fiancé?" Ike says as he looks out the window.

"Enough already!" He knows it's Ardishir; he saw him getting screamed at by Maryam last night. "It's so strange you haven't met Ardishir yet."

"He was busy getting nacho cheese sauce," Ike says with a laugh.

We greet Ardishir at the front door, and I'm filled with happiness as two of my very favorite people in the world shake hands for the first time.

"I hear congratulations are in order," Ike says.

"Thank you, yes." Ardishir beams. "And you, too, of course. Congratulations on your marriage! We wish we could have been there, and we'd like to throw a party for you."

"That'd be great," Ike says. "Although let's wait until my parents are a little more copacetic with the idea."

Copacetic. I have no idea what that means. Before I can ask, Ardishir replies.

"Yes, Tami told us about that." He furrows his brow sympathetically. "I'm sorry it's caused problems for you with your family."

Ike grins happily at me. "Tami's worth any trouble."

"Can I get us some tea?" I ask.

"Tea would be wonderful," Ardishir says.

"I don't suppose you have any coffee?" Ike says.

"I'm sure we do," Ardishir says. "Somewhere. Instant, maybe."

"Never mind," Ike says. "When in Rome, et cetera."

While I'm in the kitchen preparing the tea, I eavesdrop on Ardishir and Ike in the living room as they talk about Maryam's pregnancy. Ardishir says ever since he found out he's going to be a father, he's become obsessed with learning as much as he can about American history. *This is going to be my child's homeland. He's always got to know how fortunate he is.* Hearing this, I get teary-eyed, for I know exactly what he means. This is how it all comes full circle, by giving your child the most precious thing your parents lost.

"Here we are," I say cheerily as I carry out a platter with a dish of mixed nuts, a huge bowl of fruit, and the tea, of course. "Hopefully Maryam will be home from work soon, too."

Ike's eyes widen. "That's a lot of fruit for three people."

"Yes, it is, Mr. American." As I serve the tea, I tell Ardishir about Haroun stopping by.

"The cashew nut was here?" Ardishir beams. "How *is* the fruitcake? I love that guy. Did Tami tell you how he was convinced our house was infested with bugs?"

Warily, Ike glances at me. "No, she didn't."

Ardishir gleefully tells him how Haroun spent about ten minutes compulsively washing his hands when he came for dinner, how he was terrified of germs and saw bugs where there weren't any and insisted he'd been bitten by a large insect *with tentacles*—he was very insistent about that—while at the dining room table, and how he accused us of not maintaining proper pest control, and how he sent my steak back to the chef at a restaurant because he was convinced it had mad cow disease. And how he avoids flying on airplanes because of the recycled air and how he won't use rest-stop toilets.

Ike's smile is strained as Ardishir goes on and on describing Haroun's many foibles. By the end, he's grimacing.

"What I don't understand," he says, "is why, if you couldn't find someone appropriate—and *hello, I was right there the whole time*—why not just move somewhere else when your visa expired, like to Canada or France or Spain or *someplace* other than Iran?"

That is a very good question.

And the answer is . . .

"I wouldn't know anybody," I say.

"So what?" Ike says. "That's temporary for a girl like you. You're outgoing, attractive. People like you. You would have made friends pretty quickly."

But . . . "Without my family? I . . . I couldn't do that."

Could I?

"Didn't you just tell me a little while ago that your worst day here was better than your best day there?"

I did just tell him that, and I meant it. It's just . . . to be so *alone.* I think of Nadia, and how she moved to San Francisco all by herself and pregnant, knowing far less English than I do. Could I not have been brave like Nadia?

"Maybe I could have moved to Canada," I say. "I *have* heard wonderful things about it, and its immigration policies are supposed to be easier than America's."

"There's no maybe about it, Tami," Ike says. "You should have. Going back to Iran shouldn't have even been an option. You should have hightailed it out of here and settled yourself there. Disappeared into the crowd someplace."

"But if I'd gone to Canada, then I wouldn't have married you." I blink sweetly at him, hoping to charm him. It doesn't work.

"Freedom is not for the faint of heart, my dear." He says this sternly, but sort of in a joking tone, too, and the line is so good it must be from a movie.

"Where did you get that one from?" I ask.

"I think I came up with it myself, actually." He grins. "But I'll have to Google it to be sure."

Haroun's visit might have bothered Ike more than he's willing to admit, because he asks if I would mind putting off our visit to the guesthouse until the next day. I do mind—quite a bit, actually—because if he's not staying with me, then he's staying with his parents, and they don't like me. But his home is what he's used to, and he scared me with his *too much, too fast, too soon* burst of emotion earlier, and I don't want to push him to do anything he's not ready to do. So I tell him I don't mind at all.

As I walk him outside to his truck, we make plans to meet at the guesthouse tomorrow morning. When we hug and kiss good-bye, he sighs with contentment and seems in no hurry to leave me, so I think maybe he'll change his mind. But no—he climbs into his truck and puts the key in the ignition.

"Good night, Tami."

"Good night, Ike."

He must catch the wavering in my voice because he asks, "You all right?"

"I was just wondering, are you going to tell your parents about Haroun?"

He grins. "Is this your scaredy-cat way of asking me not to?"

I can't help but smile. "I suppose it is."

"Don't worry about it," he says. "Just leave my parents to me."

We kiss good-bye all over again, and after he drives off, I go back inside to find Ardishir waiting for me on the couch. He pats a spot next to him for me to sit.

"Tami," he says.

"Ardishir," I say back playfully.

"Ike's great," he says. "He's an absolutely great guy."

His words warm my heart. "Thank you."

"He's one in a million," he says. "A true prince among men."

"He is, isn't he?"

"But I have an issue."

I swallow hard. Ardishir so seldom takes issue with anything, and when he does, he's someone I listen to very seriously.

"Anyone can see he's crazy about you." At his words, I smile broadly, but Ardishir's face is gently reprimanding. "You must have known it, too. Or felt it. You were developing a friendship with him for three entire months. You *had* to have a sense of how he felt about you." His look grows even firmer. "You should have told him about your situation."

As I begin to say I didn't know how, he holds up his hand to stop me. "None of that," he says. "This is your life we're talking about—*your life*! You needed to be brave enough to move to Canada—he's right—but before that, you needed to be courageous enough to give him the opportunity to help you. If Maryam hadn't gone to him, you'd be heading back to Iran right now, all because you were too afraid to trust your feelings."

Actually, I'd be marrying Haroun right now, but besides that, he's right. My insides burn with shame. I'm the Cowardly Lion. "I don't know that my feelings are trustworthy, Ardishir."

Because I mumbled this, he makes me repeat myself and shakes his head when I do.

"You *had* to have a sense he'd help you," he insists. "I've known the guy for under an hour, and it's obvious he's a straight shooter. That's just it—he is. He would've heard you out. He would have considered the options, and he would have made his decision. If it wasn't right for him, he wouldn't have married you. But it's remarkable to me that you never even gave him the chance. What's *up* with that, Tami?"

I take a huge breath. "I knew I loved him, but . . ."

Ardishir persists. "But what?"

I knew I loved him.

I did.

"But I don't know," I say miserably, realizing exactly what the problem was: I loved Ike, but I didn't see how he could really, honestly, truly love me. What have I done in my life to be worthy of his love?

Ardishir narrows his eyes. "What's going to happen when your sister's not there to save you?"

"Ike will save me." I say this in a joking tone, hoping we can move on from this uncomfortable conversation, but Ardishir taps me on the knee.

"This is important," he says. "Not something to joke about. You were setting yourself up for an unhappy ending. You know that, don't you?"

"Now I do."

"You didn't at the time?"

I avert my eyes from his and look at my hands, which I'm twisting together, pressing flesh against bone in my search for some small way to put myself in physical pain. "I guess I did."

Ardishir reaches and covers my hands with his, putting a stop to what I'm doing.

"Don't do it again," he says. "Don't ever do that again. The world will eat you alive if you let it, Tami—so don't let it. You choose your own ending. Even if it's only choosing your frame of mind. We all choose our own endings, and it's important to me—very important—that you choose a happy one."

"I want that, too," I say. "I want it very much."

"Well, then, fight for it," he says. "You should know by now that no one just hands you your happiness—or your freedom, for that matter. You've got to go out there and fight for them, and keep on fighting—sometimes until your dying day. But they're worth it, even if you have to die for them. The glory is in the struggle. Never forget that. The glory is in the struggle."

Chapter 9

The next morning, when Ike comes over to the guesthouse, he brings with him a duffel bag full of essentials . . . and a dog.

He's told me about his dog, a golden retriever named Old Sport, but I didn't see him that night at his parents' house, and I'm a little worried about why he's brought him now.

Old Sport rides right alongside Ike in the truck and climbs over him to get out first. Once down, he jumps up on me, pressing his paws against my stomach. I squeal and jump back, crossing my arms in front of me for protection. I'm not used to dogs, especially big jumping ones who slop their tongues all over the place!

Rose, on the other hand, with whom I've been enjoying tea and who came with me to greet Ike in the driveway, gets down on her old-lady knees to have an eye-to-eye conversation with Old Sport. "You're a good dog, yes, you are!" She rubs him behind the ears. "Aren't you? Aren't you a good dog?"

"Morning, ladies." Ike kisses me on the cheek. "You didn't tell me you're afraid of dogs."

"I'm not afraid of dogs."

He laughs. "You looked a little afraid there."

I'm not—not exactly. The thing is, not many people have dogs for pets in Iran. It's mostly a cultural thing, the belief that dogs are dirty and carry disease. Here, I've seen many, many people take their dogs even to outdoor restaurants and let the dog lick their hand and in the next moment eat with that same hand—this is definitely not a Muslim thing to do! For me, I don't fear dogs for their lack of cleanliness—that seems like a holdover from the older days. It's just that they're unfamiliar to me. I don't understand what a person would *do* with a dog, why they would *have* one. And don't they bite?

Old Sport is now stretched out on his back, blissfully enjoying the rubdown Rose is giving him, wagging his tail against my foot, *whack, whack, whack*. I move my foot out of the way.

"Want to see the guesthouse?" I ask Ike.

"Absolutely." He puts his arm around my shoulders and I put mine around his waist, and together we walk to the guesthouse. I love this—this simple moment—that we can have our arms around each other out in public and nobody cares. Nobody even notices. This is exactly how it should be everywhere, a world full of people minding their own business.

Ike's glance around the guesthouse takes all of maybe three seconds. "You're kidding, right? This is beyond tiny. It's as small as my place." His eyes skim the patio, and then he looks back to the main house. Through a kitchen window, we see Rose inside, filling a watering can at the sink. She sees us and smiles. "It's not very private, either. How am I supposed to ravish you with her right there?"

At his use of the word *ravish*, I blush. At the idea of it, actually. *To be ravished by Ike.* I wonder what that would feel like. He's been very gentle so far, on our one night together, as I suppose is necessary with someone of my experience. But one day, I vow—one day soon—I will be ready and worthy of being ravished.

"Come on, Ike." I tug on his shirtsleeve. "It is too bigger than your place, and there are curtains on the windows. I love it here. And also, we don't want to spend much money on housing right now so you can use your savings for the coffee shop. This isn't so much money. Only four hundred and fifty dollars per month, and that includes utilities. Rose is giving us a very good deal."

"That *is* a good deal. Frankly, it's an unbeatable deal, unless—" He gives me a mischievous look. "Unless you want to move into my guesthouse with me."

"Oh, right!" I laugh. "Like your parents would allow that!"

He looks around the backyard again. "This is fine, I

guess. It's cute. Colorful, certainly. And Old Sport seems to like it."

Old Sport is sitting at the edge of the goldfish pond, entranced by the fat fish swimming idly in circles. I wonder if he'll try to eat them.

Ike gets an amused look on his face. "Do you like my dog?"

"Sure, I like your dog."

"Rose's cats don't seem to mind him."

"This is true." And since Rose spent about five minutes telling Old Sport what a good dog he is—*Oh, yes, you are. You're such a good dog. Did you know what a good dog you are? Well, you are. Yes, you are!*—I suspect she'd be fine with him living here. I know exactly where Ike is going with this. "The cats seem fine with him," I say.

"So?" Ike gives me his most irresistible look. "Could we give it a try?"

I take a big, worried breath. I feel the same concern about Old Sport that Maryam feels about her baby: I have no idea what to *do* with it. How to take care of it. Make sure it's okay. Make sure it has what it needs. Keep the house clean with it shedding all over the place. Keep the house *smelling* good with it . . .

"How many times a day does a dog use the bathroom?" I ask.

Ike bursts out laughing. "A dog *doesn't* use the bathroom."

I poke him in the arm. "I know *that*. I mean, who cleans up after him if you're at work all day?"

"I'll take care of all dog issues," he says. "I'll feed him, bathe him, clean up his crap. Everything."

Okay, but . . . "What does he *do* all day?"

"Oh, you know. He reads the *Wall Street Journal.* Makes a few phone calls. I'm sure he'd do the grocery shopping if you asked him nicely."

Fighting my smile, I narrow my eyes. "Will you say yes to the guesthouse even if I say no to the dog?"

"Of course I will," he says. "I'd do anything to make you happy."

I groan. "That's very clever, Ike. How can I say no to the dog after you've said something as sweet as that?"

He grins. "I'm betting you can't."

He's right. And so reluctantly, I agree we can give it a try.

"All right!" He swings me around. "You're going to love him. He'll be your best friend. I just know it."

"Maryam's going to hate this. She probably won't even visit if there's a dog here."

"Now that would be such a shame."

My mouth drops open. "You really don't mind having people mad at you, do you?"

"It's our path, remember?"

"That's right," I say. "Yours, mine, and the dog's."

We go into the guesthouse and have a good look at it. It's basically one small room that makes up both the kitchen and the living room, plus a small separate bedroom and, inside that, a bathroom with a shower, no bathtub. But it's *so cute.* It's so *non-Persian.* So nothing like my house in Iran, so nothing like Maryam's house here. This casita is young. Fresh. Lively. Most of the walls are painted yellow, and each window frame is a different color—one orange, one purple, one green. Tissue-paper flowers spring from tall blue pottery. The French doors that lead to the patio are turquoise, and when Ike props both doors open, it makes the space seem twice as large.

A sombrero hangs on a wall for decoration. "I feel like I'm at a Mexican restaurant," Ike says, taking the hat off the wall and putting it on my head.

"¡Hola!" I say. "Would you like some tortilla chips?"

"That depends." He grins. "Do you have any nacho cheese sauce?"

Funny husband! I move to swat him in the arm, but before I can, he sweeps me off my feet. "Ready to be carried over the threshold?"

"Over the what?"

"The threshold," he says. "The doorway."

"I'm already inside, Ike!"

"I guess it's not a Persian tradition." As he carries me outside, he explains. "Crossing the threshold means, symbolically, starting something new—crossing over into a new life or a new adventure. And when you get *married*, the groom carries the bride over the threshold—the doorway—of their new home."

Okay, the thing is—I feel the same way about this as I did about Ike getting down on one knee to propose. It's sweet, but uneven. If it's symbolic, it's somehow symbolic in a way I don't like. "Isn't the bride capable of crossing the threshold on her own two feet, at her husband's side, maybe holding his hand instead of being carried by him?"

"Look at you. Ms. Feminist. Come on," he says. "Let me have my moment. I'm trying to be romantic here."

That's right—I forgot that for Ike, life is like a movie.

As he carries me across the threshold, my sombrero bumps against the doorway and gets knocked off my head.

"Oops." Ike tries to correct that mistake, but in doing so he swings me around so my feet knock into the other side of the narrow doorway. *See, we should have walked through it together.*

"Not very graceful," he says. "Sorry."

But I love that he tries so hard.

"Don't be sorry." I kiss his cheek. "Who needs grace when we have love?"

We go to the main house and tell Rose the good news that yes, we will rent the guesthouse. She, in turn, tells us that of course Old Sport is welcome, too. Along with the lease for us to sign, which she says is unnecessary for her but will help us with the immigration officials, she gives us a gift basket that contains a bottle of champagne, two glasses, and a box of chocolates. We thank her for the gift, sign the lease, Ike writes her a check for the first month's rent, and within minutes, he and I are officially living together as husband and wife.

Now what?

"Now the fun begins," Ike says when I ask him this question. We're back in the guesthouse, standing in the kitchen, holding hands, and—I don't know how Ike feels, but I feel very awkward. "Should we unpack? That'll take all of about two minutes."

It does take all of about two minutes to move our clothes to the dresser (Ike gets the top two dresser drawers, while I get the bottom three). He only brought a few things, and I don't have much more. We take longer with my special items that I brought from Iran. They're not many, but they are meaningful. My favorite headscarf, given to me by my students on my last day as their teacher. A book of poetry by Ferdowsi, given to me by my dear friend Nima. My Googoosh CDs. My candle. And my world map.

"My sister gave me this," I say as I pull it out from its cylindrical tube. It was bothersome taking it as a carry-on all the way from Iran, but I couldn't have left it behind. "She gave it to me as a going-away gift when she married Ardishir and moved to America."

Maryam circled Tehran in black marker and wrote *You Are Here.* She circled Tucson, too, and wrote *Maryam Is Here.* Then she drew a thick black line that connected us across the miles, across the ocean, and wrote above it, *Together again someday.*

"And now you are," Ike says when I explain about the map.

Yes, thanks to you. "But my parents aren't."

Ike gets a hammer and nails from the tool compartment in the back of his truck and puts the map on the bedroom wall for me. Once it's up, he steps back and puts his arm around me and we stand together, looking at it.

"The map's outdated now." With his finger, he traces a path from my name in Iran all the way over to Maryam's in Tucson. "We'll have to change that."

"Do you have a marker in your truck? We could change it now."

"I probably do." While he's looking for it, I stare and stare at the map until all the borders become blurry, like I used to do back home. It's prettier that way. When he comes back with a thick red marker, I write my name next to Maryam's and cross out my name in Tehran. Instead, I write in *Maman* and *Baba.* The distance between us is considerable. *They are there*, I think as I put my finger on Tehran. *They are there when they don't have to be.*

How to get them to come?

"I'm so mad at my mother," I confess softly, for this is a new emotion for me, and it makes me feel ungrateful. "All my life, they've talked only of their desire to see their daughters living in America. More than twenty years of this talk I've heard! How much of it was necessary, if we all could have left long ago?"

Ike wraps his arms around me. "I'm starting to realize that mothers are strange people."

"Maryam is keeping her pregnancy a secret from them," I say. "Don't you think that's wrong?"

"I'm not going to get in the middle of that," he says. "Although I think in general, secrets do more harm than good."

"I just . . . I have to believe that if they could be here in time for when she has her baby, they would be."

"Well, they certainly can't if they don't even know about it."

"Right." I agree. "And Maryam's not going to tell them."

I want him to say, *Tell them, Tami.* I want him to give me permission, to tell me it's the right thing to do.

He doesn't, exactly. Although he does, sort of.

"I find it's helpful to visualize the outcome I want for something," he says. "Like my coffee shop, in that perfect, ideal location. Open soon, filled with customers, cool music playing, you and me there together, side by side. I *see* it. It's *going* to happen. And how I get there is far less important than *that* I get there. Does that make any sense?"

"You're telling me I should tell my parents about the baby?"

He shakes his head. "Focus on the outcome. What's the outcome you want? Visualize it. Verbalize it."

"I want them here," I say. "That's the outcome I want."

"Go on," he says. He encourages me—Ike, who has so much more experience than I do when it comes to working toward a dream. "What exactly do you see when you see them here?"

Dare I? To put a dream in specifics is a very scary thing. To visualize it is to make it real, and when it's real and doesn't happen, then it's a dream denied. Then, it's crushing. Soul-destroying. It's far easier emotionally to keep my dreams half formed. But it's probably not very effective. I look deep into Ike's eyes—we face each other and hold hands the same way we did when he proposed—and the purity in his gaze, the absolute faith he has in me, gives me the courage I need. And so I tell him my most secret dream.

"I see Maryam in the hospital, after she's had the baby. And she did great, and the baby's healthy and so, so beautiful. And she's holding it in her arms, and Ardishir's standing by her side, and everyone's so happy. It's already a perfect moment." My eyes tear up, for I'm actually seeing this happen, and I don't think my heart has ever been so happy. "I'm there, too, and the door opens, and my mother steps inside, and Maryam didn't know she was coming, but I did. My mother steps through the doorway and my father's right behind her, and my sister looks at them, and then she looks at me, and *I did this.*" Tears overflowing, I'm giddy with the image. "Me, Tami! The one everyone hides things from. The one they all think is so fragile, she can't even be told the truth. I brought everyone together. This is my gift, for my sister and my parents and for myself, too. Can you see it, Ike? Can you ever see it happening?"

"Absolutely," he says. "You can do anything you put your mind to."

Chapter 10

He inspires me, Ike does.

Soon after he leaves for work, with my new resolve I tap on Rose's back door. She says of course I can use her telephone to call Iran and of course I can reimburse her later. She's cooking soup on the stove, but offers to leave the kitchen so I can have privacy. I assure her it's not necessary, as I'll be speaking in Farsi and she won't be able to understand anyway.

I dial the international code for Iran and then my parents' number, and even as I hold my breath while the phone rings, my heart races with nerves. So much has happened since I last spoke with them.

"*'Alo?*" It's my mother's soft voice.

"*Maman, salaam, che tore?*"

"Tami! We've been waiting for your call. Congratulations on your marriage! Your sister filled us in on all the details. It sounds like it was quite romantic! We're so proud of you, Tami Joon—so glad everything worked out."

My throat swells with the relief that comes from knowing I've fulfilled her greatest wish. I have to clear my throat before I can speak, for the mother's love in how she says my name is something no one else can ever replicate. It's a love I couldn't bear to lose. I have to be careful how I go about convincing them it's time to summon the courage to, if nothing else, start the process of filing the paperwork to leave Iran. Baby steps are okay. We all started with baby steps.

"You'd love Ike," I say. "I wish you could meet him."

"Will you send pictures?" she asks.

"I have a better idea. You and Baba should come." I say this quickly, before I lose my courage. "Come here. Meet him for yourself, not just in pictures."

After a pause, Maman says, "You know that's not possible."

"I don't know what's possible," I say. "I only know what I've been told."

I'm sitting at Rose's kitchen table. Rose is at the stove, slowly stirring the soup she's making for someone in her church who is ill. At my words, she looks up at me and smiles her sympathetic smile. I'm sure she heard the ache in my voice; yearning sounds the same in any language.

My mother asks, "Are you all right, Tami Joon? Is anything wrong? Didn't everything work out well?"

"I miss you," I say. "I wish you were here."

You should have been here for my wedding.

"Maybe someday it will be possible, *inshallah*," she says.

"Inshallah." I swallow over the bitterness that comes when I say that word. I swallow over my bitterness as years of stories run through my head: We were happy, once upon a time. Iran was a beautiful place to live, once upon a time. It will be again, someday.

Someday, our family will be together in America, *inshallah*.

Inshallah—God willing, God willing, God willing.

But what, a voice whispers inside me, *what do* we *will?* Where does God's power leave off and our own personal power begin?

These stories, these beliefs, this silly wistful word *someday*, have kept my parents stuck—paralyzed—for far too long. If they truly do not need to remain in Iran, then they mustn't accept it as their fate. It's my duty as a daughter to help them see this. But my mother—I fear she never will. I fear she believes the best is far behind her, that it's been beaten out of her.

"Is Baba there?" I ask. "Can I talk with him, please?"

When my father gets on the phone, we exchange greetings and I accept his congratulations on my marriage. I don't have to tiptoe with my words to him like I do with Maman, so I repeat to him what Maryam told me and ask if it's true—could they, in fact, potentially come to America? My father falters in his reply.

"Maryam should not be talking of such things at such a happy time." Baba's voice is lowered, and I know he has walked away from my mother to hide his words from her ears.

My heart falls and hardens at the same time. "It's true, then?"

He clears his throat. "You are our little black fish," he says. "You go where your parents cannot and swim in the larger, happier world."

Can I truly be happy when I know my parents aren't?

"Is it true, Baba, that possibly you could come? Please tell me."

"You're a newlywed," he says. "You should worry about your husband's happiness, not ours. We're happy enough."

But they're not. There's no way they are.

"It's amazing here, Baba. I know you haven't forgotten what freedom feels like."

"Of course not." There's a sad silence, and when he speaks again, his voice is full of yearning. "Once freedom is in your soul, it never leaves. But to pursue freedom, one needs both courage and hope. Your mother has neither. She's a bird unable to fly. She wants you to have everything she lost by coming back. For her, that's enough."

"Baba, it's *not* enough. What will she live for now? What dreams will carry her forward? Maryam says not to bother, that there's no way Maman will ever be willing to even try. But you and I—"

"You can't force a person to be happy. Sometimes people grow comfortable with their sorrow," he says.

"You and I must not give up hope for her happiness," I insist. "We have to make this happen."

He sighs, and I wonder how many conversations he and my mother have had over the years about this topic. The subject must exhaust him. But he's tougher than Maman. I can't allow him to give up.

"Do you remember that little blue perfume bottle you gave me, Baba?"

"Of course," he says.

When I was five years old and we were back in Iran—Maman would already have been imprisoned and released by then—my father gave me for my birthday a small blue perfume bottle filled with grains of sand. In fact, it might have been the same one I'd been playing with when my mother came home from prison that day. *This*, he said when he gave it to me for my birthday, *is sand from America. When you are older, you have a special job to do. You are to take this sand and return it to where it belongs. You are to return it to America.*

He never says the word *America* without a tone of reverence. Like my mother, he loved it here. Unlike her, he never wanted to leave. Yet he had, for her.

And now she won't come back, not even for him.

When my father gave me my visa and airplane ticket to America three months ago, he put them in a gift box, and along with them he included that little blue bottle of sand and reminded me of the promise I'd made to him when I was five: I was to return the sand to American shores.

"I want you with me when I sprinkle the sand back onto the shores of the San Francisco Bay," I say to him now. "So hurry up and come. I'll wait for you."

Again, there's silence on his end, and in the silence I

grow panicky that he's going to tell me not to wait, to go ahead without him, and I know that if he says it, my heart will break. To prevent this, I say, "Maryam said you have the visa applications already filled out. Is this true?"

In a soft voice, he tells me yes, they are in his dresser drawer.

"Mail them, Baba."

"I can't," he says. "I made a promise to your mother."

"I made a promise, too, Baba, and I have no problem breaking it. I'm going to tell you a secret I'm not supposed to tell."

"Maybe you sh—"

"Maryam's pregnant." At my father's joyful gasp, I add, "You can't tell Maman! Maryam doesn't want her to know yet. But Baba—you're going to be a grandfather! And wouldn't it be great if—"

I stop, for I can't even say it. *Wouldn't it be great if you could hold that baby? And if my mother, too, could hold Hope in her arms?* To Ike, maybe I could say this dream. But to my father, it's too big to say out loud—because if he gets his hopes up and it doesn't happen, I really worry it might destroy him.

I clear my throat and continue. "Do you see why I broke my promise, Baba? Do you see why you have to break yours, too? It's within our grasp, to have our whole family here. Three generations! It's so close we can almost touch it."

"I don't know, Tami." But along with his uncertainty, I hear a new hope, and because of this, I know I'm right to persist.

"God doesn't give us the pain without also giving us the medicine, Baba." This is a Persian proverb. "We can fix this. It's time for our family to be happy again, and the way to do that is by mailing those applications. If they're approved and Maman still says no, well, then at least you'll know for sure what you're giving up. But you've got to try. At least, you must do that."

He sighs, like this is too difficult a request.

"Please, Baba. I miss my kind father." Tears stream down my face, for I do miss him, so much. "Come, Baba. Together we'll go to San Francisco and return our special sand to where we took it from all those years ago." I can *see* this happening. I can smell the salty air and feel the ocean breeze. And my father's strong hand in mine—I can feel that, too, as together we hold the little blue bottle and together we sprinkle out the sand. It will be an ending for us, and a beginning, too. "Please, Baba. We need you here. We need our father."

He clears his throat. Perhaps he's imagining the same thing I am. Perhaps he smells the same ocean air as me.

"You're a good daughter," he says finally. "I'll see what I can do."

My heart gasps with hope when he says this. We say our good-byes, and for the first time in my life when it comes to my parents, I hang up the phone feeling better than I did at the start of the conversation.

"Sorry," I say to Rose. "I'm sorry for crying in your kitchen!"

"It must be hard to have your parents so far away," she says.

"It is," I say. "I just really want . . . well . . ." It's difficult for me to say what I want out loud. What I want is for my parents to see me happy. For them not to have to wonder, or to ask, but to see with their own eyes that I am, in fact and finally, simply, hugely *happy.* Is it selfish to want this? Maybe not, because I think if they were here and could see this, it would make them happy, too—happy all the way into their souls.

"Nobody knows you like your parents, for better and worse," Rose says. "That was probably the hardest thing about losing mine."

Who knows you, Rose? Who knows the secrets of your soul?

I don't ask, because maybe no one does, and if this is true, it must be something she longs for. I don't want to put sad thoughts into her head.

"It seems like in America, people almost . . . create their families," I say. "Do you think this is true?"

She smiles. "I think so, yes. I have my church, my bridge club, my knitting circle, my book clubs. My sister, my nieces—and you, of course!"

"Thank you for letting us live here," I say. "It means so much to be close to you and get to see you so often. No more just when I walk by on my way to school!"

"But don't worry," she says. "I'll make sure you two newlyweds have your privacy."

"Oh, don't worry about that!" I'm blushing to think of her thinking of *us* having sex in her guesthouse. That's not an image I want in her head!

* * *

Back in my casita, I pull out from my suitcase the few photographs I have from our family's time in America and sit on my new bed and sort through them. There's one of me eating French fries at McDonald's, sitting on my father's lap. I'm about three years old, and my father's young eyes glow with happiness. There's one of me being pushed from behind on a baby swing by Maryam at the children's playground at Golden Gate Park. There's one of me naked in the Pacific Ocean, running from the cold waves and squealing in delight.

There's another from that day at the ocean.

In this one, I'm wearing a pink one-piece swimsuit with a big yellow daisy in the middle. My mother holds me. My legs are wrapped around her waist, and my head rests on her shoulder. A wave washes over her feet. She looks straight into the eye of the camera. My mother's skin is tanned, her long hair windblown. She knows nothing yet of segregated beaches and confiscated passports and shrouding oneself from the sun's warmth and men's eyes. All she knows is the beauty of this day. The sun. The waves. The sound of the ocean. The sexy confidence of a bikini top and cutoff shorts highlighting the strong-muscled legs of an able woman. Bare feet. The wind dancing through her hair. Big gold hoop earrings and bright red lipstick. Red nail polish, too. Remarkably beautiful, she looks so happy. So happy and so free.

This is not the mother I know.

The mother I know has always worn *hejab*, has always covered herself in the regime's mandated head covering.

She has always ducked her head and averted her eyes when passing men in the street, walking with the gait of a broken, defeated woman.

I don't remember the carefree, unburdened mother in the photograph at all, but I've missed her every day of my life, even so.

The mother I know has always been sad.

But now, after my phone call with my father, I look at that photograph and think, *Maybe again.* Maybe, if everything works out exactly right, I might come to know a happier version of my mother, rather than merely the ghost of who she used to be.

I call to her, across the ocean: *Come, Maman.*

Come and wake up your luck.

Chapter 11

That night, Ike and I drink the entire bottle of champagne and eat the entire box of chocolates. He doesn't ravish me—we're still working our way to that—but the evening passes very pleasantly in every regard. I sleep well—so well, in fact, that the next morning, when I half hear heavy breathing next to me in the moments before I'm officially awake, I assume it's Ike.

"Heh, heh, heh."

"Mmmm," I say back in dreamy pleasure and stretch my arm to put around him.

"Heh, heh, heh."

He's breathing very strangely. I open my eyes to see if he is okay, and instead of Ike beside me, it's Old Sport lying in the middle of the bed—right next to me! I can't help it—I scream. Old Sport watches me, giving me a look like, *What's the problem?* Ike's at the bedroom door within seconds, wearing faded jeans and a pale green T-shirt, the sleeves of which end at the halfway point of his biceps. He's got his thumbs hooked in his front pockets, and he looks immensely handsome, perfectly American. And he's laughing as hard as I've ever seen him.

"Ike! It's not funny! I'm naked here!"

This just makes him laugh harder. "Don't worry," he says. "I don't think you're his type."

I pull the covers as tight as I can, although Old Sport's big dog body makes this challenging. "Please make him go away."

Ike sends Old Sport outside and then sits on the edge of the bed and smoothes my hair. "Poor baby. I'm sorry."

"You're still laughing," I point out.

"I know, but . . . I went to get us bagels and when I got back, he was in the bed. I just couldn't resist letting him stay."

I knee him in the back. "Next time, resist."

"I will." He kisses my forehead, then asks, "Are you always this grumpy in the morning?"

I move to knee him in the back again, but he scoots up from the bed. "Kidding, kidding! Hey, I've got bagels and tea for you outside. It's a beautiful morning."

It's also just six thirty. "Do you always get up so early?"

"The world belongs to the early risers." Ike tells me that before he got the bagels, he ran five miles. "What are *you* going to do today?"

"A delicious amount of nothing," I say. "Except I do

have English class. It's the first day of our new session. If that's . . . is it okay for me to do this?"

"To do what?" Ike says, leaning against the doorway. "Take your English class?"

"Yes," I say. "I mean, I can't do much else yet—get a permanent job, or take university classes—until my immigration paperwork comes through, and so I might as well keep working on my English, right?" Even though my language skills have gotten much better in the three months since I first arrived, I'm still tripped up by words every day—many times each day, actually. It's constantly tricky as a foreigner, because no matter how much you've studied English before arriving, people change the most common words into something unrecognizable. Truly, it's the casual words and phrases—simple things such as how people say *Hiya* and *Buh-bye* and *Seeya*—that most confuse me.

Ike frowns at me a little. "You don't need to ask my permission," he says. "Do whatever you want. Do what makes you happy."

"Well . . . they *are* all my friends."

"You don't need to justify anything," he says. "If you enjoy it, do it."

"You're sure?" I say. "I mean, I should still have plenty of time to cook dinner, and clean, and—"

"Oh, God, don't." He comes back to sit on the edge of the bed. "Don't become this wifey-wife. Okay? That's not what I want from you. I'd hate it, in fact. Your priorities shouldn't be cooking and cleaning—those should be last on your list."

That's not what Maryam would say. She'd say a wife should cook for her husband and take care of his needs. "Yes, but someone has to—"

Ike shakes his head. "This place is tiny, which is a real advantage, actually. There'll be very little cleaning to do. We can bust through it in an hour once a week, tops. And as far as cooking—well, this kitchen doesn't lend itself to cooking. It lends itself to eating out, which is fine with me. Or grilling, which I love to do. We should buy ourselves a— Oh, wait! Hold on. I got something for you, but I left it in the truck. Hold on. I'll be right back."

While he gets up and goes outside, I quickly throw on jeans and a camisole. Because Ike likes my hair up, I put it in a ponytail. I wonder what he's got for me. A wedding ring?

I can't wait in the bedroom—I'm too excited—so I go out onto the patio where his coffee and my tea and our bagels are waiting for us, and inhale the desert-fresh air. It's chilly and warm at the same time on this early April morning, and standing here barefoot on the patio, waiting for my husband, seeing my table set for two, I can't help but marvel, *This is my life. My beautiful, beautiful life—a life that almost never was.* I can't believe I almost lost this—that this exact morning, this precise moment, almost never happened.

My heart soars as Ike comes around the corner, and his smile is equally ebullient. *We did this! We made this happen!* He comes up to me, grips my shoulders, kisses my forehead, and says, "Okay. It's in my back pocket."

It could be a wedding ring. A wedding ring would fit in his back pocket, even if it's in a box.

"So . . . I should . . . ?"

He grins. "Reach into my pocket and get it, yes."

"Kiss me first." After he does, I add, "I love you, you know."

"I love you, too, Tami. Now reach into my pocket and get your gift."

A ring, a ring, let it be a ring.

My heart is skipping beats from the excitement as I reach around him and pat his back pockets, first one and then the other. There's nothing in either, except for . . .

It's not a ring.

"A cell phone?" I pull it out. Yes, it's definitely a cell phone. Okay. A cell phone, not a ring. I'll admit it: I'd rather have a ring.

"I bumped up my service to the family plan." Ike looks pleased with himself. "Because you're my family now."

Okay, this is seriously sweet.

I already have a phone my sister gave me, with prepaid minutes, but this one is special, because this one is from Ike. I press it to my heart. "Thank you, Ike! This is so great! Thank you! Thank you so much!"

"You like it?" he asks.

"I do, yes! Very much! And a family plan—that's perfect!"

"We've got unlimited text and minutes between us," he says. Again very proudly.

"You're very practical!"

When I say this, Ike shrugs like it's no big deal, but I can tell he's secretly pleased that I've noticed his practical side. And how cute is that?

We enjoy our breakfast on the patio, and then, all too soon, it's time for Ike to go to work. He changes into his Starbucks khakis and white shirt, and I walk him to his scooter. By scooter, Starbucks is maybe five minutes away, and I love that he's so near. I kiss him good-bye and walk to the end of the driveway and wave until he's out of sight, feeling very wifely as I do. And then I send him a text message with my new cell phone: *I miss you already.*

After this, I go inside and shower, forgetting about the message I sent until I'm done showering and dressing in the bedroom. I decide today is a sundress kind of day, not a jeans-and-cami day, as I'd worn at breakfast. This way, the next time Ike sees me, I'll look fresh and new to him. When the phone vibrates on the dresser, I jolt and then grab for it. *Miss U 2*, Ike has messaged back. *C U later?*

It's bad enough figuring out the English words for everything. Now I've got to add this shorthand text-message code?

Yes! I text back. *On my way to class.*

Sorry I banged your head yesterday, he texts back. I smile, remembering how he carried me over the threshold with that silly sombrero on my head.

I text back, *You can bang me anytime.*

His reply is quick. *LOL. Looking forward to it.*

I puzzle over that acronym, *LOL*, until I realize it must mean Lots of Love. How sweet! I send one last message back: *LOL here, too.*

It's my first full day as a married woman living with her husband, and my goal is simply to embrace it. My sundress is yellow and bare-shouldered, and I wear my hair down so it covers most, but not all, of my shoulders. I think this might be sort of sexy—subtly sexy. My toenails are a pretty pink with bling sparkles on them, and I have found for myself a comfortable pair of high-heeled flip-flops, which will be fine for walking to English class. I'll stop to see Ike on my way, and I'll give him a public display of affection. I'll apply for a library card today, too, now that I have a permanent address, and I might even go with Eva for a margarita this afternoon, *just because I can.* It'll be an easy, perfect, ordinary day. A day to catch my breath. A day that tells the world: This is how free people live.

I tidy up the bedroom, and when I emerge, I nearly scream for the second time that day when I find Ike's mother standing at the open half door. How long has she been there? Dealing with her—especially alone!—is *not* in my plans for an easy, perfect day.

"Oh, hi!" I rush to unlock the door and let her in. "I hope you haven't been there long. I'm sorry, if you called, I didn't hear you."

She wears a blue linen dress that makes her eyes shine. Her hair is styled, and she wears lipstick and eye shadow. The only other time I saw her, she had an end-of-day look about her, but this morning she is fresh and sparkling.

"You were singing." She smiles. Smiles, at me! "Is that a hobby of yours?"

"Oh, no. I just . . . sing when I'm happy."

And when I think I'm alone! I wonder if she will be the sort of mother-in-law who drops by unannounced all the time. I hope not!

And yet, it's encouraging that she's here.

"What a beautiful dress," she says. "I can certainly see why my son finds you attractive." She holds up a tin bread pan. "I heard your sister has a craving for bananas, so I thought she might enjoy some banana bread. How exciting that she's pregnant—please offer her my congratulations."

I'm absolutely *tingling.* She, my mother-in-law who definitely decided the other day to dislike me, made banana bread for my sister! If she wants to pretend the other day never happened, I'm very happy to go along with that.

"Thank you! That's so nice!" I take the bread from her. It's still warm and smells wonderful. "I know my sister would like to invite your family over for dinner soon."

Mrs. Hanson maintains her smile as she looks around. "Ike's at work?"

"Yes. Yes, he's at work until three. Would you . . . like some tea, or coffee? Please, have a seat!" I gesture to the kitchen table. "I'm sorry my hair's wet and, oh! I'm barefoot!" I slip on my fancy flip-flops, which are by the door. "I—" I stop myself from saying *I didn't know I'd have a guest*, and instead ask, "How are you? How is your family?"

"We're fine," Mrs. Hanson says. "And coffee would be lovely."

Only then do I realize that not only do I not have coffee, I don't even have a coffeemaker. This is *not* good daughter-in-law behavior. "Oh! Um. Well. I'm very sorry, but I haven't quite gone shopping yet. Would you"—I glance through my window to Rose's house, but there's no movement there—"like a glass of water, maybe?"

"No, thank you. I didn't expect you'd have anything to offer." Mrs. Hanson's tone flattens. "Could we just talk? Outside, maybe?"

Still carrying the banana bread, I follow her to the patio table and sit across from her and smile, smile, smile. I'm worried by the change in her tone and how she said she didn't expect me to have anything to offer. It sounded ominous, and to make matters worse, Old Sport, who ever since the incident of lying next to me in bed this morning has kept out of my way, claiming a spot in the backyard in the shade of a lemon tree, lopes over and settles at Mrs. Hanson's feet, telling me with his eyes that he's chosen sides and the side he's chosen is hers. Traitor!

Mrs. Hanson looks at me with obvious discomfort. "Oh, boy," she says eventually. "You're quite lovely. This is going to be difficult."

Don't, I think. *Please don't make things difficult.*

She carries a tote bag for a purse and reaches into it, pulling out a small bottle of Arrowhead water. She really *didn't* expect me to have anything to offer! But then again, I remind myself, many people in Tucson carry around bottled water wherever they go.

"It's going to be a hot one." She unscrews the cap and takes a drink. "Does it get hot in Iran? It should—it's the desert, right?"

"It gets very hot there, yes." I neglect to tell her, as I do my friends who ask the question, that the Tucson heat is far preferable to Tehran's, if only because of the lack of dress requirements here. Women in Tucson can barely bring themselves to wear short sleeves—yet even in Iran's summer, we have to wear not only a headscarf and regular clothes but also a manteau, a raincoat sort of covering that the government has decided on our behalf will help us preserve our modesty.

She holds out the bottle of Arrowhead. "Would you like a drink?"

"No, thank you."

"Your English," she says. "It's really very good."

"Thank you. I'm taking classes which are very helpful."

"And you're so polite, too!"

In my country, this is all part of *tarof*, this politeness on both our parts. However, I know from being in America that this sort of back-and-forth complimenting is not required—which makes me wonder why she's doing it. And yet, I'll continue on as long as she does. "Thank you for welcoming me into your home the other night. I very much enjoyed your lasagna, and your family is very nice."

"Yes," she says. "Well. We're all of us very upset about what's going on here."

My smile freezes. My whole body freezes, actually, despite the ninety-degree heat. "I'm sorry to upset you," I say. Ike may not mind having his family upset with him, but I do. In Iran, one of the most important jobs of a wife is to take care of her in-laws and try to make them happy, even if it's an impossible task—which it very often is.

Mrs. Hanson peers at me, trying to see through my eyes all the way into my heart.

"I feel for your situation," she says. "I honestly do."

Then she shrugs, which tells me that maybe she really doesn't. "I know you're in a tough position, and I don't blame you for not wanting to go back. It sounds like women have very tough lives in Iran. The thing is . . ." She raises her chin. "It was wrong for you to get married like you did."

"It wasn't . . . what's the word . . . ideal," I acknowledge. "I very much would have liked for you to be at our wedding. My family, too. My sister says maybe we can have another wedding ceremony and bring the two families together."

"Oh," Mrs. Hanson says, "that's so not going to happen."

"Oh," I say, my hopes plunging. "Okay."

"The thing is—" She gives me a mean mother-in-law look. "It's illegal, what you're trying to do. Ike could go to jail! And you could be deported. I saw an immigration lawyer yesterday, and he flat out said he wouldn't even *consider* taking you on as a client because you're so *obviously* engaged in marriage fraud."

She saw a lawyer?

She saw a lawyer?

Tears well in my eyes, threatening to spill onto my face.

Marriage fraud.

Jail.

Deported.

These are horrible words, all of them. "Please, I don't know what you mean."

"You know *exactly* what I mean." Her hatred for me is sharp, and shocking. Her words slice my insides, tear them to shreds.

"I don't," I say. "It's not illegal to marry someone you love."

"Oh, give it up." She leans too close. She's a predator, and I'm her prey. She'll devour me at any moment. "You may have fooled Ike, but you haven't fooled me. You sit there looking so pretty. So quiet, so respectful. But underneath it all, you're a master manipulator."

Feeling a blush spread across my face and neck, I look desperately to Rose's house, needing an ally, as this is far from a fair fight, but she's not anywhere in sight. *Help me out here. Somebody, please help me out. Ike. Maryam. Somebody.* I look at Old Sport, who's lying on top of Mrs. Hanson's feet doing his usual *heh, heh, heh.* Couldn't he at least come lie at *my* feet? But no. There's no one to take my side. I'll have to speak for myself.

"This is the path that Ike and I have chosen," I say, as firmly as I can. "And—"

"Oh, stop with the path! If I hear about this stupid path one more time from either of you, I'll—" She leans toward me. "Just—enough already. Okay? I have your number. I know what you're up to, and it's not going to work. You've involved my son in what amounts to a federal offense. So don't tell me you're in love with him, because that's *not* a loving thing to do. Now—" Her voice again turns friendly. "Have you filed your residency paperwork yet?"

The answer is no, we haven't, but from the change in her tone I know instinctively not to tell her this. This is what she came to find out. The banana bread was an attempt to give me a false sense of security, to lull me into thinking I was safe. Interrogators do this sort of thing in Iran, too—they try to make you feel comfortable so you say things they'll then use against you. I know better than to be tricked in this way. *And this isn't a prison*, I remind myself. *I can leave at any time*. I *should* leave, right now.

"Thank you for visiting," I say, standing up. "Please excuse me, but I must leave for my English class."

"Sit back down," she says. "We're not through."

My knees are quivering, but I stand resolutely. "No, thank you."

She rummages in her tote bag, pulls out a business card, and shows me the back of it. "See this? This is the phone number to Immigration Enforcement. This is the number I call to have you deported."

Immediately, I sit back down.

"That's better," she says. "Now, we're going to come to an understanding, you and I."

I think I already understand her well enough. She, however, has yet to try and understand me.

"Ike came to me," I tell her. "This is something you have to know. I had my airplane ticket back to Iran. I was ready to leave. It cost very much money, too. Thousands of dollars. I wasn't trying to trick him. I never even told him about my visa situation."

"No, you had your sister do your dirty work for you."

The problem with talking to mean people in a language you're just learning is you can't very easily ask them to explain what certain words mean. I didn't understand *master manipulator* or *I have your number*, and I don't understand *dirty work*, either. This is why my English class is still necessary. To help me deal with people like her.

"I prayed about this," she says. "I prayed about what to do."

I cringe, for there are few things I dislike more than when people say things like this. To me, it always seems that what they're really doing is looking for justification to do whatever it is they intend to do anyway. "And what did God tell you to do?" I ask.

With a look of serene righteousness, Mrs. Hanson pats my hand. "To ask you to leave."

Oh, really? "Where am I supposed to go?"

"Back to Iran," she says.

Not for one instant do I believe God told her this.

"I don't think God recognizes borders," I say. "I don't think God cares one bit about the silly lines men draw on their silly maps."

She narrows her eyes. "You don't belong here."

I narrow my eyes right back. "I belong with my husband. I belong with Ike."

"You haven't *earned* it," she says. "To immigrate to America, there's a legal process to follow, and you haven't followed it."

"There *is* a process to follow," I say. "You're right about that. But I *am* following it."

My understanding of the law is this: If I came to the U.S. on a tourist visa for the sole purpose of getting married in order to stay, that would be illegal. But if I came for a visit and just *happened* to fall in love—well, then it would be okay. The immigration people would let me stay.

The problem is, I did both. It's true, my family specifically tried to arrange a marriage for me so I could remain after my visa expired, but we were unsuccessful. It's also true that I fell in love with Ike—despite my best efforts not to, in fact—and that he proposed, and that I accepted.

Now, I'm not going to tell the immigration people about my original intention, and I'm sure Ike won't, either. But Mrs. Hanson might—which leaves my precarious fate in her unfriendly hands.

Chapter 12

After Ike's mother makes a few more immigration-related threats, she leaves. I don't see her out. Instead, I remain at the patio table, stunned and horrified. Her last words were to reassure me it was nothing personal, what she was doing; it was her job as a mother to protect her son and really had little to do with me at all. I believe her—of course it's nothing personal. How could it be? She doesn't know me. She doesn't look at me and see me for who I am. Because of where I'm from, when Mrs. Hanson looks at me all she sees is trouble.

So much for catching my breath. So much for embracing the day. Thanks to her, I can do neither. What is it about mother-in-laws? Why are they so often unkind? I think it's about power. It all comes down to power, all the ills in the world. People with power never want to relinquish it. To maintain it, otherwise decent people turn cruel. I've seen it too many times in my life to believe anything else.

I look at Old Sport, still lying near Mrs. Hanson's chair, and think maybe this is why people like dogs. They don't care about power. They just want you to pet them and like them, and being with you is all they need to be happy.

"Come here," I say, wiggling my fingers to attract his attention.

Old Sport obliges, getting up from his comfortable spot and coming over to me. Then he watches me and waits, wagging his tail.

"I'm sorry I screamed in your face this morning," I say. "I'm just not used to having a dog in bed with me. Or anyone, actually. So I'm sorry, okay?"

Heh, heh, heh.

"I'll get better at this," I say. "At being a dog owner, I mean. It's probably not so hard, right? How about . . . should I . . . pet you?" I hold my hand over his head. "Is that okay, if I pet you? You won't bite me, will you?"

Heh, heh, heh, he says, which tells me nothing, but his tail wags faster, which I understand to be a good sign. And so I pet him, and as I do, he plops down onto my feet.

"I'm going to have to go to my English class soon," I tell him. "So I'm going to have to move my feet, okay? You're going to have to get up in a minute. I just wanted to give you some advance warning about that . . . okay?"

Old Sport doesn't acknowledge that I've said anything. Instead, he watches a pair of birds splashing in Rose's birdbath.

I'm very impressed that he isn't rushing over trying to eat them. I think it shows maturity on his part. *Good dog.*

"Old Sport?"

He looks back to me. *Heh, heh, heh.*

"What should I do about Ike's mom? Do you think she'll ever give me a chance?"

I take his silence to mean no, she won't.

But *he's* here. Old Sport likes me, and dogs have a sense about people, don't they? So maybe I'm *not* such a horrible person as Mrs. Hanson thinks.

"I do love Ike, you know," I tell him. "I love him like crazy." Old Sport's wagging tail whacks against the patio's flagstone. He believes me. I dig my hand into Mrs. Hanson's loaf of banana bread—there's no way I'm giving it to Maryam—and scoop out a handful. I offer it to Old Sport. "You want this?"

He's on his dog feet instantly, and I'm all of a sudden terrified. *He can't eat out of my hand. That's just . . . too gross . . . too much.* I toss the chunk of banana bread a few feet from me and am greatly relieved when he bounds over to it. I use it as a diversion, too, and go inside to wash my hands and load my backpack with my camera, lipstick, and the pair of walking shoes Ike gave me soon after we met. It strikes me that Ike is a funny gift giver—shoes and a cell phone. Even his willingness to marry me—he's romantic in his practicality.

By the time I set off for class, the temperature is greater than ninety-five degrees Fahrenheit, with not a hint of cloud or breeze, but I hardly notice the heat. I hardly notice anything.

Any other day, after crossing Campbell Avenue at Third Street, I'd pause to watch the soccer game on the center grass on the University of Arizona campus, played by intent, shirtless men who come from every imaginable continent. I'd pause to watch the band practice on the south lawn and the cheerleaders with their high-ponytail hair and pom-poms as they practice flips and cartwheels and show off their strong, tan legs in short, bouncy skirts. I'd notice the people at the bus stop, the students on bicycles and skateboards. I love the free life here very much and never tire of people-watching, but today, it's all relegated to the background. Today, it feels dangerously at risk.

After passing through the gates leaving campus, I cross Park Avenue and am on University Boulevard, with its restaurants and clothing stores and coffee shops—most notably, the Starbucks where I first met Ike—my first, favorite, and forever barista. I'd had a plan, this morning. I was going to get in line and act like the person I was three months ago, when we met for the very first time.

That day, I stepped inside Starbucks, closed my eyes, inhaled the deep coffee smell, and in my memory was taken back to my grandmother's home in Esfahan—my only relative who always made coffee. I spent many days there as a child, skipping through the citrus trees in her courtyard, hopping from brick to brick, young enough that *hejab* was not yet required of me, young enough not to have to sit with the grown-ups inside, as Maryam did, and listen to them say the same things over and over again about what a failure the revolution was, how it wasn't smart to have traded one corrupt leader they knew well for someone it turned out they did not know very well at all. They talked of lessons learned: Beware of the charismatic man who speaks the words our hearts long to hear, who railed against the Shah's misdeeds and corruptions and excess and promised to create a more just society—without ever explaining that he would silence his critics by executing them at a rate of four or five per day. They talked of sanctions and hostages and inflation and frozen bank accounts and the war with Iraq and how the Americans were supplying Saddam Hussein with mustard-gas weapons to kill the soldiers of Iran.

I hated these conversations—they went around and around and depressed all the grown-ups. My mother—this is strange for me to think back to, now that I know more about her past—would sit in a straight-back chair with her knees tucked to the side and her lips pressed together. I always thought she must find their words as dull as I did, for she didn't participate in these discussions but rather only sat compliantly, waiting for the visit to end, while I would happily play outside in the courtyard, collecting pecans that had fallen from the trees, until my grandmother called me inside. As I'd step into her warm kitchen, the smell of her coffee would overpower me—just as it did at this Starbucks halfway around the world. That first day, I was flustered at having to order for myself in English. Ike was so nice to me that day, and on every day since.

Today, when he sees me, his face lights up. He arranges with his coworker and friend Josh to take a quick break and comes around the counter, kissing my cheek in greeting. "Hey, you! Having a good day?"

Um, no. Not exactly.

"Your mother brought me banana bread to give to Maryam," I tell him.

"Really?" He tilts his head, curious. "That's unexpected."

"Yes, it was very unexpected." I can't criticize her, not out loud anyway, so I try to communicate with my eyes that her visit was not a pleasant surprise.

Ike gets it. "Hey, come here." He takes my hand and leads me outside, around the corner of the building to a side walkway. Then he kisses me, pressing me against the wall, anchoring me.

"That was a pretty funny text message you sent." He lifts my hair and kisses my neck in three spots, each below the other, giving me delightful chills.

"Text message?" I murmur back, waiting for the fourth and fifth kisses—this could go on forever and be all right with me. I've completely melted into the moment and left his mother far behind. It's amazing what a few soft kisses can do to a girl.

"The one saying I can bang you anytime." He pulls back to look at me, amused. "You have no idea what that means, do you?"

My blush starts even before I figure it out. "Do I want to know?"

"You should know the context, I suppose." He fake-whispers it in my ear, then laughs. "I mean, I wouldn't want my wife going around telling other guys they can bang her anytime."

I get a mental picture of myself obliviously saying this to Josef, to Danny, to Edgard—to any of my male friends from English class—and start to giggle. "I'm going to ask Danny to teach us more slang this semester," I say. "Especially this sort of slang."

"I'm sure Eva can teach you if he doesn't."

"This is a good point." Eva's got the foulest mouth of anyone I know. It's a matter of great delight for her to shock me with her crude language.

"So what'd my mom want?" He watches me closely as he asks.

"Well . . ." I hate to ruin this lovely moment. I wish I didn't have to tell him. Even more, I wish it hadn't happened. "She saw a lawyer who told her our marriage is—what's the word?—*fraudulent*."

He pales. "She didn't."

"And she's carrying around the telephone number to the Immigration or Homeland Security people in case she wants to call and have me deported."

His eyes darken with anger. "She wouldn't."

"It was horrible, Ike. Just *horrible*."

He takes a step back and runs his hand through his hair, smoothing it, even though it's already very smooth. I can tell his mind is circling around the news over and over.

"I explained about the path, but—"

"She left a message for me earlier asking if I'd filed Form I-130 yet. That's the green card application, I assume?"

"My sister has all the immigration paperwork in a file for us," I say. "I'm not sure what that particular form is, but she'll know."

"Let's file what we can today," he says. "And then we'll pay my mother a visit."

I really, really don't want to do this.

"Don't you think it might be better if you see her alone?" He shakes his head. "Ike, she really wasn't very nice. She told me I should go back to Iran. That I don't deserve to be here. That I haven't *earned* it." As I choke on my words, I think, why can't I speak with Ike's steadiness? Or Eva's brashness? Or Ardishir's reasonableness? My words always come out so shaky, so emotional, so laced with fear. I hate this about myself.

Ike takes my hand. "My mother's completely out of line. She's just trying to intimidate you, and you can't let her."

"She was pretty convincing."

"That's what intimidation is all about." He tucks my hair behind my ear. "And that's why you have to come with me when I go see her. You can never make things easy for people who make things hard for you. Never—understand?"

I say yes, I understand.

And I do—in theory, anyway.

"Now, go enjoy your class," he says. "And afterward we'll get that paperwork filed, and then we'll go talk with my mother. And it'll all be good."

I let out a big, stressful breath. "You really think so?"

"Absolutely." Ike grips me in a huge hug. "Don't give her more attention than she deserves, which is very little at this point."

"But, Ike"—I need to see his eyes, so I pull back from his embrace—"if I could just somehow prove to her that I love you, that I'm not doing this just for—"

"Absolutely not," he says. "You don't need to prove anything to her. She's not the judge. Not the jury."

"But she *is* your mother." And *my* mother-in-law.

"You want to prove how much you love me?" Ike moves me back against the wall and lifts my hair off my neck again, readying to resume his distractingly soft kisses.

"Yes," I murmur, pretty sure his suggestion will be bedroom-related.

But my new husband once again surprises me. "Don't give up on us," he says. "That's all I'll ever ask—that you fight for us. That you never walk away from what we have. That you don't let anyone scare you away."

I pull him close and hold him tenderly. The thought of our being apart is too horrible to contemplate. It is only here, with him, that I feel whole, and safe, and good.

"I will remember the path," I vow.

He laughs—already this is becoming a joke between us. "You do that."

Then he kisses my neck and I shiver deliciously on this already hot day, and after we kiss for a while more, he goes back to work and with a much lighter heart, I continue on to English class.

Chapter 13

I'm early for class, so I have time to apply for a library card. I've wanted one ever since I attended my first English class here, and I've spent many afternoons going up and down the aisles, peeking at titles and reading pages here and there, feeling like I'm getting away with something. Now I'll be able to take books home and savor them. Books amaze me.

Books are ideas. They're expression, inspiration, provocation.

The Bible, the Torah, the Koran—all books of stories that people use to get or keep power. They do more, of course. They provide comfort. They inspire. They justify—both good and evil behavior. I think a well-told story is more powerful than any person ever could be, because people die but stories can be handed down century after century, year after year. They can hold people captive; they can set people free. I think it's the stories people tell that, in the end, will bring down regimes.

Now that I'm to live in America, I want to read what free people read, and my plan is to start with Ike's favorite book, *The Great Gatsby.* The librarian, when she learns this is the first library card I've ever applied for, comes around the counter and helps me find the book, which is filed in the fiction section under the author's last name. Then she shows me how to use the self-serve checkouts, which I think are very nice for privacy reasons, and she even gives me a sticker that says, MY VERY FIRST LIBRARY CARD. I proudly affix it to my chest, thank her, and dash down the stairs with my new book to the conference room where my English class meets.

Agata and Josef are already there, and they cheer as I enter. I haven't seen them since Las Vegas, and we're now even more bonded in our friendship, because we all got married on the same day, by the same Elvis Presley impersonator. Danny, our ponytailed hippie instructor, looks up from organizing some papers at the head of the table and comes over. He throws his arms around me, lifts me off my feet, and twirls me around.

"I heard the good news!" He sets me back down, then impulsively hugs me again. "This land is your land, baby!"

"Can you believe it?" I say. "This land *is* my land!"

"Absolutely, I believe it," he says. "You deserve every happiness. And it wasn't an arranged marriage! I can't tell you how happy I was to hear that. You're just . . ." He tilts his head, and I can tell he's trying to find words that won't offend me. "That's not who you are. I didn't want that for you."

"I didn't want that for me, either." I'm so glad I can finally admit this.

We chat a bit more before he introduces me to the new members in the group, a married Chinese couple named Alicia and Chen, who are graduate students at the University of Arizona. They're sitting with notebooks and pens ready. I say hello; they say hello back. I say welcome; they say thank you. And we all smile, smile, smile. I remember back to my first day of class—how I envied the other students' obvious camaraderie and was eager to become part of the group, yet nervous about having to speak. I wonder if they feel the same way today as I did back then.

"How long have you been in the U.S.?" I say.

"We have been here since January," Chen says. "Four months."

Longer than me!

"And do you like it here?"

"Very much," Chen says with a broad smile. Alicia nods and smiles, too. I wonder how being married is different here than being married in China, and how being in America has changed their relationship.

"Welcome to the class," I say. "I'm sure you will find it very much fun. Most of these people have taken the class for years."

"It's a good group," Danny says.

"Will everyone from the last session be here again?" I ask.

"Everyone except for Edgard," he says. "He decided to

take some medical-translation classes at the community college. He's hoping his green card will come through soon and then he'll take his medical exams."

"This is good," I say. "Good for him." In Peru, he was a doctor, but since he's been in the U.S., he's been washing dishes in a Guatemalan restaurant on Fourth Avenue. This has always made me feel sad for him, to go from being a doctor to a dishwasher, but he has never complained about it. "And no Nadia," I add.

"No Nadia," Danny agrees. "Which is a good thing, right?"

"Very good, yes," I say. "I spoke with her on the phone, and she has not yet had her baby, but very soon, she says."

"Good for her," Danny says. "She made a smart move."

"Yes, she's very brave," I say. "And Eva? She will be taking this class, too, yes?"

"She'll be here." Danny grins. "God help us all."

I laugh and explain to Alicia and Chen about Eva. "Eva is a German woman, and she says some very . . . what's the word?"

"Obnoxious?" Danny offers.

"Outrageous," I say. "She says some very outrageous things. Please don't let her offend you."

"She *vants* to a-fend you," Josef says. "She is *not* good girl." He smiles at me. "Tami, she is very good girl."

I smile at him and then notice that he is set up to sit behind Agata rather than next to her. This is how they sat last term, before they were married, when they pretended they didn't have feelings for each other.

"Why don't you sit next to your wife, Josef?" I say.

"Because I vant to sit next to you," he says.

"Agata?" I ask.

She waves her hand like this is a question not worth her time. "He talks-a too a-much." I laugh, because beneath her grumbling, Agata very much enjoys the attention Josef pays her. "Ve are here to learn to talk to others. Ve already know how to talk between us."

Josef covers his heart with his hands, very dramatically. "Yes, ve speak the language of love! Ve make love like teenagers!" While Agata rolls her eyes, Josef throws back his head and laughs his old-man laugh. When he notices my embarrassed face, he opens his arms in an unapologetic manner. "Vat? You are a newlyved. You know how it ees."

I feel my face redden. "Well . . ."

"Well, vat?" Josef demands.

"Yeah. Well, what?" At the voice, I turn to the doorway. It's Eva, my foulmouthed friend. "Don't *tell* me you haven't had mad, passionate sex with that husband of yours yet."

I'd like to at least pretend to be offended at what she's said, but I can't. I can only laugh. Eva is *too rude.* Yet as far as my sexual relations with my husband are concerned, I just don't want to talk about it. I know I have lots to learn, but no way do I want my entire English class trying to teach me! I'll leave that to Ike, and maybe to my sister, and maybe, just *maybe*, occasionally, to Eva. But not to the whole class.

"Is that a wig?" I say, hoping to distract her. Eva's got a plunging neckline on her sexy halter top and superhigh heels, paired with denim cutoff shorts. There is nothing unusual about this. But her hair's different. It's a pretty light brown instead of its usual blond, and it's maybe five inches longer than it was in Las Vegas, and quite a bit fuller and prettier.

"You like it?" She strikes a pose. "I'm so damn bored in this town that I'm running out of things to do."

"You could get a job," Danny says.

"Right." Eva gives him a look. "Can you really see me taking orders from anyone?"

After she sits down, we spend the next two hours getting to know Alicia and Chen by asking them questions about themselves, their families, and China. Then our talk turns to restaurants, and we discuss how strange it is that there are no small drinks in America—the smallest drink is actually a medium drink, and then it goes to large and extra-large and then often to something called supersize, which is a truly crazy amount, enough for a whole family to drink for a week. We practice ordering from an American-food menu—How did you want that burger done? Ketchup, mustard, and onion? And did you want fries or coleslaw? And to drink? Regular or diet? There is so much to learn about living in America—so many questions to be asked! So many choices to be made!

When Ike and I arrive at Maryam's house later, we find her inside, sitting on the couch—crying. Only, *crying* isn't the right word. *Weeping. Sobbing.* These words are better to describe her. Horrible pictures race through my imagination of all the bad things that might have happened to my parents back in Iran. And who is there anymore to help them? Or the baby! Is there a problem with the baby?

"Maryam!" I race to sit beside her. "What's wrong?" I slip into Farsi, where when I speak I don't have to think so hard. I've been told that one day I'll begin to dream in English, but as yet my dreams are in the language of home, and I'm glad for this. My dreams sometimes are more real than my reality. "Please, are you okay? Is the baby okay? Are you hurting? What can I do, please? What is it?"

Maryam gestures to the large-screen television against the wall. "Sammy just left her baby at the convent! Can you believe it? She gave away her baby!" She also speaks in Farsi, which leaves Ike unsure of what's going on.

I follow her eyes to the television, incredulous. I've been living here for three months, and I've never known my sister to watch or talk about a television program and become upset. I've never known her to watch TV in the daytime. And yet here she sits, curled up with her legs under her on the couch, wearing no makeup, with her hair uncombed. Still in her pajamas, she looks pale and tired.

Ike stands back near the door. "Is she okay?"

"She seems to be upset about the show."

Ike starts to laugh. "Hormones."

"But . . ." Maryam shifts to English. "It's not even her baby! It was switched at the hospital!"

"Gee," Ike says, "I wonder if she'll ever learn *that* piece of information?"

Maryam's eyes widen at the thought. "I'm sure she will! Don't you think?"

Ike laughs. "That was a joke. Of course she will. And then she'll get amnesia and forget, and then she'll remember again, but then she'll forget again, and this'll happen about twenty times in the next twenty years."

"It's stupid, I know." Maryam says this sheepishly, but she turns back to the show. I look at her in wonder. Her behavior is very, very strange.

"What show *is* this?" I ask.

"*Days of our Lives*," Ike says as he comes to join us in the seating area, taking Ardishir's favorite armchair.

"It's a soap opera," Maryam says. "You should watch it with me. It'll help you learn English."

I say to Ike, "*You* watch *Days of our Lives*?"

He grins and shakes his head, no. "My sisters do, and my mom, too. It's kind of a family thing, but only in the summer. There's not a heck of a lot to do in this town outdoors when it's so hot, so they stay inside and eat ice cream and watch *Days of our Lives*. They've been doing it for years. Even Camille watches. Then they update me and my dad at dinner every night."

His brightness falters. I'm sure we're thinking the same thing—that he probably won't be having fun family dinners with them for a while. I reach for his hand and squeeze it in sympathy.

"Since when have *you* watched it?" I ask Maryam, wondering if she's planning to shower today, or at least change from her pajamas before Ardishir gets home.

Maryam is usually so snap-snap with her days, going from here to there, filling them with manicures and shoe shopping and getting her hair done and her weekly massages—not to mention her part-time job as a manager at Macy's, which she has simply to have something structured to do. I find it nearly impossible to understand when she has the time to watch a daily soap opera, and it just doesn't suit her personality. I, on the other hand, am completely the sort to watch shows like this. In Iran, I was addicted to *Madare sefr darajeh* and tuned in every Friday night to see the very sexy Shahab Hosseini.

"Since you went on your trip last week," she says. "I was so tired from everything that I took a few days off work. And then I got hooked on this show." She presses the remote control to turn up the volume, and her eyes are riveted on the screen. "There's another good one on right after this."

Ike must think my sister is so weird. He's seen only these extreme emotional sides of her, either yelling or crying, nothing in between—which is *not* Maryam. She's professional and polite, but her pregnancy is really changing her. I would have expected her to be a better hostess to Ike, to offer him tea and fruit and nuts and sweets and to ask after his family and to inquire as to how we're settling into our new living arrangements. But none of this happens! The show is clearly more important to her than we are.

"If it's not too much trouble, Maryam, could you give us the form Ike needs to file for my residency?" I say. "We want to mail it today."

She doesn't take her eyes off the television. "There's no rush. Why today?"

"Why not today?" I keep my tone light. "The sooner it's filed, the sooner I can get a job."

"You have a job."

This is true, as Ardishir has offered to have me work as a receptionist and billing clerk in his orthopedic surgery office a few mornings a week, filling in for an employee who is on maternity leave.

"I mean a real full-time job. Not a family job."

"You should work at Macy's with me," she says.

"Maybe," I say. "So . . . the papers, please?"

Maryam's eyes are back on the television. "At the next commercial, okay?"

Ike and I fill out the forms, get them in the mail, and then pay a visit to Mr. Hanson, as Ike wants to know if his father played any role in his mother's nasty visit to me this morning.

Mr. Hanson is doing an addition on a house in a neighborhood called Poets Corner, where the streets are named after poets. We drive there in Ike's pickup truck. The framing is up and the roof is on, and inside we find Mr. Hanson putting up drywall in what is going to be an indoor-outdoor room, with a fireplace and screened windows that face the pool. Loud classical piano music plays from a radio beside him.

"Hey, Dad." Ike leads the way over to him with me not too close, but not too far behind, and turns down the music. "How come you're doing the drywall? Where are your subs?"

Mr. Hanson steps back from the wall and wipes his

sweaty brow. He nods at me. "They couldn't come, and I didn't want to lose a day."

"You should have called me," Ike says.

His father matches Ike's level gaze. I'm very nervous as I wait for him to respond, because whatever he says next could determine how pleasant or unpleasant the conversation will be. "I figured you're busy," he says.

"I'm never too busy for you, Dad."

There's yearning along with maturity in Ike's voice, and I want to cry for him. He tries so hard for people, and he loves his family so much. They'd make a good Persian family—they're that close. The first week I met him, he told me his father was his best friend, his truest confidant. I know how hard the past days must have been for him, to lose his father's support.

His father must know it, too. "I guess I could use some help around here," he says. "I've got another job waiting and the market seems to be slowing, so I'd like to get it going before they decide to cancel. If you could take over as contractor here, I could start work on that one. There's not all that much left, just the walls and the floors . . ."

"And the cabinetry and all the finishing touches." Ike grins. "That's a lot of hours."

"And some decent money," Mr. Hanson says.

When Ike looks at me, I smile to let him know it's okay with me. It's a good way to strengthen his relationship with his father, and I know this is how Ike has made most of the money he's saved for the coffee shop, by what he calls flipping houses with his father.

"Let me see if I can cut back my hours at work," Ike says. "The semester's ending, which means it's slowing down for the summer, so maybe I can go down to twenty hours."

"Don't quit completely," Mr. Hanson says. "After this next job, I've only got one more on the schedule—although I'm sure something will turn up."

"I can't quit, anyway." Ike says. "I'm a married man now. I need the benefits."

His dad smiles. Smiles! In that smile, I see how Ike will look twenty-five years from now. Kind. Handsome, with healthy, hard-earned smile wrinkles. Maybe he'll even have a son, just a few years younger than Ike is now. And maybe they'll be best friends, too.

Ike shifts the conversation to why we came. "Do you know what Mom's up to?"

"What do you mean?" Mr. Hanson asks, somewhat warily.

"I mean, do you know what she did?"

"I know she saw a lawyer yesterday." Mr. Hanson keeps his eyes carefully averted from mine.

"Do you know what she did to Tami today?"

Mr. Hanson shakes his head.

"She dropped by unannounced and basically told Tami to abandon the marriage and leave the country." Ike's voice has hardened. "She threatened to have her deported. And I need to know, Dad: Were you part of that?"

Ike's chest rises and falls as he waits for his father to answer. Mr. Hanson, for his part, turns to me with a troubled expression, and then goes back to his drywall supplies and starts putting them away. "Things might not go as well as the two of you hope." He doesn't look at either of us, but rather cleans off his scraper. "There's some sense to the idea of locking in your losses early. I think that's what your mother's trying to get at."

I'm a bad investment. That's the point he wants to make.

"Were you part of it, Dad? Part of her threat?"

Mr. Hanson looks at me. "Are you sure it was really a threat and not just a suggestion?"

See this? she'd said, holding up the business card. *This is the phone number to Immigration Enforcement. This is the number I call to have you deported.*

"It was a threat," I say.

He looks at me for a long moment.

"Dad."

"I didn't know your mother was going to do that," Mr. Hanson says. "Although, in fairness, I don't know that I would have stopped her if I had."

Ike gives him a serious, imploring look. "I swear to God, there are probably going to be five, maybe ten times *in my life* when I come to you and say, 'Hey, Dad, I really need you to be here for me. Right now, in this moment.' This is one of those times. It's that old deathbed argument again, and I'm sorry to throw it at you, but thirty years from now, forty years from now—"

"Or tomorrow," Mr. Hanson says. "I could die tomorrow."

I gasp. This is not something that should be said out loud!

"Or tomorrow," Ike agrees. "Although let's hope to hell not."

"You're right," Mr. Hanson says, not needing him to continue. "I don't want to regret my behavior here, and I already do." He faces me directly and says, "You were a guest in our home the other night, and I acted badly, and I apologize. Sincerely. I was caught off guard, and I wasn't at my best."

My forgiveness is instant. "That's okay. I know you're worried for Ike. You acted this way out of your love for him."

"The thing is, I trust him," he says. "I trust his judgment. He's a good kid and a better man. It's just . . . you never stop worrying about your children. You'd always—" He clears his throat. "You'd always go to your grave for them, to spare them any real suffering."

Mr. Hanson's eyes are pained as he looks at me, almost imploringly, seeking my understanding. I nod to let him know I do understand, even though I'm not yet a parent myself.

"My son loves deep and he loves hard," he says. "So if you're scamming him, taking advantage of him—I'm not saying you are, but I just have to say—"

"I'm not." I say this quickly so he doesn't have to continue. "I promise, I'm not."

"You see, Ike still thinks the world is good." Mr. Hanson's voice is strained with emotion.

"The world *is* good," Ike says.

His father swallows hard. "Sometimes it takes just one

thing, one very bad, horrible experience, to make a person question that, and I don't want this"—he looks at me—"I don't want *you* to be that thing."

What, I wonder, *was his horrible thing?*

"I love your son with all my heart," I say. "And I know what you mean about one bad experience changing how you see the world—I know this from my mother—and I'm not going to be the person, or the *thing*, that changes Ike in this way. I love him too much."

"Good." Mr. Hanson nods, his voice thick. "That's good."

To Ike, he says, "I'll work on your mother. I make no promises, but I'll speak with her." He flashes a sudden grin that's startlingly like Ike's. "I'll remind her how it is to be young and in love."

Chapter 14

The next several weeks pass very pleasantly. Ike and I have great fun living together and quickly establish our routines. He gets up early and takes Old Sport for a run, and then we have a breakfast of fruit and bagels on the patio before he goes to work. He's cut his hours at Starbucks and divides his time between there and working for his dad. I spend my mornings either helping Ardishir in his office or joining Rose as she runs errands and works on projects around the house. In the afternoons, I attend English class.

As Maryam ends her fourth month of pregnancy, her mood swings even out, and I'm very glad for this. I go along with her as she shops for a crib and maternity clothes and a car seat and baby clothes—there is so much to do to get ready for a baby! Especially if the woman already has some money and already likes to shop. Ike begins to roll his eyes when she calls to tell me the least little things—how she has indigestion and keeps having to use the bathroom and how her fingernails grow so fast—but I love to share every moment of my sister's pregnancy. Ardishir and I paint the baby's room a pretty light green. Maryam makes us use nontoxic paint and even so, she leaves the house while we paint, although she checks in by phone every half hour to see how it's going. After I agree to throw a baby shower for her, she talks about it every day, several times each day. She registers at five different stores and buys books for me about the different games and activities we can do. It's fun to see her this way, as our growing-up years weren't very festive.

In the mail, Ike and I get a letter from the U.S. Bureau of Citizenship and Immigration Services saying our application has been received and that another notice will be sent soon with a date for our immigration interview, which means that so far everything is going as it should in this regard. With my first paycheck from working in Ardishir's office, I buy a bicycle from the Ordinary Bike Shop and begin biking to class. In the early evenings, Ike and I bike around Reid Park, often packing a picnic for dinner. I love the hot spring breeze and how it works its way through my hair and the smell of the golf course grass and the *thwack* of the tennis balls as we pass the courts. I love, too, how my thigh muscles become well defined as the weeks go on, but most of all, I love my new bike. It's what Ike calls a *retro* bike, by a company called Schwinn, and it's sparkly blue with wide tires and a basket on the front and a cheerful brass bell, which I sound each time I pass a jogger or walker. Even though it's not too practical, each day I wear one of my new spring knee-length skirts when we go biking because, somehow, wearing them makes the outing feel even more American, and I put on sleeveless tops *just because I can.* America—the land of spaghetti straps and flip-flops. My kind of place!

There's so much to do, so much to explore, so much of Ike to get to know. We go to the towns of Bisbee and Tubac and also visit Kartchner Caverns, and one night, instead of bike riding, we drive to a place called Gates Pass and eat cheese and drink wine as we watch what must be the most beautiful sunset in the world, and when it's over we lie on a futon mattress in the bed of the pickup truck and make plans for our future. I've noticed that in the last few weeks he has stopped mentioning his coffee shop and instead has begun thinking of travel adventures for us to take, such as hiking to the bottom of the Grand Canyon, and river rafting in Colorado, and even backpacking in South America—once I have my residency papers. All of this sounds very good, very exciting to me, although I can't help but feel bad about his coffee shop. Rose and I often shop at the Trader Joe's across from Ike's perfect location, which is still available, still waiting for him. Every time I see it, I feel a horrible guilt from my belief that I have ruined his dream.

The situation with his parents could be worse. It could also be better.

Mrs. Hanson makes no more visits to the guesthouse, announced or unannounced, and since Ike's discussion with his father, she's stopped saying anything at all about our marriage. Ike stops over at his parents' regularly, and I even go with him once to pick up Camille, who wants to visit Old Sport. Mrs. Hanson comes out of the kitchen to say hello, and her eyes communicate no obvious dislike for me. I take this as a hopeful sign that maybe Ike is right and that over time perhaps I'll be welcomed into the family, which is something both Ike and I want very much.

I maintain this hope right up to the day that Jenna, Ike's old girlfriend, comes back to town.

Then, in an instant, I lose my newfound hope.

Then, in an instant, I realize I could lose everything—not only Ike but America, too.

Chapter 15

It happens one afternoon on a beautiful spring day that sparkles with sunshine.

It's after class. Eva and I have walked to Starbucks (since I have my bike with me, I do what Eva calls taking my bike for a walk), and just walking puts me in a good mood. This is one of those things about being free that you can't fully appreciate unless you've lived its opposite. In Iran, something as innocent as walking down the street with girlfriends—the fact of young women having fun together, of maybe laughing too loud—can draw all sorts of attention and cause all sorts of problems. But not in America. America is not about keeping other people down.

When we arrive, we join the just-off-work Ike and Josh at a patio table and quickly fall into an easy conversation, which is more or less a continuation of the one we all had the day before—a lot of talk and laughter about nothing much at all. It's all so perfect, so fun, and it feels like it will last forever, this sort of happiness, this sort of easy, free day.

I should have taken a photograph.

"No way," Ike murmurs at the sight of her. "No friggin' way."

He looks at her as if she's a mirage, a shimmering gift of water in a very thirsty desert, as if the sight of her is simply too good to be true. Then he pushes back his chair, stands, and goes to her. It's like he's floating from how light his heart is at the sight of her.

It's Jenna. I know this instinctively.

She waits for him in her short denim skirt and sparkly red high-heeled sandals that match her pedicure. In between the skirt and the sandals are impossibly long and forever-tan legs, the exact sort of muscled female legs I so badly want for myself. Her long, sleek blond hair beckons him. Her too-white model's smile beams at him. Her palms lift upward, as if to say, *Here I am, Ike. Yours.*

When they embrace, there's no space between them, and they embrace for a very, *very* long time—or maybe it just feels that way because I'm unable to breathe. I'm remembering what Mrs. Hanson told Ike when Jenna left, how if you love something, you must set it free, and if it comes back to you it's yours. I wish more than anything that Jenna had stayed away.

"This chick is trouble," Eva says. "I'm telling you right now."

Her words aren't necessary, for I can tell all on my own

that Jenna is far more than simple trouble. She's a thief—a beautiful thief, the very worst kind—and she has come to steal my husband.

"Get over there," Eva says. "Mark your man." To Josh, she asks, "Who is she?"

"I have no idea. And if I do, I'm not telling." It's clear from his low-level chuckle that he knows her. It's clear, too, by the glimmer in his eyes that he likes her.

"It's Jenna," I say. "Ike's old girlfriend."

Eva knocks her arm into me. "Get *over* there."

"I can't just—" I fall silent as they step apart—not by much, not by nearly enough! It's like there's a magnet pulling their hearts together. Why, oh why, can't I catch my breath?

They don't exchange words at first, but talk with their eyes instead.

Ike's: *I don't believe this—what are you doing here?*

Hers: *I came back. For you.*

His: *But I thought you were gone forever.*

Hers: *I couldn't stay away.*

"Ike!" Eva calls out. "Come introduce her to your wife!"

For once, I'm grateful for her obnoxiousness, because I'd begun to think Ike had forgotten all about me. At Eva's words, his forehead wrinkles and he gives me a look of confusion, as if he's forgotten who I am. *I'm your wife, Ike! Your wife!*

He nods vaguely, as if he's heard the screaming in my mind, and turns back to Jenna. I can't hear what he says, but I imagine him choking on the words *I'm married now*, saying them with regret, for Jenna is the easy one to love, the one whose presence wouldn't cause problems with his family. Jenna is the one he loved first.

"I don't feel well," I murmur.

"Oh, no you don't." Eva elbows me, hard. "Act like a grown-up for a change. *Toughen up*, chickee-poo."

She's the one who left, I tell myself. *You're the one who stayed. You're the wife. You're the wife. You're the wife.*

It seems like a pretty bad sign that I have to keep reminding myself of this.

Jenna's green eyes are troubled as Ike leads her to the table. She's *beautiful*—absolutely, inarguably so. She and Ike would make perfect American babies. She's taller than him, with broad, strong shoulders that make her waist look tiny. Ike introduces us. "Tami, this is Jenna. Jenna, Tami."

Awkwardly, I get to my feet. "Hello. It's very nice to meet you."

"It's nice to meet *you*." Jenna extends her silken-soft hands with their French-manicured nails. But it's her *eyes* that are most troublesome—a man could get lost in them for days. "I didn't know Ike got married!" she says.

"Well, he did." Eva doesn't try to keep the snarl from her tone.

"This is Eva," Ike says. "A force unto herself. And Josh. You remember Josh, of course."

Jenna gives Eva a cursory nod and focuses on Josh, a far friendlier face. "Joshie! Nice to see you!"

Josh sits up from his slouch, takes her hand, and pulls her down so he can kiss her cheek. "Hey, welcome back! Where-all have you been?"

"Oh, you know." Jenna's smile is generous. It seems to include the whole world. "I've been flitting here, there, everywhere."

Ike smiles. "Flitting—that's the perfect word to describe you."

"Did you say flit?" Eva asks. "Or twit?"

Josh laughs, and I would, too, if I knew what Eva meant, because I'm sure it's deliciously rude, but neither Jenna nor Ike seems to have heard her. Jenna tilts her shoulder forward at him, as if to say, *Aren't I just so cute to describe myself so perfectly?* The problem: She *is* just so cute! Even as she's flirting with my husband, I can't help but think this—she's cute, and beautiful, too, a deadly combination.

"Have a seat." Ike gestures for Jenna to take his chair, and she does, as if it belongs to her, as if she owns, too, this table we've been sitting at for all these weeks, all these months. This is the table where Ike gave me my walking shoes! *It's not her table!* But that's the thing about beautiful, confident people—there's power in their beauty. They feel entitled to anything they want. The last thing I want is to sit next to her, because by any comparison, I lose—in confidence most of all.

"So how was the great European adventure?" Josh asks, as Ike gets an empty chair from another table.

"It was, well . . ." Jenna glances at me, and her smile falters and she bites her lip, and for the first time, I see how hard this is for her, to have to pretend she's not upset. She probably wants to slink away and cry—that's certainly how I feel. "It was very European."

"Imagine that," Eva says.

I feel a tiny measure of relief as Ike places the extra chair next to *me,* not *her.* I'm now between them. My knee is right here. Ike could easily put his hand on it, but he doesn't.

"This is quite the triangle," Eva says. "*How* do you two know each other?"

"Eva, please don't start with your shit," Ike says, his voice mildly stern.

"We dated in college." Jenna's green eyes glow spookily.

"Fuck buddies," Eva says.

I gasp. Ike is tensed with anger, like he was when his parents insulted me. I brace myself to hear him defend Jenna's honor, but it turns out she can defend herself perfectly well.

"We were a little more than that," she says. "We lived together for over a year."

I gasp again.

Ike looks at me. "You knew that, right?"

I shake my head no. I definitely did not know that!

"I'd have to say we didn't make very good roommates." He smiles to reassure me, to tell me the fact that they lived together for more than one year is no big deal. But it is! It is a big deal!

"That's an understatement!" Jenna laughs. "Does he still leave his wet towels on the floor? That used to drive me nuts!"

Ike does, in fact, leave his towels on the floor, but it's not something I'd ever complain about, and certainly not to her. "Ike is very nice to live with."

He reaches for my hand, squeezes it, and gives me a smile

that tells me I'm nice to live with, too. I return his squeeze gratefully—very, very gratefully, for while he neglected to mention they'd lived together, I remember all too well how he described the end of their relationship. *She wanted to get married,* he said. *I said I'd wait for her, that she should go and I'd stay and get the coffee shop off the ground. But she said she knew that if she went, she wouldn't come back . . . that she wouldn't be the same person a year down the road and she had to be free to see where life took her.*

It sounds like you really loved her, I said.

He nodded. Yes, he'd loved her. *But she was right,* he said, his voice strained, nearly cracking. *She didn't come back.*

And yet, here she is. The bird he set free has flown back to him.

"How long have you two been married?" Jenna asks, studying me too closely. Witches have green eyes, don't they?

"About five weeks." I sound weak. I *am* weak. "Almost six."

Jenna tilts her head at me. "And you're . . . new to America?"

Is ours a green-card marriage, is what she's asking.

"I've been here a little more than four months."

Her smile is friendly. "Well, you sure managed to snag yourself a good one. They don't come better than Ike."

"She didn't *snag* him," Eva says. "If anything, he snagged her."

Josh makes a sound of two cats fighting, but no one finds this funny.

"*How* long are you in town for?" Eva asks.

Jenna levels her eyes at Eva, not intimidated by her at all. "Oh, I'm back for good."

"For good?" Ike looks from Jenna to me and then back to her. "What are you going to do for a job?"

"I have a few ideas about that." She tilts her head at him, then, saying something by the gesture, and I feel very much in the way, seated here between them. Even in public, part of their world is private. Inaccessible. Ike and I are still holding hands, and I squeeze his very tightly. It's a squeeze of terror, for I think I might be losing him. "What about you?" Jenna says to him. "What are you doing still working here? You should have your coffee shop open by now!"

There's unmistakable tension in his voice as Ike says, "I've hit a snag."

"Snag." Eva snorts. "That's such a bullshit word. Let's all stop using that word."

Jenna ignores her and raises an eyebrow at Ike. "A snag of the financial variety?"

"You could say that," he says. And then to Eva, he says, "Snag."

"How are your parents?" Jenna asks. "And your sisters? I miss Camille!"

"They're all good," Ike says. "Izzy's just her usual cool self, and Kat is . . . well, you know Kat. She manages to keep the whole house on its toes. It's all about her."

"And how's Paige?"

"Oh, Paige." Ike's voice is wistful. "She's still my precious girl. Almost too nice. Kat just runs right over her, and Paige just lets her. I worry she's getting lost in the shuffle."

"She's a gentle soul," Jenna says. "I hope she goes into nursing or hospice care or something—one of those care-taking professions."

"So far, she still wants to be a kindergarten teacher," Ike says.

"Well, Lord knows she's got the patience for it," Jenna says. "And Lord knows I don't! Tell them all I say hi, will you? Maybe I'll stop by one of these days."

"They'd like that." Ike's voice is falsely neutral. "Do you have a place yet?"

"I'm staying at the Hotel Congress at the moment." She gives Ike a too-long look with her too-green eyes.

"You can crash on my couch if you want," Josh offers.

"Thanks, but I like it at the Congress. For now, anyway. I've got special memories there." Ike's neck is red, something I've never seen before, and I feel absolutely nauseous imagining their special Hotel Congress memories. Jenna smiles at his reaction. "So, Ike . . . just how much do you need to get your coffee shop open?"

I swear, there's something sexual in the way she asks it. *Just how much do you need?*

"Way more than I have." Ike fiddles with his disposable coffee cup and locks eyes with her.

"Such as . . . ?" Jenna raises her horrible, cute, kiss-me shoulder at him. "How much?"

"I'm about a hundred, hundred twenty-five thousand short."

"Whew!" she says.

"Right," Ike says. "It's not going to be happening anytime soon."

"I thought your parents—?"

"Turns out I don't want to take their money," he says. "I mean, they're going to need that for my sisters' college. Tuition's not getting any cheaper."

"But I thought they—?"

"Nah," Ike says. "It's just not happening."

"Well," Jenna says. "So."

Ike smiles as if he's missed this familiar expression. "Well, so, what?"

"Well . . ." She glances at me before focusing once again on Ike. "I have my grandmother's inheritance money, remember, and so if you're . . . I don't know . . . looking for a partner, we should talk."

Ike probably doesn't even notice that his grip on me slackens, but I do. "Jenna, are you *serious*?"

"It's time for me to get serious about *something* for a change, don't you think?" She blinks her perfect eyelashes at him. "The money's not doing me any good just sitting there. I've got to put it to work."

"You've got that much?" Ike says.

"I've got that much."

They proceed to have a private, eyes-only conversation right in front of the rest of us.

Jenna: *This means we'd get to see each other every day.*

Ike: *You think we can handle being around each other?*

Jenna: *We'll see, won't we?*

"Ahem, bad idea," Eva says. "Never go into business with someone you used to fuck, or you're going to get fucked."

Ike narrows his eyes at her. "Is that right?"

"Yes," Eva says. "Besides, someone's wife might have an issue." She kicks me under the table. "Right, someone?"

Suddenly, all eyes are on me.

"Oh," I say. "Hmmm. Well."

"I wouldn't want to cause any trouble," Jenna says.

"Yes, you would," Eva says.

Josh laughs. I don't. Neither does Ike. Neither does Jenna. Josh stops laughing.

"Tami?" Ike says. "How do you feel about the idea?"

He looks at me with sympathy—looks and looks, waiting to hear what I'll say. I don't know what he's thinking, but it seems to be too complicated, or maybe too private, for words.

"I don't know what to say," I finally tell him. "I'm sorry, but I just don't know."

But even if I don't know what to say, I do know how I feel: Bad. Horrible. *Not good.*

I feel like maybe Jenna is the answer to his prayers, that she's his destiny. I feel like I'll lose him.

I feel like maybe I already have.

Chapter 16

Back in Tehran, when I was younger, Maryam used to leave me at home while she did the shopping. It was during the war with Iraq and there were shortages of everything, and so there were very long lines. Shopping for a few items could require an all-day effort. Having her little sister along was too much for Maryam to worry about, so she'd set me up in front of the television, put on *The Wizard of Oz* for me to watch, and then she'd leave. I wasn't completely alone—my mother was always home, but she rested in her bedroom in the afternoons. I loved *The Wizard of Oz*, but I hated the flying monkeys. When they came on, I'd bury my head against my knees and press my hands over my ears to drown out their screeching sounds.

Sometimes this worked, but other times my fear would get the best of me. When that happened, I'd slip off the couch and go into my mother's darkened room and silently get into bed with her. No matter what time of year it was, she kept a small fan running on the dresser, chilling the room, and she'd cover me with her blanket and kiss my forehead and hold my terrified hand in her calm, cool one. With her on those afternoons, I wasn't afraid. In her bedroom, I felt like I was tucked away somewhere safe.

This is what I need today—to be soothed. To feel safe and accepted and loved in a way I feel only with her.

I need my mother, desperately.

I call her from Rose's house, using the telephone in the kitchen. Rose isn't home, but she keeps a key under a watering can in the backyard in case I need to use the laundry or make overseas phone calls—for any reason, or no reason at all. As I dial our home in Tehran, it strikes me that I'm the same age Maman was when we left America, with my little hand clutching her smooth, slender one. I hate that her happiest days are decades behind her.

"'Alo, Maman?"

"Tami Joon, *Salaam*! How are you? Are you well? Is your husband well? And Maryam and Ardishir, how are they?"

"Everyone's fine, Maman. Everyone misses you." I wish I could tell her how precious Maryam looks with her bulging stomach and how she could be a model for maternity clothes, but Maman *still* doesn't know about her pregnancy. I can only hope she'll forgive me later for keeping Maryam's secret. "How's Baba?"

"He's fine, we're fine," she says.

"Maman?" Tears blur my eyes, my throat constricts, and I can't continue.

"*Chi shoda*, what's wrong?" Maman tempers her panic as best as she's able, but it comes through nonetheless. "Did somebody get hurt?"

"No one's hurt, Maman. It's—"

"It's what, Tami?"

"Ike's girlfriend came back to town." Saying it loud pushes me over the edge, and my tears come out in a rush. "Oh, Maman, I don't know what to do!"

"A girlfriend, Tami Joon?" Maman's voice is strained, stressed. "You never told us he had a girlfriend. What's this?"

"She's not his girlfriend anymore," I quickly say. "But she *is* beautiful, and . . ." *And he still loves her. I know he does.* "Maman, she wants to go into business with him. She wants to be his partner in the coffee shop, and he wants it, too, and . . ." *And my heart is broken because of it. Because of his wanting.* "And I just don't know . . ."

"Oh, Tami. My poor girl."

Her maternal comfort almost causes me to cry again. "Maman, I don't know what to do. I'm so afraid of losing him."

Ike and I had an odd and uncomfortable night after we left Starbucks, a night I wish I could scratch from existence. He was quiet and seemed sad, while I was quiet and terrified. *You looked like the sky was closing in on you*, he said.

And you looked like you'd seen an angel.

I'd thought this but didn't say it—afraid, I suppose, that he wouldn't dispute it.

We shared a lounge chair and spent a long time on the patio. We talked back and forth, not saying much of anything. He was uncharacteristically indirect, for hours, until he finally said, *If there's a way for us to make this work, I want to make it work.*

Then let's find a way to make it work, I said, feeling like I was signing my own death warrant. I still feel that way now. I don't have the right to deny Ike his dream, and yet I'm almost certain I'll lose him if he goes ahead with Jenna as his partner.

There's a long silence on the phone until at last my mother says, "Did I ever tell you why I made us all go back to Iran, Tami?"

I gasp, for *of course* she's never told me. No one in the family talks about this period of time, and yet the story lives on: She wanted to be part of the revolution sweeping Iran after the fall of the Shah, to help usher in a new era of justice. Many people wanted this.

"Well, because you wanted to make things better," I say. "You thought—"

"I thought your father was having an affair."

"What? Baba? No, Maman! Come on!"

"At Berkeley, your father had become friendly with an American woman, a neighbor of ours," Maman says. "I didn't trust her, and I didn't trust your father *with* her. He was so in love with all things American, it only made sense this would apply to beautiful blond American women, too."

Jenna's blond.

"Oh, Maman." My heart breaks for her. "I'm sorry. I didn't know this."

"I figured if we went back to Iran, he'd have to give her up." Her voice is soft. "I was just young, and suspicious, but he never betrayed me. Your father never did anything wrong. We came back for nothing."

Leaning against Rose's counter, my eyes sink closed. They went back because of a woman. Because of my mother's suspicions about a woman. What a waste. What a waste of all our lives. "Didn't you talk with him about this at the time?"

"I talked with him, sure. And he denied it. But I didn't believe him," she says. "I saw the way he looked at her." Just as I saw the way Ike looked at Jenna. I sigh. Women know these things, even if their husbands don't—or if they do, but won't admit it. Women always know.

She continues. "But now I think, even if he had fallen in love with her, even if he wanted to be with her, even if he had left us . . . we would have been okay. Maybe I would have remarried, or maybe not, but really, everything would have been fine."

This conversation cannot *really* be taking place. All this time, I thought my parents were deeply in love. *At least they have that*, is what I always thought. I guess maybe I just wanted to see things that were never there.

"You don't . . . love him?" It comes out in a whisper.

"I love him very much," she says quickly. "I always have."

"But, then—"

"I would have survived without him." After a long pause, she adds, "In coming back, I gave up too much."

This must be what she thought about in prison. After she'd been stripped of everything, especially her dignity, she must have decided that the price she paid to save her marriage had been too high. It's what she must have thought afterward, after her release, all those afternoons, as she lay in her darkened bedroom, as the world outside her windows turned so hateful, the walls closing in on her like a python its prey. She must have remembered the wind dancing through her hair at the ocean that day, her skin browned from the sun. She must have remembered herself, sparkling. Laughing. How she was barefoot in the sand. Beautiful in her freedom.

"I'm sorry for you, Maman," I say. "I'm so sorry for what you suffered."

"When men lose their dreams, it destroys them," she says. "They can't help but hold it against their wives."

"So what are you saying? That I should—"

"Things aren't any better here since you left," she says. "Iran is no place for you to make a life, Tami."

"Maman—"

"You must keep your husband happy," she says. "No matter what. That's very important right now. It's the most important thing. If he's happy, this will come through during your immigration interview. He must be happy at least that long. Longer if possible, yes, of course—but at *least* that long."

"I should put my marriage at risk to pass the immigration interview? Is this what you're telling me?"

But I might lose him, Maman! I might lose the only man I've ever loved—the only man who's ever loved me!

"One bad decision can ruin a life." My mother's words are gentle but firm. "A woman must never trade her freedom for her marriage, Tami Joon. Believe me, no man is worth it. But freedom? Freedom's worth it. Freedom is *everything*."

Chapter 17

To further complicate things, a letter from Immigration Services arrives in the mail telling us that our immigration interview has been scheduled for the seventh of September, four months from now. In four months, we'll know for sure. In four months, my life will either really begin . . . or really end.

I'm alone when the letter arrives. I've skipped my English class because I don't want any more of Eva's opinions about Jenna. She might convince me to do the wrong thing, and, as my mother said, sometimes it only takes one bad decision to ruin a life. Instead, I spend the afternoon trying to read *The Great Gatsby*, but when I'm supposed to be imagining Gatsby's face as he stands on his grand lawn, looking out to the green light of Daisy's estate, I imagine Jenna, yearning in a similar way to be reconciled with her beloved. Yesterday I'd felt sympathy for Gatsby, but today he seems like a horrible, unwelcome interloper.

Four months.

Couldn't you wait four months to open your coffee shop, Ike? Couldn't you just see, on your own, that taking Jenna's money is a very bad idea?

When men lose their dreams, it destroys them. My mother's words pound my mind all day long. They are incessant. Relentless.

I take Old Sport for a walk, hoping the scenery might distract me. We start out in the direction of Himmel Park, but once there, I decide to continue on to Trader Joe's to pick up some ingredients for dinner—I'll make lasagna, Ike's favorite, or maybe spaghetti. He likes that, too, and it's much easier to make. I tie Old Sport to a bike rack out front, make a quick circle through the store, and am back outside within a few minutes. On the way in, I carefully avoided looking at the available storefront that Ike so badly wants for his coffee shop, but on the way out, I forget and look right at it. I can't help but notice the bright red convertible parked in front of it.

Oh, no. Is someone leasing it? This *would* solve my problem, at least temporarily. But then again, maybe not. Maybe Ike and Jenna would spend more time together looking for another place, driving around in . . .

Wait.

I don't know what makes me think it. Women's intuition, maybe, but my heart begins to pound. *What if the red convertible is Jenna's, and what if she's inside the coffee shop with Ike? What if they're doing something they shouldn't be doing?*

I'm across the parking lot, too far to see inside with clarity, and the late-spring sun beats down on me and I really think I might throw up right here on the pavement. Should I go over there? What should I do? What if I'm right, and they see me? What if I'm wrong, and all my behavior proves is how incapable I am of surviving the addition of Jenna into our lives?

Old Sport is on his feet, waiting for me to untie him so we can continue on our way. And it would be so easy, wouldn't it, to walk away and never know? It would be far easier than facing up to my fears. It's probably not them; that would be too coincidental.

I could just stay here and wait and see who comes out. And if it were Ike and Jenna, I could wait and see if Ike tells me or not. But I don't want to play tricks on him—no more than I'd want him to play tricks on me. And I'm just not brave enough to go over there. I'm too afraid of what I might find.

Instead, Old Sport and I go back the way we came, with me berating myself the entire way home.

I prepare spaghetti for dinner, adding fresh onion, garlic, and basil to a jar of Trader Joe's marinara sauce. I set the table outside on the patio and chill a bottle of white wine. I shower for a second time that day because the smell of onion and garlic has seeped into my skin, and I put on a dress Ike always compliments. I'll pretend I never saw that red convertible. I'll pretend everything's okay.

When I hear his scooter pull into the driveway, I hurry to greet him. "Hello, Ike!"

Where have you been? Have you been with her?

"Hey, you." He watches me approach and then kisses me. "I like the way you move in that dress. It's very sexy."

This is not something a husband who's just been with another woman would say. Is it?

"That's me—very sexy." My light laugh is totally fake.

"How was your day?" He climbs off the scooter and grabs his backpack from the floorboard.

"Well, our letter from Immigration came."

"No way! Great news! And?"

"We have our interview in four months. It's the first week in September."

"That's excellent." His happiness seems genuine. "I thought we'd have to wait forever. At least a year."

I smile. "A year's not forever, Ike."

"It is when you're waiting for something," he says. "The waiting place is a terrible place to be."

Like your coffee shop—is that what you mean?

"I'm making spaghetti," I say.

"Ah, yum," he says. "That sounds great." He puts his arm around me and we go right to the patio. He opens the bottle of Chardonnay and pours us each a glass. "To September," he says.

"To September," I agree. We drink, and then he sits heavily in his chair, sighing as he does. "You look tired."

"I hardly slept at all last night," he says, and I know this is true, because I didn't either. We held hands in the darkness for most of the night—him, deep in his thoughts; me, deep in my fears. He takes another swallow of his wine. "I went to the bank today and talked to them about getting a loan."

My heart surges. "This is a good solution!"

"Yeah, well, they basically laughed me out the door."

Laughed me out the door. This must mean . . . ? I take my place across from him. "I'm sorry, Ike."

He looks at me for a moment before speaking, then says, "I talked with Jenna today, too. Showed her the place."

It *was* her, then. It was them, there. Of course she drives a red convertible; that is such a Jenna thing to do. She's a girl from a Hollywood movie; she's the girl everyone wants. *Did you put your arm around her like you put it around me when you showed me the place, Ike? Did you show her where my photographs will hang on the walls?*

I swallow these horrible, jealous thoughts. "Did she like it?"

"She did," he says. "And her offer still stands."

Her offer to steal you away?

"She really has that much money?"

"I guess so," he says. "Money definitely does not seem to be an issue with her."

He presses his lips together. I wonder if this means something *else* is an issue with her.

"Would she be a, how-do-you-say, *silent partner*?"

Ike grins. "I don't think Jenna knows how to be silent."

She's my opposite, then, because I don't know how to speak up.

"Ike . . ."

"Yeah?"

If only he could see that this partnership is doomed to fail. If only someone other than me in this horrible triangle would recognize how dangerously we are upsetting the balance of our relationship. Ike must see it. He must!

I have things to say, certainly—things I've been planning and practicing for the past several hours—but I'm in no hurry, because what I want to say and what I need to say are completely different. And so carefully, without either of us mentioning Jenna, we talk about a possible timeline for when—*if we move forward with this plan*—Ike would quit his job at Starbucks. The sooner he does, the more likely the shop could be open in time for the students coming back from summer vacation. In Tucson, few restaurants make a profit in summer, as the town empties of snowbirds and students.

"Now's the perfect time to make a move," he says. "We've got a window of opportunity that won't be there in the fall. Don't you think?"

I don't think this, actually. No matter what Ike says, the timing *isn't* perfect. It's horrible. Six months from now, once I had my permanent residency, if Jenna showed up, I'd say no, this is not a good idea, that our marriage means so much more than a coffee shop—how can he not see this? Six months from now, I could be working full-time at a job and would happily give him every dollar from every paycheck until he had enough to open his business on his own. Six months from now, if he left me for Jenna, at least I'd be able to honor my mother's hard-earned wisdom about not trading one's freedom for a marriage. But six months is a long time to wait for someone so eager, so ready, to make his mark on the world.

"You really want this, don't you?" I say. "You really want to go into business with Jenna?"

"I want my coffee shop open," he says. "And I want that location."

"Do you think your parents might change their minds about giving you the money you need? Maybe if you explain to them about this window of opportunity?"

"I, ah . . ." He coughs. "I stopped by to see my dad today, thinking the same thing. But it's a no go. They feel—*you know*—that I'm not making such good decisions lately, and I might not be at the top of my game. Or, shall we say, that I'm not as mature as they thought I was."

"Oh, Ike, I'm sorry." I know this sentiment must have hurt as much as the refusal of the money. "Did you mention to him about Jenna?"

"I didn't," he says. "Because I'm pretty sure I know what he'd say."

"He'd tell you to open the shop with her."

"No, actually, I think he'd say not to." He pauses. "Not if my marriage is really important to me."

Ouch.

Ouch, ouch.

"But you want to, anyway."

"I want that location," he says. "It's really ideal, and Tucson doesn't have many really good ones. It's not the easiest town to open a business in."

"Maybe we could move somewhere, then! Like Phoenix or Denver or . . . anywhere, Ike! Just think of it—we could go anywhere we want!"

He shakes his head. "I love Tucson. I'd never leave it."

Never? Really? This is yet another thing I didn't know about him. "You don't mind the heat?"

"I love the heat," he says. "I'm a desert rat. Born, bred, and someday I'll be buried here. I couldn't leave. I *wouldn't* leave. Tucson's part of me. It's part of who I am."

Ike from Tucson. If I'm married to Ike, then I'm married to Tucson.

"Well, okay." I had no idea he felt so strongly about his hometown. "Tucson it is."

"And I've got to make my move, Tami. It's time. I don't want to be working at Starbucks the rest of my life, or get some other job just to get a job. I'm antsy. I'm ready. I thought I was about to do it, and then . . ." He looks at me apologetically and doesn't say what I know he's thinking, *And then you came along.* "I'm afraid if I don't do it now, I never will. I'll get sucked into something else, some decent-paying job that'll never make sense to quit for something as risky as my own business, or we'll decide to use the money as a down payment on a house. Right now's the perfect time. We're in a perfect position. We have nothing to lose."

What about each other, Ike? We could lose each other.

"I want you to do what makes you happy," I say.

"Having my coffee shop would make me happy."

"Then you should do it." My throat aches to say it.

"All right, then, I will," he says, although the look in his eyes tells me he suspects there's a caveat. Which there is, of course. There are a few, actually.

"But do you think . . . do you think maybe I could be part of it, too? Part of this coffee shop adventure?"

He brightens, surprised. "You'd want to work in the coffee shop?"

"Why not? I like coffee shops. I met my husband in one, you know."

His smile is broad. "I do know that, as a matter of fact, and I'd love for us to do this together, Tami. That's an excellent idea."

"Do you think Jenna will agree?"

He shrugs. "It's part of the deal. A nonnegotiable part of the deal. She can take it or leave it." He peers at me. "Are you sure you're okay with that, though? You didn't seem very comfortable around her at Starbucks."

"I was just surprised, that's all."

That's not all. It was the way you were looking at her.

"She's super nice," Ike says. "She's got this philosophy that you can make a complete stranger's whole day better just by the way you interact with them. Just by making them laugh, or looking them in the eye and making a real connection . . . whatever. She'd just find a way—" He laughs at some private memory. "She could come across the most bored gas station attendant in the world in some Podunk town, and she'd stand there and charm the pants off him until she made him laugh. It's like a personal challenge. She always gives you that extra minute. She always leaves you feeling . . ." He shrugs, perhaps realizing he's said too much. "She's also flightier than hell. You can't make plans with her for anything."

Is this someone you should go into business with? I want to ask. *Is this a good business decision, Ike? Or is this a decision of the heart?*

"Ike, why didn't you marry her?" I try to ask this as a friend, not a wife.

My husband's eyes have never been bluer as he says, simply, with a one-shoulder shrug, "She's not you."

"Would it bother *you* to be around Jenna all the time, Ike?"

He leans forward. "I'm a married man, Tami. I wouldn't betray you. I never would."

This is good to hear, but it wasn't my question.

I take a deep breath. "I want you to know—" When I stop, he raises his eyebrows, urging me on. "I mean, I know nothing for us has been . . . normal. How we've done things, I mean—how we got married like we did, fast, and without knowing each other very well. I know it's not typical for how an American would like to get married—and it's good. I think the American way is better. And I know that if I were a different person—from a different place, I mean, if I wasn't from Iran . . . If I was from *here*, I mean. If I were an *American*, we'd only just be dating right now. You'd be . . . you'd be my new boyfriend, not my new husband."

"Yes? And?" His face tells me he's not too impressed with what I've said so far.

"Well, then this would be a more balanced choice for you."

"What choice are we talking about?"

He knows. He's just making me say it. His expression dares me to. My chest rises and falls double time as I work up my courage.

"If you want to be with Jenna," I say.

"Instead of . . . ?"

I cringe. *Instead of being with me.*

"You're okay with me choosing Jenna over you. Is that what you're saying?"

His voice is icy, and I look at him imploringly. "I want you to be with the person you want to be with. I don't want you to suffer for having married me."

"Wow." Disgust spreads across his face, and he presses back in his patio chair as if I have an ugly smell he's trying to escape. "I don't know what to say, Tami. What do you want me to say, after you've made this oh-so-generous offer? Am I supposed to thank you? Do you want me to be happy, grateful, that you're basically *abdicating* your position as my wife?" He laughs in a this-is-not-funny-at-all way. "God. What the hell? Jesus! You probably don't even know what *abdicating* means! I'm dealing with someone here who—"

"I want the best for you, Ike."

His eyes drill his anger into me. "And you don't think that's you?"

"I know you loved Jenna. You still do, Ike."

He shakes his head no, but I think he's fooling himself, or maybe it's that he's just too decent to admit it. He does still care about her. This isn't intuition or the worries of a jealous wife. It's an obvious fact—the way he looked at her yesterday was filled with not only the same sort of love he shows for me, but also nostalgia, and yearning, too. Eva saw it, I saw it, and I'm sure Josh did, too. Plus, Ike was far away from me last night, all night. His body was with me, but his imagination was filled with her.

"It doesn't make you a bad person for feeling this way," I assure him. "Remember how you told me what your mother said to you when Jenna left? How she was a bird you had to set free, and if she came back to you, your love was meant to be?"

"That's just a stupid cliché, Tami."

"Maybe she's your destiny, Ike. Who am I to get in the way of your destiny?"

"Maybe *you're* my destiny. Did that ever occur to you?" His eyes are . . . what's the word? Insulted. "She's not my destiny. We choose our destiny."

Yes, well, that's such an American thing for my American Boy to say.

"The timing's just a little bit tricky, isn't it?" I say.

"You're starting to seriously piss me off." He glares at me. "I value plainspokenness, Tami. You should know that by now."

A woman can't trade her freedom for a marriage. That is the plain fact here.

"Will you help me get my residency?" I say. "No matter

what? If you want to be with her, I mean? Could you at least promise me that?"

"God damn it," he says.

"I know. I'm really very sorry."

"You *don't* know." The edge in his voice is pickax sharp. "If you don't want Jenna around, say it. Say forget it, no coffee shop with her, and I'll forget it. But none of this *Oh, if you want to be with her, go ahead.* That makes me feel—*God.*" He presses his lips together. "I choose you, remember? We've already had this discussion. I choose you above all others. Above my parents. Above any former girlfriend who happens to show up. No matter what, I choose you. That's what being married means. So *why* are you so willing to give me up? Why are you so willing to let me go at the least little potential problem?"

"I'm not, Ike!"

"Aren't I worth fighting for, Tami? Isn't what we have worth fighting for?"

"Of course it is!"

"Then why won't you?"

"That's not how I meant for it to come across, Ike. It's just that—"

"Stop."

"I *know* you're worth fighting for."

"You're worth fighting for, too," he says. "That's the missing link, isn't it? That's what you don't get. And don't tell me you do, because when you pull crap like this—*oh, if you want Jenna, go ahead*—or when I hear stories of some of the stupid-ass shit you did to find a husband, I look at you and think, *Who did I marry?* It's sure as hell not the girl I thought I knew, and it's sure as hell not the girl I fell in love with. I mean, I always knew you were shy, but really, this is ridiculous. This isn't shyness. It's something well beyond that. It's like a crater in your heart where your sense of self-worth should be."

I'm in tears. "Ike—"

"Let me tell you something, Tami." He stands, making clear that he's readying to leave, readying to get as far away from me as he possibly can. "I can't talk to you anymore right now."

"Okay." *Oh, my God. He's leaving me, and not even for her.* "I understand. I understand you're mad. But please don't go."

"I'm worth fighting for," he says.

"I know you are."

Please, don't leave.

"You're worth fighting for, too," he says. "And I wish like hell you'd start acting like you know it."

"I will." With my imploring, tearstained eyes, I try to pull him back down in his chair, try to convince him to stay. "I love you, Ike."

But there's resolve in his eyes as he whistles for Old Sport. No sympathy, and I don't see any love, only a new hardness toward me, a new wall between us. I sit perfectly still, legs crossed properly at the ankles, hands folded together with their newly pink-manicured nails—*I did this for you, Ike! So you'd think I'm beautiful, so you'd be proud to be seen with me! Can't you see I'm trying?*

He gives me a look that says he does see me. He's just not

impressed. "If our marriage falls apart, Tami, it's not going to be because of Jenna. It's not going to be because of my parents. It's not going to be because of Immigration, and it sure as hell isn't going to be because of me. You know what that leaves, right?"

Ashamed, I shake my head no, although I do know. Of course I know.

"It's going to be because of you." His voice catches and he swallows hard before continuing. "It's going to be because you don't think you deserve to be happy. And that sort of thinking is bullshit, and it has consequences, and one of those consequences is that you'll lose me. We'll lose each other. You understand? I can't live this way. I *won't* live this way. I won't love you better, or harder, or deeper, than you love me. We've got to be equals. Equals in our love."

I look up at him, standing there, so strong. So sure. So right and so direct and so *real*, with the sun setting behind him, trying its pastel-watercolor best to steal the moment with its beauty, but it's impossible. It can't be done, because Ike's a god to me, a literal, true, life-on-Earth god to me. And he expects me to be his equal?

"I'll try," I promise. "I will try my best."

"Trying's not enough." His disappointed look says, *Don't you get it? Didn't you hear a word I said?* "You've got to *do.* You've got to *be* what we both need for you to be, or we've got no chance together."

I nod, unspeaking. What more can I say but that I'll try? Faith is a hard thing for me. People have tried to force me to have faith my entire life, and I would if I could—life would certainly be easier, yes, to go along and simply believe what other people tell you to believe, right? But you can't force faith. You can't force faith in religion, and you can't force faith in yourself. You either believe or you don't, and the ugly truth is that Ike has far more faith in me than I have in myself.

But even his faith is not absolute. I see it waver as he watches, as he waits for me to affirm myself and express my ability to be the sort of wife he needs. Old Sport has made his way over and stands by Ike's side. Old Sport is waiting for Ike, and Ike is waiting for me, waiting for me to give him a reason to stay. And I wait, too, for myself to say the words he needs to hear: *I am good enough for you. You are as lucky to be with me as I am to be with you.* But these words are a lie. I don't believe them. I can't say them.

Instead, I sit perfectly still and watch as my world-weary Ike collects his keys from the patio table and turns from me. There's not even a kiss good-bye, not even a backward glance. Like a scene from a sad movie, Ike and Old Sport drive off into the sunset in their beat-up truck and leave me behind, alone in the dying daylight. My heart is breaking, but I think maybe this is how it should be, for a part of me has always known that when night came, I'd find myself alone.

Chapter 18

"This is cute," Ardishir says in his misguided attempt to comfort me. "Your first fight as a married couple. That's all this is, each side just letting off a little steam. You've both been on your best behavior for so long; you're just settling back down on earth with us mere mortals. Couples fight sometimes. It's the nature of the marriage beast."

We're at his house in the living room. After Ike left, I threw myself on our bed and cried, cried, cried. I kept expecting him to come back—any minute!—and find me there, weeping into my pillow. He'd feel so bad. He'd have apology flowers and he'd try to get me to look at them and see how pretty they were and see how they meant he wasn't mad anymore—but I wouldn't look at them. I'd be so upset that it would take more than just flowers to make things okay again between us. I'd keep crying until he felt *really* bad. And he'd kiss me—sweet little kisses everywhere until finally I'd calm down, maybe even start to laugh from how they tickled. But he never came back.

Two hours I waited, and by then I had such a bad headache from crying that I took a double dose of aspirin and came here. Honestly, I'd rather seek comfort from Rose, but she wasn't back from her book club. When I arrived, Maryam was on the couch reading *What to Expect When You're Expecting*, and Ardishir was in his favorite chair reading a biography called *John Adams*. Both set their books aside, and I told them everything, the whole horrible story of Jenna's appearance and her offer to go into business with Ike, and about our fight and the horrible things Ike said to me.

And now Ardishir has the nerve to tell me it's cute.

"It's not cute," I say. "He was *really* mad."

"Of course he was really mad!" Maryam says. "Are you crazy, telling him he can be with that . . . that . . . that *woman*? Men like you to show a little . . . oomph. They like you to show a little possessiveness. A little jealousy!" Ardishir raises an eyebrow, like, *Oh, really?* "What were you *thinking*?" she goes on. "Seriously, Tami. Where did you *get* such a horrible idea?"

She won't like my answer.

"From Maman," I say.

"Maman?" Maryam looks like she wants to throw her *What to Expect* book at me. "Maman doesn't know anything about keeping a man happy!"

"Now, now," Ardishir says.

"Why would you go to Maman and not me? Who's here for you? Who's always been here for you?"

"She did help me, actually," I say. "Her advice was really good."

"This is what you call helpful, driving your husband away?" To Ardishir, she says, "Don't you *now, now* me!"

He smiles. "I don't think Squishy appreciates your anger, and I don't think Tami does either."

Maryam's hand goes to her swollen stomach.

"Squishy?" I say. "This is your name for the baby?"

Maryam rolls her eyes with a smile. "I'm not wild about it, but it's better than Squid, which is what he was calling the baby last week."

"Hope," I say. "I really love the name Hope."

"We don't know it's a girl," Ardishir says.

"I can't believe you're not finding out! This is critical information!"

"Right, for shopping purposes, I know!" Maryam says. "But Ardishir doesn't want us to find out. He wants a surprise in the delivery room."

"An extra dose of good news," he says. "All we need to know right now is that we're having a Squishy." Ardishir's eyes gleam. "A beautiful, healthy little Squishy."

Smiling, I glance down at my cell phone again. Nothing. "Should I call him?"

"Yes," Maryam says.

"No."

"Why not?" I ask Ardishir.

"Men need their space."

"Oh, please," Maryam says.

"We do." He grins. "Why do you think my office is so far from home?"

"What if he's with her?" I ask.

Maryam gasps. "Tami, he wouldn't! This isn't good! Do you think he is?"

"This is what I'm saying—maybe he *is* with her!"

"He's not," Ardishir says.

"Well, then, where is he?"

"Maybe he went to his parents' house," Maryam says.

"That's not good either! They hate me! They think he *should* be with her!"

"I thought you said his father has been decent to you," Ardishir says.

"Well, he has, but—"

"And his mother hasn't done anything rude since that one time," he says.

"But she—"

"She's just worried about her son," Maryam interrupts. "This is natural, for a mother to worry. They're your in-laws. It's important to think the best of them, and to win them over. We should have them over soon. We really should. Don't you think, Ardi?"

"But if he goes there, in this mood . . ." In desperation, I look to Ardishir. "He's never raised his voice to me before. Maybe he won't come back."

"Well, then he's a baby," Maryam says. "Call him. Find him, go to him, bring him home. This is what he wants.

Men are like little boys who run away from home. They want you to find them and bring them back."

I give Ardishir a questioning look.

"He does seem to want you to show a little initiative," he says. "So if it'll make you feel better, by all means, give him a call. Just don't snivel. No sniveling."

Snivel? This is a new word for me, but after Ardishir mimics me being babyish, I understand what it means. I dial Ike's cell phone, and it goes straight to voice mail. "I think he turned off his phone."

"Leave a message," Maryam says.

"Yes, Ike. This is Tami." *Your wife, where are you?* "Please call me when you get this message."

I hang up, satisfied with my nonsniveling tone. Ardishir, however, is laughing at me.

"Send a text," Maryam says.

"Don't," Ardishir counters.

"Gah!" I say.

I decide to send one that's brief and to the point and that will definitely show him—well, lots of love! I type *LOL. LOL. LOL*, hit the SEND button. I visit for a while longer with Maryam and Ardishir, all the while half expecting Ike will send me a similar message back. But he doesn't, and the hour gets late, and I'm supposed to work in the morning, although I'm sure Ardishir would understand if I took the morning off, but I don't want to leave him without the help he needs, and so when it gets to be eleven, I ask if he'll drive me back home.

I love riding in cars at night. I always have, especially

with my window down, and the fresh air tonight makes me feel better. "Thank you for listening to me snivel tonight," I say.

Ardishir smiles. "You weren't sniveling. You're just a bit emotional, which can get in the way sometimes of having a . . ."

"Mature discussion? Yes, I know."

"I guess Ike's telling you to toughen up a little bit."

I smile. "That's what Eva said to me, too. *Toughen up, chickee-poo.*"

"The world's not going to end if Ike doesn't open that coffee shop right now," Ardishir says.

"But he wants it," I say. "And if I wasn't in his life, he'd have the money he needs from his parents and he'd open it for sure. And I *want* him to have his shop. I want that for him. It's as important to me as it is to him."

"Were his parents just going to give him the money, or was it going to be a loan?"

"I'm not sure," I say. "I didn't think it was my place to ask."

"Well, Jenna would give the money in exchange for half ownership, right? Is that the offer on the table?"

"I think so, but do you really think that's a good idea?"

"Knowing you, I think it's a horrible idea. But it's good to know Ike's willing to take on a partner." Ardishir shifts in his seat and glances at me. "I have a little money, you know."

I stare at him, remembering something Maryam told me once—that Ardishir's family has money behind the money and bank accounts behind the bank accounts. "You have a lot of money, don't you, Ardishir?"

He smiles. "You could say that."

I've always liked how he never shows off his money. He does buy the best of things, but he doesn't buy too much. Their house is beautiful, and it's big, but it's not flashy. It's classy.

"Are you saying you'd loan Ike the money?"

Ardishir shakes his head. "I don't want to loan him any money."

"But you couldn't just give it," I say. "He wouldn't accept it. You'd be a partner with him, somehow?"

He shakes his head again. "I don't want to be a partner in a coffee shop. But I would like my sister-in-law to be an entrepreneur. That's still the best way to get rich in America. I'm thinking I could make some money available to her at very favorable terms."

"You mean—" My heart swells as I realize what he's offering. He's so good to us, so good to me. "But I've never run a business before. I'm probably not a very good investment risk."

We're just a block from home, and he holds off on answering until we get there. He pulls into the driveway where Ike's truck should be but still isn't, idles the engine, and gives me one of his long, mentoring looks. "When have you not succeeded at anything you've tried?"

I'm the only one in this car, and he's looking right at me, so he must be talking to me. But . . . excuse me? He can't *really* be talking about me. "I haven't exactly tried much of anything in my life," I say. "Ardishir, what if he never comes back?"

"Ike's not the sort of guy who's going to cut and run," Ardishir says. "He's in it for the long haul, and he's trying to make sure that you are, too. Now, didn't you earn your college degree?"

"Well, yes," I say. "Of course. You know I did." Rose peeks out from behind her living room curtain to see who's in her driveway. I wave to her, and she waves back before disappearing behind the curtain again. "I love Rose."

"Stop changing the subject," Ardishir says. "Didn't you get a good job as a teacher?"

"Well, yes, but . . ."

"And didn't you leave that job on your own terms once you realized it no longer was the right job for you?"

I smile, for I'd never thought of it that way before. I'd only thought I failed. "That's one way of looking at it, I suppose."

"And didn't you somehow manage to get a coveted visa to America?"

"Well, yes, but that was—"

"And didn't you find a way to stay?"

"Only because—"

"And didn't you marry a great guy who loves you very much?"

"You mean the guy who has since left me?"

"Ah, ah, ah!" He holds up a hand to stop me. "To me, it looks as if you have achieved or are in the process of achieving some very impressive things. To me, an investment in

Tamila Soroush is a very good investment. I think it's an A-plus investment."

Wow.

"Ardishir!" I sit up taller, trying to assume the posture of someone who is an A-plus investment. I do, actually, suspect I'd be a good business owner. Ever since the idea of working in the coffee shop occurred to me, I've become more and more excited about it. I've thought how it would be smart to have a spreadsheet detailing the profit margin on each item of food or drink we sell, and to run our specials based on this. Besides the business aspect, I also can imagine working there with Eva, keeping it fun, bringing Ike's vision to life. His grand plan is to have not just one, but a chain of local coffee shops, and so he'll need someone to manage the one while he opens the others, won't he?

Maybe I can be that someone . . . if he ever comes back.

Chapter 19

Ike stays away the entire night, but when I wake up from a very troubled sleep, I see that at least he sent me a text message shortly after two o'clock, although it's not at all nice: *What the hell's so funny?*

A flame of anger sparks in me. Who does he think he is, to talk to me this way? And why does he think that *I* think anything's funny? Nothing's funny! This is serious business! I think of several rude comments to type back to him, but I don't. Instead, I text, *Where R U?* leaving off the *LOL* this time—that'll show him!

By the time I've showered, dressed, and tidied up, I've received no reply. I want to text again, *Where are you? Where are you? Are you with her?* but I know this will only anger him further, and so I force myself not to.

I go outside and wait on the sidewalk for Ardishir to pick

me up, and I'm frustrated, because not only is it rude of Ike to stay away like this and to send mean messages, but everything's changed and he doesn't even know it! He has no idea that he doesn't need Jenna or his parents anymore. All he needs is me and my money from Ardishir, and he can make his coffee shop dream come true. I finally have something to offer him, and he's really not being very nice to me right now. I bet he'd be nicer if he knew.

When Ardishir pulls his black Lexus to the curb and I climb in, he gives me a concerned look. "He's not back yet? Or did he just leave early today?"

"He's not back."

Ardishir whistles. "Maryam would *not* let me get away with that. There'd be hell to pay if I ever tried."

I love my morning drives with Ardishir. We have such nice conversations, just the two of us, and I appreciate getting his perspective on things without Maryam butting in. He drives me to work on the three mornings a week that I fill in for the woman on maternity leave, and I usually take the city bus back home, unless Maryam picks me up to go shopping, which is pretty often, as there's always something she wants to buy or consider buying for the baby.

"What would Maryam do?" I really want to know, because I definitely don't know what I'm supposed to do—it isn't okay that he hasn't come home!

"I have no idea," Ardishir says. "I'd never do it."

"So it's bad that Ike thinks he can do this?"

He gives me a sidelong glance. "What do you think?"

I sigh. "I think it's probably pretty bad."

"Changing the locks would not be inappropriate at this point," he says. "To teach him a lesson, if nothing else."

"Do you think he's trying to make me mad? To see what I'll do?"

"I doubt it," Ardishir says. "I think he's just so wrapped up in whatever he's feeling that he's not considering you at all right now."

"Jerk," I say, quickly adding, "Him, not you!"

Ardishir smiles. "It's hard, becoming a couple."

"Was it hard with you and Maryam?"

Now he laughs out loud. "I'll plead the Fifth on that one!"

"The Fifth?"

"The Fifth Amendment to the U.S. Constitution—you can't be made to incriminate yourself or testify against yourself in a court of law. The idea dates back to England in the late sixteenth, early seventeenth century, when it was common practice to torture people to get information from them, or to get them to confess to something."

Late sixteenth, early seventeenth centuries—in normal countries, physical coercion was outlawed centuries ago. Not years, not decades—*centuries.* "You mean like still happens in Iran?"

I say this ironically, but Ardishir raises an eyebrow. "It's not just Iran, but yes. Torture can be a pretty effective way of getting what you want out of someone. Or, it can be a way of totally disregarding everything you profess to stand for and making yourself look like an ass in the process. It depends on the country."

Once we arrive at his office, I take my position at the receptionist's desk and get to work greeting clients and answering the telephone and filling out insurance paperwork. I leave my cell phone right in front of me, but Ike doesn't call and doesn't call, and even though I'm very busy, my anger builds throughout the morning. Who does he think he is, to treat me this way? This is not how a husband treats his wife! I decide to call and tell him this. No more waiting around for him. And if he doesn't answer . . . well, let's just say some very unpleasant things might be said on his voice mail.

But thankfully, he does. "Hey," he says.

This is how you greet your wife?

"Where were you last night, Ike?"

"Listen, Tami, I'm at work. I don't have time for this discussion right now."

My new husband can be a real jerk when he wants to be.

"I'm at work, too, Ike, and I understand you're busy, but you can give me a one-word answer. Where were you?"

"What's all this LOL shit you keep texting me?"

A flame of anger surges inside of me. "I don't believe you just said that!"

"I don't believe you think this is funny," he says.

"I *don't* think this is funny!"

"Well, then, why do you—" He pauses, and then, unexpectedly, he laughs. "What do you think *LOL* means, anyway?"

The instant he says this, my eyes sink closed and I know I've made yet another mistake with my English. "What does it mean, please?"

"LOL. Laughing Out Loud."

"I thought it meant Lots of Love." I roll my eyes as I think back to the numerous ways I've used this inappropriately, such as when I told him he could bang me forever, and all the times I've texted him to ask when he'd be home for dinner—LOL. "You must have thought I was crazy this whole time!"

He chuckles. "No, just very happy."

Now I'm laughing, too. Kristen, the other billing clerk, in whom I confided, gives me the thumbs-up sign and a hopeful look that causes my laughter to fade, as it reminds me that things are still *not* okay between us. "Ike, where were you last night?"

"Where do you think I was, Tami?" The edge is back in his voice.

He knows what I'm worried about, I can tell. I shouldn't have to say it. "If I knew, I wouldn't ask. Why don't you just tell me?"

He sighs. "I really do have to go. We'll talk later, all right?"

"No, Ike, it's not all right!"

"Well, it's going to have to be. It requires more of an explanation than I have time to give."

With that, he hangs up. Hangs up—on me, his wife who has the money he needs to open his precious coffee shop! *You don't hang up on your wife without saying good-bye. You don't hang up without saying I love you.* This is what I should call back and tell him, but I'm sure he wouldn't answer. I could text him (leaving out any mention of *LOL*), only if he didn't reply, then I really *would* have to change the locks, and I don't want to do that, so instead, I spent the rest of the morning ignoring him just as earnestly as he ignores me.

But I'm fuming. *Fuming.* I'm mad as I say good-bye to Kristen and Ardishir. I'm mad the whole bus ride back to central Tucson, and I'm mad the whole six-block walk home from the bus stop. I'm so mad I don't know what to do with all my anger.

It's only when I arrive home and find *her*—Jenna—sitting in *my* chaise lounge on *my* patio, petting *my* dog, whom Ike must have dropped off on his way to work, that I know what do to with all my anger.

I aim it—like a bullet to the heart—directly at her. She looks so perfectly pretty in her sleeveless white T-shirt and red miniskirt that I'd like to claw out her pretty green eyeballs. I set my purse down on the patio table and face her with my hands on my hips. "Please stop petting my dog," I say. "And please get out of my chair."

When she first saw me, Jenna looked chastened. But now, her brows furrow. Not like she's intimidated, more like she's curious. *Was she with him, was she with him, was she with him last night?*

"This isn't your dog," she says. "It's Ike's."

The nerve of this woman!

"What's mine is Ike's, and what's Ike's is mine," I say. "That's what being married is all about."

"Is it?" she says. "Really?"

"Well, no," I say, feeling very stupid. "Of course not."

Smiling, Jenna gives Old Sport one last pat on the head,

but she remains in the chair. "Could you sit for a minute?" She gestures to the second lounge chair and shifts so we will be face-to-face instead of side by side. "There's something I need to tell you."

I remain standing as it comes to me in a rush: If Ike was with her last night, *I don't want to know.* I just want my chance with him, the chance to be the wife he needs. To be the wife, the friend, the partner, the lover that he needs. I want the chance to get it right.

"I don't want to hear what you have to say," I tell her shakily. "I really don't think I do."

"You need to." She looks at me steadily. "For your own good, you need to."

She's right. I know this, even as I don't want to accept it.

With huge amounts of dread pulling me down, I sit. As we look at each other face-to-face, woman-to-woman, something like empathy fills her eyes. "You really love him, don't you?"

"I wouldn't have married him if I didn't."

She nods, accepting my answer, and looks at me for another long moment. "When I went to Starbucks the other day, I already knew that you and Ike were married."

"Okay," I say slowly, confused. It's not much of a response, but I can't think of anything better, and besides, I know what she's said is only the first part of what she's going to tell me. So, okay. Get on with it.

"I know," she says, "because his mother told me. Elizabeth told me what happened."

I flinch. All of a sudden, it feels like a little bit of evil has joined us on the patio. "How? When?"

"She called my parents and got my contact information," Jenna says. "I was in England at the time. I'd just gotten back from India, actually. I stayed at an ashram. You know what an ashram is?"

I shake my head, no.

"No? It's a—well, never mind. Suffice it to say that when I got her call, I felt like it was a sign that this is what I was supposed to do."

"To come back and ruin my marriage?"

"I know, right?" Jenna says this wryly. "Of course it wasn't a sign. It was a test. I was supposed to *resist*, not succumb."

At this point, I have no idea what she's talking about.

"She's convinced you married Ike just for your green card," she says next.

Ah. Now we're back on familiar ground.

"Yes, I'm aware of this." It's my tone that's wry now. "But she's wrong."

"I know she is." Jenna nods her agreement. "I watched you for the better part of an hour before Ike caught sight of me. You're on cloud nine together, the two of you. I don't think I even would have gone over to your table if he hadn't seen me. I thought maybe that, too, was a sign. That he'd seen me."

"I'm sorry, *cloud nine*?"

"I have no idea what that refers to, actually," she says. "Cloud nine versus cloud eight or cloud seven or cloud one." She laughs adorably. "But my point is: It's obvious you two are in love. You can tell just by how you look at each other. Did you know, for instance, that you have the habit of tucking your hair behind your ear whenever you lean forward to hear something he's saying to you? It's very flirtatious, in its way."

I blush to be caught at what I'd thought was an enticingly subtle gesture.

"It's very sweet," she says. "It suits you. Everything about you is sweet. You love him, I know. The thing is"—here Jenna pauses and looks at me pointedly—"the thing is, I love him, too."

Chapter 20

Ike's mother called his ex-girlfriend all the way in England and encouraged her to come back and claim him for herself. This is just great. It had really seemed for a while now that once Mr. Hanson talked with her after she'd threatened to call Immigration and report me, Mrs. Hanson was leaving us alone, and perhaps even coming to accept me—but I see now that she had just changed her strategy and instead looked for a way to ruin what we have without directing the blame at herself.

Not nice.

And now Jenna's telling me she loves my husband. Also not nice.

"I'll fight." I resolve this in my mind at the exact moment I say it. "I won't let Ike go without a fight."

"I'd hope not." In the cool, level look Jenna gives me, I

see confidence and massive amounts of strength. She's capable of beating me in any fight that requires those qualities, of that I'm sure. "But you don't need to," she says. "I'm leaving."

"You are?" A broad smile erupts on my face; I can't help it. "Really, you're leaving?"

Jenna nods. "It wouldn't be a healthy situation for any of us if I stayed. You love Ike, I love Ike, Ike loves . . ." She gives me a grim look. "Well."

And here we are, at the heart of the matter. I say the words she had the decency to hold back. "Ike loves us both."

Jenna clears her throat. "That's probably right."

It's definitely right.

"Please," I say quickly. "Were you with him last night?" I don't want to know, but I have to find out. It would crush me, would kill me, but I need to know. Jenna's look of confusion seems genuine, but I don't know her well enough to say if it is. "We had a fight and he left," I tell her. "It was our first big fight."

"About . . . me?" She's kind of cringing, like this would be a bad thing—but again, I don't know her very well. She could be hiding her hopefulness.

"It started out about you," I say. "But really, it was more about me."

She leans forward and her eyes spark. She wants me to go on, but there's no way I will. If I tell her how weak Ike thinks I am, how he doesn't think I'll fight for our marriage, Jenna might change her mind about leaving.

"Were you with him?" I ask again. "Please tell me."

"No, we weren't together."

Her eyes are honest. They're not the eyes of an enemy.

"Thank you for leaving," I say. "This is an honorable thing you're doing."

"Yeah, well"—Jenna gives a little quarter-laugh—"honorable would have been not coming back in the first place, right?"

I won't argue with that! "Do you wish you'd never left?"

"Left what, Ike? Or Tucson in general?"

"Ike, I suppose." (Ike, definitely!)

"I'm not sure I know how to answer that." She looks around Rose's backyard. "This is a pretty yard. Do you know the lady who lives here?"

"How do you know it's a lady?"

"You can just tell," Jenna says. "It's the colors, I suppose. A man wouldn't paint his flowerpots purple and pink, or put polka dots on them, right? And also the tables—they're feminine."

She's right. The chairs are curvy-backed, like a musical treble clef.

"My friend Rose lives here," I say. "And you're trying to change the subject, yes?"

Jenna gives me a level look. "In answer to your question, I think I would have regretted not going on my trip more than I regret having gone." She shakes her head, correcting herself. "What am I saying? I don't regret going at all! Not for a minute!"

"Even though . . . ?"

"Even though I lost Ike as a result?"

Well, yes. I nod.

She shrugs. "I don't believe we have just one true love. I mean, I've been around the world now, and I can say for a fact that Ike's a truly great guy, and yet other guys are great, too. Not better than Ike, but . . . just as good—for me, anyway. Probably. And he *is* such a homebody. . . . You just . . . I don't know. I had to go, or else I would have wondered for the rest of my life what I'd missed. You can't be afraid to do big things in life, whatever your version of a big thing is. You just have to have faith that everything will work out for the best."

Ah, that word *faith* again. It taunts me. How do you *do* it—how do you lose that fear? How do you develop that faith? "You weren't scared, traveling alone?"

"Well, I'm never alone for very long." Jenna's smile comes again, so naturally, so enticingly. Of course she's never alone for long—she's irresistible! "What's that saying? 'A stranger is only a friend you have yet to meet.' "

She obviously didn't go to Iran on her travels. The Revolutionary Guards are *not* the sort of strangers who'd ever become your friends—although the Iranian people are. But no wonder Ike was so surprised I didn't consider going to Canada when my U.S. visa expired: Jenna would have. I need to be more like Jenna and less like me.

"Does Ike know you're leaving?" I ask.

She shakes her head. "I just decided a few hours ago, actually. A friend of mine called and offered me a job as a river rafting guide in Colorado."

"Oh!" So she's not leaving only because she's nice. She's also being flighty, like Ike said she was. "You leave when?"

"Today," she says. "I'm just going to hook up with some friends for lunch first, and then I'm off. But I came here for a reason. There's something else you should know." Jenna gives me a look that makes my stomach drop. "You know the money I said I had for the coffee shop?"

"Your inheritance from your grandmother."

"Right," she says. "That was the story, but it's not the truth. I don't have nearly that much money left. It's Elizabeth's money."

I gasp. "No! It can't be."

"I'm sorry, but it is," Jenna says. "She was going to give me the money on the condition that I partner up with Ike. That's really why I came here today—to warn you. She's out to get you, Tami. She wants you gone, and she'll do anything—absolutely anything—to make that happen."

Sometimes when you're down, you think your heart can't sink any lower. But it always can. I look away from Jenna, to the pretty little fountain in the pretty little patio garden as it trickles peacefully. I'm so happy here. *I've been so happy here.*

"Why does she hate me so much, do you think?" I avert my eyes. "Is it because of where I'm from?"

"It's just . . . they have a special relationship, Ike and his mom." Jenna sighs. "I think it goes back to . . . well, for a while—maybe Ike's already told you this, but he was an only child until he was about five. Then his mom got pregnant again, when he was in kindergarten."

I look at her, curious. The math doesn't come out right. His oldest sister is only eighteen, and Ike's twenty-eight.

"She lost the baby, right near the end," Jenna says. "The cord was wrapped around its neck—it was a boy. Charles B. Hanson, if I remember correctly. They were going to call him Charlie. Charlie Bongo Hanson. From the way Ike tells it, he was phenomenally excited about having a brother. Bought stuffed animals for him. Chose the safari wallpaper for his bedroom. He even picked out the middle name, Bongo." She laughs. "What parent would let their kid be named Bongo? Well, Ike's parents would, because they so badly wanted Ike to be happy about the baby. And he was. And then, there was just . . ." Jenna's eyes flatten. "Well, bad things happen sometimes when you're pregnant. Sometimes babies just don't make it."

My heart clutches with this reminder. *Maryam's baby will make it. Maryam's baby will thrive.*

"What Ike remembers most is the feeling of how overnight they went from being a happy family to being a sad one," Jenna says. "That's hard for a kid to process. No more baby brother, and the whole vibe of the house changed. And just imagine poor Elizabeth. She was a labor and delivery nurse at the time—not since; she couldn't do it afterward—and she totally blamed herself. She thought she should've known something was wrong in time to save the baby. Thank God for sweet little Ike. You know? There was no reason to go on, otherwise. That's what she told me once, that Ike was the only thing that got her through, the need to be there for him. And of course, all Ike wanted to do was make his mama smile again."

I yearn to be with him suddenly, to hold him close and

mourn for the little boy he was, who lost his happy mother. I know exactly how that little boy felt; I lost my mother, too.

"Ike's good at saving people," I say.

I should know. He saved me.

"Yes," Jenna agrees. "And now she's trying to save him. Not that he needs saving," she adds quickly. "But she's fierce in her love for him. Even when she eventually went on to have the girls—I mean, she's great with them, no doubt, but she's got a special place in her heart for Ike. She'd do anything to keep him from getting hurt. Majorly hurt, I mean."

The kind of hurt I'm apparently capable of inflicting.

"You hurt Ike, too," I remind her. "And she seems to like you just fine."

Jenna shrugs. "I'm a known quantity, I guess. And she is capable of forgiveness. It just doesn't come as easily when the offense—alleged offense, I should say—is committed against Ike. She was a nightmare when we broke up." She shudders. "I basically had to break up with the whole family. It was all a little unhealthy, to be quite frank. In the end, I was glad to get away. She gets so . . . mother-bearish. And Ike just kind of went along with it."

"That surprises me," I say. "I see him stand up to her all the time."

"Then he's changed and grown." She grins. "It wouldn't surprise me if he's been in therapy."

Or maybe there was just a part of him that wanted you to go.

"Does Mrs. Hanson know you're leaving?"

"Oh, yeah. She had a few choice words for me." Jenna's eyes are dark emeralds. "And she somehow coerced me into promising I wouldn't tell Ike about her role in getting me back here. I still don't know how she managed that."

"She's a . . . what's the word . . . ?"

"Bitch?" Jenna suggests.

I smile. I can't help it. This is something Eva would say. "A persuasive woman."

"Yes, she is." Jenna gives me a conspiratorial smile. "But I never promised not to tell you."

It takes me a moment to understand what she's suggesting. "You want me to tell Ike?"

"He should know, don't you think?"

I sit back, startled, unsure how to reply. I think that if he knew, Ike might never forgive his mother. And despite everything, I don't want that to happen. He is as wonderful as he is partly because of her love. To lose the certainty of that love . . . well, it would change Ike. Harden him, somehow, and I love his soft-yet-also-strong heart just the way it is. And yet how am I to fight Mrs. Hanson on my own? If she really won't stop—and doing something as horrible as this tells me she won't—what can I possibly do to protect myself from her?

"I suppose maybe he should know." For my sake, he should. But for his own sake? I just don't think so.

"Well, I should go." Jenna slaps her pretty, manicured hands on her pretty, muscular thighs, readying to stand. And all of a sudden, her selfishness strikes me full-force.

"Are you going to say good-bye to Ike? You will, right?" It's not that I want them seeing each other, but it's the decent thing for Jenna to do, and Ike will be hurt if she doesn't.

She stands and shakes out her long blond hair. "Walking away from him takes every ounce of strength I have. Seeing him again, saying good-bye . . . it's too much. It would just be . . . too much." She smiles a brave, sad, dramatic smile that makes me want to roll my eyes. "Tell him I'll drop him a postcard sometime, would you?"

A postcard, Jenna—really?

You show up with selfish intentions, stir up all sorts of emotions in my husband, make him an offer he can hardly refuse, get his hopes up for his coffee shop—and now you want me *to tell him you'll send him a postcard sometime?*

She's like Daisy Buchanan in *The Great Gatsby*, a character I've been unable to admire—a dazzling, careless woman who walks away from the messes she makes without so much as a backward glance, leaving others to clean them up.

"Ike deserves better than that," I say as firmly as I can. *Daisy.*

"Ike's getting better," Jenna says. "He's getting you."

Chapter 21

After Jenna leaves, I sink back into my patio chair and let the late-May sun melt into my skin. I'm so exhausted, emotionally and physically, that I actually fall asleep for a little while, until Old Sport barks and wakes me up. Rose is home, and the sound of her car in the driveway is what's gotten him so excited. I'm excited, too—Rose is busy for an older, unmarried woman, with all her clubs and volunteer work and lunches with "the ladies," as she calls them. I'm so fortunate I even met her all those months ago when I hid my shoes in her yard, for she's home far less than I expected when I moved into the guesthouse.

I dash to the pink gate that separates the car part of the driveway from the entrance-to-the-backyard part of the driveway. She gives me a friendly wave.

"Tea, Rose?"

"I'd love that, Tami. Meet you in five?"

"Meet you in five." I smile from happiness at the familiarity of our relationship. That's our most-often-used expression: *Meet you in five.* We squeeze in time for tea as often as possible with our respective coming and going, usually daily and sometimes even twice a day. If we're both home and one of us wants to have tea with the other, we'll sit at the table on Rose's back patio, letting the other know we're available without being intrusive. This is nothing we ever talked about; it's just the pattern we fell into. But if one finds the other already outside, or just arriving home like Rose is now, we do our *Meet you in five.* Whoever initiates is the one who makes the tea. While I like preparing tea and always use the very nice tea set Maryam gave to me, I prefer it when Rose prepares it because then we use her mother's china, which Rose inherited. She more often shares stories about her mother when she drinks from these teacups, and I love to hear stories about her mother. About anyone's mother, actually!

When, over our tea, I tell Rose about my fight with Ike, and about everything that has happened since, she listens—as always—in exactly the way I need: closely, sometimes with sympathetic nods. She listens with love, Rose does. Love, and acceptance, too. I don't leave anything out—what I said to Ike and how angry he was with me, about Jenna's coming to see me and telling me how Mrs. Hanson won't stop until she ruins my marriage to Ike.

I end by asking, "Should I tell him what Jenna told me, Rose?"

"I'm sure that must be a difficult decision," she says, keeping with her policy of withholding her opinion for as long as possible. I like this about her—she forces me to talk through my problems, and frequently I talk myself into a decision, which she then always says sounds like a good one. Without even knowing she does this, Rose is teaching me to trust myself, that I have within myself the answers I need.

"Ike would want me to tell him."

"Probably," she says.

"But he's very—how do you say?—black and white about things." I'm incorporating last week's lesson on slang. "Very cut-and-dry. This way or that way. No gray areas."

"You're concerned that he'll sever ties with his mother."

"He might, yes. But he loves his family very much, and I know he *really* wants to have good relations with them, and this will only hurt in that regard."

"It might be easier for you if he did sever ties with her," Rose says.

I pour Rose more tea and let my mind fantasize how nice it would be if I never had to deal with Mrs. Hanson again. But . . . "Ike wouldn't be happy that way."

"Well, maybe this is the last of it." Rose shakes her head. "If she only *knew* you. If she could only see you with Ike, how good you two are together. How *right*. She really couldn't find a better daughter-in-law than you."

"I wish you were my mother-in-law, Rose." *Or even my mother—I could have learned so much, growing up with you. How to be independent, for one thing.* "She doesn't even know me, and she hates me, but you were nice from the first moment we met. You invited me for tea that very first day, remember? After I acted so stupidly!"

Rose's eyes gleam. "It was fun to watch you out my window as you hunted around for your walking shoes! When I found them, I couldn't imagine who'd left them, or why. I didn't know what to think—they were brand-new! Hidden in my tall native grass!"

I smile and blush thinking back to that day. Ike had given me the shoes after seeing how I limped from walking to and from English class in boots that hadn't yet adjusted to my feet. I was afraid if Maryam saw them—a gift from a man—she would insist on chaperoning me on my way to and from English class, and my walks were my favorite times, the times I felt most free. And so I hid the shoes he'd given me in Rose's front yard, and when I went back the next day, they were gone. I was on my hands and knees searching for them in the long grass when she approached. Holding them up, she asked, *Looking for these?* Then, once she learned why I was hiding them, she put a basket on her front porch and invited me to leave them there from then on. And she invited me for tea, and we've been friends ever since.

"You've always been so kind," I say. "Thank you, Rose, for everything you've done."

"You're welcome." She pats my hand. "I've always found you to be irresistibly charming, and that's what confuses me so much about Ike's mother. I have to believe that if she got to know you even the tiniest bit, she'd come to think so, too."

"She can barely stand to be in the same room as me."

"Maybe when she sees how you're providing Ike with the money he needs to get his shop open, she'll have a change of heart," Rose says. "It shows your long-term commitment. After all, if your intention were to leave him once you got your residency, you wouldn't invest your money in the business."

"She'll think I'm trying to buy him," I say. "Or bribe him."

"If she were your mother-in-law in Iran, what might you do differently?"

I feel my face redden. If she were my mother-in-law in Iran, I'd cater to her every whim. And here, I haven't even officially invited Mr. and Mrs. Hanson over for dinner yet. No wonder she hates me! "I haven't made enough of an effort, have I?"

"You've done just fine," Rose says. "But I'm thinking of this phrase, *kill 'em with kindness*, which more or less means if you keep on being nice to her and issuing invitations and making an effort with her, at some point she'll feel compelled to be nice back. I can't imagine that her family will let her get away with being mean for too long. Plus, maybe she really *will* come to like you, or at the very least, tolerate you."

I sigh, for I don't have much hope that Mrs. Hanson will change her mind about me, but Rose is right: What's important is that I try. I'll continue to smile through her meanness. I've certainly had enough practice; you do it all too often as a woman in Iran.

* * *

Back to my immediate problem: making things right with Ike. After tea with Rose, I put on a gorgeous new skirt I got while shopping with Maryam, one that Ike hasn't yet seen. It's calf length and flouncy, colored a swirling mix of gold, red, and purple. I pair it with a purple camisole, marveling as always at how nice it is to bare my skin to the world after being denied the ability for so long—*and look, the world keeps turning*—and I choose makeup that's especially glittery, and then, in my high-heeled sandals and Ray-Ban aviator sunglasses, I bike to Starbucks.

When I enter the coffee shop, Ike has thirty minutes left on his shift. I see him before he sees me, and I feel immediately bad for him because he looks so very tired, and also world-weary, not at all like he's excited about the conversation we'll soon have. But that's okay. I'm enthusiastic enough for us both. I'll make things right with him, and then I'll begin to kill his mother with my kindness. I love the idea that kindness can be a form of aggression.

Ike is working the machines, making the drinks and serving as backup for the counter person, so I approach and wait.

"Tall latte," he calls out, placing the drink on the high counter and noticing me, finally. "Hey, you!" I seem to be a pleasant surprise, thankfully. "You look gorgeous. What are you doing here—no class today?"

"I'm waiting for my husband." When I give him my best smile, he can't resist smiling back. I'll kill him with kindness, too. "I have good news to share with you, Ike. News so good it can't wait even one minute from when you get off work, so I'm skipping English class."

"Tell me now," he says. "I could use some good news."

I shake my head. "I'll wait for you over there." I point over my shoulder at the armchair near the window. "I love you, you know."

"I do know." His eyes both soften and sadden. "I love you, too, for what it's worth."

For what it's worth?

"It's worth everything, Ike."

He nods like maybe he's too emotional to respond verbally and focuses back on his work. As I watch him for the remainder of his shift, I fall further in love with him by the minute as I imagine him as a child—so earnest, so loving. I love him for what he lost, his baby brother, Charlie Bongo, and for what he saved, his mother's happiness. I wonder what he did that I was unable to do with my own mother. I wonder if there's anything I could still do for her, or if it's really too late, as Maryam believes.

After Ike's shift ends, we leave my bike locked in the rack and walk, holding hands, to Friendship Chapel, a little nondenominational chapel on campus that I sometimes slip into on my way to and from English class. It's getting so hot out lately, and the chapel has become my refuge, cool and nearly always empty. When I go there, all the English that's been crowding my brain, fighting to overtake my Farsi, moves to the back of my mind, and it's just me again, thinking in the language I know best. Visiting the chapel has become my time to remember home. I think of my mother, my father, my old room. I'm so different from who I was back then. I'm so much happier now that I'm almost ashamed sometimes that I should be so happy when others are still so sad there. That I actually get to live the sort of life people in Iran can only imagine, one where we're just *left alone.* Where we're *celebrated.* Where we're thought of as good and valuable. At the chapel, I close my eyes and see the Alborz Mountains, the Caspian Sea. I see the street signs in Farsi. The highlighted bangs and dark headscarves. I see the good, good people I miss so much. All of what's good about home, and some of what's bad, I remember in this chapel. Today's the first time Ike has joined me here. Until today, it's been my secret hideaway.

We slip into a pew halfway from the front and face each other. I expect him to ask me what my news is, but instead, he says nothing for a long time. He simply looks into my eyes as if he's studying a beloved painting hanging in a museum, something he can look at but never touch. But he can, and he should, and why isn't he?

"How're you doing?" he finally asks.

"I'm doing great."

"I was at my family's cabin on Mount Lemmon last night," he says. "I should have told you. I don't know why I didn't. I just found myself—I don't know . . ."

Annoyed with my lack of faith in you?

But if there's anyone I have faith in, it's Ike. "It's okay," I say. "Last night was rough for both of us."

"I was having a bit of a crisis," he says. "I don't ever want to have another night like last night."

That makes two of us. "Jenna came to see me a little while ago."

Ike's eyes widen with what looks to me like alarm. "What did she say?"

Crush, the world is crushing me. What do you think she said? What are you afraid she said?

"Ike?"

He sighs from something that could be exhaustion or could be dread. "We need to have a very direct conversation, Tami."

Oh, no. Jenna lied—he was *with her last night!*

"Okay," I say shakily.

He takes my hand. "I've thought through what I need to say to you today, what I need for you to hear, and some of it might hurt you, and that's not my intention, Tami, but—" He searches my eyes—for permission, it seems.

"Go ahead," I tell him. "I can take it. I'm tough."

He smiles at my claim, which we both know isn't exactly (okay, at all!) true, but still, his eyes hold pain. "All right. Here goes." His eyes bore into mine. "You're making it easy for me to leave you."

His words stab my heart. I grip his hand. "No, Ike. I'm not."

"You are," he insists. "You're making it easy for me to leave you."

I shake my head. "I'm sorry if that's what you took from what I said yesterday, but it's really not what I meant. I *don't* want you to leave me. I would die if you left me."

"You wouldn't." He brushes a strand of hair from my forehead. "And I know that by telling me I could be with Jenna if that's what I wanted, you were being kind and generous and loving, in your own, special Tamila Soroush way. But you've got to realize"—his eyes darken—"I did love her. I loved her a lot. And despite what you may have heard or misheard or presumed from my mother about how it ended, it wasn't easy, certainly, but it was a mature breakup. It was two people who had different—" He stops, smiles. "I'm not going to say different *paths* here, but we had two different—" He laughs. "I keep reaching for the road analogies, I guess. Two different roads, or paths, or what have you. She had her own things she wanted to do in life to . . . honor her soul, or whatever . . . and I didn't feel the same need to do those things, to travel the world at that particular point in time. But I didn't *not* love her. And we weren't not good together."

His eyes implore me not to be offended, and I'm not. I don't think who you love is something you can help. Sometimes it's just something you have to *deal with*. "It's okay, Ike."

"If you think in movie terms, Jenna and I had different plotlines. But we didn't have conflict. And, Tami, here's the part I've got to say, the part you should know: If you weren't in the picture—if you'd gone back to Iran or if I'd never met you at all—and she showed up like she did, well . . ."

"You'd be with her. I know this, Ike. I *know*."

"She did flat-out tell me I was the reason she came back," he says. "She told me yesterday, when we were at the coffee shop. She made it very clear—" He stops and his face takes on a shamed look.

"You don't need to say it," I say. "I know. I felt it. When you were at the coffee shop, I was at Trader Joe's, and I saw her car. I knew you were inside together. I knew she was— I knew you were—"

"Nothing happened," he says. "Absolutely nothing happened. There was an attempt made on her part, but . . ." He's trying to see if I believe him, and I nod that I do. "Tami, to come home from something like that, which required a lot of willpower on my part, and then have you basically say I could have—" Another heavy exhale on his part. "Well, like I said . . ."

Jenna tried something at the coffee shop, to kiss him or maybe even more, and Ike wouldn't let her. He pulled away while part of him wanted her. I know this; I feel it in my bones. And then he came home, with her perfume probably still lingering in his memory, and I, dumb girl that I am, offered that he could be with her if he wanted to.

"You're right," I say. "I *was* making it easy for you to leave me. I'm sorry. I was a . . . what's the word? An *idiot*."

He smiles. "Well, your intentions were good."

"But that's not enough, is it?"

He shakes his head. "We've got to *commit*, Tami. That's what marriage is, or should be. It's what mine *has* to be—an unbreakable commitment. We've got to cling to each other like we're the other person's life preserver and our boat's toppled in the ocean. *It's you and me out there.* You've got to hold my hand like you're never going to let it go. That's what I need to see from you that I'm not seeing."

Tears fill my eyes as I grip his hand tighter than I ever have before. "I won't let go, Ike. I promise. I won't let you go."

He nods and clears his throat. "I demand that of you, Tami. And it's what I'll give you in return. I thought we'd already covered this ground. I think that's why I was so frustrated yesterday, so angry. Didn't we already have this discussion? Didn't we already make this commitment?"

"Fighting, making demands—this is all new to me," I say. "My family has tried to protect me my whole life. Any fighting that needed to be done, my father and Maryam did it for me. Anything unpleasant, they kept from me. They . . . what's the word? . . . they *conspired* to protect me." I look at him earnestly. "I'm not making excuses, Ike, but I think this is maybe why I'm so weak. I want to be strong, though. I really, really do. It's just . . . people can't grow strong overnight."

"Sure they can," he says. "People become strong by refusing to be weak."

Oh, my God, his confidence! "You really think it's that easy?"

"I'm not saying it's easy," he says. "But it *can* happen overnight. It can happen in an instant. We are who we are because of the choices we make, and we always have a choice."

"How do you *know* these things, Ike? How can you be so sure?"

"I know myself," he says. "And what's true for me is true for everyone. If one person in the world can be strong . . . if there's one Gandhi, one Martin Luther King, Jr., one guy who refuses to move out of the path of the military tank in Tiananmen Square . . . or, you know the best example I can think of? In the Civil War, at the Battle of Gettysburg, there was this one guy, a college professor from Maine—I can't remember his name . . . Chamberlain? I think that was it. Chamberlain and his men, at the Battle of Little Round Top. They'd fought all day. They were out of ammunition, they'd suffered lots of casualties, and they were about to be attacked again, and if they lost—if they lost the hill they were defending—the entire Union Army would have been surrounded and this country as we know it might very well not exist. There was so much at stake. And there was *no way* Chamberlain's men could win . . . and yet they won, because they summoned the strength they had within themselves. You've *got* to see that movie, Tami. *Gettysburg*, we'll watch it sometime. *'Bayonets!'*" Ike raises an arm like he himself is going into a bayonet battle and he enjoys a moment of imaginary glory before peering at me. "My point is, we have all these great stories to pull from—stories of strength—and therefore, we know we can be strong in our smaller, everyday ways. Right? Deep down, we all have the same capacities."

Sitting here in this peaceful chapel, with its pretty marble floors and its many flickering candles, it feels like Ike is delivering to me a message from God. I do believe in the power of stories. What he's saying feels good and true and right in a larger-than-myself way, and I know there are so many things in this world we can't control—where we're born, what family we're born into, when and where floods and earthquakes and wars occur, or what they might do to us in prison—but we do own our hearts and our minds. Everything inside of us, we own, and *that's* where we find freedom. *That's* where we find God's glory, in our choices to be strong, or kind, or brave. My heart pounds at the realization that in order to have true faith in God, I have to have faith in myself. And I *want* this faith. I *want* to have faith in God. *I'll get there*, I vow. I don't think I'll get there overnight, like Ike is suggesting I can, but I will get there one day.

"For now, at least, I'm strong enough to hold your hand," I say to Ike. "I'm strong enough to hold on and not let go."

"I know you are," he says. "And that's all I ask." He raises my hand to his lips and kisses it—so, so gently. "That's all I'll ever ask of you, Tami. Hold my hand. Don't let go. Don't give up."

Chapter 22

Three days later, I clutch his hand underneath the table. I'm terrified.

We're in the lounge at the Lodge on the Desert, waiting for his parents to arrive. They requested this meeting after Ike told them I'd be providing the money he needs for his coffee shop. I've asked Ike probably close to a thousand times why they want to meet with us, but he refuses to speculate and doesn't seem too concerned. He's certainly not terrified like me, but then again, he doesn't know what his mother did concerning Jenna. I do—I'll never forget—which is why I asked Maryam and Ardishir to join us.

But so far we're the only ones here and it's one o'clock, the time our meeting is supposed to start. *Please hurry, Maryam,* I call to her in my head. I need my sister's fierce loyalty, and my brother-in-law's even-keeled wisdom. Maryam is passionate, and Ardishir is rational. I'm just scared.

Ike's parents arrive right on time. Mr. Hanson holds open the door to the lounge for Mrs. Hanson. Behind her, he looks around until he spots us. His blue eyes look tentative. Mrs. Hanson is the one who's smiling as she approaches, but I know better than to trust this. *Where is my sister?*

Ike and I, seated next to each other, stand as his parents approach. Ike kisses his mother's cheek, while Mr. Hanson kisses mine. We exchange pleasantries and then we all sit. When a waiter offers to get us drinks, Ike and his father order draft beers. I ask for a Diet Coke, and Mrs. Hanson chooses iced tea.

"Tami invited her sister and brother-in-law to join us," Ike says after the waiter leaves. "I'm sure they'll be here soon."

"Oh, that wasn't necessary," Mrs. Hanson says. If Eva were here, she'd say it damn well *is* necessary. I only smile. I'm still resolved to kill her with kindness.

"They're looking forward to meeting you," I say. "They've both heard so much about you. My sister's going to love your earrings!"

"Thank you," Mrs. Hanson says, touching one of her dangling silver-and-turquoise earrings. "They were a Christmas gift from my kids."

"Speaking of, how are the midgets?" Ike asks.

Mrs. Hanson updates us: Camille has tested into the gifted program at her school for next year; Izzy, about to graduate from high school, accepted a job for the summer as a lifeguard at a camp in Oregon; Kat is begging her parents for her own car, which isn't going to happen; and fourteen-year-old Paige has fallen in love.

At the news about Paige, Ike's neck veins tense. "She's too young."

"I agree," says Mr. Hanson.

Mrs. Hanson smiles. "I don't think she's actually even spoken to this boy yet. She's just swooning from afar. She's on the phone with her friend Molly incessantly: *Did he have product in his hair today? Isn't it just so sexy how he sort of snarls his upper lip when he talks to teachers? Isn't it* so cool *he's in a band?*"

"Don't let her date until she goes off to college," Ike says. "Please. I'm serious about this."

"Kat and Izzy were both dating by her age," his mom says. "I can't very well forbid it with her."

I'm enjoying this conversation—I love how teenage romances don't need to be kept secret from parents in America, but I can hardly focus for glancing out the window to the parking lot, willing Maryam and Ardishir to show up. They know this is important to me, and I can't imagine what's caused them to be late.

"Kat and Izzy could punch a guy's lights out if they needed to," Ike says. "But Paige, she's—" Ike stops, his jaw tight. He has a soft spot in his heart for Paige. She's what he calls *the sensitive one* in the family. I don't know her well, but she seems shy, maybe uncertain of herself. "Well, Paige is Paige, and I'll kill the guy who hurts her."

"You and me both," Mr. Hanson says. He and Ike raise their glasses of beer to this idea.

Mrs. Hanson turns to me. "When do you expect your family to arrive?"

"I'm sorry." I give her my most apologetic look. "They should have been here by now. Maybe I should call . . ."

"Let's just get started, why don't we," Mrs. Hanson says. "And then we'll share with them the good news once they arrive."

Good news? I'd like the sound of that, if only I trusted her.

"News?" I say.

She sits up straight and announces, "We've decided to give Ike the money for the coffee shop as we initially agreed. Our emotions got the best of us for a time, but we're calmer now, and we know it's the right thing to do."

"Really?" Ike smiles a huge smile. "That would be . . . that's just—well, it's *huge*." He stands, moves around the table, and gives each parent a kiss and hug. "Thank you, Mom. Dad. *Thank you*. I can't tell you how much this means to me." He sits back down and covers my hand with his, beaming. "Wow. This is amazing. Fantastic, isn't it, Tami?"

He has no idea I'm falling apart.

"Well, it's . . ." It's rotten, is what it is. I mean, it's nice, maybe, but it's awful, too. Because this makes Ike a partner with *them*, not me. In the past days, Ike's dream has become my dream, and *oh, God*. His mother's going to probably want to work there, doing the baking or working the cash register or something, and there's no way I could ever tell her what to do like a boss sometimes has to—and would I even *be* the boss anymore if none of my money is used?

When Mr. Hanson's watchful eyes catch mine, I look away, to the window, desperate to escape, desperate to be rescued. "I don't know what's keeping my sister," I say. "Excuse me, please." I reach for my purse and stand. "I should make sure they're okay."

Conscious of everyone's eyes on me, I walk away, outside and to the parking lot. I look up the street in the direction from which Maryam and Ardishir should be coming, hoping in vain to see their arriving car. There are no messages on my cell phone, and so I dial Maryam's, which rings four times and then goes to voice mail. I hang up and call Ardishir, but his goes to voice mail, too. I feel tenser with each ring that goes unanswered. I call their house, which they better not still be at, but the machine comes on there as well. I dial back Maryam's cell phone. This time I leave a message. "I hope you're on your way," I say. "Things aren't going well and I need you!"

I'm dialing Ardishir's cell phone again to leave a similar message when Ike joins me outside.

"Everything okay?" he asks.

"I don't know," I say. "They're not answering, and I'm getting worried."

"No, I meant—I'm sure they're fine. I meant, are you all right with this?"

"With us accepting your parents' money?"

"Yes, right."

"Oh, well . . ." My heart melts as I look at him, standing there all blue-eyed and broad-shouldered. "I thought we'd settled on using Ardishir's money."

"Yeah, but that was a loan," he says. "This is a gift that doesn't have to be repaid."

"Do we really want to do that?" I ask. "Accept such a large gift?"

"Hell, yeah," he says. "My folks want to help get all their kids established firmly on their feet as adults, doing what they love without the burden of a huge debt. It means a lot to them, to be able to help us. Just about everything my dad and I made flipping houses was supposed to be used for my business, and now that they've reconsidered the . . . the . . . the wisdom of our marriage, I *want* them to be able to help in the way they've always intended."

"But that's the thing, Ike. *Have* they reconsidered the wisdom of our marriage?"

"You don't think so?"

"Don't you think it's a little strange for them to make this offer only now, after my family stepped in and solved the problem that your family caused? This could be their way of, I don't know . . . of *not* accepting me."

Ike's jaw is set. I've offended him. "I doubt this has anything to do with you, to be quite honest. It's about them and me, and us reestablishing the strong relationship we had, up until . . ."

He stops, but the rest of his words are in his eyes.

"Yes, Ike. Go ahead, you can say it. You had a good relationship with them until I came along," I say. "But I don't think that's your mom's motive, or at least her only motive."

"Well, then, what do you think her motive is, Tami?" His tone is edgy, challenging.

"Don't be mad at me, Ike. I'm just trying to tell you how I feel, which is what you always say you want me to do, right?"

His posture softens immediately. "Yes. I'm sorry. I do want to know what you think." He grins. "This is just one of those instances in which I wish it happened to be exactly the same thing I think."

I smile. "I wish that, too."

"But it's not," he says. "So what do you think?"

I think this is your mother's latest strategy to get rid of me, after her last one of throwing Jenna at you didn't work out the way she thought it would.

"I think your mom doesn't like me any better today than she did yesterday or a week or a month ago. She still hates me, and I think that maybe this is her way of—what's the word? Keeping influence over you. I like the idea of us being fifty-fifty partners, and it won't be that way anymore if you use their money."

"Yes, it will," he says. "Of course it will."

"It won't feel that way," I say. "At least not to me."

"Well, yeah, but you're—"

"I'm what, Ike? A total and complete wimp?"

He smiles. "No. You're just wrong," he says. "And if you come back inside, I'll prove it to you."

Going back inside is about the last thing I want to do, but I can't very well refuse, so we go back, hand in hand.

"Is everything okay?" Mr. Hanson asks when we get back to the table.

"Everything's fine," Ike says. "We just need to discuss your offer a little bit further."

"I meant with Tami's sister and brother-in-law," Mr. Hanson says. "Are they all right?"

"I'm sure they're fine." I smile at him gratefully for his concern.

Ike and I are sitting down by now, side by side again, with Ike's arm around my shoulder. "So, anyway," he says, tapping on the table with his free hand. "I guess we need to understand what your motives are in offering us the money."

"We gave you our word, Ike, and we mean to keep it." Mr. Hanson looks solidly at his son.

"I appreciate that," Ike says. "Probably more than you'll ever know. But we have the money we need now, from Tami's brother-in-law."

"We're not offering you a loan," Mrs. Hanson says. "This won't have to be paid back. Isn't that what he's offering, just a loan?"

Ike raises an eyebrow at her. "It's not *just* a loan, Mom. Ardishir was the only guy who ponied up when no one else would. Not you, not the bank. He came through for us in a very generous way. And if he hadn't, would you be—?" He looks firmly at his father. "Why are you making this offer? And why now? Why not three weeks ago?"

Mr. Hanson clears his throat. "It's taken time for us to—"

"It's the prudent thing to do," Mrs. Hanson interrupts. Mr. Hanson narrows his eyes at her.

"Prudent," Ike repeats. "What do you mean?"

Mr. Hanson answers. "Until we know what the future holds, we believe this is the wisest course for all concerned."

"I see," Ike says. "And what is it you think the future holds, Dad?"

"I don't know," he says. "That's the problem with the future. It's impossible to know, and it's certainly all too often unpredictable."

"Well, Tami and I are confident the future holds great things for us," Ike says.

"And some people are confident, even in this day and age, that the earth is flat," Mrs. Hanson says. "Being confident doesn't mean you're right."

"Jesus Christ, Mom," Ike says. "What are you worried about? Tami's immigration situation? Because everything's progressing in that regard. It's not going to be a problem."

"You don't know that." Mrs. Hanson puts on her smiling, banana-bread face and turns to me. "Tami, please know this is not a criticism of you. We think you're lovely."

I smile at her lie. This sort of false kindness is something I'm very used to from Iran, where people seldom say what they really think. Even so, my intense dislike for her bubbles to the surface.

"You think *Jenna's* lovely," I say, correcting her. Just as quickly, I gasp and cover my mouth. I hadn't really meant to say that!

Mrs. Hanson startles backward. "Jenna? Who said anything about Jenna?"

While Ike and his dad are looking at me to see why on earth I brought up Jenna, Mrs. Hanson glares at me, threatening with her bloodthirsty eyes. I've seen this look on people before—on the *bassidji* in Iran, where the worst thing you can do is let them haul you away, to get you alone, where anything can happen—where they can devour you, where they can make you disappear. If we're going to have a confrontation, we'd better have it in front of witnesses who can offer me some protection.

"I forgot to tell you, Jenna was in town this past week," Ike says, which I'm sure isn't true. He didn't forget. "She said to tell you hello."

"Your mother already knows Jenna was here," I say. "In fact, they got together, more than once. At least that's what Jenna told me. We had a long conversation right before she left."

"I'm surprised you didn't mention it, Mom," Ike says, and then adds, "I'm surprised you didn't mention it either, Tami."

"And *I'm* surprised that no one mentioned it to me," says Mr. Hanson.

Ike looks to his mom at the same time she's shooting me a warning look. It doesn't go unnoticed. "Mom?"

She says nothing.

By now, the arm that Ike's got around my shoulder is rigid. "What exactly are you suggesting, Tami?"

I know right then from the tense resolve in his eyes that Ike really has made his choice, and he really has chosen me. He would wrestle with a tiger to keep me from harm; he would not forgive his mother, ever, for what she tried to do. I feel trapped by his eyes, asking me for the truth, but now I'm filled with regret. I didn't mean for it to come out this way. I didn't mean for it to come out at all.

"I'm not suggesting anything," I say.

"Then why bring it up?" Mrs. Hanson says. "Why bring up the fact that I visited with Ike's old girlfriend for a few minutes and neglected to mention it? Maybe I was trying to spare the two of you some awkward moments. Maybe I was trying to *help you* by not mentioning she was in town. Did you ever think of that?"

At that, I have to laugh, just the tiniest bit. "Right. Of course. You were just trying to be nice to me. I can't imagine why that never occurred to me. How exactly did you happen to see Jenna? How did that meeting come about, if you don't mind my asking?"

Mrs. Hanson has tiger eyes—she wants to devour me.

Mr. Hanson covers his wife's hand with his own. "Let's go back to the money," he says. "This really is a business issue. A business decision."

"But it's not your business," Ike says. "Not anymore."

"Doesn't it make sense to keep legal entanglements to a minimum for a while? Just until"—Mr. Hanson looks at me apologetically—"until we know for certain that Tami's going to be here for the long haul. Which I, for one, hope you are."

I smile at him in thanks for his kind words, but Ike's not feeling quite so generous.

"Our *marriage* is a legal entanglement, Dad," he says. "And—"

"What happens if you can't stay?" Mrs. Hanson asks me. "What happens to your share of the business, then? Is your family willing to just *give* Ike the money?"

"I'm not going anywhere." As I say it, my cell phone rings. I scramble for my purse and see it's Ardishir. "Having said that, excuse me please. Let me just— Hello?" I stand and walk away from the group. "Ardishir?"

"Tami, hey. Sorry we're missing your meeting. Is it going okay?"

I glance back at the table. Ike and his mother are leaning toward each other, clearly arguing. I strain to hear. "I thought you were going to call it Ike's Coffee Shop!" she's saying. "What are you going to call it now—Ike and Tami's?" She says this like it's a horrible-sounding name.

"Elizabeth," Mr. Hanson says.

"Where *are* you, Ardishir? I'm dying here without you! You would not believe—"

"The baby's fine," Ardishir says. "Your sister just had some stomach cramps, and we thought we should get to the doctor. But she's fine. Everyone's fine. She just needs to stay off her feet for a while."

"Oh, Ardishir!"

Back at the table, Ike stands. "I've about had it with you," he says to his mother.

"You're my son," she says. "I'll never stop trying to protect you."

"I better go," I whisper to Ardishir. "I'll call you later."

"I don't need your protection," Ike snaps.

I've ended my call and stand frozen, not wanting to walk back into what is now a very heated conversation. I wish I could tiptoe away, but I can't do that either, so I just stand still and pretend to be invisible.

"And I don't need your money, either," Ike goes on. "I need your support. *And* I need you to be decent to my wife, because *she's not going anywhere.*"

"Oh, yes, she is, son," Mrs. Hanson says. Meanwhile, Mr. Hanson is holding his head in his hands, like this conversation has gone exactly where he'd hoped and prayed it wouldn't.

"*I've had it,*" Ike says. "If you're forcing me to make a choice between you and Tami, I choose her. You've got to know that by now."

My heart begins to swell with love until Mrs. Hanson retorts, "You don't have to choose, Ike." She pauses for effect and takes a long sip of her iced tea before continuing. "I can just about guarantee that the government will do that for you."

Part Two

LET US LINGER HERE A WHILE
IN THE FOOLISHNESS OF THINGS

Chapter 23

Immigration Interview: ELEVEN WEEKS AWAY

Ike and I meet the leasing agent at the coffee shop. We sign the papers for a five-year lease (wow!) and give him the deposit. We have officially accepted Ardishir's loan offer and officially rejected Ike's parents' gift. The night we get the keys, we set a table for two in the middle of the empty café. By candlelight, we drink champagne and giddily plan our grand opening. We dance (badly) around the restaurant. As Ike twirls me, visions of my framed photographs spin through my mind, finding their places on the walls of our café. I wish *this* moment could be photographed and then placed on the wall, captured forever, for like my photographs it, too, feels like an act of rebellion, a tiny declaration: This is what free people do. They make their dreams come true.

★ ★ ★

Maryam has quit her job at Macy's so she can stay off her feet for the baby. The day of our meeting with Ike's parents, she'd woken from a nap with a stomachache so severe it made her feel like her insides were being pulled out of her by an unknown, evil force. She was sure she was losing the baby, as she had the others. After her doctor examined her, he said it was nothing serious, that the baby was fine and it was only that her ligaments were stretching. This did nothing to calm Maryam, and she's finding it very hard to feel hopeful about the baby.

I can tell Ardishir is nervous, too, even though he's acting like Mr. Calm and Reasonable. Already very considerate of Maryam, he's become even more so—bringing her tea in bed, running virtually every household errand, and calling her every few hours. Within days, he's begun to drive Maryam crazy.

Deciding on a name for the coffee shop proves very difficult but also very fun. We hold a wine and cheesecake party in Rose's backyard one night and invite our friends and families to help us come up with a good name.

Ike's whole family comes, except for Mrs. Hanson, who claims to have a migraine headache. I'm pretty sure it's the thought of me that causes it. At the party, I'm busy with my camera. I take a picture of Mr. Hanson with Maryam and Ardishir, the three of them talking, laughing, their faces illuminated by a string of lights woven through tree branches. Mr. Hanson holds Camille in his arms, and Camille is entranced by my sister—maybe by her glittery jewelry, or maybe by her beautiful smile. This is a picture I'd like to send my parents, except it would show Maryam's pregnancy, so I can't. I take others that I *can* send, such as a shot of my friends from English class with their arms around each other's shoulders, and another of Ike with his sisters. He and the older girls stand in a line and hold Camille sideways across them, while she giggles her little-girl laugh.

The whole night is filled with laughter, and we have a very good time thinking up names for the coffee shop.

Eva suggests Ass-Kicking Coffee. I could have guessed she'd pick that!

Camille suggests Stinky Coffee Breath. Paige suggests Cozy Coffee. Maryam suggests Coffee, Tea, or Me. Rose suggests the Irish Coffee House and says we could also serve Irish whiskey and Baileys. Our friend Beth suggests Sips, which I like, and also Sip by Sip, which I like even better because it's like we're inviting people to take life sip by sip and savor all the good parts.

Our friend Lisa suggests Steamin' Cup after her favorite coffee shop from when she lived in Wisconsin. I like this but worry about people not wanting to be steaming in Tucson in the summer, and I think the same thing about Carol's suggestion of Hotter Than Tucson. Several people suggest names with strange letter combinations, such as Kismet Koffee Kafe and Kashmir Kafe, and I worry that people will think I don't know how to spell. There is also Coffee

Oasis, Enchanted Café, Desert Brew, the Desert Spoon. Jitters is suggested, and Carpe Coffee, and Wildcups because we're near the University of Arizona, whose sports teams are called the Wildcats. I like all of these. It's so hard to choose! But when our friend Tonia gives her suggestion, Ike and I look at each other and we just know it's the right name. It speaks to our coming together—not just Ike and me, but what we hope for all the cultures of the world. It speaks to our shared humanity, to our universality.

It speaks to the capturing-freedom photographs that will hang on the walls. It says that we are, all of us, more alike than different.

Our coffee shop will be called . . . drumroll, please . . . Common Grounds.

Immigration Interview: TEN WEEKS AWAY

Ike and I spend the entire week driving around town, going to various government buildings and law offices and banks and accountants' offices. I had no idea there was so much to do when you're opening a business! Every day Ike starts by making a list of tasks and puts maybe ten items on it, but those ten really break down into fifty, or maybe one hundred. You need a security system—what kind? Which locksmith? Do you want cameras? Alarms on the doors? To be able to monitor the shop on the Internet when you're not there? How many sets of keys? What's your budget? It's crazy! I'm learning so much from all the conversations Ike and I have with people about the business that it seems my English class isn't the best way for me to practice my English anymore, and that it's maybe not needed. Still, I go a few times per week, mostly because I want to see my friends.

Also, I keep working for Ardishir several mornings a week. One day, he bursts out of his inner office into the waiting room, where, thankfully, there are no clients waiting to see him. With his shoes on, he leaps onto his nice black leather couch and, with one hand raised in a fist, shouts, "'Gentlemen may cry, "Peace, peace"—but there is no peace. The war is actually begun! . . . Our brethren are already in the field! Why stand we here idle? . . . Is life so dear, or peace so sweet, as to be purchased at the price of chains and slavery? Forbid it, Almighty God! I know not what course others may take; but as for me, give me liberty or give me death!'"

Tilly, the billing clerk, and I exchange an amused glance. This sort of scene has become increasingly familiar, as Ardishir's new interest in American history has turned into something of an obsession.

"Who said it? Do you know?" He jumps down from the couch. "If we have a boy, I'm naming him after this great American. Take a guess. Who do you think it was?"

I, of course, have no idea. I don't know many names from American history, and Tilly, who watches every reality show there is, but not the History Channel, isn't the type to know either. Ardishir knows this. This is just part of the routine.

"Thomas Paine?" I guess. This was last week's grand

speech—*It is always to be taken for granted, that those who oppose an equality of rights never mean the exclusion should take place on themselves.*

"No!" Ardishir comes up to the reception counter and takes a chocolate Hershey's Kiss from the sweets bowl. "Today's American is mostly remembered for his rousing speech convincing the Virginia colony, the largest colony, to join in the American Revolution, but his contribution to the cause of freedom went well beyond his give-me-liberty-or-give-me-death speech."

My brother-in-law, the college professor.

"I still don't even know who you're talking about," I say.

"Patrick Henry!" Ardishir says. "He urged Virginia to oppose the Constitution because he thought it eroded the *very* liberties we fought so hard for. History has proven him quite the prophet! I thank Patrick Henry for the Bill of Rights!" He raises both arms in hurrah. "To Patrick Henry!"

Gamely, Tilly and I raise our fists. "You're such a nut," I say.

I'm beginning to think he's even more of a nut than Haroun!

Immigration Interview: NINE WEEKS AWAY

Speaking of Haroun . . .

It's a beautiful, perfect, no-care-in-the-world day I'm spending with Eva when we run into him. That's not exactly correct—we don't exactly run into him. It's more like he hunts us down.

It's a Saturday, and Ike and his father are constructing a wall at the coffee shop, so Eva and I go to the Fourth Avenue Street Fair. I love it; it is very much fun. I've never seen such a large crowd in Tucson, walking up and down the street, over and over, looking at all the things the street vendors have for sale, such as tie-dye shirts and handmade jewelry and wind chimes and the like. And the food! We try a little bit of everything—gyros, tamales, bratwurst, and over the course of an hour, we drink two beers each, which is one too many for me.

We're sitting at a shared picnic table near a stage where rock bands perform, but the band is on break and the other people at the table have just left. Eva, in a slinky green dress that looks more like lingerie than clothing and a pair of midcalf cowboy boots that I love and yet another wig of long red hair, sits across from me. She's telling me in graphic detail about the lovemaking she heard going on in the apartment next to hers last night, and what she would like to do to the man involved if she had the chance, and I'm staring at her, openmouthed, wondering as usual how she can be so . . . so *Eva*—what would her parents think to hear her?—when he, Haroun, comes straight at us.

"Tamila Soroush."

Oh, *God*. I never thought I'd have to hear his voice again. There's something snide about it, too, which apparently Eva does not notice. Before I can say anything, she flips her fake red hair over her shoulder and looks at him seductively. "Ooh, a Persian dude. Have a seat, Persian dude."

I make big eyes at her to tell her this is a very bad idea, but she's not looking at me. Haroun, with his perfectly straight white teeth and his sparkling brown, solicitous eyes, both of which could fool a woman—especially a woman who's had two beers—into thinking he's handsome, into thinking he's not dangerous, gives her a charming, Persian-clever smile. "Oooh, you're a hottie," she says, sliding over to make space for him on the bench. But he's *not* a hottie. He's fastidious and obsessive; this is the reason for his trim look. Each morning in his home gym he does one hundred sit-ups, one hundred chin-ups, and one hundred push-ups, followed by forty-five minutes of cardio exercises (no way would he go to a health club—too many germs) because he has determined this is the best way to maintain health and avoid illness. And sure, he looks healthy, physically. But he's not healthy in his head.

Eva gives me a mischievous look to let me know she intends to have some fun with him. I shake my head no, but as usual, she ignores me and asks him, "How do you know our Tami?"

"This is Haroun," I say quickly.

"Oh, dude, you're the—" To her credit, she stops. But then she says, "You didn't tell me he was so yummy, Tami."

"That's me," he says. "Yummy. A dessert, a regular fruitcake. Or so I hear."

My heart freezes in shock. How could he *possibly* know we called him this, along with pistachio nut, macadamia nut, peanut, and any other nut Ardishir could think of? He couldn't have. It must just be an odd coincidence, same as the fact that we ran into him at all. But if running into him really *was* a coincidence, he could have walked away when he saw me. I certainly would have if I'd seen him! Oh, God, please don't let him be following me! I do *not* need an obsessive-compulsive stalker in my life!

I give him my friendliest smile. "How are you, Haroun?"

"I'm fine, thank you." He doesn't smile back.

"Ooh, there's a chill in the air!" Eva says. "A chill in the air and it's ninety-eight degrees. Bring it on, people!"

Unlike me, Eva loves confrontation.

"We should go." I glance at the wrist my watch would be on if I wore a watch. "It was so nice to see you!"

"You're not wearing a wedding ring." Haroun gestures to my still-bare ring finger. "What happened—did you break his heart, too?"

"Zing! Pow!" Eva puts her fists into a punching formation. "Sha-zam!"

"I'm still married. Thanks for asking," I say.

"Please convey to him my regards." Haroun gives me that small, self-satisfied smile Iranians use when they're being disingenuous. And who can blame him for hating me?

"Haroun, I owe you an apology. I'm so very sorry for what happened," I say. "I'm so sorry I disappointed you."

"*Disappointed* me?" His eyes bulge. "You used me. You—"

"She fell in love," Eva says. "Get over it."

"Love." Haroun's upper lip curls into a snarl. "She's not in love. Her American is just convenient. Marriage of convenience strictly okay—right?"

Eva looks at me. "You're right, he is cuckoo. Is he making any sense to you?"

I shake my head, but something is jiggling in my brain. I've heard that phrase before.

"We should go," I say again.

"I don't appreciate being called an obsessive-compulsive neat freak, Tami," he says, narrowing his eyes at me.

"Of course I'd never call you that." I say this calmly, but my heart is racing. *What does he know, and how does he know it?*

"There she goes, lying again." Haroun looks at me like I'm a dirty dog he'd like to kick.

"Dude, seriously," Eva says. "Get over yourself."

Ignoring her, he reaches into his back pocket and pulls out his wallet. From it, he withdraws a carefully folded sheet of computer paper. He smirks at Eva and hands the paper to me. "I don't appreciate this, Tami. This is *kolah bardari*. A scam, a fraud."

I unfold it, and when I see what it is, I gasp.

Single Persian woman looking for a good man to marry.

It's the Internet advertisement that Eva ran on Persian-singles.com when it became clear that Haroun was going to propose to me. She was sure the germ-phobic Haroun would never have sex with me because of the unsanitary nature of the act. She was sure I'd die a virgin, and that was unthinkable to my sex-obsessed German friend. And so without my knowledge, she placed a very blunt advertisement on the matchmaking site . . . which eventually led to my meeting Masoud and breaking off my almost-engagement to Haroun.

This is something he was never supposed to see.

Single Persian woman looking for a good man to marry.

Save me from current prospect, an obsessive-compulsive neat freak! Visa expires in April, but desperately want to stay in America! Marriage of convenience strictly okay. I'm young, sexy, will look great by your side. Save me, marry me!

No wonder he's furious!

"Haroun, I'm *so sorry.* I—"

"What is it?" Eva grabs the paper. Her eyes widen as she reads the ad.

"I don't forgive you," Haroun says.

"What makes you think Tami wrote this?" Eva says. "Maybe some other chick was in a similar situation, and—"

"It was Tami," Haroun says. "I know it for a fact."

"Dude, *I* did this. This is *my* work of art." Eva waves the singles ad in Haroun's face. He grabs it from her. "Tami had nothing to do with it. She didn't even know about it, so don't get all boo-hoo about her making fun of you. She wasn't. I was. Boo-hoo. Get over it, Mr. Victim. What do you even carry it around for? How pathetic is that?"

"Eva!"

"I carry this around so I never forget," he says.

Eva rolls her eyes. "You're such a drama queen."

Tact, Eva, tact!

"You're a good person, Haroun," I say. "You deserve to be with someone who really, really loves you."

"That's all I was doing," he says, clearing his throat. "Looking for love." He carefully refolds the ad. "That's why I was on that Web site. That's how I came across the ad." He looks at me, and the pain in his eyes breaks my heart. "I wasn't going to let what happened with you be a setback for me. You know?"

I remember back to the day he got down on one knee and proposed, the day I told him I'd already married Ike. *The world is so beautiful, isn't it?* he'd said. *The greens are so green and the blues are so blue and the reds are so red . . .*

Poor Haroun.

Poor, poor Haroun.

He tries so hard.

"I know you'll find your happiness, Haroun," I say. "I promise you will."

His eyes are dark and angry again. "No one will marry me now."

"No one knows the ad's about you," Eva says. "Think about it, genius."

"I was in love with you," he says to me, ignoring her.

I shake my head, for what he says isn't true. We never had that . . . what is the word? . . . that spark of attraction. That flame of love. He was in love with the idea that I would cure his loneliness. That by marrying me, he'd somehow become . . . normal. He wouldn't have, but nonetheless, his affection for me was sincere. In the whole finding-Tami-a-husband project, Haroun was the only one whose motives were one hundred percent pure.

He's also the only one whose heart was broken, and I'm sorry for that. I'm very, very sorry. But I can tell from the unforgiving look in his eyes that my being sorry is not enough.

I can tell it's not nearly enough.

Immigration Interview: EIGHT WEEKS AWAY

At Maryam and Ardishir's first birthing class, Ardishir, who was helping Maryam practice her breathing, hyperventilated and nearly passed out.

At the second class, the instructor, who was quite large, got down on her hands and knees to demonstrate some exercises that could take away lower-back pain, and then she couldn't get back up. Ardishir got the giggles and couldn't get rid of them, so they had to leave the class, which both embarrassed and infuriated Maryam.

At their third class, after Ardishir fell asleep during the relaxation exercises, Maryam fired him from his birthing-room duties.

"He acts like this pregnancy is all about him!" she says one day when we're out shopping—maternity clothes for her and summer skirts for me.

"Well, it's half about him, yes?" I say.

She looks at me like I'm crazy. "Whose womb is this baby in? I'm housing it! Growing it! Feeding it! Getting swollen feet and gaining weight because of it! It's *more* my baby than his, at least at this point."

I put out my lower lip into a sad pout on Ardishir's behalf. "But he puts gas in your car for you. And gives you back rubs. And he reads to the baby—that's so sweet!"

"Yeah, big old boring history books that put me to sleep!"

"He goes to the McDonald's drive-thru for you to get your Big Macs," I remind her. This is one of her cravings, along with nacho cheese sauce and Three Musketeers candy bars. "And he doesn't make fun of you for having to use the bathroom all the time."

"Are you kidding?" she says. "He teases me *all the time.* I've asked him to stop, but he won't. I can't count on him for anything!"

This must be her hormones talking again. "Ardishir's completely reliable."

"Well, just in case, will you be my backup, if he can't handle his responsibilities in the labor and delivery room?"

"Oh, Maryam!" I throw my arms around her. I've been hoping she'd ask. "Nothing would make me happier, nothing at all!"

And this is almost true. The only thing that would make me happier is having our parents there, too.

Immigration Interview: SEVEN WEEKS AWAY

All summer long, Ike, Rose, and I have had movie nights at her house. Ike, the expert movie-picker, has chosen the movies, while Rose has made popcorn and I've brought big movie-theater boxes of candy, purchased for one dollar each at Walgreen's. I like all the candy I've tried, but my very favorites are Junior Mints and Milk Duds.

So far, we've watched conspiracy-theory movies such as *The Manchurian Candidate*; bringing-down-the-government movies such as *All the President's Men*; love-between-men movies such as *Brokeback Mountain*—none of which would ever be permitted to play in a theater in Iran. I've enjoyed them all, but my favorite movie so far has been one that was made nearly thirty years ago called *The Jazz Singer*, about a Jewish man, a cantor, who loves his father and wants to respect him, and he loves his wife, too, but he longs to be a singer of more than just religious music. Unfortunately, neither his wife nor his father supports him in this endeavor. While I watch the movie, my insides are clenched for him—I so want him to succeed! His story reminds me of Maryam, who told me recently that one of her biggest memories from when we went back to Iran is how one time she was in our bedroom playing Olivia Newton-John on her stereo and very loudly singing along, practicing her performance in the mirror, when Baba burst into the room and made her stop. He didn't want the neighbors to hear our family play Western music; you never knew where anyone's loyalties lie, and someone might report us. Maryam told me she never sang again and put aside all her dreams of being a famous singer.

That's why I want this Neil Diamond character to succeed.

In all cultures, people have dreams, and in all cultures people are fully alive only when they're striving for them. This is why people come to America from all around the world—we come here to flourish. We come believing that nobody will tell us to stop singing, or to stop taking pictures, or to stop doing whatever it is that gives our souls joy. In America, people say *yes.* They say *go for it.* Having the opportunity to be true to yourself—that's the American dream.

After the movie, I download the Neil Diamond song "America" onto the iPod that Ike gave me for our one-month-of-being-married anniversary. He thinks this is very funny, since the movie and the song are so old and somewhat silly to him, but I feel like they've been written just for me. *Everywhere around the world, they're coming to America. Every time that flag's unfurled, they're coming to America. Today!* Oh, how I cried when he sang that at the end of the movie!

This song becomes a sound track to my life. I listen to it constantly and take many more pictures than I had been, because, who knows? Maybe that's where my true talent lies, and if does, then I owe it to myself to develop it. Tucson has a neighborhood called Barrio Viejo, which is one of the oldest neighborhoods in town. One morning when Ike goes for his run, I bike there and take pictures in the dawn light of cats in windowsills, of colorful doors on old adobe buildings, of tin watering cans used for vases—even shattered glass beer bottles sparkling in the street take on an artistic quality. Wearing my iPod on my way to English class, I play the song "America" over and over, shouting the chorus in my head. I'm a character in a movie. I'm living the American dream. Anything is possible.

It's in this Hollywood-inspired spirit that I call my father. "Baba, hello!"

My father says, "You sound happy, Tami Joon!"

"I am happy!" In my head, I sing, *dun, dun, dun—Freedom's light burning warm. Freedom's light burning warm.* "I'm in America, who wouldn't be happy here?"

"How is your sister? Is she doing okay?"

"She's fine, Baba. Do you have any good news for me? Have you received your visa paperwork yet?"

There's a pause, and then my father says, "Not yet, Tami Joon. I'm afraid we might have a long wait ahead of us."

But today, I think maybe not. *They're coming to America. Today!*

"Who knows?" I say. "You might get your paperwork today, Baba!"

"It didn't come in today's mail, Tami Joon."

"Well, there's still time for you to be here before Maryam's baby is born. I'm not giving up hope."

"For that to happen, everything has to go perfectly. Since when does anything work perfectly in Iran?" he says.

"This is a good point," I say. "But still. Let's choose hope."

Immigration Interview: SIX WEEKS AWAY

One morning, I'm alone in the guesthouse hiding from the heat when there's a tap on the door. I open it to find sweet Paige, Ike's fourteen-year-old sister.

"Hello!" Ike's sisters all love to do the kiss-on-the-cheek greeting—they think it's so cosmopolitan—and so this is how I greet her. "Ike's not here, sweetie, I'm sorry."

Paige blushes. "That's okay. I was out on my bike . . . I'm looking for a birthday present for my mom, and I thought, you know, maybe you'd want to come with me? To Fourth Avenue, maybe? I'm really bad at picking out gifts."

I'm so touched she thought of me. Ike's sisters stop over a lot to visit Old Sport (and us, too, I hope!), although never alone like Paige is today, and Ike and I have been going to his parents' house for dinner most Sundays. And even though Mrs. Hanson still barely says a word to me, I know his sisters are on my side—they don't even try to hide it from their mom—and I think little by little, we are all starting to wear her down. Rose is right about killing someone with kindness: It's hard to be mean to someone when all they are is nice to you, and so I like to think that Mrs. Hanson is starting to feel a little silly. She does listen when I talk to Mr. Hanson, Ike, or the girls, and every so often, I catch her smiling at something I've said. I hope that maybe once I have my residency and I'm still with Ike and he hasn't gotten in trouble for being married to me, things might be better between Mrs. Hanson and me.

I invite Paige inside and offer her some iced tea, which she gratefully accepts. She sits on the couch, leaning forward with her elbows on her knees, her knees together and her feet separated. She's very cute in her long braids and Converse sneakers, although her limbs are gangly and it's clear she's awkward in her body, not yet used to her feminine curves. She has no idea how beautiful she is.

I sit next to her and place my cool hand on her sun-hot back, marveling that I've always wanted a little sister, and now I have four! "What are you thinking of getting your mother for her birthday?"

"I don't know." She says this like she wants to cry. "Camille will make her something cute, and Kat and Izzy will get her something cool that costs a lot of money, and I have hardly any money, and anything I do won't be cute, it'll just be *stupid*!"

I rub her back a little bit. "I have some money. I have as much as you need." She looks at me gratefully, like this is the nicest thing anyone has said to her in a long time. And then her eyes moisten. "Paige, sweetie! It's all right, we'll think of something!"

"It's not that." She sniffles. "I'm just so stupid!"

"You're not stupid. You're a smart girl." She studies me closely to see if I really think this or if I'm just trying to make her feel better. "You are, Paige."

She sniffles again. "Can I braid your hair?"

"Of course." Camille loves to play with my hair, too. Almost every Sunday, she sits me down on the floor, with her on the couch, and brushes it before putting it in goofy pigtails that stick up all over the place. I don't even care that I look silly—it feels so good to have a little kid's hands touching me. Paige's request to braid my hair reminds me that while her body is changing, she is, in so many ways—good ways—still a child, still an innocent.

I get a comb, barrettes, and elastic bands from the bathroom and come back to our little living room. "Should I sit on the floor?"

She nods, and so I stretch out at her feet and relax my back against the couch.

"I like your nail polish," she says as she starts combing my hair.

"Thank you." I wiggle my hot-pink toes at her.

"Did you do them yourself, or did you get a pedicure?"

"It's a pedicure," I say. "My sister always wants me to come along when she has anything done, which is pretty often since she quit her job!" We've begun calling Fridays our beauty days. Depending on our needs or desires, we get massages or mani/pedis or various waxings (and sometimes all three!), finished off with a round of shopping, for which Maryam inevitably pays, saying she's making up for all the years she couldn't do this with me in Iran. Being the sister of someone who's married to an independently wealthy and also successful orthopedic surgeon has its perks.

"I've never had a pedicure," Paige says.

"We should go sometime," I say. "I'd love to treat you. Maybe that's what you could do with your mom for her birthday—a pedicure and lunch?"

"My mom hates stuff like that." She begins braiding. "She can't stand spending time or money on something so *impractical*." I recognize her mother's chastising tone when she says that last word.

I laugh. "I must really make her crazy, then! I'm pretty sure my nails are a different color every time I go over there!"

"Not you so much—she thinks you're really pretty," she says. "But she's always on Izzy's case about stuff like that."

"Well, then we'll have to think of something else for her birthday."

"Besides, Ike takes her to lunch for her birthday. He does it every year."

I wonder if I'll be invited along this year. I decide I won't go if I am. I'll let them keep up this special tradition. I wonder, though: What should I get her?

"Can I ask you something?" Paige says.

"Of course."

"How old were you the first time you . . . you know . . . had sex?"

I inhale sharply. So *that's* what this is about. This is the reason for her visit. This is the reason she has me sitting on the floor, braiding my hair, so I'm facing away from her as she asks this personal question.

"Oh, Paige." *She's fourteen!* "Are you . . . Did you . . . ?"

"No," she says quickly.

"Will you tell me what's going on?"

The words spill out of her in a rush, like they've been dying to get out for so long. She tells me about the boy she likes, Garrett. It's the same boy Mrs. Hanson told us about at Lodge on the Desert that awful day, the one with lots of gel in his hair, who snarls his lip when he talks to his teachers, who is a guitarist and singer in a rock band . . . *and who is seventeen years old.* When Paige tells me this, I'm so glad Ike isn't here. He'd throw a fit, which is probably why she came when he wasn't home. For all I know, she biked by the house ten times until she saw that his truck was no longer in the driveway. Paige and Garrett aren't even officially dating. He says she's too young for him, so they're FWB, friends with benefits. But he's so *nice* to her, and when he looks at her, he makes her feel beautiful. When they're together, neither one of them can *get enough.* Paige says she loses herself when she's with him, that she can hardly control herself.

And he wants to have sex, of course. He always has condoms, and he always lets her know he has them. She doesn't know how much longer they can go, realistically, before they'll have sex, even though she always thought she'd wait until she was in college.

She's been braiding my hair the whole time she's been talking, finishing a braid, then unraveling it and redoing it. I, too, am glad we're not facing each other as she tells me all this, because I've never felt like such a foreigner as I do right now. I'm sure hers is the story of a typical American teenage girl's first love—but who am I to give advice? Ike's the first man I've loved—the only man I've loved. He's the only man I've had sex with, and almost the first I kissed, as I don't count the various neighborhood boys with their pushy, grimy hands who'd reach for me with lustful eyes in the shadows of our streets in Tehran. I kissed a few of them, but only because it seemed like the quickest way to get them to leave me alone. One close-lipped, unaffectionate kiss in an alleyway could fuel their fantasies for years, it seemed. But love? Lust? Really, these feelings are as new to me as they are to Paige. I get all my sex tips from the *Cosmopolitan* magazines I read at the library!

"Would it be wrong of me?" she asks. "Lots of girls my age already have."

I sigh. My heart would break for her if she went ahead with this idea. Young teenagers in America wear call-girl makeup and push-up bras and thong underwear and they watch things on television you could be arrested for in Iran, but in so many ways, they're still such innocents. Life has its cruel ways of breaking people, but if American teenagers her age have had a good family life, like Paige has, they've not yet been damaged. They haven't lived in a police state; they haven't known of family members being tortured. And I'm not saying having your heart broken by a boy after you've had sex with him is in any way comparable to these things, but sex for someone who's inexperienced brings with it powerful, complicated emotions that I can only hope to understand one day. I sure don't now. Would it be wrong? That's not a value judgment I want to make.

"If he broke up with you right now, today, how would you feel?" I ask her.

"Oh, my God, horrible!" Paige says. "Don't even ask me that—I can't stand to think about it!"

This friends-with-benefits deal seems like it's better for him than it is for her, since she wants him to be her boyfriend. "Have your parents met him yet?"

"Not yet," she says. "They'll just tease me."

"Your parents would tease you?"

"No, but my sisters would. They always do. Nothing's private in my family."

"So you meet him out somewhere?"

"Yeah. Sometimes I hang out with his band when they rehearse, or sometimes he waits for me to get off swim practice."

"Does he have other friends with benefits?"

"We don't talk about it," she says. "But I don't think so."

And here I thought *I* was naïve.

She's finishing up my second braid again, and to prevent

her from unraveling it, I say, "Done, my dear?" She wraps a band around it, and then I get up and sit next to her on the couch. I stroke her cheek like my sister sometimes does to me when she feels bad for me. Because that's how I feel—bad for her. Horrible for her.

"Sweetie, I think this boy might break your heart."

Paige's eyes well with tears and she nods. She knows this, too, deep down.

"I think he'll break your heart whether you have sex with him or not, because . . . well . . . besides the difference in your ages, I worry that he doesn't know how special you are."

"That's the thing," she whispers. "I'm not, except when I'm with him."

"I didn't grow up thinking I was anything special either," I say. "Even though my father always told me I was, I never believed him. But it's good he told me this, because it made me never want to let him down, to never do anything that might cause him to be disappointed in me. Even coming to America—it was really hard for me to do, to leave everything behind. I was very scared, but I did it because I wanted to make my parents proud."

"You must think my problems are so small," Paige says.

"Not at all, sweetie! Not at all!"

"They are, compared to yours."

I firmly shake my head. "I only said all that to help you see that more people than just this boy, Garrett, think you're special. Your parents do. Ike does. I'm sure your sisters do, and I do, too. And they care about what happens to you. And we don't know exactly what Garrett wants *for* you—we only know what he wants *from* you, yes? But these other people really want the best for you, and so you should think of them. You should think if they'll be proud of you if you do what you're thinking about doing, or if they'll be disappointed."

She clears her throat and nods. Not like she's happy with my answer—more like she's wondering if she'll ever be able to have a private moment with Garrett again without imagining her father's stern face watching her. I, for one, hope she can't!

"Do you know what I think?" I take her hand. "I think Garrett's probably a really nice boy, and he's probably really fun to be with."

"He is," she says. "He's really, really nice."

"I think you should take things slow," I say. "Very, very slow. Even just holding a boy's hand—that's a pretty awesome thing to do, isn't it? To walk down the street and not have a care in the world. To share an ice cream cone, or have a picnic in the park . . . to go to movies and on bike rides . . . those small pleasures really are the most important ones. They're what so many girls all around the world never get to do. And so *you* should do them."

"I should because they can't?"

"You should because dating is all about finding out who you are and what you like and what you want, which is why governments like mine forbid it. They don't want women and girls to know who they are because it might not fit in with what *they* need for us to be. But they shouldn't get to define us. We should define ourselves. No boy, and no government, should do that for us. Right?"

"Right." Paige nods, although she still looks unsure.

"So if you always thought you should wait until college before being so physical with a boy, then maybe you should wait. You shouldn't be the girl who has sex with a boy at fourteen just because he wanted to. Does that help at all?"

"I guess." She smiles and looks a little relieved. "But I sure wish I had your confidence."

I smile. This is the first time in my life someone has admired my confidence!

Immigration Interview: FIVE WEEKS AWAY

"I met this woman from Canada who had to have a *vaginal exam* at her immigration interview," Eva says one day as we are walking back from class. "Can you believe it? A *vaginal exam*! No lie! A *Canadian*! What the hell?"

Eva has not had her immigration interview yet, either. Maybe I got mine scheduled for sooner because I'm Iranian, I don't know, or maybe because her husband is in the military and overseas, but she hasn't even gotten the date for hers yet. She's only filled out the first forms and had her fingerprints taken. But like every other not-passed-the-interview-yet person, she pesters everyone who has.

Other immigration horror stories people tell me:

There is the one about the man from Egypt who, when

asked his wife's mother's maiden name, didn't know. He failed the interview and had to go back to Egypt.

There is the one about the pregnant Mexican woman who followed her boyfriend to America. Her boyfriend was a U.S. citizen, but she was not. She gave birth to her baby in the U.S., was arrested at the hospital, and driven back to the other side of the border, which left her baby with the gift of U.S. citizenship but without a mother. She never even *got* an interview.

Even poor Nadia has her immigration-interview horror story, but hers is due mostly to her horrible husband. The night before their interview, Lenny threatened to say all sorts of lies about her, such as that she'd been a prostitute in Russia and that she'd left several children behind which he hadn't learned about until later—all cruel lies. But if she got her green card, then she could get a job, which he wanted to happen because why should he work when he could sit around all day in his grubby T-shirt drinking beer, feeding his Internet pornography addiction, and sending the wife he hated out to work instead? Nadia said there was no way the interviewer believed they married for love, but she thinks he took pity on her because she was pregnant. Nadia says now that if she hadn't been pregnant, she would have left Lenny on her own.

But for every horror story, I hear three more from people who say the interview is no big deal, that as long as you have all your paperwork in order and are living with your spouse and have a bank account together and seem to be in a real relationship, then the interview is just a formality that doesn't last more than ten or fifteen minutes.

These stories—the ones with happy endings—are the ones I cling to. Ike and I not only live together, not only have a shared bank account, we also have a shared business. I have made a substantial investment in our relationship by going into partnership with him. Plus, everybody says they can tell just by looking at us that we're madly in love.

And they're right!

Immigration Interview: FOUR WEEKS AWAY

Maryam calls me, too upset even for tears. "It's happening again." Her voice over the phone is a weak, mournful whisper. "I'm losing this baby. Oh, God, Tami, I can't *do* this again. I don't have it in me to go through it again."

Her stomachache has come back and there's been some bleeding, and her hope is already gone. I cling to mine and plead for her to hold on, to close her mind to bad outcomes and just *hold on.* Ardishir is far away at work, and I'm so close, and even while I'm telling her to hold on, that just because there's some spotting it doesn't mean she's lost the baby, even as I'm saying this, I'm crossing the backyard to Rose's house and tracking her down in the laundry room. I'm covering the phone and saying, "Please, Rose. I need your help. It's Maryam. It's the baby," and we're on our way immediately, and I soothe Maryam on the phone as we drive to her. I fill her mind with the tasks we will do and the thoughts we will think until these tasks are done—positive thoughts, only positive thoughts. If there's to be sorrow, it will not be yet. We'll hold on to our hope until the last possible moment, and we'll hold on and we'll hold on, until the doctor tells us to let it go. "But it's not over," I tell her. "Until this baby's last little heartbeat, *it's not over.*"

I say all this as if I believe it, and in fact, I do. We create the gods we need, and my god simply would not do this in this moment, at this time. My god would let my family have its happiness for once, and this is just a test of our will, of our strength, and as we drive to Maryam's, at the same time I'm reassuring her, I remind my god of this, that this is our moment for joy. I'm not asking for forever; I'd gladly trade my forever for my sister and for *exactly right now.*

Now, I know as well as anyone that a woman's prayers aren't always answered. Sometimes, not even the prayers of an entire country are answered. But for once, mine are.

We get to the emergency room, where an ultrasound clearly shows the baby moving, weaving her little fingers as if dancing a dreamy dance.

"She's doing just fine," the doctor says.

"She?" Maryam's smile is broad. "We're having a girl? And she's okay?"

The technician nods. "You want to listen to the heart-beat?"

All three of us listen in turn—Maryam, me, then Rose. *Thu-thump, thu-thump*—her heart beats strong and true.

Ardishir arrives in a frantic rush.

"We're having a girl!" Maryam says. "Come listen, Ardi. She's fine. She's perfect!"

His eyes tear up as he listens to his daughter's heartbeat. "Good girl," he whispers. "You're my good, good girl."

But there has been this stomachache, and there has been this dark spotting. Thankfully, the baby is not the problem—Maryam's cervix is. She's two centimeters dilated. At only twenty-eight weeks, Maryam's body is going into labor before the baby's ready. The official diagnosis: an incompetent cervix.

Maryam, so good at so many things, who hates to be bad at anything, is furious. She needs something called a cerclage, a stitch to close her cervix. For this procedure, she's admitted to the hospital overnight. The next day, the doctor prescribes weekly shots of progesterone to help prevent early labor. She and her incompetent cervix are placed on bed rest, indefinitely.

Because their master bedroom is upstairs, far from the main action of the house, Ardishir sets up the guest bedroom off the kitchen for her and brings in the large television from the living room so Maryam can watch her American soap operas and her Persian news stations on the satellite television. With her world shrunken so small, she quickly becomes bored (as well as boring), and cranky, and needy. She's got opinions about everything, including the coffee shop—what colors the walls should be, how we should advertise for employees, how we should wear uniform shirts with the business logo (a steaming mug—which, according to her, not that we asked, isn't flashy enough), and so on. I begin to leave my cell phone at home so I don't have to take her constant calls.

But Rose is so good with her. She visits Maryam each afternoon, and together they knit booties and blankets for the baby and listen to books on tape. They play cards and Scrabble and over the long hours they become very close. Throughout this whole experience, it's saddened me that Maman has known nothing about Maryam's pregnancy, that she hasn't been able to—hasn't been given the opportunity to—offer Maryam the comfort she needs. It seems like an insult. As hard as it's been, this experience has brought us closer, all of us—Maryam, Ardishir, Rose, myself, and even Ike—and yet it's left my parents ever farther apart from us.

And every week when I call them, my father has no news about their visa application. It gets so I can hardly bring myself to ask anymore, because his answer always makes me so sad. We need them, I need them, but especially Maryam needs them.

Immigration Interview: THREE WEEKS AWAY

"Just act natural," Ike tells me as we approach the border patrol checkpoint on Interstate 8 on our way to San Diego. We're taking a much-needed long weekend off from our coffee shop preparations after several frustrating weeks of unfairly failed inspections, and problems with sign permits and emergency exit signs, and toilets that flush on the left instead of on the right, and on and on. I don't think I'm exaggerating much when I tell people it would probably be easier to open a business in Iran than in Tucson. In Iran, you could just pay people off, but in Tucson, it's almost as if these city workers get kickbacks for *not* letting new businesses open. We're driving from Arizona to California and the Pacific Ocean, but when Ike suggested this trip, he didn't say anything about a border patrol checkpoint, and I begin to shake with fear as we approach it.

"How do I act natural?" I ask. "What should I do?"

"Nothing," Ike says. "Just sit there." He glances at me, then leans over and opens the glove compartment, pulling out an old pair of sunglasses. "Here, put these on. You look terrified." He half laughs. "You look guilty!"

"I *feel* guilty." I can't help it—in Iran, you *are* guilty. Always, no matter what.

"I promise, it's no big deal," he says. "Just relax."

I try, but the men have guns. There's one car ahead of us, and an officer is bending over, looking at each passenger, a woman and two kids, questioning them. Clearly, they are a family going on vacation, so what's taking so long? If *they're* suspicious to the officer, what on earth will he think of me?

"You didn't happen to bring your immigration paperwork, did you?" Ike asks this question very casually, so casually I know there's nothing at all casual about it.

"No!" My entire body is frozen from panic. "Do I need it?"

"No, no. Never mind, you don't need it," he says. "I shouldn't have asked. Just relax. We're a married couple on a weekend away. We're just like everyone else."

This is where he's wrong. Being from the axis-of-evil Iran, I'm *not* like everyone else. Not to a border patrol officer anyway, whose job is to keep the borders safe from . . . well, from people like me.

The officer steps back from the vehicle in front of us and waves it along. As it's our turn, Ike rolls down his window.

The officer peers at us.

"Good morning," Ike says.

"Morning," the border patrol officer says back. "Where are you folks traveling from?"

In my heart, I gasp. I cannot tell him Iran. I simply cannot.

"Tucson," Ike says.

The officer looks at me. "Both of you?"

"Yes, both of us." It's only because I know Ike so well that I hear the false cheeriness in his tone. He's heard the border patrol horror stories, too. By now, everyone has.

The officer keeps looking at me, and I know he can tell something's wrong. Fear has its own physiology, a certain smell, and he's smelling it. If I don't do something fast, he's going to tell me to step outside the vehicle, and then I'll be surrounded by officers, with the guard dog barking at me, wanting to tear into me, with hundreds of people in the cars behind me watching, saying to each other, *I wonder what she did wrong. Drugs, you think?* Or, *I bet she's an illegal.* Or, worse, *She's probably an illegal alien*, as if I'm not only *not* legal, but also that I'm an alien from another world! Ike will try to help, but they'll take me away while holding him back. I can't let this happen. I've got to get rid of this stench, this fear. I've got to save myself.

I fall back on Eva's fake-it-'til-you-make-it advice: I'm twenty-seven years old. I'm married. Young, beautiful, happy. I'm afraid of nothing, for I've done nothing wrong. Kindness oozes from me. I'm a friend to everyone, a threat to no one—especially not to this friendly officer and his friendly dog. He probably thinks I'm a Mexican, and so I have to talk. Sure, I have an accent, but it's not a Spanish one. I take off the pair of men's sunglasses I've been wearing, which are wrong for my face anyway, and smile at the officer.

"We're on our honeymoon," I tell him brightly. I give a little wave with my left hand so he can see my wedding ring, which matches the one Ike is wearing on his left hand, which is resting on the steering wheel. We got these last week, finally—simple gold bands. Sadly, there was nothing very romantic about it. We were having dinner at North at La Encantada and I mentioned we needed to have wedding rings before the immigration interview. After dinner, we were walking through the ritzy outdoor mall and Ike steered me into Tiffany's. We bought the cheapest bands they had, because right now a walk-in freezer for the coffee shop is more important than flashy wedding rings, but, hey, at least they're from Tiffany's!

After I wave my ring at the officer and tell him we're on our honeymoon, he says, "That right?"

"That's right." Ike taps his ring finger on the steering wheel so it makes a clicking sound.

"All right, then. You'd better get on with it." The officer slaps the frame of Ike's rolled-down window and steps back. "Congratulations."

"Thank you! Thank you so much!" I give him my best smile, but the officer already has his eyes on the driver in the car behind us. He—an employee of Homeland Security, a representative of the United States government—has judged me innocent, deemed me worthy. This is good, a good omen, I'm sure of it.

We stay at a hotel in Mission Beach where President Nixon used to stay and the weather is so perfect and the ocean so beautiful and there is so much life going on that I say to Ike several times, "Tell me again: Why aren't we living here?" I love Tucson—it's very special, probably there is no place like it in the world—but I'm a big-city girl. I miss the fast pace of Tehran. Tucson is a great place to catch your breath, but San Diego is great for everything. I gawk at the women in bikinis . . . at the grocery store! Ike gawks at me in a bikini (a sexy turquoise one), but I wear it only at the beach. I feel self-conscious even there, so no way would I wear it to a grocery store! And the tattoos—they're everywhere! Everyone seems to have one. At first, I don't understand why people would get them, why they'd mark their bodies in this way. I understand their desire to express their individuality—I understand this desire quite well—but it seems like this attempt to be original just . . . isn't, not when everyone else also has them. And yet, on our third night, after doing what Ike calls barhopping, we each get one—tiny tattoos on our hip bones, for no one except each other to see, hearts with the other's name inside. Thanks to all the peach-flavored wine coolers I drank, it hardly hurts at all.

On the last day, it's nearing sunset and Ike is surfing. I'm happily watching him from shore, having already resolved to take swimming lessons once we're back in Tucson so that next summer I can join him. I like the idea of riding the waves rather than fearing them. In front of me, a little girl plays with her father. She's three years old, maybe four, in the water up to her ankles. She faces her father, who faces her, in the water up to his knees. Over and over she points and yells, *Look out! A wave!* And he keeps saying, *No, there's no wave.* And then one smacks into him and he reacts with surprise each time, and she laughs and laughs. They do this for thirty minutes, maybe more. It makes me wonder if my father was playful like this, if he made me giggle like this, when we lived in America and visited the ocean. I bet he did. I bet he was that sort of father, for that happy little while we had as a family in America. And I bet he'd be that sort of grandfather, too, for Maryam's baby and, one day, for mine—if he could be here for them.

He swam in the ocean all those years ago, in the very same ocean my husband swims in now. I'm almost certain of it, because he swam as a teenager in the Caspian Sea. I've heard the stories of my handsome, wild father before he met my mother. I've seen the photographs, I've seen how he glistened in the sun. I watch Ike, and he glistens, too.

I think they'd like each other, my father and Ike.

I think they'd like each other very much.

Immigration Interview: TWO WEEKS AWAY

Maryam, thirty weeks along and finally off bed rest, arrives at the coffee shop with a color wheel and a paintbrush and some sample-sized cans of paint for us to test on the walls. When Ike sees her unloading them from her car, he grits his teeth.

He's in a grumpy mood, and I don't blame him. Our least favorite inspector just left, having refused to sign off on a permit to have the gas turned back on. The plumber had turned it off while he was changing out some fittings, but the gas company happened to come by to read the meter, saw the valve was off, and locked it. Now the only way to get it back on is to go back to the city and have it reinspected. The inspector's name is Le-Rick, but we call him Le-Dick. He's got a beer belly and an outdated ponytail—a frustrated hippie, Ike calls him—and you can tell just by looking at him that he hates his life and his job. He walks around the store making notes on his clipboard, criticizing everything. When he did his pressure test on the gas line, the pressure dropped. This could turn out to be something small, or it could turn out to be a $1,500 repair; we just don't know. And even though Le-Rick was only here to inspect the gas line, he got mad at Ike for having changed out the hood over the grill. He said the floor drain wasn't done right and the hand sink shouldn't be where it is—even though the health inspector said there *had* to be one in that spot *and* had already signed off on the floor drain. I keep telling Ike these people must be looking for bribes, but he says no, they're just all assholes.

And now Ike grits his teeth at my sister as she waddles into the shop with her color wheel and paint cans. Ike loves Maryam's Persian food, but he doesn't care for her many unsolicited opinions.

"I'll take care of things with her, love." I rest my hand on his forearm for a moment, hoping it will calm him. "Why don't you call the plumber?"

"I'm going to call my dad first." He cracks his neck. "Hopefully, he'll know how to cut through the bullshit."

He says hello to Maryam before disappearing into the back. I give her a bright smile. It's so good to see her on her feet again; we all feel triumphant.

"Guess what? Ardishir's aunt is coming to visit from Canada!" she says. "Homa Nasseri. You'll love her; she's so funny. She's coming to help with the baby! Ardishir's so happy! She called him at his office to tell him, and he brought home the biggest bouquet of flowers he's ever given me, and his eyes glowed all night. He's like a little kid waiting for presents! I didn't realize how much he must be missing his family, too. It's too bad his parents can't come, but they're too old to travel so far anymore."

His parents live in Tehran, too, a few kilometers from mine. That's how Ardishir met Maryam, while on a visit home to see them.

"It's an important time for both of you," I say. "Of course he wants his family here."

I'm happy for them, but I want *my* family here. Homa

Nasseri will stay for several months, I'm sure, and she'll be of great help, but she'll take the bedroom that would have been my parents', and then if they *are* able to come, where will they stay? We'd find room, of course, but Homa Nasseri's visit is like an admonition, a reminder of how unlikely it is that my parents will ever come.

"Look what I brought!" Maryam holds up the paint cans. "This one's a rustic red, which I think would look great on that wall, and then you could complement it with a dusty gray with silver flecks. Let's try them, yes? Maybe on that wall?" She indicates the main wall customers will see as they enter the shop.

"Oh, well . . ." I hide a sigh. I'm tired of her involvement, too. "Ike already knows what color he wants. It's a really pretty golden color."

"Gold's so last year." Maryam holds the cans out for me to take. "Here. These are nontoxic. You can put them on right now and it's not bad for the baby. I'm sure Ike would appreciate seeing other colors, even if he thinks he knows what he wants."

Ike doesn't *think* he knows what he wants. He *knows* what he wants.

"Maryam, you know how Americans have such a need for individualism?"

"No," she says.

I laugh. "Yes, you do." We talk about it all the time. "You know, how they break away from their families and create brand-new lives for themselves."

"That's not individualism," she says. "It's selfishness."

"It's not," I say. It's *The Jazz Singer.* "It's *living*, American-style—life on their own terms. Ike's a lot like that. It's really important for him to make his own decisions."

"That's why you, as his wife, have to guide him into making the *right* decisions," she says. "I'm just helping with ideas. I'm not trying to—" She stops talking and grimaces. With her right hand, she massages her stomach like she's trying to get the baby to shift position. Something about the gesture alarms me, and I step closer.

"Are you okay?"

"Yes, sure," she says. "She's just elbowing me. It's better now." But Maryam is pale, and her skin is stretched tight like she's trying not to wince.

"Are you sure?" I say. "Is it that stomachache feeling again?"

"It's nothing," she says. "Just heartburn. I shouldn't have had those jalapeños for lunch."

Ike wanders into the front of the store. He's on his cell phone, but he pauses and raises his eyebrows at me, questioning if Maryam is okay. I give him a look back, telling him I don't know.

"What if you're in labor, Maryam? We should go to the hospital!"

"I'm not in labor." She walks toward the wall she wants me to paint, but halfway there, she stops and again presses her side. From behind, it looks like she's going to crumple to the ground. Both Ike and I rush over and lead her to a chair.

"I'm fine," she insists. "I just need to get off my feet for a while."

"We need to get you to a doctor," Ike says.

"I'm not going into labor," she insists. "I'm taking those shots, remember? It's just my ligaments stretching again."

"Ligaments stretching *is* labor," Ike says. "They're stretching so the baby can get through the birth canal."

Maryam's eyes tear up. "That's not what's happening."

"One way to find out," Ike says.

"It's too soon," Maryam says.

"They can stop it," I say. "They can probably stop it, if you go in right now."

"I can't go on bed rest again!" Maryam wails. "I have too much to do! I have to get ready for Homa Nasseri's visit, and there's my baby shower, and your interview—I've got to help you get ready for that! And there's—" She moans, straightens, and tries to smooth away her pain.

Ike sits in the chair next to her. "The goal is a healthy baby, Maryam. Right? That's the end goal."

"I have a doctor's appointment tomorrow," she says. "I'll see what he says then."

"Maryam." I give her a stern-sister look.

"The baby's *fine*, Tami." She grimaces. "She's just shifting position, that's all."

But I don't think so. I think the baby's struggling. I think maybe she's being strangled by the umbilical cord like so many of those sad stories we've heard. I look at Ike, and it's clear he's thinking the same thing, and I remember what happened to his little brother, Charlie Bongo, and *it can't happen to Baby Hope.*

And yet Maryam has that stubborn look on her face that means she's not going to listen to us, as if sheer willpower will make everything okay. I know it's fear that's driving her, but I don't know what to do about it. What she needs is a mother's guidance. And since our mother's not here . . .

I lock eyes with Ike. My heart pounds like it always does at the very idea of his mother and the memory of how she tried to ruin our marriage. But she *was* a labor and delivery nurse, and that's exactly what my sister needs. "Would you call your mother, please, Ike?"

Maryam protests, but Ike nods and moves away from us to make the call. Less than fifteen minutes later, Mrs. Hanson arrives and convinces Maryam she must go to the doctor. Just as Maryam feared, she's placed on hospital bed rest for the remainder of her pregnancy. Secretly, I'm glad. I like to know the baby's safe and that help is always near.

Immigration Interview: ONE WEEK AWAY

This week, the movie we watch is *Green Card* with Andie MacDowell and a really ugly French actor named Gerard Depardieu. It's funny and charming and I pay very close attention. Afterward, Ike and I begin questioning each other in earnest in preparation for our upcoming interview.

Here are some facts about Ike: His middle name is Howard, which is also his mother's maiden name. He will only use Crest toothpaste and Tide laundry detergent, original scent. Disorganization stresses him out. Every morning, he plans every task he wants to do that day and prioritizes the order in which he'll do them, using an A-B-C, 1-2-3 system. He had chicken pox when he was seven years old and he had his appendix taken out in college. His favorite type of beer is Hefeweisen, and his shoe size is eleven. He likes the side of the bed closest to the door. He likes plain vanilla ice cream with strawberries on top. He likes me in my turquoise bikini, and he likes prettily pedicured toenails. He likes to see movies at the theater in the afternoons, and he doesn't mind seeing them alone. He likes running and racquetball. He pushes himself in everything he does.

Here are some things about me: I like walking barefoot through the grass at the University of Arizona campus mall. I like watching kids play soccer at Himmel Park. I like seeing Ike shirtless. I like *all* bumper stickers—I like the very idea of bumper stickers—and I especially like the one on my neighbor's car: *Well-behaved women rarely make history.* I like live music, any kind, but especially I like women singers. I like watching Ike play Texas Hold 'Em with his poker friends and seeing the way his Tiffany wedding band looks so good on his left hand. I like being outdoors late at night, when our side of the earth has rotated away from the throbbing summer sun and the pavement stops radiating heat. I like lying back on our patio lounge chairs with Ike and watching the stars, talking about everything and nothing. I like front doors open to the world. I like seeing my neighbor lady walk down her driveway every morning in her hanging-open robe and curlers in her hair to collect her newspaper. I like the lack of smog here, the absence of Tehran's early-morning noise and its too many pairs of judgmental eyes. I like American grocery stores, the bigger the better, and fashion magazines. I like the sight of little girls jumping rope. I like ringing the cheerful bell on my Schwinn bicycle and waving to people. I like wearing short skirts and high heels. I like how people mind their own business. I like being left alone.

Immigration Interview: TOMORROW!

"Well, Persian Girl," Ike says. "This is it. Are you ready?"

I smile at him. I asked him this same question once, and I still remember his answer. "No," I say, like he'd said that day on the airplane, on our way back to Tucson from getting married in Las Vegas. "But what the hell, let's do it anyway."

We're at Common Grounds, holding hands across the table. It's night, dark out, but we've left the lights off because the super-expensive and very cool Common Grounds sign was finally delivered and installed today, and we're basking in its spooky purple glow. We've hired our employees and the restaurant is ready to open. All that's left is for the city inspector to grant us the certificate of occupancy, which we hope will happen tomorrow after the interview. And then, we can open the day after that if we want.

It'll be the first day of the rest of our lives.

It's not true that I'm not ready. I am. *We* are—all of us. My father has filed their paperwork and is waiting. Maryam waits, too, safely in her hospital bed at University Medical Center, thanks to the no-nonsense efforts of Ike's mom. Maryam's not happy about being on bed rest again, but she's relieved that her doctors have been able to stop her early labor and keep the baby in her stomach. We know that every day counts. Every day, the baby gets stronger and more able to thrive in the greater world.

That's how I feel about myself, too. In the seven months I've been here, in the four months I've been Ike's wife, I've gotten so much stronger. America has infiltrated my soul and allowed me to grow, to blossom, to bloom. Ike has helped me be the very best version of myself, the best person I'm capable of being. That's what real love does—it inspires.

He flashes his trademark grin at me. "Favorite food?"

I smile back—he knows I know the answer. "Lasagna. My favorite animal?"

His smile broadens. "Old Sport, of course. Do you think at this point there's anything we don't know about each other?"

We spend a minute staring into each other's eyes, looking for anything new, anything unexpected, but our knowledge of each other is complete. We've done our homework. We've been tested—by Ike's parents, by Jenna, by the considerable challenge of opening a business together—and we've flourished. Despite my nervousness about tomorrow's interview, I feel certain of its outcome.

We've already triumphed.

Tomorrow is just a formality, just one more beautiful day in what will be a lifetime of beautiful days.

Chapter 24

It's almost morning.

The big day.

I don't feel quite so invincible anymore.

I feel like I want to cower in the corner, like I want to slink away in shame. Who am I to ask for refuge? How do I deserve this chance more than the millions of others who want their freedom, too, but who'll never have an opportunity?

This is my scared self talking, the one I thought I'd banished. She came back in the darkest hours of the night, after Ike was asleep, after the whole world was asleep. Old Sport and I snuck outside and curled up on a patio chair. The moon was full, the air perfect, and as I looked around Rose's backyard, which she lights at night with white holiday lights and which she has so graciously shared with us, I would have given anything to freeze the moment, to hang suspended forever in the beautiful limbo of what has been and what might yet be. We all have those moments, I think—those perfect moments when we realize we could die right then and it would be okay, for we've had our happiness. We've had our moments of glory, and we realize they're enough, that no one's promised us an entire lifetime of them.

It was last night that I finally felt as if I understood my mother, and understood, too, why she doesn't fight to come back. It's because she already had her once-upon-a-time. She already had her happily-ever-after. She already had as much as anyone ever has the right to expect, and much more than most people will ever get.

I have loved it here so much.

I fall asleep before the darkness becomes dawn, and when the alarm sounds and Ike reaches for me with his warm, sure hand and suggests we have good-luck sex before our interview, I tell him I can't, that I think I might throw up.

"I have a bad feeling about today, Ike."

He pulls me close and shushes me. "That's just your fear talking."

But I'm not so sure. There's a difference between fear and dread, and this is dread, the same feeling I'd get in Tehran when I'd find myself alone in an alley with a group of low-class men, anticipating with certainty the jeering and jostling that never failed to follow. Fear is something to overcome, but dread is something to be endured, and that's how I feel now. Today is going to be horrible, and it can't be avoided, and I'll never meet Maryam's baby and I'll never bear Ike's children, and knowing this, I begin to cry—tearlessly, so the interviewer won't see the evidence of my sorrow. I won't give him that satisfaction.

Ike holds me and kisses me and whispers that it's going to be all right. I don't have the heart to tell him it's *not* going to be all right. I let him comfort me; I let him have his last moments of hope.

When we can stay in bed no longer, I go through the motions of showering, dressing, and making myself pretty, even though I feel completely dull inside, like a used-up, punched-around floppy doll. Ike continues to think it's just nerves, and I continue to let him, and he chats casually to help put me at ease, looking handsomely American in pressed khakis and a black polo shirt.

Oh, how I've loved him.

We join Rose for orange juice and muffins. I don't eat much, and I can tell she's worried about me. I clasp her to me as we're leaving, since you never know when you'll say the last good-bye. I've heard stories that if you fail your immigration interview, they can take you away immediately. It doesn't usually happen, I'm told, but it can, and so I embrace her extra tight and breathe her in and try to memorize the feel of her curved shoulders, the old-lady-soft skin that covers her jawbone, the creaky, fragile bones that often cause her pain.

When we separate, her eyes are moist. "You'll be fine, Tami. I'll see you soon."

I won't be fine. If I fail the interview, I lose my Rose.

If I fail the interview, I lose everything.

"I'll see you soon," I tell her, wishing so much it were true.

The office where we're to be interviewed is near the airport, and the drive takes a few minutes longer than we anticipated because of a bad car wreck on Kino Parkway. The VW bug didn't stand a chance against the semitrailer truck. Still, we arrive fifteen minutes early. We go through the security screening inside the entrance, and Ike takes my hand as we walk to the waiting-room lobby. He's got an extra spring in his step. In his mind, this all turns out well—there is no other possible outcome. He mentions a ski trip he'd like us to take in February, at a resort in Utah. I tell him yes, I'd love to go. I let him keep up the pretense because this is one of his qualities that I love most: his American optimism.

The waiting room is large and empty, and we sit on an ugly wooden bench, and I'm certain we're being watched, that there are cameras or one-way mirrors with powerful unseen eyes behind them, judging us from a distance. Everything we say feels false. *Did you pay that invoice for the electrician? . . . Yes, I did. . . . Remind me we need to pick up milk on the way home. . . . Pick up milk on the way home . . . very funny, buster. . . .* What has always been natural between us now feels forced. It's as if we're playacting at being married.

Tiny bits of nervous sweat break out along my hairline and I press my fingertips into it, trying to make it look like I'm smoothing back my hair. On my lap is a binder I've put together of all the documents we might need, such as our marriage certificate, bank statements, credit card statements, the lease to the guesthouse, the leasing contract for Common Grounds. Everything has both our names on it. I also have pictures of us together, a scrapbook of sorts—of our Elvis-impersonator wedding in Las Vegas, of us lying on the beach in San Diego, of us painting the coffee shop (we stuck with Ike's color choice). There's one of me on the back of Ike's scooter. There's another of us on our bicycles. There's one of us having a Persian dinner at Maryam's, and another at one of Ike's Texas Hold 'Em nights, and several from the party we threw when we were naming the coffee shop and both our families (except for Ike's mother) were there. I flip through the binder, trying to see the photographs through the eyes of the interviewer, and no matter how hard I try, I see nothing suspicious, nothing other than two people in love with life and with each other.

Ten o'clock comes and goes. Ike hates to be late, hates to be kept waiting—it makes him snippy—and yet we are. He tries to sit perfectly still, but his left leg shakes, imperceptibly to the eye but not to me, as my leg is pressed against his. I put my hand on his thigh to steady him.

"Are you nervous?" I whisper.

"About what?" he asks with a smile, slipping his hand into mine. His is warm and safe and it's the hand I want to hold for the rest of my life.

After a thirty-minute wait, a pale-faced Hispanic man with an unfortunate haircut appears in the doorway of the waiting room. "Soroush?"

Quickly, we rise. "That's us," Ike says. "We're Soroush."

The man nods a greeting. "I'm Cesar Hernandez."

He doesn't look mean. I couldn't say he looks nice, necessarily, but he doesn't look mean, either. A layer or two away from sloppy, he wears navy pants that have been through the wash too many times, tattered loafers, and a less-than-white oxford shirt, open-necked, no tie. He offers no hand for a handshake. I wonder if he was born here or south of the border, and whether that matters in how he'll make his decision.

We follow him down the hallway to his office, where he gives us the meaningless smile of a bureaucrat and offers us each a chair. He sits behind his desk, while we're on the other side, across from him. He flips open a file folder and scans its contents. My body is so tense I feel as if all my muscles have locked up, and I'm afraid to even look at Ike. We've waited so long for this day, and now it's here, and is it really happening? *This is it. This is everything.* This man—this Mr. Hernandez with the bad haircut—will decide the fate of my marriage, the fate of my life. He has such power over us. Who is he? Does he have a wife? Does he think people are basically good or basically not so good?

He looks up and catches my eye. "Nervous?"

"A little bit," I say, giving him my best Julia Roberts smile.

"That's natural." He almost seems to fall for my smile but then catches himself and shifts his attention to Ike.

"So," he says. "Tell me how you and Tamila met."

For this question, Ike is well prepared. No matter how many times he tells the story of how we met, he never loses his emotional undertone, and he doesn't lose it now, either. He tells Mr. Hernandez how he saw me for the first time that day at Starbucks, when I was hot and thirsty and limping from my new boots as I walked to English class. *She was a vision of beauty,* he tells Mr. Hernandez, *a disheveled vision of beauty.* I can't help but laugh. Only to him. I was so nervous, on my own in America for the first time, and Ike was the first American man I spoke to. It was a conversation filled with confusion—he gave me a sample of tea and I didn't understand it was free. There's always a price, right? I kept trying to pay, but Ike kept telling me no. He retells the story sweetly—Mr. Hernandez smiles as he listens!—and then Ike's voice slows and deepens as he explains how he noticed my terror of the policemen who approached me, and how he made sure I was okay afterward, and how he offered to help me practice my English after he got off work. *And that,* Ike says, *was the start of a beautiful friendship.*

Mr. Hernandez idly confirms some of the details from our application—that my sister has been in the U.S. for a long time, that I lived here when I was a small child, that my sister's a citizen.

He looks up at me again. "And you like it here?"

"Very much, yes. I'm very happy here."

"And you'd like to stay." He says this as a statement, not a question.

"Oh, yes," I say. "Yes, please."

He smiles. "What was your intention when you first came on your tourist visa?"

This is the tricky part. I'm careful to keep my eyes on

him, careful not to look at Ike. "I came to visit my sister. It had been a very long time since I'd seen her."

"So your intention was strictly for a visit?"

The top of my scalp feels prickly. I'd like to scratch it, but is a scratch more than just a scratch at a time like this? "Yes," I say, intertwining my fingers to help me resist the urge to scratch. "I came here only for a visit."

"You intended to go back when your visa expired?"

"Yes," I say.

"And yet here you are." His tone now is not as friendly.

Ike reaches for my hand. "I wouldn't let her go."

"What did she offer you?"

"I beg your pardon?" Ike says.

"Nothing," I say.

"You offered love and devotion," Ike corrects me. "That's not nothing."

But somehow, I don't think this is what Mr. Hernandez means.

"Tell me how your marriage came about," he says to me.

"Sure," I say. We've practiced this, too. "I'd gone to Lake Havasu and then Las Vegas with my friends from my English class, and it was very much fun, and we were in the hotel room before we went out for the night, and there was a knock on the door, and it was Ike. He'd gone to my sister's house to see me—to propose—and when I wasn't there, he drove straight to the airport and flew to Las Vegas to find me."

"Sounds romantic," Mr. Hernandez says.

"It was," I say.

What *really* happened is that my engagement to the horrible Masoud ended the day of what was to be our wedding. Ardishir went back to Haroun to see if he was still willing to marry me, but he said no. We bought my ticket back to Iran, and I left on the trip to Lake Havasu and then Las Vegas with my friends, a farewell trip. While I was gone, Maryam went to Ike and explained my visa situation. Ike then flew to Las Vegas and proposed much as I already described. But I change some of those details, and some, I omit. The way I tell it, I make it sound like a scene from a movie—which, really, is what it felt like and how I choose to remember it.

For a long, awkward moment after I tell this story, Mr. Hernandez says nothing. And then he asks Ike, "Is this all true?"

Ike nods. "All of Tami's friends were there, so we have witnesses if you need them."

"Why the rush to get married?" Mr. Hernandez asks. "You hadn't known her very long."

"That's easy," Ike says. "Because I was—and still am—completely, madly in love with her. I had a limited window of opportunity, right? If she went back to Iran, I'd lose her forever. That wasn't an acceptable outcome. It was either marry her or live without her. Like I said, it was an easy choice."

"What did your parents think when you got married so suddenly?" Mr. Hernandez asks.

Mrs. Hanson. What did she do? Sweat breaks out on my hairline again. *Mustn't wipe it.* I keep a doll's smile on my face, like this is not at all a disturbing direction we're heading. *Mrs. Hanson loves me! Everything's fine!* This is what my doll's smile says.

Unfortunately, it's not what Ike says.

"I can't say they were thrilled," he says. "But everyone who knows Tami comes to love her. They just wanted to make sure I knew what I was doing. I told them I'd never been more sure of anything in my life."

Mr. Hernandez accepts Ike's answer with a nod. "And when you proposed, I assume you were under the impression that Ms. Soroush loved you as well? That she loved you as you loved her?"

"What does *that* mean?" Ike says. "Of course she did."

"Did she offer you money in exchange for marrying her? Such as . . . oh, I don't know . . . money for the business you hoped to establish?"

Mrs. Hanson told him this!

Ike sits straight, then leans forward and rests his hand on Mr. Hernandez's desk, tapping it with his index finger. "She offered to love, honor, and cherish me." His voice is steely. "It was an offer I'd be an idiot to refuse."

But Mr. Hernandez gives him a look that suggests maybe it's the opposite—that Ike would have been smart to refuse my affections. He waits an endless minute before asking in a matter-of-fact, gotcha voice, "Do you think Ms. Soroush loved you more than she loved her other fiancés?"

Other fiancés.

"Excuse me?" Ike sounds very far away from me.

Other fiancés. Other fiancés.

Mr. Hernandez repeats his question. "Do you think Ms. Soroush loved you more than she loved her other fiancés?"

Only one. I only had the one, and how does he know this? Maybe he's testing us. Maryam warned that they might go fishing for information. She said be careful. She said stick to the story.

"I did not have fiancés," I say.

"It's okay, Tami," Ike says. "It's nothing to be ashamed of."

"So you knew about them?" Mr. Hernandez asks.

This could be a trick! I shout a warning to Ike in my mind, but he doesn't hear.

"I knew about them, yes."

"You knew at the time you married her?"

Ike lowers his chin and considers the question. He keeps his hand on the desk and with his shoulders so strong, but bent like this, he looks like a wounded warrior, but only for a moment. Soon, he looks up and makes confident eye contact with Mr. Hernandez. "Yes. I did."

"It didn't bother you? She had more fiancés in the span of three months than most people have in a lifetime. She's either extremely fickle, or . . ." Mr. Hernandez raises an eyebrow. To me, he says, "You left out quite a large part of the story."

"Excuse me, please," I say. "I don't know what you're talking about."

"*Of course* it bothered me," Ike says. "But you've got to know Tami. You've got to know the situation. There was more going on than meets the eye. There were a lot of cultural factors at play that wouldn't, at first glance, make sense to an outsider."

"I deal with cultural issues all day, every day," Mr. Hernandez says. "I'm well aware of differing cultural mores regarding marriage."

"Well, then you understand," Ike says. "That's what this was. Her family's very traditional. They were trying to arrange a marriage for her, and she wanted no part of it. That's it. End of story."

"Oh." Mr. Hernandez chuckles. "There's quite a bit more to the story."

"There's not," I say. "I promise there's not."

"Are you aware of the consequences for providing false information in this interview?" he says.

"It doesn't matter," Ike says. "We're telling you the truth."

Mr. Hernandez raises an eyebrow and asks me, "So your family wanted you to get married? They wanted you to get married and to stay in America, is that right?"

"Yes," I say. "That's right. But I . . . I didn't . . ."

"You can't hold someone responsible for the behavior of their family members," Ike says.

"I was going back to Iran," I say. "I promise I was. I have my ticket right here; would you like to see it?" I make a move to find it in the binder, this beautiful binder that contains the proof of our marriage, the proof of our love, but Mr. Hernandez waves for me to stop. He has no interest in it.

"I'd rather see your ticket to Chicago," he says. "Did you bring *that* with you?"

I gasp. *He wasn't just fishing for information. He already knows!*

"Chicago?"

"Yes, Chicago. The ticket I'm referring to is the one your fiancé, Masoud Farkhi, purchased for you. Remember him? You were supposed to go to Chicago with him after your wedding, the one that was to take place just days before your visa expired?"

How, how, how does he know about Masoud???

I open the binder and locate my ticket to Iran. I pull it out of its protective sleeve and hand it across the desk to Mr. Hernandez. "I was going back. See? My ticket cost several thousand dollars. I wouldn't have bought it if I didn't intend to use it."

"Mr. Fakrhi spent several thousand dollars on a wedding ring," he says. "Surely, he wouldn't have bought it if *he* didn't intend to use it. Would you like to see the receipt for that? I have it."

No. No, I wouldn't.

He's been in contact with Masoud?

"This isn't how it looks on paper." Ike's voice trembles. "You've got to understand Tami, and then it makes sense. She's super shy, super polite, and she finds it very difficult to stand up for herself. And her family's tough! Her sister's really pushy. But she said no. To her credit, she finally said no. It was late in the game, granted, but she did, and it was a huge moment for her. She would rather have gone back to Iran than marry someone she didn't love. I find that honorable. *Very* honorable."

Mr. Hernandez listens to what Ike has to say; then he looks at me. "So you're telling me you're the victim of your very traditional family, and you think I shouldn't judge you based on what they were trying to do. Is that right? Is that what you're saying?"

"Yes, please," I say. "This is what I think."

He gives me a long, considering look.

"All right," he says finally. "Fair enough."

I let out the breath I hadn't realized I'd been holding. "Thank you!" I say. "You're very kind. You're very decent."

"Not so fast." He pulls out a single sheet of paper from his folder. "I'll judge you on this."

Ike takes the paper that's offered and reads it, expressionless. My chair is far enough back that I can't see what it is.

"Did you know about *this*?" Mr. Hernandez asks him. "I can't imagine you think *this* is honorable."

Ike sniffs, then hands the paper to me. I search his eyes for our common ground, but I can't find it anymore. When I see what's on the paper, I know why.

Single Persian woman looking for a good man to marry. Save me from current prospect, an obsessive-compulsive neat freak! Visa expires in April, but desperately want to stay in America! Marriage of convenience strictly okay. I'm young, sexy, will look great by your side. Save me, marry me!

My eyes sink closed. I'm dead. It's over.

"Why don't you read it out loud?" Mr. Hernandez suggests, but there is absolutely no way I'll read this out loud. I can't even stand to read it silently.

"I didn't write this!" I say. "It was my friend Eva. She did this without my knowledge."

"You're not one to take responsibility for your actions, are you?" Mr. Hernandez says.

You could balance a stack of coins on Ike's shoulders. They're that rigid.

"How did you find this?" he says. "I'm sorry, but I have to ask. I have to know."

"I was wondering when someone would." Mr. Hernandez smiles. "As it turns out, we received a phone call about the two of you. We received a tip on the fraud hotline. It seems that someone doesn't think very highly of what you've done."

Ike's mother.

I still have nightmares about her on my patio in her blue linen dress. She brought her deceitful banana bread and rummaged through her bag and pulled out that business card and showed me the back of it. *See this? This is the phone number to Immigration Enforcement. This is the number I call to have you deported.*

She did it. She called. She did exactly what she said she'd do.

Stunned, I look to Ike.

Poor Ike.

His eyes are closed and he's shaking his head. He can't believe it, can't believe his own mother would do something so awful to her own son. But I can, for I know better than he that a mother's love can be toxic sometimes, even when it's well intentioned.

Chapter 25

"Ike's mother has always hated me," I say to Mr. Hernandez. "She's done some horrible things, and she's not as nice as she seems. Please, you can't believe what she's told you."

"Tami," Ike says.

"What?" I say. "She has, Ike. You don't even know all she's done."

"*Who called the hotline?*" Ike demands. "Was it my mother?"

Mr. Hernandez smiles. "Haroun Mehdi called the hotline."

Haroun!

I look at Ike, astounded. "Haroun's *crazy*," I say. "He's—"

"He says he was your fiancé."

"He was never my fiancé! You can't trust *anything* he says. He's—"

"He says he was." Mr. Hernandez shrugs. "I tend to believe him. He was humiliated when you left him for Mr. Fakhri. He was so upset, apparently, that he went to significant lengths to track him down. It seems they bonded over their broken hearts, or at least over their failed engagements."

"Please, can you just—" I practically throw my photo album at Mr. Hernandez. "*We love each other.* Ike and I love each other. Can't you see that?"

I hate crying. I wish I wasn't, but maybe it's a good thing because I know most men can't stand to see women cry, and maybe this is why Mr. Hernandez finally is willing to look through my photographs—at the pictures of us in San Diego, of me in a bikini for the first time in my life. Of us dancing in the coffee shop, the photo taken on a timer, one of my first slow dances with a man (the other time was also with Ike, at a country-western bar). Of Old Sport, the first dog I've ever liked, smothering me on our patio chair. Of us at Gates Pass, watching the sunset from the back of Ike's pickup. Out at a bar with my ESL friends that night we saw Danny sing in his band.

"This is a *life* we have together," I say. "Can't you see that?"

Mr. Hernandez finally looks up. "I believe you love your husband," he says, nodding. "And I believe your husband loves you."

"Oh!" I sigh, so relieved. *"Thank you."*

"But that doesn't mean you can use a tourist visa to get married so you can apply for residency."

"That wasn't what I did," I say. "It really, honestly wasn't."

"The evidence suggests otherwise." He gestures to his file folder. "We have at least two known fiancés prior to your marriage to Mr. Hanson here. We have records of money changing hands." Upon seeing my confusion, he holds up a bank record of a money transfer from Masoud to Ardishir, my dowry of sorts. "We have plane tickets to Chicago bought with his credit card, in both your names. We have a contract spelling out when and under what conditions your residency application was to be filed. We have an admission on his part—"

"I didn't sign that contract!"

"But you considered it," he said. "At the very least, you considered it, and that speaks to motive."

"But—"

"And we have that very damning ad you ran on the singles Web site."

"I didn't run that ad."

Mr. Hernandez holds up his hand. "We don't need to go around and around on this. It's okay. I have the information I need. Thank you very much for your time, and you can expect to receive our decision in the mail within a few days."

Just like that. He hands back my binder.

"But please—"

"I have my next appointment."

"We have more to talk about." Ike's voice is thick. "There's so much you don't understand about Tami. If only you knew her—"

"I know enough to know she's a lovely person," Mr. Hernandez says.

"Look at that binder," Ike says desperately, taking it from me and trying to hand it back to Mr. Hernandez, who doesn't accept it. "Look at the stuff in there. We *live* together. We have a *bank account* together. We're opening a *business* together—in days, we're opening it! We're together *all the time.* Our marriage—" After a pause, he continues softly. "Our marriage is the most real thing I know. It's the only thing I'm sure of. The only thing in this crappy world that makes any sense to me."

I almost cry out. Since when does Ike think the world's crappy?

I remember his father's words: *Ike still thinks the world is good. Sometimes it takes just one very bad, horrible experience to make a person question that. And I don't want you to be that thing.*

But I am.

I am that thing.

"Please," I beg. "Isn't there anything we can do?" I search my brain for something that might help our case. A vaginal exam, like that woman from Canada had to get?

No! But there must be something.

"I know!" I say. "We have tattoos! See, look. Both of us." I jump up and lower the waistband of my skirt to show Mr. Hernandez my heart tattoo with Ike's name inside. "Ike, show him yours, too."

Ike looks at me like I'm crazy. "Why would I show him my tattoo?"

"We wouldn't have gotten them if we didn't love each other." I look to Mr. Hernandez. "They're permanent! They're forever!"

He laughs. "I can't grant you residency based on a tattoo."

"But, please. Ike's my family, even more than my family's my family. Please, Mr. Hernandez!"

He sighs. "Have a seat."

Quickly, hopefully, I do.

"I'm going to tell you a story," he says. "About the day my daughter took her test to get her driver's license. Do you have your driver's license? Here, I mean?"

I shake my head no.

"Well, there's a written portion and then there's the road test," he says. "My daughter did great on the written portion. She aced it, and she did great on the road test, too, except for one small mistake. When she was parallel parking, she scraped the side of the car in front of her, the one she was trying to fit in behind. Just barely, she hit it. It didn't even leave a scratch. Well, the instructor, he was really nice about it, but he said, you know, that as a matter of policy, if you strike a car on your road test, no matter how slight, there's simply no way they pass you. There's just . . ." He shrugs. "No way. You see what I'm saying?" He eyes me. "In driver's test terms, you're lurching down the road here, hitting virtually every car in your path, whether it's parked or moving. One of these mistakes alone might have disqualified you—fiancé number one. Fiancé number two. Money being exchanged. Internet ads being placed. A rushed Vegas wedding. You can say what you want, and I do believe you love each other—I'll grant you that. But all evidence indicates that your intentions were in violation of U.S. immigration law, and that's what

I have to base my judgment on. You understand? It's not personal."

It's not personal.

Do I understand this?

The funny thing is, I do understand. If a country gives you a tourist visa, they want you to come as a tourist, and then go home. That's what you promise when you sign up for the visa. It's a reasonable process and a reasonable law, and I appreciate the fact that he's being so . . . reasonable. I don't like his decision. I hate it, but at least it's not *arbitrary*. This is all I want for Iran. If Iran would just have reasonable laws and enforce them reasonably, none of us would ever want to leave. It's our home, and we want to be proud of it. But instead, we're made to feel like exiles in our own country. All a person wants is to be treated with decency. That's all anybody wants. So *thank you*, Mr. Immigration Official, for treating me in a way I've never been treated by my own government. Thank you, even though you're telling me I must go.

"I understand," I tell him.

"Well, I don't." Ike's eyes are blazing. "She's not a threat to anyone. She's a *great person*."

"I'm not saying she's not a good person," Mr. Hernandez says. "But that's not what I make my judgment on. Now, I almost never do this, but you're both very nice people, and here's the thing—I have never before told anyone they've failed their interview while they're here in my office. There's just no point. It'd be a nightmare. Constant headaches. It might even be dangerous for me. So I keep the interview pleasant and smooth, and I send a letter with my decision after they've left. You see why I do this?"

We failed. He's telling us we've failed. Oh, poor Ike. His jaw is clenched. His fists are clenched. His heart—that's clenched, too. *I'm so sorry, Ike.*

When neither of us answers, Mr. Hernandez continues. "You'll be receiving your letter in a few days. When you do, you have a major decision to make." He looks at me. "You can accept it and leave the country voluntarily. If you do this, then in ten years' time, you can try again. You can file a visa of some sort. Tourist or marriage or otherwise, and it'll be considered with no prejudice against you because of this situation."

"Ten years," I say, stunned.

"You're young," he says. "It's not as long as it seems."

Ten years. I look over at Ike. He might have gray hair by then. He'll certainly have children by then—several children, with another woman, another wife! And they'll be so beautiful and he'll be such a good dad, and he'll have his chain of coffee shops. And me? What will I have?

"Don't send me back to Iran," I plead to Mr. Hernandez. "A *day* there feels like a death sentence—ten years would kill me."

I'd be like Maman, all the time seeking refuge in my bedroom, yearning for days I can't get back.

"We're going to appeal," Ike says. "You can't do this. You don't understand us. You don't know what we mean to each other. We mean *everything* to each other."

"I believe you," Mr. Hernandez says. "And I'm still denying your application for residency, based on the grounds of marriage fraud."

"We'll fight this," Ike says. "We'll go to court, and we'll fight."

"You absolutely will not win," Mr. Hernandez says. "Your appeal will be denied, and at that point, your wife's deportation won't be considered voluntary, and she'll never be able to come back, not under any type of visa, no matter how much time has passed."

Baby Hope. I'll never get to see Baby Hope.

This world, it's too cruel.

"And *you*—" Mr. Hernandez looks sternly at Ike. "If you go to court, you might not get off so easy."

"How is this getting off easy?" Ike's trying very hard not to shout. "How is *losing my wife* getting off easy?"

"You could be sent to prison."

I gasp.

"Bullshit," Ike says.

"Being a participant in a fraudulent marriage is a felony offense."

"Falling in love?" Ike says. "That's a crime?"

"Ike." I reach to take his hand, but he pulls it close to himself. His eyes are the same color as my perfume bottle of sand, a splintered-glass shade of blue.

"Ike didn't do anything wrong," I say. "Please, you can't send him to jail!"

"I'm not sending him to jail," Mr. Hernandez says. "But he was an accessory to what the evidence suggests is a fraudulent marriage, entered into for the purpose of gaining U.S.

residency. It doesn't often happen that the U.S. citizen is jailed, but if you get a judge who's having a particularly bad day, it certainly could. So I advise you to think long and hard about what you'll do next."

But there's no need—no need to think long or hard. I know already we can't go to court—Ike can't put his future at risk.

So that's it. Stunned, I sit there a moment longer.

That's really it. America doesn't want me. As much as I love America, America does not love me back.

Part Three

GO AS FAR AS YOU CAN SEE, AND WHEN YOU GET THERE, YOU'LL SEE FARTHER

Emma Lazarus, "The New Colossus"

Not like the brazen giant of Greek fame,
With conquering limbs astride from land to land;
Here at our sea-washed, sunset gates shall stand
A mighty woman with a torch, whose flame
Is the imprisoned lightning, and her name
Mother of Exiles. From her beacon-hand
Glows world-wide welcome; her mild eyes command
The air-bridged harbor that twin cities frame.
"Keep, ancient lands, your storied pomp!" cries she
With silent lips. "Give me your tired, your poor,
Your huddled masses yearning to breathe free,
The wretched refuse of your teeming shore.
Send these, the homeless, tempest-tost to me,
I lift my lamp beside the golden door!"

Chapter 26

Maman Joon, Tehran

He comes to me, my husband.

He comes to me with quite a story.

Maryam is pregnant, he says, just weeks away from giving birth.

Hamid! This is wonderful news. Oh, this is lovely.

She has been hospitalized, he tells me, and holds up his hands to halt the traffic of my panic. She's fine; it's only that the baby is impatient—she is ready to come screeching into the world, a new American citizen, to be born in the land of the free.

My husband loves this phrase, *the land of the free.*

When he tells me this, I'm in my mother's cane-backed

chair near the window, warming myself by the stale sun of the late afternoon. I've been looking out upon the courtyard, at the stone fountain that hasn't worked in forever, and at my geraniums in their flower boxes, which thrive no matter how neglectful I've been. He has pulled a chair over from the dining room and set it close enough so that our knees touch. He looks young today. Not so old. He looks like a man in his mid-fifties, which, in fact, he is.

This is wonderful, Hamid. So wonderful for Maryam.

How he came to know this before me, I won't ask. In a marriage, in a life, some questions are best left unspoken.

It's great for us, too, he says. We're to be grandparents, Azar! Grandparents at last!

The untainted joy in his eyes makes him seem a stranger. We'll be grandparents from afar. We'll call from across the ocean. This is not what my husband wants; I know this. And so what is the reason for such purity in his joy?

I have more news, he says. In his hand is a thick brown envelope, which he holds out to me. I have more very good news.

My heart quickens. Is it Tami? This is a big day for her; she has her immigration interview today. Do you have good news about Tami Joon?

He shakes his head, none yet. The good news is about us, he says. For a change, I have good news about us. Open it. See what's inside.

My heart falters, skips a beat. There's a gap between what I want and what can be, and the gap has been there for so long I hardly notice it anymore, except in moments like these—moments that provoke hope against all better reason.

Tell me, Hamid. My eyes hurt today. They hurt too much to read.

A veil of disappointment descends over his eyes. Could you please for once just do as I wish?

Then bring me my glasses, I say. (Let nothing ever be easy.)

He rises to retrieve them, starts away but then turns back. They're our visas, he says. They're airplane tickets with our names on them. Inside that envelope is our way out. For once, we finally have good news for ourselves.

What's this? I say, my mind a fog. I've heard him; I just don't understand. Every year for very many years, we traveled to the embassy in Turkey and applied for visas to America. Every year for very many years, we were always turned down, with no reason given. We never told our children we made this annual journey, for it was best, we always thought, that we suffer in silence when we received the inevitable rejection. In recent years, we stopped going. It seemed there was no point. Yet a few months ago, Hamid wanted for us to try again. Poor Hamid, burdened with hope. I said no, Hamid. Our life is here. This is not a life, he said.

Maryam is pregnant, he says again. And you're depressed, and I love you, but I can't go on this way. I'm going to America, he says. We got our visas, and I'm going to be with our daughters, and I'd like very much for you to come with me.

Meaning, he will go without me if he must.

What does a wife say to something like this?

While mine was not, his visa was once approved—once and only once. He could have left long ago, but he stayed.

He stayed.

He stayed for me.

And now you should go for him. This is whispered to me; I'm not sure if the voice is mine or perhaps my mother's, but in either case, it's a forgotten voice, and yet familiar all the same.

He could have left long ago.

Maryam didn't want to tell you about the baby because she worried you'd bring bad luck, he says now. I know this, of course. It's why I didn't ask.

She thinks I'm cursed, I say.

But you're not, Azar Joon.

Hamid takes the envelope back from me and sits back down. He looks older again, resigned. He thinks he knows what I'll say. I'd like to surprise him, to see for a second time today pure joy in his warm caramel eyes. I reach for his hand, and absently, he strokes the back of my palm. He's been doing this since ours were teenage hands. His still look young. They're still strong, still capable. Mine are old-lady hands now, too much bone and not enough flesh, and yet he caresses them as he always has. It's perhaps the one thing about us that hasn't changed.

Will you help me? I ask. If I decide to do this, can I count on your help, Hamid? I'm afraid of everything now.

His throat thickens; he cannot speak. He nods, my kindred spirit, my kind heart. Yes, he will help me. Thank God for this, because I've been paralyzed for so long. Anchored to my sorrow like a sunken ship.

For so long I've felt like nothing, Hamid. I don't know what I'm good for anymore.

He looks at me, and I wonder what he sees. The poets would have embraced me once, but I'm not pretty anymore. My eyes used to dance, but now they're only half alive. And my soul—well, it's been nearly three decades since I sent it away, a green balloon on a lonely, icy-skied day. A balloon untethered rises; it does not return; it cannot be captured. It is carried away by God's wind and eventually dies its own death, on its own terms. In this way, it remains forever free. Lying on a cement prison floor, knowing what they'd do to me, I kissed my soul good-bye. I let myself go. What they did in Evin Prison, they didn't do to me, but to the shackled, blindfolded body of a soulless stranger. It was no one I knew.

My daughter in America is reading *The Great Gatsby*, struggling with that common question: Was Gatsby, who was in love with not a woman but a memory, great like the title of the story suggests? Who cares if he was great, I have wanted to say to her. He was American—always dreaming, always reaching, always believing the best is yet to be. That's what Americans do. That's what makes them great.

When I left America, I brought back with me a book called *Atlas Shrugged*. So very different from *Gatsby*! I thought it was brilliant, once upon a time; I was so easy to persuade back then, so easy to be convinced. When someone tells you through their actions, through their laws, that you are worthless, that you have no value, that you have nothing unique to contribute to the world, it's tempting to say, *That is fine.* If you feel that way, I will stop trying. I will not vote in your facade of a democracy. I will produce nothing for you. I will not, by any degree of participation, give the impression that I support what you are doing to my country. And while it's unfortunate that you don't value the beauty that is me, that is fine, because I no longer wish to give it to you, anyway. I will refuse to contribute. Refuse to create. Refuse to dream. All I will do is shrug—at you and at your hypocrisy.

But when we think this way, who, in the end, is harmed the most?

You are. I am.

Stalled, the whole world is.

There's this baby, now, on the other side of the world. Not content to remain tucked away in my daughter's womb—not even born yet!—she fights for her independence. Already, I like this baby. I'm sure she could teach me a thing or two. But the question remains: What am I good for anymore? What could I teach her?

You have arms, don't you, Hamid says. Your arms can hold a baby—that's something.

I smile. That is something.

You have a voice, don't you?

Of that, I'm not so sure. It was smothered long ago.

You do, he insists. And I know that baby would love to hear you sing. You can comfort this baby when she's in need of comfort. As you used to comfort our daughters.

My vision blurs from tears. This is good; I haven't cried in many years. I sang lullabies to my daughters, and I'd like to sing to this new baby, too. I'd like to smell her baby smell and for her little fingers to vise-grip mine. I'd like her to fade to sleep with her heavy-lidded eyes locked onto my gaze. I'd like to see her toothless smile, to hear her gurgling laugh. I'd like her to adore me. I'd like to cheer her on as she wails unabashedly, demanding that her needs and wants be taken seriously. Very much, I'd like to be part of her life.

I still remember all the old lullabies, Hamid.

I know you do, he says. I know you still remember.

In his eyes, I see his love for me rekindled. I have given him a glimpse of the woman I used to be.

I take the envelope from him. My eyes are not so tired anymore. I take from it the visas, the tickets. My name is on the visa. It's really there. *It's really there.*

For so long now, America has been a meteor to me, a bright star that shoots to a place I could not follow. It has been Gatsby's green light.

But suddenly, finally—it's within my reach.

Chapter 27

I think sometimes of all the people in this polluted city. If you took away the sputtering traffic, the relentless car horns, the obscuring veils, the heavy curtains, the high walls—if you took them all away, what would you see?

You'd see everything. Peace. Desperation. Love being born. Loneliness slowly killing. You'd see music. Dancing. Laughter, pain, drugs, despair, secrets being kept and revealed. In the streets, we're all alike, all the same. That's the plan, anyway. But there are poets in the bedrooms, artists in the kitchens, lovers in the living rooms. In one of the apartments, there is a woman of fifty-five years, who yesterday would have told you she was inescapably dying in her cool, dark bedroom, dying from the inside out.

Her mother died in a cool, dark bedroom, too. From

tumors, the doctor would have said. Much of her family would have said she died a good death, at peace. But her daughter knows better. I, her daughter, know better.

When I was in prison, this was my greatest regret, that I'd caused my mother such grief. Grief is a cancer; it can kill just as surely. I came to know my mother very well while I was at Evin, my mind's eye remembering back to every mundane conversation, every ordinary dinner, every shared task of every day, of every year. Every memory strung together, seeing her, at last, as only one mother can see another. *Who will mother the mothers?* I wondered. Who *can*, except for the daughters?

And there I was, being of no use to anyone.

There may be relief, but there is no glory in death, and my mother did not die well. She died bitter. Disappointed. The world was worse when she left than when she entered it. The revolution that was supposed to be so glorious was music turned down, it was eyes to the ground, it was joy suppressed. The government became the *zanjeer zani*, the whips against our backs. My mother's country had tortured her daughter. It had sent its young men to a worthless war. It had sacrificed one nephew to battle; another had lost both legs. *They're not martyrs*, she'd say, refusing to accept the religiously convenient terms. *They're just dead boys.*

After being released from prison, like a porcelain doll I smiled unflinchingly through all the wasted words, through all the pointless questions: *What happened? How did we not see this coming? Where is the justice? What can be done?* I myself had only one question. Only to my mother could I ask, *Who will suppress the sadists?*

This is not a question that would occur to free people, or to people who've never been their victims. The police do, of course. The police and the courts and the prisons suppress the sadists. This is what happens in any normal place, in any honorable country.

The Shah was brutal, too. He sanctioned torture to keep his power, as does this newest regime, but he didn't sanction it in the name of God. He wasn't that indecent; he wasn't that clever. In the span of only a few months, Iran became a government of, by, and for the sadists. Even today, it astounds me how quickly this happened, at how quickly a country can lose its way.

When I was released from prison, like a porcelain doll I could smile through everything, except my mother's death. *Who will love me when you're gone?* I'd whisper, holding her frail hand. *Who will love me like my mother does?*

Only to her could I ask the unanswerable questions.

After her death, I was utterly alone. In spite of my husband and my children and my cousins and my dwindling group of friends, I was utterly alone. I'd look in the mirror sometimes—not as I used to as a self-absorbed girl, practicing poses and pouts for hours on end—but as a woman living a lie, as a body without a soul. I'd ask the woman in the mirror, the one with haunted eyes, the one I didn't know, *Who or what will save me now?*

Today, decades later—finally—I look at the woman in the mirror, the one with gray-black hair and a new light in her eyes. Hope is elusive; I know she still has dark moments ahead of her; and I want her to remember my admonition, and so I frown at her.

Enough, I say sternly. *Stop asking the unanswerable questions.*

You can kill yourself, asking them. And this woman, with a suitcase packed, with a new grandbaby on the way, all of a sudden has a lot to live for once again. She must go, ever forward, in search of joy.

I've lived lazily for so many years, but now that I'm days away from leaving, perhaps never to return, there is so much I have to do! There are the practical matters, such as arranging for one cousin to check on our home, and selling our car, and taking care of some banking needs. Those are tasks written on a list and checked off, one by one.

There are many other things to do in the few days before I leave, although they aren't written on a paper list, but rather within my heart. Like taking a subway to my old neighborhood, where I grew up, and walking the streets I used to walk—past Shahnaz Pahlavi, the all-girls' high school I attended, when the Shah was still in power, and going to Nonvaie, the bakery where my family always bought our bread. America doesn't have many bakeries like this, with oven pits making the bread fresh, enveloping the street with the most delicious smell. I buy a feast of bread for myself and Hamid and we enjoy it with cheese and olives, a picnic in the park. What I have for so long taken for granted now grows precious, as I see Tehran once more, finally, with the eyes of a lover saying farewell forever.

I spend several afternoons at the Tajrish bazaar to buy

gifts—a mirror with a candleholder for Tami and Ike, a gold necklace for Maryam's baby, and a silver tea set for Maryam that I will have to fit in my suitcase somehow.

I go to Behesht-e-Zahra, Tehran's big cemetery, to visit my parents' graves, buying gladiolas and two bottles of rose water from the attendant. It's windy, as it always is at the cemetery, and I pass by families gathered and by women weeping in front of gravestones. I visit my father's grave first, at the eastern part of the cemetery. He died when I was young; I hardly remember him at all. I pay my respects by washing his gravestone with the rose water, but I don't stay long. It's my mother I most want to honor; it's my mother I will miss the most.

I wash her gravestone as well, and then I find a pebble on the ground and use it to tap her gravestone three times, *tap, tap, tap*, bidding her spirit to join me. The wind stills for a lingering moment, and sharply, I sense her presence. Filled with an aching longing—how can I leave her behind, who will visit her now?—I tell her about the journey I'm soon to make, about the great-granddaughter she is soon to have, and how I hope this new baby will have my mother's kindred smile.

Maybe one day, I whisper, life will be better here and I'll bring her to visit you. I will show her how to wash your gravestone with rose water, and while she does, I'll wash it with my tears.

Maybe we'll do this, Maman. Maybe we'll do this someday.

Chapter 28

TAMI JOON

Where does a woman go when she has nowhere to go?

Where does she go when no one wants her?

This is my situation. America doesn't want me, and I don't want Iran.

You're not going back to Iran. Ike said this on the car ride home. It was pretty much all he said, besides, *I can't talk about this right now.* I heard that several times; the rest of the ride passed in brittle silence. When Ike is very upset, he needs to be alone. I understand. I try not to take it personally. I only wish that I could be with him when he needs to be alone.

He drops me off at the hospital to see Maryam. He's going to Common Grounds for what we hope is the last inspection, and after that, he's going for a few hours to his family's cabin on Mount Lemmon. He said we'd talk later, and he promised not to stay away all night.

I take the elevator to the seventh floor and walk down the too-familiar corridor to my sister's private room. She's in the recliner by the window, wearing her golden silk robe. She caresses that baby bulge of her stomach as she looks out the window and sings a song from our family's favorite movie. *Somewhere over the rainbow, way up high. There's a land that I heard of once in a lullaby.*

She's singing to the baby—to her baby, to our baby.

Somewhere over the rainbow, skies are blue. And the dreams that you dare to dream really do come true.

I listen from the doorway. Her voice, this song, takes me back to our childhood. For many years, Maryam and I slept in the same bed at night, and we'd sit up, cross-legged in the dark, after the lights were out, and she'd braid my hair like Judy Garland's was in the movie as Dorothy, and she'd sing to me. This is one of the songs she sang, and when she did, she was singing about America. America was our over-the-rainbow place, where our dreams really could come true.

I'd gladly stand in the doorway listening to her sing all day rather than tell her the bad news, but she senses my presence and turns.

"Tami! How did it go?"

"We should watch *The Wizard of Oz* soon," I say.

"We haven't watched it together in a long time, have we?" she says. "Gosh, it must be fifteen years."

I hate those flying monkeys.

"I really like that song," I say.

"If I don't sing it quietly, it's really off-key."

I smile. Yes, I remember this.

She smiles, too. "So, how did it go? How soon do you find out? I'm sure you did great!"

Maryam is glowing. Despite her incompetent cervix, pregnancy agrees with her. I hate to tell her. I hate to do this to her.

I cross the room, and when I get to her, I kiss her on both cheeks. "Are you comfortable? Would you like to get back in bed? How are you feeling today, anyway?"

She takes my hands to focus me on her question. I kneel in front of her. We speak first with our eyes, neither of us strangers to bad news about our family members.

"It didn't go so well, Maryam."

She smiles sympathetically. "You probably did better than you think."

"No, it's . . . he already told us. He denied our application."

"What? No!" Her brown eyes flash with surprise and anger. "You had everything you needed. You did everything right! I'm sure he was just—"

I hold tight to her hand. She's always been my lifeline, now I must be hers. "We failed the interview, Maryam. I didn't get my residency. I have to leave."

Sounding like a wounded animal, she howls, "NOO-OOOOOO!"

Her room is near the nurses' station, and within seconds, Noreen, Maryam's favorite nurse, is in the room.

"What happened? What's wrong?" She approaches Maryam and takes her wrist to determine her heart rate. I slip back, shaken. It's horrible to hear a loved one wail, and more horrible yet to be the one who caused it.

"My sister has to leave the country!" Maryam cries. "She's telling me she has to leave, but it can't be true!"

"Oh, no," Noreen says. "We were all sending positive thoughts your way this morning. Is there . . . There's nothing that can be done?"

"I don't think so," I say.

Noreen gives me a sympathetic look, probably the same sort she gives to dying patients, then lets go of Maryam's wrist. "Don't let your heart rate get too high," she says. "That'll cause stress for the baby, okay? Do some deep breathing. Center yourself."

Maryam nods. "I think I should get back in my bed."

Noreen stays while Maryam gets up from the recliner and climbs back into bed. I tuck close around her the peacock blue cashmere blanket she brought from home.

"This can't be happening!" Maryam says once Noreen leaves. "Why can't we ever get a break, just once?"

"The baby is our break," I remind her. "The baby is our good fortune. Really, that's the most important thing."

"But you're her aunt, and you have to be here! How is Baby Hope supposed to know you?"

I sit on the edge of her bed and reclaim her hand. "There's an appeals process, but the interviewer told us not to bother, that there's no way we'd win. He knew everything, Maryam. He had a copy of that stupid Internet ad Eva ran. He had the contract Masoud tried to make me sign. I couldn't believe it—Haroun called the fraud hotline! Haroun did this! Plus, he was in touch with Masoud!"

"The interviewer?"

"No, Haroun! Can you believe it? Doesn't he have better things to do than try to ruin my life?"

"I'm going to *kill* him," Maryam says. "That stupid, nutty, fruit-cakey man. I will kill him."

"I'll help you," I say. "How should we do it? Should we let a poisonous spider loose in his house so it crawls up his leg at night? That would be real justice!"

"I'd rather shoot him through the heart," she says. "This way, we'd see him die."

"Good point," I say. "Only he doesn't have a heart."

"This isn't *fair*!" Maryam says. "It's not right! You were lost to me for so many years. I can't lose you again!"

Her sobs are quiet, but her whole body shakes. This can't be good for the baby.

"I know, I know." I soothe her. "But you'll be so busy with Hope that you won't even have time to miss me."

"Don't say that," she sniffs. "Of course I will!"

"But it'll be different this time, with me gone. It won't be so bad, because you won't be alone."

"It's going to be a million times worse!" she says. "I can't lose my sister again!"

"Well—maybe I don't have to go so far away," I say. "I think I have an idea. I can't stay, but that doesn't mean I have to go back to Iran. I just have to leave America. And if I leave on my own—voluntarily, no challenging the decision—I can come back in ten years."

"Ten years is forever, Tami!"

"Not really," I say. "Hope would just be turning ten. That's . . . not so bad."

"But you could win in court, yes? Maybe the judge would let you stay?"

"How would I ever win?" I ask. "Is all that evidence against me going to magically disappear? They could have Haroun testify, for all I know. Maybe they'd even have Masoud fly in from Chicago. He's gay, Maryam! He has a longtime boyfriend. There's no way he was marrying me for love. The judge would just laugh in my face."

"He's gay?" Maryam's eyes widen. "You never told me that."

"I was embarrassed, that's why! I was ashamed of myself for even considering marrying someone who's gay just to get my residency. That's . . . It was *stupid.* The whole thing was so stupid, Maryam, and if I go to court and lose, Ike could go to jail."

"They're not going to send Ike to jail."

"They could," I say. "The interviewer told us it was possible, and I'd never forgive myself if that happened. And also if we lose, I'd never be able to come back to the U.S.—*never.* Is that a risk we want to take? I sure don't. This way, at least there's still hope for someday."

"Still hope for Hope." Maryam continues to sniffle but she seems to come to terms with the situation. "So where would you go? Canada?"

I nod. "That's what I'm thinking. I haven't talked to Ike about it yet, but there's a way to immigrate to Canada pretty easily—and legally—as an entrepreneur. You just have to take a certain amount of money in and use it to start a business." I cringe because I hate to ask for anything, but . . . "I know you and Ardishir have already been so generous . . ."

"This is not a bad idea," she says. "Many Iranians go to Canada. In fact, there are so many in one part of Toronto they call it Tehranto. And it's a *beautiful* city! Ardishir and I went there for a conference once. It's *beautiful.* And so much more fun than Tucson! A much bigger, more cosmopolitan city. This is a good idea, Tami! We could even buy a townhouse there, and I can spend summers there with the baby! And would you sell the coffee shop here, or would Ike fly back and forth, or what? You should keep them both, and be international entrepreneurs and have an international marriage! It'll help you come back in ten years, too, if you already have a business here. Tami, this could work! It could really work!"

My heart is pounding so hard. It so badly wants to have hope again. "I don't know if that's something Ike would want to do," I say. "He loves Tucson."

"Are you crazy?" Maryam says. "Of course he'll do it. He loves *you* a lot more than he loves Tucson!"

There it is, that flutter of hope back in my heart. "You really think?"

"Of course—why not? Look at the deal he's getting! He gets to stay with you, have his business here, start a new one in Canada—there's no downside for him, Tami."

"He does like to ski," I say, recalling how he mentioned earlier today about wanting to go skiing in Utah this winter.

"See? He could ski all winter!" she says. "And it's really not too far to visit. It's no different than if you lived in New York or Boston. It's just a long plane ride, with one or maybe two transfers. We can visit all the time, and Ike can come back and forth . . . maybe he has to stay here a few months longer than you because of the shop, but that's okay, right? That's not the end of the world. Going to jail, or being sent back to Iran—*that's* the end of the world. And then, in ten years, you can come back!"

I like this idea. I like it very much, and I think Ike might like it, too. It's more complicated than what we have now, and I know he likes things to be simple, but we can't keep what we have now, anyway. That's not an option, so . . . why not, Ike? Why not give it a try?

I'm back at home having tea in the backyard with Rose when Ike returns, looking weary and broken. I start to get up and go to him, to kiss him hello, as usual, but something about his approach stops me. He watches me warily, as if I'm someone he hardly knows. As if I'm not his wife.

Rose, on the other hand, does go to him. She pats his cheek and announces she's going inside and would he like any coffee. He says no, thank you, he doesn't feel like any coffee. He takes her chair and sits back in it with his legs spread and his fingers intertwined.

"You don't feel like coffee?" I say, smiling. "You always feel like coffee."

"Listen, Tami," he says. "We need to talk."

"We do," I agree.

"Can I ask what you're smiling for?" he says. "Did we not just attend the same immigration interview?"

"I'm smiling because . . . Ike, how would you feel about moving to Canada with me?"

I lean forward to convey my excitement, but he does the opposite, startling backward.

"Canada?" he says. "Are you serious?"

I can't tell from how he said it if he meant it in a good or a bad way. I decide he meant it in a good way. *Are you serious!?!?!*

"Sure! We could open a coffee shop there. A whole chain, maybe. It's colder—people probably drink more coffee in Canada, wouldn't you think? I talked with Maryam, and they're willing to lend us the money—we were thinking Toronto, but, really, anywhere's fine. We could go wherever you want, and then in ten years, we move back here. What do you think?"

Ike is expressionless. "What about the shop here?"

"We'll hire a manager for it."

"With what money?" he says. "We weren't going to be drawing a salary for at least six months, probably longer, remember? We might have money in the bank, but that's all to carry the cost of the coffee shop until it can carry itself. We need that for cash flow. We can't afford to hire a manager. You know perfectly well that we're in the sweat-equity phase of the business."

"Ardishir will help out with the money," I say.

"Wouldn't it be easier for you to go to court and appeal the decision?"

I was afraid he'd say this. "We won't win, Ike."

"You don't know that." Now he's the one who sits forward, and I'm the one who shrinks back. "We try again, and we keep on trying. That's what we do."

"You want to be arrested, Ike? You want to put your future at risk like that?"

"No one's going to arrest me," he says. "Hernandez was just trying to scare us."

"Well, it worked."

"Yeah, but it doesn't take much to scare you," he says. "That's pretty much your standard operating procedure, remember?"

Excuse me?

"I knew you were going to do this," he says. "I sat up there on the porch at the cabin, and I just knew it. I knew you wouldn't fight. I couldn't come up with any possible circumstance under which you'd agree to go to court. You're going to slink out of town like a beaten-down animal, and you're going to go through the same thing again somewhere else. Because wherever you go, there you are, Tami. Until you learn to fight, you're never going to get what you want."

I will not cry. *I will not cry.*

"If I thought I had any chance of winning, Ike, I'd fight with everything I had."

"You *do* have a chance of winning," he says. "That's what

an appeal is—it's a fresh look at the situation. Hernandez didn't even . . ." He shakes his head in disgust. "Some judge out there is going to look at the fact that we're crazy in love with each other, and we have a business together. We have contracts together. Leases. We have family in town. You're not going to be a drain on society. You're not some sort of risk to the country, Tami. There's got to be some sane judge who's going to recognize that!"

"That's not what this is about," I say. "It's about taking advantage of someone's generosity. That's what I did. The government didn't have to give me a visa in the first place, but they did. They said, hey, yes, sure. You can come see your sister for three months, absolutely! Just, when your visa expires, understand that you have to go home. I didn't keep my end of the bargain, and they have every right to make me leave."

"Whose side are you on?" Ike's voice is raised, angry. "I don't think there's a lawyer out there who could argue against you better than you just argued against yourself."

"It's the truth, Ike."

"I thought you married me because you loved me."

"I *did* marry you because I love you."

"I'm your *husband*," he says. "And I'm a citizen. They *don't* have the right to keep my wife from me. Who's the government to tell me who I can love? They need to get the hell out of my bedroom."

"You want to go to court so you can tell them that."

"Damn straight I do."

"But guess what?" I say. "You can go to court, and you can say those things, and you can fight on principle, but you're still going to lose. *We're still going to lose.* And when we do, we lose control of what happens. They might arrest you. They'll definitely arrest me."

"You don't know that," he says. "You're just talking out of fear again instead of facts. They might give you months before you'd have to leave!"

"And maybe not," I say bitterly. "You live in a world, Ike, where you think your best-case scenario is what's always going to happen. That you'll get the result you want, or that you deserve. But let me tell you the worst-case scenario, okay? It's pretty ugly. Worst-case scenario is that you get arrested and get out of jail in, I don't know, maybe three months, maybe a year, maybe you even get out on bail the same day. Me? I don't have it so good. They handcuff me, arrest me, put me on some military plane and take me to God knows where, some immigration detention facility where no one can find me, or they dump me in Iran, or . . . who knows? *We just don't know.* You say we create our own destiny, but not by going to court we don't, and that's why moving to Canada—now, voluntarily—is the right thing to do. Don't you see that?"

He slams his fist on the table. "*I don't want to move to Canada! I don't want your family's money!* I want to make my *own* way in the world. I don't want to get by on the generosity of other people."

"Is it so wrong to let other people help you?"

"It is when you can take care of yourself," he says. "And that's all I'm asking you to do. This is not a new issue, Tami. It's the same old one—your unwillingness to do what's hard for you to do, which is to stand up and fight for yourself. To fight for *us*." He sits forward and softens his tone. "I want you in court. I know it's going to be hard for you. I know you'll shake like a leaf and your knees will knock and your voice will quiver. But that's your truth, Tami, and there's beauty in it. Freedom's not for the faint of heart—remember I told you that once?"

But I *am* faint of heart. "I'll lose, Ike." Tears stream down my face.

Not his, though. His eyes are dry and piercing, so blue I can hardly stand it. "You lose by not fighting, Tami."

I lose *him* by not fighting. This is what he's saying.

"Can we just go to Canada, Ike? Please? It's the last thing I'll ever ask you to do for me, I promise."

"Tami, I can't." His voice breaks. "I can't ignore the basic, fundamental problem between us anymore. We're at a point in our relationship—a crossroads, if you will. And if you're not willing to do this for me, then I'll lose respect for you, and if that happens, we can't make a life together no matter where we are." His eyes are both loving and earnest, and very, very determined. "I need to see you strong, for once. I need to see you fight, for once—to fight for us. Because if this life we have together—here in Tucson—isn't worth fighting for, Tami, then what is?"

Chapter 29

Four days later, the letter arrives, bearing the news we knew it would. *Your application for residency has been denied.* A court date is set for next week; it's not a date I intend to keep.

Half of me is in shock, a not-unfamiliar feeling. My childhood took place during a time of war, Iran versus Iraq, and during that eight-year period, our entire country walked around shell-shocked—mourning profusely for all the dead soldiers, of course, but shell-shocked just the same. You can see only so much destruction, so many bombed-out houses, so many limbless men, so many orphaned children. You can see only so much, and then it ceases to register anymore. You block it out so you can go on. That's me, now, again. Shell-shocked. I've fought my own small war for independence, and I've lost.

I've cried my tears. I've told myself to be grateful for the good times we had, that these extra months in America have been a gift—and I am grateful. All the same, I've surrendered to the inevitable. It always did seem too good to last.

But while part of me is in shock, the other part is very focused on what I need to do, which is find a way to get to Canada. Six months ago I couldn't have done it. I couldn't have moved to a new place alone and created a whole new life. Now I have no doubt that I can. And if Canada doesn't work, I'll go to Europe, or to Mexico, or I'll become a nomad, a citizen of nowhere. The silly lines drawn on silly maps have nothing to do with me. I'll respect no border.

I'm tough, aren't I?

Not really, but it helps that Ike's making it easy for me to go. He's never home, and when I turn up at the coffee shop, he finds an errand to run, a reason to leave. It seems we've lost our common ground. There's always something between us—literally. In bed, it's Old Sport. In the driveway, it's the door of the car. At the coffee shop, it's the counter, or a table, or an armful of binders. Anything to block the natural, physical pull we used to have. The last time Ike thought I was leaving, he said, *Let's not waste a single minute.*

What happened to that, Ike?

I'm prepared to go, but there are a few good-byes I must say, and a few things I must do, the most important of which is to host Maryam's baby shower.

We have it in her hospital room a week earlier than intended, and from her bed, my sister is the beautiful queen of the party. We have a catered lunch from the Tucson Tamale Company and a Welcome Baby chocolate cake from Cakes by Clara. Maryam gets so many adorable items for the baby, so many cute outfits. My gift is a handcrafted plaque for the baby's room that says *Home Is Where Your Story Begins.* This makes Maryam cry. We play all the games she wanted us to play, such as Baby Shower Bingo and Baby Pictionary. Ardishir is the only male in attendance, and he plays along good-naturedly. Among the guests are Maryam's two favorite nurses, Janine and Noreen, as well as friends from Maryam's old job at Macy's, along with her Persian women friends from the community. My contingent attends, too—Rose, Eva, Agata. My friends know what has happened to me, of course, but we keep it from the other members of the party. We must make time for celebration, even in the midst of tragedy.

The plan is this: I'm going to San Francisco to visit Nadia and to meet her new daughter. Also, I have that promise to fulfill for my father, that bottle of sand I must sprinkle on the ocean shore. These are the reasons I've given Ike. But here's my secret: When I get on the plane to visit Nadia, I won't be coming back.

San Francisco is a sixteen-hour drive from Vancouver, Canada, or a three-hour flight. From San Francisco, I'll be going to Canada, I think by car so I can see more of America. Only Maryam and Rose and Nadia know this. Nadia has even agreed to go with me and stay until I'm settled.

Two women and a baby, on the loose in Vancouver. Sounds fun, yes? The others, I'll tell once I'm across the border. I don't want any last-minute, white-knight gestures from Ike, although that seems unlikely in any case. I'm pretty sure he won't come after me in San Francisco like he did in Las Vegas. When he's willing to talk to me, he still insists I should go to court. Ardishir agrees with Ike, although as yet he hasn't been able to find a lawyer who thinks I have a chance. None of us will change our mind, and none of us has anything new to say. All we're doing is making each other miserable.

The morning I'm to leave, I ride my bicycle to Ike's parents' house. Ardishir and I prepared legal papers transferring my half of the coffee shop to them upon receipt of the amount of money I've invested so far. My intention is to put the envelope in their mailbox without having to talk to anyone, but as I'm slipping it in the box out front, I hear Camille call out, "Auntie Tami's here! Hi, Auntie Tami! Mommy, Auntie Tami's here!" She waves at me from behind the screen security door that keeps her safe inside.

"Hi, Camille!" I wave back from the street. "I have to go, I'm in a hurry, but say hi to everyone for me, okay? Can you do that?"

As she nods, Mrs. Hanson comes up behind her. She's the one person I didn't want to see, for while she isn't the one who reported us to the fraud hotline, she might have. She's certainly capable of it.

"I left some papers for you," I call to her. "Some papers concerning the shop."

Mrs. Hanson puts her hand on Camille's shoulder and says something I can't hear. Then she unlocks the door and approaches me. For the first time since I've known her, she looks uncertain. I don't say anything. I'm done trying with her. She can be the one to speak first.

When she gets to the mailbox, she opens it and takes out the manila envelope I just put in. She doesn't open it and doesn't ask what it is, although she probably knows. She searches my eyes. "Paige told me about the talk you had a few weeks back, about sex and that boy, Garrett. I want to thank you. It sounds like you gave her some good advice."

"She's too young," I say. "Too young and too innocent."

Mrs. Hanson nods. "When I asked her why she sought you out for a talk, instead of coming to me, do you know what she said?"

I shake my head.

"She said she went to you because you don't judge people." She swallows hard after she says it.

"I try not to," I say.

"She also told me you were the one who took the photograph she gave me for my birthday." This is true—we enlarged the picture I took at our coffee-shop-naming party, of the older Hanson siblings holding Camille sideways. "It's beautiful," Mrs. Hanson says. "It really captures the essence of my children, and I thank you. It'll have a spot on our fireplace mantel forever."

"I'm glad you like it." I say this politely, but I'm swallowing my bitterness.

"Tami . . . I'm sorry." Mrs. Hanson looks at me with

the crystal blue eyes Ike inherited from her, and in them I see sincere regret. "I'm sorry I judged you so harshly. I was wrong about you. You make my son happy. What more could a mother want? You've been so nice to us." Her eyes moisten. "I'm sorry that I've been so mean."

Ardishir is driving me to the airport, and when he pulls into the driveway, I take my carry-on bag to the car and tell him I'll be right back, that I need to say good-bye to Rose. I find her in the kitchen, washing dishes with her Persian lime-scented dish soap. "It's time, Rose. I'm leaving."

She reaches for a towel to dry her hands and comes around the counter to embrace me.

"Be safe," she says. "And Godspeed. I'll see you soon."

"You'll look out for Ike?" She nods, and I know she will. My Rose will take care of my Ike. "Encourage him to stay in the guesthouse where you can keep an eye on him, okay? And where he can look out for you, too. I worry about you, being alone."

"Don't worry about me," she says. "You're never more than a phone call away."

We embrace one last time. It won't be the *last*, last time—she has a passport, and I expect to see her again very soon. If I'm to be a nomad, at least I know my friends will follow me.

In the car, Ardishir is distracted. In some ways, he seems to have taken this turn of events the hardest. He's called everyone he knows, looking for help or an overlooked point of law, or a lawyer who is confident he could plead my case successfully. So far, the silver lining has eluded him, and my failure weighs heavily on his mind. I'm sad for this. With the baby so close to being born—perhaps days—he should feel only excitement. I regret so much that I caused this moment to be at least as bitter as it is sweet. For Ardishir, I wish him only life's sweetness.

"Are you ready for your aunt's arrival?" I ask on the drive over to the coffee shop, expecting it will make him happy, for I know how much he's looking forward to her visit.

But instead, he grips the steering wheel. "Sure," he says. "Of course."

"You're not? Is something wrong?"

He takes his eyes off the road to give me a probing look. "I heard Maryam on the phone with her friend in San Francisco."

My heart races. "What did you hear?"

"Not enough," he says. "Just enough to make me wonder. You are coming back, aren't you? Even if you don't go to court, you'll be coming back to Tucson, right? For however much longer you have?"

"Of course, Ardishir."

I'm not sure he believes me, but thankfully, we've arrived at Common Grounds, so this discussion will end. For a moment, I sit in the car and look at it, this coffee shop that was supposed to be mine—that *was* mine, for a time. Now, looking at it today, I feel foolish. It was so hopeful—so cocky, so arrogant—to think I could open a business with

Ike before I'd gotten my residency. I've managed not to spend much time here since the immigration interview, but Ike's here, and as much as I don't want to—as much as it will kill me—I have to say good-bye.

"I'll wait in the car," Ardishir says.

"You're sure?"

He nods. "I have some phone calls to make."

But instead of starting to make them, he leans his head against the window.

"Ardishir?"

"This isn't right," he says quietly. "America would be lucky to have you."

I lean over to kiss his cheek. "I was lucky to have America, and I'm so glad your baby's going to be an American citizen."

He looks from me to the neon sign out front. "It's a nice idea, Common Grounds. It's a good name for a coffee shop."

"Make sure to buy all your coffee here," I say. "Help Ike succeed."

"I've no doubt he'll succeed," Ardishir says. "He's got that special something."

Ardishir is right about that.

"Still, buy your coffee here," I say. "And your tea, too. I chose the tea selection. It's the best you can get."

My heart races as I approach the shop. I'm pretty sure I'll miss this place as much as I'll miss the people, except for Ike, who's so much a part of it that many of my best memories are of this place, with him. We held hands by candlelight at a special table we declared ours, dreaming of our opening day. I even knew what I'd wear—impractical high heels, my new blue baby-doll top, a denim skirt, and a flower in my hair. Even now, I can picture myself dressed like this, with an apron around my waist, offering bakery samples from a basket. I was going to make rose-water scones and call them a Persian delicacy, even though I invented them all by myself.

We made love in the stockroom. In the office, too. This was long ago, the first few weeks we had the shop, and to this day, my stomach flutters from the memory every time I go in either one. I wonder if Ike's does, too. I wonder if it always will.

I step inside and call to him. "Ike?"

I know he's here. His truck's out front and the door's unlocked.

His voice arrives before he does, angry, complaining on the phone to some contractor or other about not showing up. Ah, it's the waste-removal people. Yet again, there's something between us, this time the phone. He acknowledges me with his eyes and stays behind the counter to finish his call.

While I wait, I go to the wall that holds the majority of my nicely framed prints, the photographic collection titled *Everyday Acts of Freedom.* The project turned out wonderfully. Enlarged, they look even more artistic and make even more of a statement. We'd talked about listing them for sale, at the unbelievable price of two hundred dollars each, and I see now that Ike has made placards for them, listing the price and the artist's name. *Tamila Soroush, Photographer.* That's me.

That *was* me. That's who I was going to be.

Tamila Soroush, Photographer.

Coffee-shop owner.

And wife, her favorite role of all.

Looking at these photographs, I feel like I'm looking at my own gravestone.

"That's it," Ike says when he hangs up the phone. "I quit."

I don't turn around. The man who says this is no one I know. Ike's not a quitter.

We've looked at these photographs together so many times, and we have a routine—I come over first, he approaches from behind, wraps his arms around me, lifts my hair, and softly kisses my neck. I link one hand back through his hair. But today, he abandons the routine. He comes up behind me but just stands there. *Where are the arms, Ike, the arms you should wrap around me? Where is the soft kiss on my neck? What have you put between us now?*

I turn, thinking maybe I will say something, but for once, there's nothing in his hands, not even his phone, not even a pen. He looks like he's lost—he looks like he's losing—his best friend, which he is. I take a step toward him, but he shakes his head just enough to keep me back.

"I don't want you to sell them," I say. "I want to know they're always here."

"I don't think this damned place is ever going to open," he says. "Nothing's coming together like it should."

"It will, Ike," I say. "You'll see. It'll open, and it'll be great."

He studies me. "So you're leaving."

"I made that promise to my father to return the sand to the ocean shore. . . ."

And besides, you won't even talk to me.

With his hands in his pockets, he scans the pictures on the wall: The one of a teenage boy with three earrings in his ear and one in his lip. The one of a barefoot, shirtless black man with crazy braids riding a unicycle and playing a flute. The one of Eva from the waist down—of her miniskirt and thigh-high boots. The one of Ike's and my intertwined hands.

"I noticed you were on MapQuest getting directions to Vancouver from San Francisco." He doesn't look at me as he says this. Instead, his eyes linger on that last photograph. "You should clear the computer's history if you're trying to keep a secret from someone."

He knows.

"Ike . . ."

He knows and he's not trying to stop me.

He looks at me. "I guess there's not much more to say, is there?"

This is not a pretty moment. It's not how I wanted our marriage to end, but I have a flight to catch, a heart to heal, a life to build.

"I love you," I tell him. "I'll never stop loving you."

"I love you, too." It looks like it hurts him to say the words, like he wishes they weren't true.

"Will you kiss me good-bye, please?"

He waits for me to step to him, but he does kiss me. It's soft and lingering, sweet and loving.

It is, perhaps, the saddest kiss the world has ever known.

"I won't sell your photographs." He brushes my hair off my shoulder. "I'll keep them right here, in case you ever make it back to Tucson."

Ten years, Ike. I'll peek in the window.

He'll have moved on by then, but the pictures won't have changed.

In the photograph, at least, I'll always be holding his hand.

Chapter 30

At the airport, Ardishir walks me to the security gate. It's only then that I pull from my backpack the gift I got for him. His quizzical look soon turns to one of suspicion. I knew it would—this is why I waited to give it to him until now. All I have to do is step past the screener and he can't follow me. "What's this for?"

"Open it," I tell him. I've bought him a copy of *The Killer Angels* by Michael Shaara, a novel about the Civil War.

He's very pleased to receive it, but his suspicion lingers. "Thank you, but why'd you get this for me?"

"I know you're bored spending all that time in the hospital, and I thought you might like it. Or have you read it? I tried to pick one you haven't read yet. One of Ike's favorite movies, *Gettysburg*, is based on this book, and—"

"No, this is great, it looks fascinating, but . . . why now?"

He narrows his eyes. "I think you're up to something. You and your sister both."

"Don't be silly." Quickly I kiss him. "I've got to go, or I'm going to miss my flight. Thanks for everything! Kiss Maryam for me!"

He grabs my wrist. "You're coming back, aren't you? You *need* to, Tami. If you never listen to another word I say, listen to me now: *You've got to come back.* Trust me on this."

"Ardishir . . ." I give him a pleading look. When he releases his grip, I wave and back away. "Don't worry about me, please. Everything will work out fine."

I'm careful not to look back as I go through the security ID check and begin the slope up to the screening area.

"Tami!" I cringe and pretend not to hear him, but he calls again, even louder. "Tami!" Reluctantly, I turn. He's far enough away that he has to raise his voice. "You know why I read all these books and watch all these movies?"

I shake my head.

He crooks his finger at me, beckoning me back, and he waits to speak until I'm close enough that he can speak intimately. "I've been trying to figure out how America managed to get things so right. Does that make sense? When it comes to freedom, I mean. Why America succeeded where so many others have failed. And I've come to a few conclusions. Want to hear them?"

I clear my throat. I do want to hear them, but I have the feeling there's a relevant lecture in here somewhere, which normally I wouldn't mind, but I don't want to be talked out of what I'm going to do, so I want his lesson but not the lecture. "Sure, but I only have a minute." I keep my bag on my shoulder, heavy though it is, to emphasize this point. It's not true I only have a minute. My flight doesn't leave for another hour.

"America got it right because the people in power understood the nefarious nature of that power." He's puffed up and says this in professor mode, holding the book I gave him like it's sacred.

I hate to have to ask, but this is an English word I don't know. "Nefarious?"

"Evil," he says. "Power corrupts, almost absolutely. And it's addictive. People will do *anything* to keep their power. As you well know."

"Yes," I say. All Iranians know this.

"It takes a special kind of person to possess power but not abuse it," he says. "That's why I admire the founding fathers. That's why I study them. They were wise enough to know that in order for their children and their grandchildren and *my child* to enjoy the freedoms they'd fought for, they had to create a government that acknowledged that the best power is limited power. And they did something that was unheard of at the time—they created a country in which the citizens owe allegiance to no leader, but rather to a set of principles. *The power resides in the principles.* Principles are what people will fight for, and principles are what they'll die for. They'll die for no man—at least no man of power. They'll die for each other, and they'll die for their children, and they'll die for their ideals. They'll die so freedom remains the birthright of every American."

My skin tingles at his words, at his passionate conviction. *God, I love it here.* America is a beautiful, beautiful place, for this very reason that Ardishir describes.

He continues quietly. "I read these books because I like the stories of all the decisions, all the choices, these people made, and how they little by little made one good decision here and another smart decision there—and when you add them up, they make a country."

"A great country," I say.

"I'm telling you this for a reason," he says. "I'm telling you because there's always a moment, isn't there? When something great and magical happens involving freedom, there's always a moment that precedes it—a moment of decision. Sometimes made collectively; other times, individually. Sometimes it's spontaneous and other times, it's well planned. When something great and magical happens involving freedom, it's because there's a moment when a person or a group of people decides to step up and be what the moment requires of them." The look he gives me is compassionate, and also matter-of-fact. "This is your moment, Tami."

I shake my head. "I had my moment. The immigration interview—that was my moment."

"Separation of powers, Tami. Checks and balances." Ardishir smiles. "That's the brilliance of it all. That guy had no business telling you what the outcome of a court hearing would be. That's not his branch of government. He doesn't control it. It'll come down to you and the judge, and the judge's interpretation of the law. That's it. No one else counts, just you and the judge. *This* is your moment, Tami. You're about to have your moment."

The question in his eyes: *Will you step up?*

Chapter 31

"Will you step over here, miss?" This is what I hear immediately after I go through the metal detector. The person who asks is a black-skinned woman close in age to my mother, and she asks politely, but my terror ignites like it always does when I have to deal with people who have power over me.

"I, well . . ." I glance back and see Ardishir watching. He shrugs and smiles, telling me it'll be fine, that this is no big deal. "Okay, sure."

She leads me to a special section—thank God it's right in public and not in a locked, windowless room!—and asks me to stretch out my arms and spread my feet. As she waves her wand, my body locks into a rigid position. I have no knives, no guns, no shoe bombs, no nothing. But still, I'm guilty. That's what moments like this always remind me of—that I'm guilty of the crime of being born. Of being born a woman in the Middle East. While the guard waves her wand, a male officer looks through my shoulder bag and carry-on luggage, the sum total of my worldly possessions.

"I'm sorry for the inconvenience," says the lady. "We're required to do these random checks."

With my foreign name, I can't help but think there was nothing random about it. I think this even though to my right is an elderly white man and to my left is a mother with a little boy and a baby. They've pulled the bottom rubber balls from the old man's walker to peer inside and they made the mom lift her baby from its stroller to examine it more closely. From the cradle to the grave, it seems we're all potential threats to the status quo.

"No problem." I give the woman a false, polite smile, then collect my bags, wave to Ardishir, and continue up the ramp to the terminal. The entire unpleasantness lasted less than a minute, but I know too well from past experience that its effects will linger.

I detour into the women's bathroom, thinking I'll catch my breath there, out of sight of the authorities, out of the public eye. But this is a bad idea, for once inside, my heart is flooded with a memory of my very first night in America, when I had such hope for my future, and I burst into tears. It's been too much—all of it. The highs have been too high and the lows have been too low and the daily indignities of life will never, ever go away.

There's a woman washing her hands, and she looks at me in sympathy. "Are you all right?"

No. I'm not all right.

But I nod and wheel my carry-on bag into a toilet stall, locking the door behind me. I've always been good at crying silently; I've had lots of practice.

On my first night, Maryam met me at the airport and dragged me into a bathroom just like this one, only on the other side of security. Thirty Persians waited back at her house to welcome me to America—one was potential husband material—and the clothes I'd worn on the plane weren't right for the party, so she dragged me into an airport bathroom and slipped a form-fitting red dress with a deep V-neck over me, slathered makeup on my face until I hardly recognized myself, slipped my feet into open-toed, high-heeled sandals, and painted my toenails a stark red. I protested that I was exhausted and in no mood for a party, but she played the part of pushy Persian perfectly and insisted that I smile my way through the night. *That's all you have to do*, she said. *Smile through everything.*

That first night in America, everything seemed possible.

Maryam. My heart cries out for her. I already miss her terribly, and I so wanted to see her as a mother—not just once a year on her summer trip to Canada, but every day. She'll be one of those crazy, overprotective moms who thinks the world revolves around her daughter. She'll be convinced her daughter is the smartest, funniest, prettiest girl ever. And she'll be right, because it's every mother's prerogative to think that about her child, and it will *certainly* be true about my niece.

I like how Ardishir said that freedom is every American's birthright, and I'll add that it's every child's birthright, no matter where they're born, to have someone believe in them—to believe they're deserving and capable of anything, that the world is theirs for the taking.

I would have thought that about my child, if I'd been so fortunate to have one.

But now I never will.

I don't think I'll ever love again. It's too painful, too hard. I'll be like Rose, the old lady who lives alone. But I don't *want* to be the old lady who lives alone—I want to be the old lady who lives with Ike, and he's letting me go without a fight. This hurts more than anything. How can he just let me go? I can't even breathe without him.

This is ridiculous, I tell myself. *Of course you can breathe. Get it together and get out of this stupid bathroom and out of this town. It was only a way station, that's all it was ever intended to be. It was never supposed to be your home—you're a big-city girl, and you'll be happier in Vancouver.*

I tell myself this only to propel myself out of the bathroom and onto the airplane. I don't believe a word of it. What I believe is that I'll miss these people every day for the rest of my life. I believe the sun will never shine as brightly as when I lived here. I believe the best is behind me.

I'm like my mother that way.

Chapter 32

Now, San Francisco is what I call a city!

I've been here before, when I was small and my parents were graduate students at Berkeley, but I was so young I have no memories of it, only the few pictures I've been given. I wonder if my parents took us to Chinatown and Castro Street. I wonder if we rode the cable cars. I wonder if we drove across the Golden Gate Bridge. We must have—who would go to San Francisco and not drive across the Golden Gate Bridge?

With Nadia and Baby Maryam, I do all these things. The only tourist destination I skip is the prison on Alcatraz Island. No, thank you—why would I want to see that?

Nadia is doing so well. I have only known her when she was in a bad relationship with a mean husband, and so this visit is special to me because she's a whole new person—the best of her old self, with the wisdom of someone who's lived through a hard time. She's been staying with Maryam's fashion-conscious Persian friend, who has taken her clothes shopping (she used to wear her husband's old beer-brand T-shirts) and for a new highlighted hairstyle (it used to be stringy and an unflattering dirty blond). Best of all, Nadia laughs. Really and truly laughs, and she's so pretty when she does! If she keeps this up, she'll have laugh lines one day. And her baby gurgles and squeals with delight at the world around her. I've never seen such a happy baby.

On my second day, Nadia borrows a friend's car and drives me to the beach. When we're in the parking lot, my cell phone rings. It's a call from Iran. My heart lurches. They must know. They must know I have to leave. Their poor hearts must be broken.

"'Alo, Baba?"

"Tami? Is that you?"

"Maman, *salaam*!" She never calls me; it's always my father who calls. "How are you? Is everything okay? Baba's okay?"

"We're fine, Tami Joon. It's you we're worried about." Her voice smoothes and soothes. "We spoke with Ardishir. I'm so sorry about your interview. I'm so sad for you."

I hate for her to be sad for me. She's already been swallowed up by sadness for herself.

"It's okay," I say. "I'm actually doing okay. I'm visiting my friend Nadia in San Francisco. Do you remember being here, Maman?"

"Like it was yesterday," she says. "Memories of places are often so vivid, yes?"

Nadia has the baby loaded into the stroller and gestures that she's going for a walk. I wander over to the low wall separating the parking lot from the footpath. I should look at the ocean, it's so pretty, but I stare at my feet instead.

"It was more than twenty years ago," I say. "Too much time has gone by."

"I love all the old Victorian houses," she says. "I always thought I'd like to live in one."

This is Maman's preferred way of talking—indirectly, around an issue, so as not to cause offense, so as not to make anyone feel bad. But I do feel bad. My mother *could* have lived in one of the pretty houses here, if she hadn't left America on what amounted to a thoughtless, jealous whim!

"I'm at the beach with Nadia, Maman. Was there anything else you called for, or can I call you back later?"

Later, like from Canada.

"Ardishir thinks you should take your situation before a judge. He's worried you won't go back home after this trip."

"Home?" I swallow hard. "I'm not sure where that is anymore, Maman."

"I would have loved to go to court," she says quietly. "After I was arrested. I would have loved the chance to go before my accusers and defend myself, with a fair and honest process. I always pictured it, in my head. I had a great speech all planned."

My heart aches for her. My throat, too, so no words can get out.

"No one ever asked me what happened," she says. "No one. Not even your father. I suppose no one wanted to cause me any grief. I don't blame them, and I didn't want to talk about it any more than they wanted to hear it. You don't want to put that burden on someone." There's a pause, and then she says softly, "Anything they could have imagined, it was a hundred times worse. You like to think you'd be strong, but . . ."

"Why didn't we leave afterward?" I ask. "We could have all lived in a Victorian house. We could have all been happy."

Such a long silence follows that I worry she's set the phone down and walked away from her disrespectful daughter. Finally she replies.

"I made so many bargains with God," she says. "So many bargains. And He let me out. He let me live. I guess I thought I didn't have the right to hope for anything more. And at first I couldn't leave. Did you know this? They held my passport for several years. And then my mother became ill. And then . . ." Her voice fades.

And then you didn't care anymore.

"I don't want to be afraid any longer." My mother's voice quavers. "You don't know what it's like, to be so afraid."

"You'd be happy here. I know it," I say. "And don't feel bad that I have to leave. You should come anyway." I swallow my bitterness at the irony that just as my mother might finally summon the courage to come, I have to leave. "Maryam needs you, Maman. She really, really needs you right now."

"Tami, don't give up," Maman says. "Don't be like me and just stop trying."

"Maman, I'm not. I promise. I'm just being realistic."

"I used to say the same thing," she says.

I already long for a cool, dark bedroom where I can hide myself away for the next twenty years. I'm already so much like Maman.

"Please don't make me feel any worse than I already do," I say.

"You should go before a judge," she says insistently. "Think of all the people who'll never get the chance to, Tami. You have a chance here. *You have a chance.*"

I look out to the ocean. The water looks cold and dark and like it could swallow me whole.

"I'm too afraid," I say.

"You're stronger than you think," Maman says as I watch a sailboat with a brilliant blue sail, the same color as Ike's eyes. "We're all of us stronger than we think."

Chapter 33

MAMAN JOON

I'm here at Tehran's Mehrabad Airport with Hamid, folding in upon myself from nerves, feeling several decades older than my true age. This is all right; I don't mind. Let them think I'm a harmless old lady. I *am* a harmless old lady! Everything that can be done to influence a smooth departure has been done. I'm wearing a chador, the most proper sort of Islamic dress for women. I'm unadorned and wear no makeup; I'll save that for America. Since prison, where each of my interrogators, each of my guards, had one, I can't stand the sight of beards, but I asked Hamid to grow one for this day, and now I remember there is such a thing as a decent man with a beard, for he has been so kind to me since I've agreed to go to the U.S., accompanying me to dentist and doctor appointments and even to hair appointments so that when I see my daughters, their first impression will be that I am, if not fashionable like their Persian and American friends, at least trying. I want them to know I'm trying.

Hamid has taken me for rose-water ice cream, which he did when we were first married. He has held my hand on the streets. He has said exactly enough, never too much, about his hopes for us in America. He wants to open a business, maybe a limousine service or a franchise of submarine sandwiches. You'll help take care of the baby, he tells me, and I agree. Yes, I'll take care of the baby, and my daughters, too. I'll be the mother they've needed all these years. And where Tami goes, I'll go, too, as often as possible, although I still hold out hope that she'll get to stay.

Be greedy, I have willed her every hour since our conversation. She's so giving. She gives far more than she takes, but this is a time for her to be greedy. They might say Americans are the greedy ones—that they're greedy for money and power—but everyone is greedy for something, if not for money or power, then for salvation, or to stop the self-loathing. *Be greedy for freedom*, I will my daughter. *Let your greed for freedom be greater than your fear.*

We pass through the airport terminal seemingly unnoticed. We're two among many, and others are so much brighter, louder, and take up more space. The Revolutionary Guards should stay busy with them, not us. We're nothings, we're nobodies. We're just two people—good

Muslims, see my chador and my husband's beard and open-necked shirt?—with tickets to London, connecting through to America, a thirty-six-hour journey to our new life.

Still, when I hand my passport to the man at the ticket counter, my knees buckle. Not everyone knows this, but there are layers to fear—often, you realize this only when you move from one layer to a new, deeper one. I've talked to myself about how my fear at the airport will be an easy, outer-layer fear; me against myself, mostly. If the worst should happen—if I'm not allowed to leave—it's because I'm not meant to.

This is what I've talked myself into believing, and yet when the woman in a chador appears at my side from nowhere when we're at the ticket counter and says, *Sister, please come with me*, I resist. She's with two other Revolutionary Guards, young men with machine guns. If this is my destiny, I'll deny it. I shake off her hold on my elbow. No, please, I must catch my flight.

Beside me, Hamid pales. He has assured me repeatedly there will be no problems for me, that many who've been in prison have had no problems leaving. They leave all the time! And I did so little wrong in the first place; there's no reason why my name would be on a list. I stood on the edge of a crowd and didn't run fast enough when the crowd dispersed. It's been twenty-five years since I offended the regime in this manner, and my punishment then was far more severe than any crime, committed or imagined. My crime back then was dreaming of something better for my country. That was my only crime: daring to dream. Ask anyone who knows me—I've been cured of that particular affliction.

"Please," Hamid says. "My wife has done nothing and we really must be going."

But the woman starts to lead me away, friendly, still, polite, still, but her delicate features are hardened by her mission. She takes pride in a job that many others find repulsive. I've sometimes hated these women the most, their piety and righteousness, their willingness to interpret an already gender-obsessed religion in their own, unique women-hating ways. These women call me sister, and yet this is not how sisters should be treated.

I almost cry out, almost whimper.

"There, there, now," the woman says. "Don't make trouble; this is nothing, no big deal. We're just going to ask you a few questions."

But the people around me, my fellow travelers, look at me in a way that tells me this isn't nothing. It's something, and it might be something big. It might be the thing that kills me. I trip over my chador as I look over my shoulder at my kind, bearded husband. He can do nothing for me now except to bear witness, and bearing witness isn't enough. I think of the mirror I used to look into, asking my unanswerable questions. *Who or what will save me now?*

You save yourself, an American would say, but some of us know better. Sometimes it doesn't matter what you say or who you betray or what ideals you cling to. There's not much I can do in this particular situation to save myself, and so the question comes to me now, again: *Who or what will save me?*

The guards escort me to a curtained area, which is flanked by more machine-gun-carrying men. The male guards leave me with the female one. In the area are other travelers, many others, all in various states of search and interrogation. This could take hours. I can't sit down. I can't be interrogated. I simply can't. I have nothing to give them; there are no questions I can answer, no games left to play. If I don't get on that plane, I'll die, regardless of what they do to me. My life is there, in America, or it's nowhere at all.

"Please," I say, grasping the woman's surprisingly soft hand. She doesn't like my touch and tries to take her hand back, but I won't let go. I can tell she's on the verge of calling for backup. "Please," I say urgently. "My daughter is having a baby."

Her eyes soften.

"I'm begging for your mercy," I plead. "Please. I must be there."

"Your first grandchild?" she says. "Is this to be your first?"

Tearfully, I nod.

"Is the baby a boy or a girl?"

"A girl," I say.

The woman smiles. "Bless her." She pats my hand. "I'm a grandmother, too, and I know a daughter needs her mother in times like this. Don't fret, sister. Save your tears for happy times. I'll make sure you get on that airplane."

* * *

An hour later, as the plane ascends—with me on it!—I think again of how I used to look into the mirror and ask that impossible question. I was pretty sure back then that I knew the answer: Nothing and no one will save me. But now I know better. Thanks to the woman who had the power to arrest me but chose not to, I know better. In the end, if we're to be saved, it will be through the kindness of a grandmother. Through the kindness of a woman, through the kindness of a stranger.

In the end, it will be kindness that saves us.

Chapter 34

TAMI JOON

After I say good-bye to my mother and disconnect the call, I walk to the shore. It's windy, but I don't mind. I love how the ocean breeze dances its way through my hair, how the wind tickles my skin. *Take me*, I say to the wind. *Take me to a place where there is no pain.* In my hands, I hold the blue perfume bottle my father gave me for my fifth birthday, the one I was disappointed to discover contained not my mother's perfume, but rather grains of sand he collected from these very shores.

I was so young then.

I didn't understand what a precious gift it was.

I look out over the ocean with far eyes, and I see my

house in Iran. I'm outside, looking toward the living room window. My parents stand inside, facing out. My father has his arm around my mother, and she leans her head on his shoulder. Their world is so small, and their regrets so large. Through their actions, they've set a powerful example for me about love, and freedom, and who I do and don't want to be.

My father captured freedom in a bottle. My mother kept the lid of the bottle shut tight for all these years. In these past months, I've learned this: Freedom cannot be held captive forever.

Slowly, deliberately, not wanting to rush this moment, I unscrew the lid of the perfume bottle. After I give it a few shakes, the sand tumbles out, catching easily in the breeze and finding its way back to the shore it was taken from so many years ago.

Watching it sprinkle its way back to the earth, I realize that what's true for freedom is also true for love. I have so much love in my heart for Ike, and if I leave now I'll have to bottle it up forever.

And that would be wrong, because love only means something if you give it away.

I'm sitting prim and proper on the couch when Ike comes home. I've been here an hour, just sitting, thinking a little bit, when I hear his truck pull into the driveway. His car door closes, and Old Sport runs to greet him, but still I sit on the edge of the couch. I'm too nervous to move. I don't know how our reunion will go. I don't know if my coming back is too little, or if it's too late.

Ike comes in, pets the dog, and sets his planner on the counter, which he then leans against. For a long moment, he says nothing, just takes me in.

"You're back," he finally says. And smiles! "I was sure you weren't coming back."

"I had to come back," I say. "I have a date with a judge."

His smile broadens. "That you do."

It seems I've said the magic words, for he comes over, holds out a hand, and pulls me off the couch, tucking me into his safe, strong arms. "I'm glad you're back, Persian Girl." He smells of fresh air and faded aftershave and the Body Shop soap I bought for him. He smells like my husband, the one I almost lost.

"I'm glad, too," I whisper. "I missed you, American Boy."

He steps back. "You're really going to court?"

I nod. "I'm really going to court."

For you, I will. For my mother, I will.

For myself, I will.

"And I'll move to Canada." He nods and swallows hard and reaches for my hands. "If things don't work out in court, I mean. I want you to know that, Tami. Your coming back . . . your willingness to fight—it means everything, absolutely everything. So you've got nothing to lose where I'm concerned. I'm with you either way, regardless of the outcome. Okay?"

Oh, my heart. I fear it might burst.

"For real?" I say.

"For real," he says. "So the worst outcome we've got still has us making babies together. They'll just be Canadian babies."

"They'll be hockey babies!" Laughing, crying, I throw my arms around him. "Thank you, Ike. Thank you so much. I was sure I was losing you."

"You were letting me go," he says quietly. "There's a big difference."

He's right.

"I'm going to be strong, Ike," I promise him. "I'm going to do my best in court—with my knees knocking and my voice quivering and all that. I'll still do my best."

"I know you will," he says. "And as an added incentive, you'll be happy to know that the inspector finally signed off on the certificate of occupancy today, the bastard."

"Hey! Congratulations!" He did it! We did it! This was the last hurdle we faced, and it was a high one. "When do we open?"

"The sooner, the better," he says. "Right?"

"Right!" I resolve that I'll be here for the opening. Even if I lose my appeal, I'll beg the judge to grant me this one wish. I want to ring up the first customer with Ike. Maybe as a joke we can offer free samples of tea. "We've got to celebrate, Ike!"

"We do." His eyes twinkle. "What did you have in mind?"

He pulls me against him in the way that always makes me gasp, and *my God*, I love this man. I'm going to grow old with him.

"Same thing you do," I say, but we don't rush to ravish each other, not at first, for it's brand new again between us. We were lost and now we're found, and with my fingertips I have to re-memorize the curve of his eyebrows, the press of his cheekbones, the thickness of his hair. With my lips, I have to reacquaint myself with the soft skin of his neck, with the underside of his chin, with his tender earlobes. I kiss his collarbone, his wrists, the precious laugh lines around his eyes. Ike stands perfectly still and lets me do all this. He's as patient with me as he can be, just like he's always been.

Chapter 35

It's midafternoon.

The big day.

I'm waiting in the hallway of the courthouse for my hearing to begin. Ike sits beside me in a camel-colored suit, so handsome.

We drove here with Rose. She's dressed for court, too, in a flowery cream skirt and a purple top. Beside me, she clutches her purse. I can't tell who's most nervous. It's pretty even, I'd say, although I'm the only one who's thrown up, twice. Thank goodness my lawyer, Mr. Robert McGuire, will take care of all the talking. Ardishir, Ike, and I met with him for a long time yesterday, and while he realistically thinks things are not likely to go in my favor, he hopes the fact that I'm a partner in a business and generating jobs for the community *with my husband, at this moment*, might be given greater consideration than it was at my interview, which focused only on what my family and friends did, in the past, allegedly without my knowledge or permission. If nothing else, it may enable me to get a different type of visa to come back sooner.

We're forty-five minutes early. I don't know why we came so early—time drags interminably here—except it was worse at home and there were more things to worry about which we have now eliminated, such as traffic and road closures or an accident that might delay us or not being able to find parking or there being a crazy-long line at security or the elevators being broken . . . and so on. It's really much better now that we're here. There's less to worry about—only the worry that Mr. McGuire might not arrive on time! But I think he's just down the street at a different federal building.

As we wait, I've been watching people come and go. I can tell who the lawyers are, since they're among the few people in Tucson who wear suits. Even most men going to court don't wear suits—some are in jeans and T-shirts!

"Hey, look." Ike points to the elevator, which has just opened. "Your tribe's here."

"Oh!" My ESL friends, they've come—my teacher, Danny, too! He's still got his scruffy beard and long hair and wears a Grateful Dead T-shirt, but he substituted khaki pants for his usual shorts, and over his T-shirt he has on a sport coat. It's more of a heavy winter one, but I appreciate the gesture. I jump up and hug each of them in turn. "Thank you for coming. Thank you so much. Danny, I'm very touched. Thank you."

He gives me one of his friendly winks. "This land is your land, baby."

"And, Agata, you look so nice! Great lipstick, that orange really matches your dress! And Josef, you're so handsome in your suit!"

Pleased, Josef stands with his hands behind his back and sucks air through his missing tooth. He has a proud-grandfather posture and announces he'll buy lunch for the entire group after the hearing. "On me," he says. "On me."

"And you," I say to Eva, who today has coal black hair and black leather everything else, "Not even for today, you couldn't . . . ?"

"Dress more modestly?" She snaps her gum. "Hell, no." She grins. "So, hey, chickee-poo—I've got a plan. When you get inside, you need to tell the judge to *fuck himself*."

I laugh. "I'm sure that would work wonders, Eva."

"I'm serious," she says. "You need to go out in a blaze of glory."

I throw my arms around her and squeeze her tight. Whatever happens, I'll never escape Eva. She'll live on in my sassy side; she'll be the temptress whispering in my ear.

I turn to Ike, who has greeted each of my friends with either a kiss or a handshake. "Is it okay for her to dress this way?" I ask.

"We'll just tell the judge we don't know her."

"No!" she says. "Tell the judge I'm the dumb-ass who ran that stupid Internet ad, and point out to him that clearly, I have no sense of boundaries." Her black leather top has a zipper, and she unzips it a little more, exposing another half inch of her already-plunging neckline. "And then I'll offer to visit with him in his private chambers and see if I can, ahem, do anything to persuade him."

"Too bad the judge is a woman," I say.

"Damn," she says. "Are you serious?"

"I'm afraid so," Ike says.

Eva shrugs. "I'd be up for a little girl-on-girl."

We laugh, all of us. No one has actually ever seen Eva do anything outrageous of a sexual nature beyond how she dresses and talks. I think it was Josef who said she's all bark, no bite.

"But we appreciate the gesture, don't we, Tami?" Ike says.

"We do."

Ike and I lock eyes and try to laugh, try to keep up the frivolity, but the moment threatens to turn terrible if we're not careful—if our eyes linger too long, for instance. The truth is, we're both terrified. Last night, again, I was unable to sleep. This time, Ike joined me on the patio. We cuddled under a blanket and tried to buoy ourselves by talking through our worst-case scenario. Mr. McGuire confirmed that if I lose my appeal, I won't be put in handcuffs, that I'll be granted some time to wrap up my affairs, and if that happens, I'm off to Canada, with Ike following as soon as possible. We'll make a life there, have our business and our babies there. We'll be happy, even though the people we love are here.

The elevator dings again and this time it's . . . Ardishir and Maryam. Maryam! On her feet and HUGE in the stomach. Every time I see her, I think she can't possibly get any larger, and yet every single time, she does!

I rush to her. "Maryam! You shouldn't be here, what are you doing? Sit, sit, have a seat!"

She waves off my attempt to guide her to a bench. "As if I'd miss this."

"But you're supposed to be on bed rest!"

"Not anymore!" she says. "The doctor says if I go into labor now, that's fine, the baby's big enough. I got my stitches out, and he's going to induce next week if I don't go into labor on my own."

"Make sure you point her out to the judge," Eva says. "Play the new-auntie card."

Maryam rubs her belly and looks around. "Maybe I *will* have a seat."

I follow her to the bench, feeling my stomach flutter again from nerves. For a few minutes, this gathering felt festive. We're dressed so fancy and everyone's working to keep each other's spirits up, but it's exhausting to maintain the pretense. I sit on the bench between Maryam and Rose. My ESL friends stand nearby, but their conversation fades. I guess it's hard for everyone.

The only one who seems genuinely excited is Ardishir. He jingles the coins in his pocket and wears a carnation affixed to the lapel of his suit. He looks this way and that, gazing around the courthouse with approving eyes.

"Why are you so excited, Ardishir?" I ask.

"Because this is your moment," he says. "And I have a good feeling about it."

I'm glad one of us does.

The elevator dings again, and this time, it's Ike's whole family—even little Camille, who runs over and gives me a hug. "You look pretty," she says.

"Thank you, Camille. So do you. Do you remember my sister, Maryam?"

Camille looks at Maryam's swelled stomach. "She's having a baby."

"Yes, she is," I say. "Very soon."

"Oof!" Maryam's hand goes to her belly and she freezes, as if from pain. "That one hurt." She does some odd-looking breathing.

"That one what?" I say.

"I don't know," she says. "A contraction, maybe?"

"A contraction! Maryam, why did you leave the hospital? You shouldn't be out of bed!"

"Come on, Tami." She slips her hand into mine. "You know I *have* to be here for my little sister. I'll always be here for you, no matter where *here* is."

I squeeze her hand. "The same for me, Maryam."

To Ike's mom, who has led her family over, I say, "Mrs. Hanson, she's having contractions. Tell her she should go back to the hospital."

"How long is it between them?" Mrs. Hanson asks Maryam.

"About ten minutes?" Maryam looking to Ardishir for confirmation. He nods agreeably.

"Did your water break?" Ike's mother asks.

Maryam shakes her head.

"She's fine," Ardishir says.

What happened to Mr. Overprotective? "Do you want your wife to have your baby in a courthouse?" I ask him.

"We have this hearing, then we have my aunt to pick up from the airport, and *then* she can have the baby," he says.

"What if the baby doesn't agree with this schedule?" I say.

"We want to be here," Ardishir says. "She's fine." He looks to Mrs. Hanson. "Besides, we have a nurse right here."

"It's probably okay for her to stay a little while," Mrs. Hanson says. "But if the contractions come any closer together, she's got to go."

Ardishir nods. "It's a deal. Thank you. You're very kind. You've been very helpful to my family."

I know he means it not just because of what she's doing now. Yesterday, in an unexpected gesture, Ike's entire family prepared affidavits in support of me. Ike showed them to me last night. "Thank you for your affidavits," I tell them all, putting my arm around Paige's shoulders. "They touched my heart."

Mrs. Hanson is wearing the same blue linen dress she did when she stopped over uninvited to see me at the guesthouse and demand I leave Ike, and America. But now, the compassion in her eyes seems sincere. "Good luck today," she says. "We're praying for you."

"Thank you," I say. "I need all the prayers I can get."

I look over her shoulder at her family. All of them are smiling at me. Mr. Hanson, in his blue suit, opens his arms to me. Gratefully, I hug him. He's been a very kind father-in-law.

The elevator dings again, and it's my lawyer.

"It's showtime," he says. "Are you ready?"

"I'm terrified," I say.

Ike puts his arm around me and squeezes. "Do it anyway."

"As if she has a choice," Eva says.

"You can be quiet," he tells her, teasingly.

"Never," she counters.

Josef points to me. "Don't-a be afraid. You are good girl. The judge, he will see this."

"It's a VO-MAN!" Agata pokes Josef. "Vhy you no listen? It's a VO-MAN!!"

I look to Rose and Danny. As usual, their quiet support gives me strength. Both look at me with eyes that say, *You can do it, and we'll be right here with you.*

"Come on." Ike steers me toward our hearing room. "Let's get this over with."

"Amen," Mrs. Hanson says from behind us. "Let's get this over with."

The hearing room is not a regular criminal courtroom with a jury box and tables for the prosecutor and defender. It's a smaller room than you ever see on television, and Mr. Hernandez from my interview isn't even here. A brown-uniformed bailiff stands inside the door, and the sight of him instantly terrifies me, even though my lawyer said I won't be handcuffed if I lose and I won't be taken away. But I have yet to conquer my fear of authorities, whether it's friendly police officers at a coffee shop or border patrol agents at interstate checkpoints or the bailiff here in court. Of course, I'm afraid of the judge most of all.

Mr. McGuire, Ike, and I sit together at the table assigned for defendants. I'm in the middle, and Ike right away reaches for my hand. With his thumb, he caresses the palm of my hand. Usually, this is comforting, but today, right now, nothing can comfort me. I'm still uneasy over the way Mrs. Hanson said, *Amen, let's get this over with*, and I'm trying to figure out why. It had a hard edge, very different from the way she said, *Good luck—we're praying for you.* But I seem to be the only one who noticed. I glance at her, and she shows me how she and Camille have crossed their fingers. But how do I know hers aren't crossed for me to lose?

The judge enters. Except for Maryam, who can't quite get up fast enough, we all stand and then sit down at her command. The judge is petite, in her late fifties, I'd guess, and wears red bifocal glasses pushed down on her nose. She's got short brown hair with a streak of gray, piercing blue eyes, and porcelain white skin. There's nothing the least bit ethnic-looking about her. Whatever immigrant blood she has is that of generations long ago. What I also notice about her: She does not seem particularly friendly. She sits on her raised bench, greets Mr. McGuire, looks from me to Ike, and then scans the rest of the group. Her eyes linger on Maryam, and then on Ike's mother.

"Did you go to Tucson High?" she asks. "Elizabeth Howard?"

"I did!" Mrs. Hanson says.

"Janis King," the judge says.

"Well, I'll be, wouldn't you know." Mrs. Hanson smiles broadly. "Tucson's such a small town, isn't it? Just a big old small town. You were in my brother's class. How have you been?"

Ike squeezes my hand. He thinks this connection between the judge and his mother is a good thing. Me, I'm not so sure. What if the judge didn't like Mrs. Hanson in high school? What if Mrs. Hanson's brother did something mean to her?

"I've been good," Judge King says. "I'm getting divorced, but . . . that's not a bad thing. What's your connection to this hearing?"

"My son is Ike, right there. He's the husband." She points him out. "I did an affidavit; it's probably in your file right there. Under my married name, Hanson."

Judge King looks at Mr. Hanson. "Is this your husband?"

"Yes," Mrs. Hanson says. "This is my husband, Alan."

Alan gives a friendly wave and then winks at me. He, too, thinks it's a good thing they know each other.

"Very well. Let's get started." While the bailiff swears us in, Judge King flips open the case file and skims it, refreshing her memory. "This is an appeal on the denial of your application for U.S. residency. On paper, this doesn't look so good." She gazes at Ike like he's the son of a friend, which I suppose he is, a few decades removed, while she gives me a decidedly less friendly look. "It appears you were trying to pull something over on this young man. And over on everyone, quite frankly."

I shake my head. No, that isn't what I was doing.

Mr. McGuire says, "What we have here, Your Honor, is a modern girl bumped up against a traditional family. She was trying to be true to herself and respectful of them at the same time."

"What she needed to do was respect the law," Judge King says.

I cringe.

"Your Honor—" Ike says.

"Did I ask you a question?" Judge King says.

"But Tami—"

"She can speak for herself if she's got something to say," she says. "Ms. Soroush, do you have something you'd like to say?"

"Oh, I . . . uh . . ." Panicked, I look to my lawyer. Should I stand up? Isn't that what people do in court? Do I really have to talk? He said he'd take care of all the talking! "I wasn't trying to trick anybody. I promise this. I . . . I've loved Ike since the first moment I saw him."

"Love at first sight, was it?" She gives me an ironic look. "And yet you were acquiring other boyfriends at the same time you were allegedly falling in love with Mr. Hanson. You believe in love at first sight—you just don't believe in monogamy. Is that it?"

After she says this, Judge King makes eye contact with Ike's mother and sustains it, and oh, my God, this is a setup! Mrs. Hanson knew this woman was our judge and she contacted her ahead of time and told her all her horrible stories about me, and then, to save her relationship with Ike, she wrote her meaningless affidavit and is pretending to like me and pretending to be sorry about my situation.

Let's get this over with, she said, knowing already what the outcome would be.

"It *was* love at first sight," I say through gritted teeth. "And I do believe in monogamy. I believe in being true to the people you love." I look at Mrs. Hanson as I say it. If she's ruined my life here, I'll tell Ike what she did with Jenna. I will tell, I will tell, I will tell. I will not let her get away with it.

Maryam makes big eyes for me to be respectful. Next to her, Ardishir gives me a worried look.

"Are you okay?" Ike whispers.

"Ask your mother if *she's* okay."

I'm shaking from my anger. Literally, shaking. Ike presses my hand. He's very pale.

"Careful with your tone," Mr. McGuire advises under his breath. "You're not doing yourself any favors with that tone."

I almost laugh. *No one's* doing me any favors. "I'm not looking for favors," I say back. "Just a fair chance."

"Is there a problem here?" Judge King asks.

I look to Eva. She smirks: Screw this.

I think of my mother, who had so much to say in her own defense and was never given the chance.

And really, why am I always so nice to people who are horrible to me? Where has taking the higher road ever gotten me?

"Actually, yes," I say. "There is a problem. There's a huge problem."

Behind me, everyone gasps. Ike squeezes my hand so hard he's crushing it, so I pull it away. Why should I be expected to be polite, to keep silent, when I'm the one who suffers for it? This isn't a fair fight, and when people collude against you and you figure it out, you shouldn't have to pretend for one minute that these people are decent human beings, because *they're not.*

"I'm all ears," Judge King says. "Tell me your huge problem."

I've lost this hearing, and I know it. I lost before it even began, and some of it was from my own stupidity, and I accept that. But I won't accept Mrs. Hanson's part in it. I shouldn't have to.

"Here's my problem," I say. Ike tries to grab my arm and stop me, but I stand and walk away from him, away from everyone. And he's right. My knees are knocking, and my heart's racing and I've made my sister cry. She sits silently, with tears streaming down her face. She thinks I'm ruining my chances, but what she doesn't know is they're already ruined.

"Who are you to judge if my marriage is for real?" I ask. "It *is* real. I'm telling you it's real. Ike's telling you it's real. No matter who's told you otherwise"—I pointedly look to Mrs. Hanson, whose eyes widen as she shakes her head no—"they don't see what goes on behind closed doors, which is love. Very much love goes on between us, and not just behind closed doors—right out in the open, too! If you'd spend only one day with us, you'd see it." I glare at Mrs. Hanson. "But you don't. And yet still, you think you have the right to judge me."

"Your Honor!" Mr. McGuire says, starting to stand. "You really—"

"Quiet!" the judge says, her eyes searing.

Stay silent, Tami Joon. Stay silent. My grandmother said this when they brought my mother home from prison, and I've been silent pretty much ever since.

"I've been quiet my whole life," I say to Judge King.

She raises her eyebrows. "You have more to say?"

I laugh. If she only knew!

I look to my tribe, the people who have made up my life here. Camille waves to me. Paige seems worried, while Ike's other sisters appear stunned. His parents look horrified. I can't even glance at Ike, but Rose's face is fretful. My sister has closed her eyes and is massaging her stomach. Ardishir shakes his head like I've made a big mistake. My ESL friends watch expressionless. They are my witnesses. They know this is about more than just this moment. Eva grins at me and makes her fingers into the form of a gun shooting. *Bang*, she's saying. *Go out with a bang.* This is why we all need an Eva in our lives—for moments like this.

I turn back to the judge.

"I do have more to say." My knees aren't knocking anymore. "I'm not going to stand here and ask for your permission to be free. That isn't your decision. I *am* free. And I'm going to stay that way no matter what, because freedom is my birthright, and it isn't negotiable."

A glance to the defendant's table reveals that my lawyer's face is buried in his hands. Ike, however, now sits up straight, watching me with interested, admiring eyes. His are the eyes I love, and looking in them, I remember that my worst-case scenario—having Canadian hockey babies—is not so bad.

I smile at him, then turn back to Judge King. "Please, I'd like to tell you about this man I know."

My lawyer tries again. "Your Honor—"

Judge King waves him silent. "I want to hear what she has to say."

I follow her gaze to Mrs. Hanson, and there's something missing in the air. An absence of evil, maybe, and it occurs to me that perhaps they *didn't* conspire together beforehand, that maybe I'm the lone gunman, turning the weapon on myself.

All of a sudden, I'm pretty sure this is the case.

But, oh, well. I'm still standing. Maybe I'm bulletproof and just never knew it.

"There's this man I know," I say again. "This very nice man. I met him when I was still very new at speaking English, and he asked me, 'Do you know, Tami, what are the three most important words in the English language?' I said, 'No, please tell me. What are these three most important words?' "

I smile at Ike. He smiles back.

" '*I love you*,' he said." Ike nods yes, but with a smile, I shake my head. "This man is really smart," I say. "But he was wrong."

Ike smiles broadly at me, unsure where I'm going but trusting that it's somewhere good.

"I. Am. Worthy," I say. "Those are the three most important words: I am worthy. Everything follows that. By the simple fact of my existence, I'm worthy."

I've thought about this a lot, lately. This is what's wrong with the world, and this is how we make it right.

"Not everybody believes this," I say. "Not every *country* believes it, and so it's really—literally—a revolutionary idea. But if you look back through history—" I pause and look to my history-buff brother-in-law, who's got great pride in his eyes. "*I am worthy.* This knowledge causes revolutions. It crushes empires, and I think it always will."

Agata and Josef nod fervently. Maryam, too. They've lived it. They know.

I turn back to Judge King.

"This is why it doesn't really matter what you decide," I say quietly. "I have a life here. I have a husband here, a wonderful husband. I have a business, a sister. Friends. A niece, about to be born. I'm so glad my niece will be born in this country. She's very lucky."

I smile at Maryam. She smiles back, then grimaces. Another contraction. I better hurry up!

"But that's all it is," I say, turning back to Judge King. "Luck. She's no more worthy than the thousands of babies born the same day somewhere else. I was almost lucky like her—I missed being born here by eighteen months. If my parents had gone to school here just a little sooner, I would have been an American citizen by birth, and then we wouldn't be having this conversation. What I'm saying is: We're all accidents of birth. It helps to remember this.

"Now, I'm going to live in freedom," I say. "Will it be American freedom? That's up to you. But you should know—my heart is here. Some of my history is here. I'm needed here, by a lot of good people. And I'll be a good citizen. I'll make America proud. It's not that I don't love Iran. I do. But I want . . . I need . . ." *What is it? What is it, Tami?* "I want my soul to flourish, to have the opportunity to flourish. And it can't flourish in Iran at this moment in time. So, please. Use your power wisely. That's all I ask. See that I'm one of your huddled masses who yearns to stand tall, and welcome me, if you can find it in your heart to do this. But you should know—I won't be destroyed if you make me leave, because we are the stories we choose to tell ourselves, and one way or another, I'm going to get my happy ending."

There's silence when I finish—no roar of approval from my friends in the gallery like you'd see in the movies. They're all of them, every single one, frozen with tension, terrified of what comes next. But not me. For once, I have no fear. I've already won.

Mr. McGuire sits at the table, waiting for a cue from the judge. Ike anchors the other end. The pride, the love, the conviction in his eyes are unmistakable.

Freedom is not for the faint of heart, Ike. I remember how you said that.

Judge King tilts her head, considering me. "I've been a judge for a long time," she says. "And I've never heard a speech quite like yours." She pushes her chair back from the bench. "It's an interesting question, isn't it, what makes someone an American? Really, how often do we think about it? On days like 9/11, we pause to consider. We hear stories of someone's grandson carrying an injured woman down thirty flights of stairs to safety, and we think about it. We hear of our firefighters going into burning buildings, to their certain deaths, and we think about it. Or we watch the Olympics, and our young athletes do us proud. We think about it then, when the American flag is raised at the medals ceremony, and when the anthem plays. Anytime our hearts swell," she says. "Right? Anytime someone by his actions or his words fills our hearts with hope, or pride—that's when we think about it. That's what Americans do when they're at their best—they fill others with hope."

"That's right," I say. "America brings out the best in people. And America allows people to be their best. *That's* what makes this country really special."

Judge King takes off her bifocals and peers at me. "Usually, my job is not very fulfilling. I don't get to say yes very often, but today . . ."

Yes? Today what? Today you're going to say yes? To me, you might say yes? I'd said all these things for myself, and for my family and friends—I was pretty sure they wouldn't make a difference to the judge. My heart, however, suddenly suspects they might have.

"You've filled me with hope," she says. "And that's saying something, because I've become a pretty cynical person over the years. Now, I don't know if your marriage is going to last. You're right—who am I to judge? I couldn't even make my own marriage last. But I do have to make my judgment. I do have to rule on this particular case. And do I think you're sincere? Yes, I do. Do I think you love your husband? Yes, I do. Do I think this country would be better with you in it? Yes, I do."

She pauses for effect. My friends and family are on the edge of their seats, ready to cheer, ready to explode with joy. This is all sounding good, very promising. Ike has happy tears in his eyes, but not me. Not yet. Especially not when I notice that Maryam is still sitting back with her eyes closed, crying and shaking.

"Please, Your Honor," I say to the judge. "This is too much stress for my sister."

Judge King smiles. "If I approve this request today, it's not the end, as I'm sure you know. If I grant you your residency today, it's conditional. Two years from now, you'll have to apply for permanent status. So you're stuck with this guy for two years. Are you okay with that?"

My smile is so wide that my face hurts.

"I'm okay with that." *This is a yes.* Somewhere in her words, I'm hearing a yes. "I'm very much okay with it. I'd like to be stuck with Ike forever."

"Well, then . . ." She winks at me. "I'm approving your application for residency." She notes something on a piece of paper and then looks back to me. "Welcome to America, Ms. Soroush."

Chapter 36

Ike reaches me first.

He grabs me and swings me around and squeezes me into a tight hug. "You did it! Tami—you did it!" He embraces me again and swings me around again, saying, *you did it, you did it*, over and over again, and I see Judge King slipping out of the room with a glance backward. Our eyes connect for one last moment and I try to say thank you, but Ike spins me too fast and the next time around, she's gone.

Then the others are there, surrounding me, congratulating me. Rose is on the outskirts, and I reach for her hand and squeeze it. I can't wait to have tea with her later and relive these moments a hundred times, a thousand times. This should be a movie, based on my true story, and we could sit on her couch together with Ike and watch it, eating our buttered popcorn and huge theater-sized boxes of candy. I wonder what the sound track would be? I suppose Ike, who has the right song for every occasion, should get to choose the sound track!

This moment *will* stand still forever—I'll never forget it. I look for Ardishir, to thank him for the what's-so-great-about-America speech he gave me at the airport, and there are Danny and Eva and Agata and Josef and Ike's whole family and holding my hand is Rose, and there's Ike, of course, but where is Ardishir? Where is Maryam?

I look through the crowd and see they haven't moved from their seats. Maryam still sits, pale, shaken, and my heart pounds to see her this way. She doesn't look good. Ardishir is kneeling beside her.

"Maryam!" I push through the group and start toward her. I sense everyone turning, everyone noticing, everyone stunned into silence. Right behind me is Mrs. Hanson, the nurse of my extended family.

"My water broke," Maryam says. I've never heard such fear in her voice. "Ardishir?"

Mrs. Hanson slips by me and quickly gets to Maryam. "You'll be fine," she says. "Your body knows what to do."

"Will you stay with me?" Maryam asks her.

"Of course," Mrs. Hanson says. She holds her hand out for Maryam to take. "Come, you'll be fine. You're about to become a mom. To experience love on a whole new level! You just have to be brave, like your sister here was just so very brave." She smiles at me.

"My sister's brave, too," I say. "She's a woman from Iran, so of course she is! Right, Maryam?"

Maryam nods and tries to smile. The bailiff holds the door open for us. Maryam goes first, flanked by Ardishir and Ike's mother. I'm right behind them, thrilled. *I'll be here. I get to be here!* This is so great! This is such a good day for our family!

There isn't room for everyone in the elevator, so the others stay behind and call out excited good-byes and good lucks.

"The airport!" Ardishir remembers when we're halfway down. "I've got to get to the airport!"

"I'll go," Ike says.

"Will you? Thank you!" I say. "And then bring Ardishir's aunt to the hospital."

"You go, too, Tami," Ardishir says.

"No, I'm going with you," I say. "No way will I miss this!"

"You need to go with Ike to the airport," Ardishir says. "My aunt won't go anywhere with a man she doesn't know."

"No, I can't—"

"You *have* to, Tami," Ardishir insists. "And don't worry, by the time we get to the hospital, you'll be at the airport. Just pick her up and bring her directly to the hospital, and you'll only be half an hour behind us."

"But"—I turn to my sister— "Maryam? What do you want me to do?" She wants me to stay with her. I can see it in her eyes. "I'm staying with my sister."

But she shakes her head. "It's okay. Go with Ike. Just hurry back!"

"You're sure?" I ask. She nods that yes, she's sure.

"I'll text you the flight information," Ardishir says.

"Text Ike," I say. "I left my phone at home."

When the elevator arrives at the ground floor, Ike and I shout good-byes and run down the hall, through security, and to his truck. "Rose!" I say, remembering that we gave her a ride to the courthouse. "How will she get home?"

"You don't need to worry about Rose," Ike said. "Rose will be fine. She can find her own way home."

I snap the seat belt around myself and say, "Hurry! *Hurry!*"

Ike isn't usually a fast driver. He's a little slow, if anything, but today he's willing to go ten miles over the speed limit. This is good but . . .

"Faster, Ike!"

"If we get pulled over, that will just take more time."

I know he's right, but around us on the interstate, trucks and cars are speeding by. "I don't think we're going to be singled out."

"Her plane's going to get there when it gets there," he says. "Us being at the airport five minutes early won't make her arrive any sooner."

"Well, I know, but—"

His phone vibrates. He retrieves it from his pocket and hands it to me. "See what it says."

It's a text from Ardishir. *Arriving at 4:40. Meet at top of stairs leading to baggage.*

It's four thirty right now, and we're more than ten minutes away.

"Ike! Please, you have to go faster!"

He laughs. "If I get a ticket—"

"Who cares if you get a ticket? If that's the worst thing that happens to us today, so what?"

He laughs harder. "You're right. Today's been pretty incredible. All right, here I go."

He takes off, passes several cars, and maintains a high speed on the exit ramp. We're back on city streets, and he makes the first few lights on Irvington and keeps going through the yellows, which he never, ever does. I laugh the whole way.

We barrel into the short-term visitors lot and run inside, straight to the stairs where we're supposed to meet Ardishir's aunt, and then stop short. We're here, we made it! It's exactly four forty. It's so fitting, so appropriate, that we're meeting her under the WELCOME TO TUCSON sign.

"Will you recognize her?" Ike says.

"I think so," I say. "I doubt there'll be any other Persians on the flight."

I look around, at all the people coming and going, their lives in motion, and *mine is, too!* "Ike, we did it!" I throw my arms around him. "I'm here! I'm here forever!"

"No hockey babies," he says.

I laugh. "No hockey babies—but babies, for sure."

"For sure," he says, and then steps back from my embrace and turns me to face the arrival gates. "It looks like the flight's here."

I scan the oncoming crowd and wait for a flicker of familiarity. I know a Persian when I see one.

"She's how old?" Ike asks.

"In her fifties, I think."

"Well, there's someone that might be her. She's very pretty and looks Mediterranean, but . . . she's with someone. Never mind."

My eyes follow his, to the side of the ramp, halfway back, and my heart starts beating rapidly. It seems to know something I don't.

"Ike . . ."

This . . . can't be . . . It can't be right. I squint at the couple.

"Ike?"

Tears blur my vision. *Why am I crying?*

"What's wrong, Tami?"

"That's—oh, my God, Ike!"

I cover my mouth with my hand, trying to hold my emotions in. My hand shakes. I might faint. It's them. It's *them.*

It's her.

"That's my mother, Ike." I burst into tears. *"It's my mother."*

"Wha—?" He looks at the couple. My parents—my mother, my father—are looking right at me. They're crying, too, and smiling through their tears.

I start walking toward them. They must be a mirage in the distance, sure to disappear when I get close. And that's why I walk so slowly. I don't want them to disappear. But then again, maybe if I get there quick enough . . . I begin running.

"Maman? Baba?"

They're about twenty meters away.

"Tami!"

My mother starts running, too. Seconds later, we collide, locking together in one huge, long, screaming, traffic-stopping hug, expanded to include Baba when he reaches us.

"I won!" I say. "I won in court—just now! Just, thirty minutes ago! I get to stay! And Maryam—she's having the baby! And, oh my God! Come meet Ike! You're here! *You're here!*"

I'm so flustered; I'm talking so fast and I'm sure I'm not making any sense. I don't know what to do, where to go, how to steer them, but there's Ike in his suit, looking like a gorgeous American model, looking exactly how I'd want him to look when meeting my parents for the first time.

"Sir." He shakes my father's hand, then my mother's, too. "Mrs. Soroush. It's very nice to meet you. I have to say—you came on the perfect day."

I'm beyond tears. The ones streaming down my face mean nothing.

"Our daughter has told us so much about you," my father says, his English perfect. "It's very good to meet you." His proud eyes glisten. "You are a good man."

Oh, to hear my father say this. It means everything. They will swim in the ocean together, Ike and my father. Ike and my father and my son, someday.

"Tami, you might want to read this." Ike hands me his cell phone. There's a text message, from Ardishir: *Baby Hope is here!*

"Maryam had her baby," I say. "She had her baby!"

"Can we go?" Maman says. "Can we go to her right away?"

"Of course," I say. But I have to stand still for a minute. I have to catch my breath. I have to look at my mother and my father and understand that this is real. That *they* are real, and that they're here.

"How did this happen?" I say.

"It's our time," my father says. "It's our time for joy."

So much has happened so fast. For so long, after dreaming for decades of somedays, within minutes, all our dreams have come true. My U.S. residency. Maryam's healthy baby. My parents, here.

It's really a little much.

I look at Ike and swallow over the lump in my throat. "You were the one who made me say it out loud." He looks at me, unsure what I'm referring to. "Don't you remember, you made me say my most secret dream out loud, the day we moved into the guesthouse?"

"Right." He nods. "The day we put that map up."

"This is it, Ike. This is that dream!"

I imagined the door to Maryam's hospital room opening, and my mother stepping through it, with my father right behind.

I imagined Maryam with the baby in her arms and Ardishir by her side, seeing my parents for the first time in over fifteen years.

I imagined my mother, moments later, holding Baby Hope in her arms.

Can you see it? I asked him. *Can you ever see it happening?*

Absolutely, he said. *If anyone can pull it off, you can.*

This is why I love him: because he believed in me even before I believed in myself.

We take the escalator down to the baggage claim. My parents' luggage is already circling the carousel, and while Ike and my father go to collect it, my mother and I stay back. She stands close and smoothes my hair, caresses my cheek. "I'm here," she says. "Can you believe it?"

"Of course I can." I smooth *her* hair. I caress *her* cheek. *This is my mother, in America!*

She looks familiar and different at the same time.

I think it's her smile that's different. It's a smile I've only ever seen before in photographs from long ago. It's the smile of the mother I've missed every day of my life, the smile of the mother I've longed to know.

I don't have to miss her anymore.

She's here. She's here!

My mother, at long last, has come to wake up her luck.

Photo by Lance Fairchild Photography

Laura Fitzgerald is the author of *Veil of Roses* and *One True Theory of Love*. A native of Wisconsin, she lives in Arizona with her husband, who is of Iranian descent, and their two children. She can be reached through her Web site at www.laurafitzgerald.com.